W9-BZW-058

"With hard-edged, imperfect but memorable characters, a complex plot and no-nonsense dialog, this excellent novel will appeal to fans of Lisa Gardner and Lisa Jackson."

Library Journal

"Absolutely chilling! Don't miss this well-crafted, spine-tingling read."

Brenda Novak, *New York Times* bestselling author

"A terrifying novel of suspense."

Mysterious Reviews

"This is a story to read with the lights on."

BookPage

DYING SCREAM

"Burton's taut, fast-paced thriller will have you guessing until the last blood-soaked page. Keep the lights on for this one."

RT Book Reviews

"A twisted tale . . . I couldn't put it down!"

Lisa Jackson, *New York Times* bestselling author

DEAD RINGER

"Dangerous secrets, deadly truths and a diabolical killer combine to make Mary Burton's *Dead Ringer* a chilling thriller."

Beverly Barton, *New York Times* bestselling author

"With a gift for artful obfuscation, Burton juggles a budding romance and two very plausible might-be perpetrators right up to the tense conclusion."

Publishers Weekly

I'M WATCHING YOU

"Taut . . . compelling . . . Mary Burton delivers a page-turner."
Carla Neggers, *New York Times* bestselling author

"Creepy and terrifying, it will give you chills."

Romantic Times

Books by Mary Burton

I'M WATCHING YOU

DEAD RINGER

DYING SCREAM

SENSELESS

MERCILESS

BEFORE SHE DIES

THE SEVENTH VICTIM

NO ESCAPE

YOU'RE NOT SAFE

COVER YOUR EYES

BE AFRAID

I'LL NEVER LET YOU GO

VULNERABLE

Published by Kensington Publishing Corp.

Outstanding praise for Mary Burton and her novels!

COVER YOUR EYES

"Will keep you up all night reading."

The Parkersburg News & Sentinel

"Burton takes the reader on another of her high-speed roller coaster rides."

BookReporter.com

YOU'RE NOT SAFE

"Burton once again demonstrates her romantic suspense chops with this taut novel. Burton plays cat-and-mouse with the reader through a tight plot, with credible suspects and romantic spice keeping it real."

Publishers Weekly

"Serial killers, vendettas, tortured souls and romance are the main ingredients in *You're Not Safe*. Beware! As one of Burton's main characters might say, she has all kinds of tricks up her sleeve."

BookReporter.com

"Mary Burton is one of the best romantic thriller writers around."

The Pilot (Southern Pines, North Carolina)

"Burton really has a way with plot lines and her delivery is flawless. *You're Not Safe* carries just the right amount of suspense, creepiness and romance, that when mixed together, creates a satisfying mystery with a shocker of an ending."

FreshFiction.com

NO ESCAPE

"A thrill a minute . . . there is no escaping the fact that with *No Escape*, Mary Burton delivers again."

The Jefferson County Post (Tennessee)

THE SEVENTH VICTIM

"Dark and disturbing, a well-written tale of obsession and murder."

Kat Martin, *New York Times* bestselling author

Please turn the page for more rave reviews!

THE SEVENTH VICTIM

"Burton's crisp storytelling, solid pacing and well-developed plot will draw you in and the strong suspense will keep you hooked and make this story hard to put down."

RT Book Reviews

"A nail-biter that you will not want to miss. Terrifying . . . it keeps you on the edge of your chair."

The Free Lance–Star (Fredericksburg, Virginia)

BEFORE SHE DIES

"Will have readers sleeping with the lights on."

Publishers Weekly (starred review)

MERCILESS

"Convincing detective lingo and an appropriately shivery murder venue go a long way."

Publishers Weekly

"Burton just keeps getting better!"

RT Book Reviews

"Terrifying . . . this chilling thriller is an engrossing story."

Library Journal

"Mary Burton's latest romantic suspense has it all—terrific plot, complex and engaging protagonists, a twisted villain, and enough crime-scene detail to satisfy the most savvy suspense reader."

Erica Spindler, *New York Times* bestselling author

SENSELESS

"Stieg Larsson fans will find a lot to like in Burton's taut, well-paced novel of romantic suspense."

Publishers Weekly

"This is a page turner of a story, one that will keep you up all night, with every twist in the plot and with all of the doors locked."

The Parkersburg News & Sentinel

I'LL NEVER LET YOU GO

MARY BURTON

PINNACLE BOOKS
Kensington Publishing Corp.
www.kensingtonbooks.com

PINNACLE BOOKS are published by

Kensington Publishing Corp.
119 West 40th Street
New York, NY 10018

Copyright © 2015 Mary Burton

All rights reserved. No part of this book may be reproduced in any form
or by any means without the prior written consent of the publisher, excepting
brief quotes used in reviews.

This book is a work of fiction. Names, characters, businesses, organiza-
tions, places, events, and incidents either are the product of the author's
imagination or are used fictitiously. Any resemblance to actual persons,
living or dead, events, or locales is entirely coincidental.

If you purchased this book without a cover, you should be aware that this
book is stolen property. It was reported as "unsold and destroyed" to the
publisher, and neither the author nor the publisher has received any pay-
ment for this "stripped book." All Kensington titles, imprints, and distrib-
uted lines are available at special quantity discounts for bulk purchases for
sales promotions, premiums, fund-raising, educational, or institutional use.
Special book excerpts or customized printings can also be created to fit
specific needs. For details, write or phone the office of the Kensington
sales manager: Kensington Publishing Corp., 119 West 40th Street,
New York, NY 10018, attn: Sales Department; phone 1-800-221-2647.

PINNACLE BOOKS and the Pinnacle logo are Reg. U.S. Pat. & TM Off

ISBN: 978-0-7860-4946-2

First Zebra paperback printing: November 2015
First Pinnacle printing: February 2022

10   9   8   7   6   5   4

Printed in the United States of America

Electronic edition:

ISBN: 978-1-4201-3216-8 (Zebra e-book)

PROLOGUE

January 25, midnight
Four years earlier
Nashville, Tennessee

Leah never slept deeply. Her brain, always on alert, skimmed just below consciousness, waiting for him to return. Not a matter of if he'd strike. A matter of when.

When floorboards creaked and a cold wind whispered in the shifting shadows of her first-floor apartment, Leah bolted up in bed. Gripping the sheets, heart slamming, she reached for her phone on the nightstand and waited, her thumb poised over the emergency 9-1-1 speed dial. Seconds passed. Was this another false alarm? Another nightmare? Or had her estranged husband finally come to kill her as he'd promised?

Adrenaline surged and rushed through sinew and bone, pricking the underside of her skin as she listened and waited.

The temptation to call the cops pulled, beckoned, screamed. But she'd cried wolf too often. Too many false alarms had been sounded. The last annoyed officer, his voice rough with frustration, had told her to count to ten before she called again.

"One. Two. Three." Her breathing quick and shallow, she listened, expecting footsteps, but hearing only silence and the *thud, thud, thud* of her heart.

God, she was so tired. She needed sleep. Freedom. Peace. She needed her life back.

During the day, Philip was always there, standing and watching. He sent her flowers. Called her cell at all hours. Left scrawled messages under her windshield wipers. *You can't escape. I own you.* Months of his relentless pursuit had stretched frayed nerves to breaking. During the day, she jumped at every creak, bump, and footfall, and at night, terrors jerked her from sleep, leaving her fully awake, tension gripping her chest and shallow breathing chasing a racing heart.

Holding her breath, she listened as she stared at her locked bedroom door. Again, she heard nothing save for the hum of the furnace.

"Four. Five. Six."

She scrambled for a logical reason to explain this latest scare. It was Tuesday. That meant her roommate, Greta, was working the late shift at the bar. Greta closed on Tuesdays. How many times had Leah awoken screaming when Greta had returned home late? Poor, normal Greta, grad student and bartender, now moved slowly and quietly on Tuesday nights, fearful any sound would send her roommate into hysterics.

Leah glanced at the clock. Midnight. Too early for Greta. She listened, heartbeat still jackhammering. Thank God, no more sounds. Had this been another dream? Another false alarm? Yes. Maybe. "Seven. Eight. Nine."

Slowly, she lowered to her pillow, clutching the phone to her chest, eyes wide open, staring at the swathe of shadows slicing across the ceiling. *Breathe in. Breathe out.*

The day she'd finally fled her marriage had begun as it always did. Fights, a barrage of questions, her promising to come home as soon as she got off work. But that morning, she'd been at her desk when a coworker had asked her about the bruises on her arm. She'd lied of course, but this time, the words hadn't tumbled freely. Instead, they soured on her tongue. Sickened, she'd asked for the afternoon off. No matter how much she'd hoped, his contrition always faded and his temper flared, quick and hot, scorching *I'm sorry* to ash.

She had no plan when she'd returned to their apartment and then quickly cramming clothes into three green trash bags. *Take only what you need. Get the hell out of here fast.* The words slammed as hard as his fists.

When she'd twisted off her wedding band and laid it on the kitchen counter, it was exactly three o'clock in the afternoon, just thirty minutes before his shift ended. She'd dragged the bags into the hallway, and when the apartment door slammed behind her, she'd actually felt free. *It's over. It's over.*

But it wasn't.

Philip had called her cell seconds after five that same day. Guilt had prompted her to take that first call as she'd sat in the shabby motel room, surrounded by her life in trash bags. He'd begged her to return. *I love you. I need you. It will never happen again.*

Of course he was sorry. He was always sorry.

He'd sent flowers. Called. Waited outside her office. No matter where she looked, he was there. *Please come back to me. I love you so much.*

Floorboards creaked in her closet, and she bolted back up, clutching her hand to her mouth, the pulse drumming under her fingertips. This time, logic couldn't silence the alarm bells, which clanged louder and angrier until reason scurried away like a frightened mouse. The last time she'd seen Philip, he'd been clutching the restraining order, furious. *This is bullshit! You don't know what you've done!*

Her fingers poised over the 9-1-1 direct-dial button, her gaze scanning the darkness. At first glance, nothing was out of place. Her door was closed. Locked along with a dead bolt.

And then, the faint flutter of movement in the shadows inside her closet. Another cold breeze from a half-open window brushed her skin. Time slowed, and even the air in the room grew heavy.

"Hello, Leah." Philip's deep voice sounded amused as he stepped out of her closet.

Philip! How had he gotten into her room? Mentally, she ran from lock to lock in the apartment, checking.

He clicked on the overhead light, making her wince at the burst of brightness. Tall, wearing a dark turtleneck, jeans, and boots, his broad shoulders ate up the tiny space of her room. He stared at her, his long fingers clenching and unclenching at his sides. Attached to his waistband was the brown leather holster that cradled a six-inch knife blade. The blade was inches from his right hand.

"Philip."

"Leah." His voice devoid of concern or fear, as it always did when he came to a decision. There would be no turning back.

Without taking her gaze from him, she hit 9-1-1. A distant "Nine-one-one, what's your emergency?" echoed from the phone.

"My husband's going to kill me," Leah said. "I live at One-Twelve Main Street, Apartment Two. Treemont Apartments." How many times had she practiced this line, imagining this moment over and over?

"Ma'am, repeat what you just said." The operator's voice was clean, crisp, and so blissfully free of fear.

Leah's hand trembled so badly she thought she'd drop the phone. "He's found me. He's in my room."

"Who's found you, ma'am?"

Unconcerned, Philip rested his hand on the hilt of the knife.

"My husband. Philip Latimer. He's going to kill me."

How long would it take for the cops to arrive? Five minutes? Ten? And how long would it take for him to cross the room and stab her? Seconds.

"How do you know he'll kill you?" The operator's voice was flat, emotionless.

"He's in my bedroom. He has a knife."

Philip knew exactly how long it took the cops to respond. He was a cop. Saving people like her was his job.

"What's your name?"

"Leah Carson. Leah Latimer." She rattled off her address again, fearing she'd be dead before they arrived.

"I'll send a car," the operator said. "Stay on the line."

The words were cold comfort. Philip had broken the protective order. He didn't care about an arrest or his career. He'd crossed an invisible line, knowing his decision was a one-way trip. His only goal now was to kill her while she could see it all happen.

Tears filled Leah's eyes as he slid the knife from its holster, the cold metal catching and glinting in the moonlight.

He moved toward the bed, slowly and unhurried. He'd slicked back his thick, blond hair from his angled face, now hardened with purpose. Once, she'd considered his face handsome. Once, she'd looked into those vivid blue eyes and seen love. Once, he'd made her feel protected.

"You're so beautiful." His deep voice was smooth, silky, as if they'd bumped into each other on a street corner on a sunny afternoon. He smelled of fresh cold night air and whiskey.

During their marriage, she'd learned to fear him most when he wasn't ranting or raving but when he was cool and controlled. "Philip, what do you want?"

"I've been telling you for weeks. But you won't listen. I want you back home with me."

With deliberate slowness, she pulled the covers over the T-shirt that strained against the outline of her breasts. "Philip. How'd you get in here?"

Keep him talking. Buy time. How much time did she need? She'd timed the route once or twice. Without traffic, it took ten minutes.

Those long, callused fingers slid up the blade to the tip. "I've missed everything about you."

"Philip, you shouldn't be here." The evenness in her voice belied her fingers tightening into a white-knuckled grip on the comforter.

His thumb circled the knife's hilt. "Why not? You're my wife. And this is our wedding anniversary."

Twelve months ago today they'd exchanged vows. "You need to leave."

"And if I don't? What're you going to do?"

"The cops are coming."

He traced the knife tip over the comforter, snagging the ice-blue fabric. "I don't care."

"Philip. Just go. Get away while you still can."

He raised the blade to his thumb and pricked the edge. Crimson blood dripped, before he slowly stroked it against the bedsheet. "You were so pretty on our wedding day. Such a beautiful white dress. You carried those pretty purple flowers. What were they called? Irises?"

"Just leave me alone, Philip. Go away. I don't want to see you arrested. It will ruin your career." Her pulse thrummed against the soft skin of her neck.

"Until death do us part, Leah. I promised. And so did you."

Keep talking. "You love your job. You're a good cop. Respected."

"Without you, it means nothing. You're mine, Leah. We're two halves of a whole. Restraining orders and cops can't keep us apart."

Chin raised, tears pooled and spilled. Stall. *Buy time!* False promises of love and devotion danced on her tongue, readied for declaration when the truth stubbornly elbowed past. "We're over, Philip. I'm not coming back to you."

He traced his hand over her leg, rough calluses on smooth white skin. Skin prickling, she flinched and rolled her leg away. Gaze darkening, he clenched the blankets in his large hand. An onyx pinky ring marked with the letter L winked in the moonlight before he yanked the covering off the bed. She was helpless, wearing only gym shorts and a T-shirt. Cold air skimmed her bare legs. Goose bumps puckered.

"Philip, please—"

For a moment, he sat as still as a statue, his terrible beauty etched in calm repose. And then, like a rattler roiled, he struck, moving with lightning speed. He climbed on top of her, the rough fabric of his jeans scraping against her thrashing legs. He pressed the knife blade to her throat.

Their gazes locked as he smoothed the steel tip over her chest to her flat belly. She flinched. Braced.

"Philip, don't. Please."

This close, his eyes, red-rimmed as if he'd been crying, bore into her. "I'll never let you go. You belong to me. I love you." His body hummed with need. Need to own her. Need to possess her. Need to hear her words of love.

More tears spilled down the sides of her face. He controlled so much in this moment. Life or death rested solely with him. All she controlled was her words. The truth. If she died tonight, Philip would know her heart. "I don't love you."

He flinched, as if the statement bit like a rattler. "You've been brainwashed. Your mother and your friends filled you with lies. Poisoned you against me."

"I don't love you." Defiance pricked as sharp as the knife's tip. "You don't own me."

Pain deepened the lines of his face, even as his teeth bared into a snarl. He lowered his lips to her ear. Warm breath against her skin raked over her nerves.

"I love you," he whispered. "I love you. Why can't you understand that?"

Out of habit, not love, she raised her hand to his muscled arm, her touch gentle, as if soothing a beast. "Philip, this isn't love."

He burrowed his face into the crook of her neck. His hand fisted her blond hair. "It's love. It is."

"No, Philip." A pathetic lie crept from the shadows. "You deserve better."

A fist pounded on the apartment's front door. "Ms. Carson! Ms. Carson! This is the police!"

The officer's voice cut through the door and relief collided with tension. The cops!

He flinched. "Shh. It's just us, the way it's supposed to be."

Her fingers hardened into a grip. "Help me! He's going to kill me!"

Philip rose up, eyed her, disappointment mingling with anger. "Carson. You told the operator your name was Carson. You took your maiden name back."

The anger-coated words stoked a flicker of guilt. His temper, abuse, was not her fault, but even after all the pain, he could so easily press the button that triggered guilt. Her weakness shamed her. "The cops are here. Go! Run while you can, Philip. Leave through the window. Just go! You don't want to go to jail."

He pressed the knife's tip to the hollow of her neck. "That would suit you just fine."

"I don't want to see you in jail." She prayed the directness in her gaze covered the lie. "You helped so many people as a cop. Let someone help you."

"I don't need a doctor. I only need you!"

"Ms. Carson!" the officer shouted. "Are you in there?"

Nothing would sway Philip. Nothing. "Yes!" she screamed.

Philip winced and pressed the tip of the knife to her neck. The tip scraped skin and drew blood.

How much longer before the cop got into her apartment? How long to slice skin? Seconds?

Blood flickered along the narrow column of her neck and dripped on her hair. "Please."

"We're meant to be together." Desperation tinged the anger.

"Just leave. While you can."

He dragged the tip of the knife over her belly, etching a red scratch along her milky-white midline.

Fear contorted her gut as keys rattled in the front door. Had the cops gotten the apartment manager's master key?

Hurry! A door opened but caught on the security chain. Her life depended on just a few more seconds.

Philip wiped the blood trickling from her neck with his forefinger and smeared it across his lips and forehead. "We live and die together."

He raised the knife and plunged it into her gut. At first shock and then agony sliced and burned through her insides as she stared into blue eyes that danced with satisfaction. He pulled the knife back and drove it down toward her neck. It skidded over her collarbone before he sliced her cheek and her arms.

Cops pounded on the door. "Ms. Carson!"

Screaming, she grabbed the blade. The edge cut her palms. Blood gushed from her hands as he pulled the blade free and raised it again. She lost count of how many times he stabbed her before he rose breathless and stood over her. He stared a long moment at the blood blooming on the bedsheets. With his rage spent, his eyes filled with fresh tears. "What have I done? God, I'm sorry."

In the next instant, he vanished through the window, leaving her alone and dying. Stunned by pain, she lay still, feeling the warm blood pool around her body.

A scream caught in her throat as her hands went to her belly, now crimson and wet. The front door finally yielded. The silhouette of the cop appeared in the door frame. "Leah Carson?"

The cop's gaze froze momentarily on the mass of blood pooling around Leah and then swept the room for threats. When he determined the room was clear, he holstered his gun and pushed a button attached to the mic on his vest. "I need an ambulance . . ."

His deep voice drifted away as her insides burned and

she fought to stay awake. She lay as still as possible, fearing Philip had severed an artery.

Her mind drifted to a sandy beach where the breeze was gentle, the sky a bright blue, and the sun warm.

"Ms. Carson, can you hear me?" Desperation edged the words. "Open your eyes."

She looked up, the blurred face of an officer with dark graying hair. Kind, worried eyes.

"Stay with me. Help is coming. Can you tell me who did this?"

Air hissed from a slice in her chest as she struggled for a breath. "My husband. Philip Latimer."

The room chilled quickly and she could hear only faint noises. A shiver passed through her body, and she imagined her spirit leaving, drifting above, looking down at a pale, lifeless body.

Her eyes closing, her mind traveled to the warm beach, where the sky winked crystal clear and the waves lapped against fine sand. A seagull squawked. A gentle breeze. So far away from the pain, Philip, and death.

CHAPTER ONE

Four years later
Saturday, January 14, 7 P.M.
Nashville, Tennessee

Tennessee Bureau of Investigation Agent Alex Morgan arrived at an abandoned warehouse located on the frigid banks of the Cumberland River. Weeds and yellow crime scene tape circled the warehouse, which was scarred with black scorch marks from a recent fire. Each window was smashed.

On cold nights, the homeless broke into abandoned structures like this one, and set paper and sticks on fire for warmth. He guessed flames had jumped, spread too quickly, and licked up the wooden rafters.

An unseen door banged open and closed in the bitter wind that cut across the mile-wide river, flapping the tape and chilling him to the bone. He turned up his charcoal-gray overcoat collar and burrowed his hands deeper into his pockets fingering a pocketknife he always carried. Fifteen minutes earlier, he'd been on his way to Rudy's, a honky-tonk on Broadway. Not a normal haunt for him, but tonight was a rare night off. And surprisingly, a date. Both rarities.

Blue lights from three cop cars flashed as three officers huddled near the ring of yellow tape.

Frozen dirt crunched and crackled under his neatly polished wingtips. Brittle grass brushed the sides of his freshly dry-cleaned suit pants as his long legs ate up the ground separating him and the abandoned metal building.

This part of the river, in East Nashville, didn't enjoy the vibrant beat of the city's West End, where the famed Broadway strip sported the neon lights of honky-tonks and restaurants. Even on a night as cold as this, Broadway had its charm, and though the streets weren't as packed as they would be on a summer night, the honky-tonks remained filled with laughter and the music of aspiring artists.

On the East Side of the river, no lights or live music beckoned. The architecture was neither charming nor historic. Instead, not-so-sexy garages, scrap metal companies, and storage facilities housed in boxy one-story metal and industrial brick buildings lined the streets.

A uniformed officer stood at the edge of the crime scene tape. The officer's thin frame, thick blond hair, and ruddy cheeks gave away his youth. He rubbed two gloved hands together and stomped his feet to stay warm.

Alex pulled his badge from his breast pocket. "Alex Morgan, TBI."

The officer frowned. He knew Alex. All the cops knew Alex. The traitor. The turncoat. The agent, who for the last three years, investigated cops. "Yes, sir. Your brother is waiting."

Mindful that the other officers were also staring at him, Alex moved toward the yellow tape. The uniformed officer didn't bother to raise the tape for Alex. Uncaring and accustomed to this kind of chill, Alex ducked under the tape and crossed the cracked and potted asphalt. If he really cared about their opinion, which he didn't, he'd have asked them to explain their resentment. Like them, he had joined the force to catch bad guys. The only difference was that he tracked bad guys who hid behind a uniform. If he cared . . .

By the building's entrance stood a tall, broad-shouldered man powerfully built, and wearing a perpetual frown. He wore a knit cap and a thick, black, well-worn overcoat that covered dark pants and heavy muddied boots. He was Alex's older brother, Deke Morgan, and he headed up the Nashville Police Department's Homicide Squad.

"Deke," he said.

His brother turned, the scowl on his face easing a fraction. "Thanks for coming."

"This is a first. A murder scene?" As an agent with the Tennessee Bureau of Investigation, it had been a couple of years since he'd shifted away from murder investigations to internal affairs. "What do you have?"

Deke handed Alex a set of black rubber gloves. "A burned torso. No hands, no feet. No head." Each word puffed out in cold clouds as he spoke.

Alex's tall, rawboned frame topped six three. Deke had been gifted with strength and bulk, whereas Alex enjoyed speed and agility. Despite physical differences, each matched the other in raw determination.

Alex yanked on the gloves. "There's a homeless problem down here. And normally, the death of a vagrant doesn't rate this kind of attention."

They'd both been in police work long enough to understand that politics followed, even in death.

"Not so sure this guy is homeless."

Deke clicked on a heavy-duty flashlight, and the two moved into the building. The scent of gasoline and charred flesh hung heavy in the room. In the far right corner, portable lights glared over the blackened remains of something that didn't resemble anything human. Fire could do that. Melt away all traces of humanity.

One forensic technician dressed in a jumpsuit and a jacket shot pictures of the body while another sketched the scene.

Alex stared closely at the body. In an intense fire, flames ate away the hands and feet first. "Extremities burned by fire?"

"Dismembered. Bone cuts are clean and precise."

Interesting. "Cause of death?"

"Gunshot wound to the chest. No large bloodstains, which makes me think murder and dismemberment happened at another location."

"Male or female?" Alex asked, his interest growing.

"Appears to be male," he said. "Someone tossed gasoline or diesel on him and then set him on fire. The flames burned quickly and hot, ate up his skin before it fizzled out."

"Clothes?"

"Body was stripped."

"Any sign of the extremities or head?"

"No. I've got an officer coming with a dog in the morning to search the area."

"Who found the body?"

"A couple of homeless guys called. They didn't give names but said where the body could be found. Officer O'Connor responded and reported it."

"No identification on or near the body?"

"No."

"Time of death estimates?"

"Don't know yet. Cold is making that a tough call. Could be a couple of days if not more."

"I'm surprised the fire wasn't reported."

"We had that snowstorm last week. Could have been missed, and judging by the looks, the building contained the fire. I expect the medical examiner will be able to tell us quite a bit more."

The facts processed, Alex met his brother's gaze. "Why am I here for a dead guy who may or may not be homeless?"

A smile flickered on Deke's bulldog face. "Always warm and fuzzy."

Small talk wasted time. "I'm trying."

That jostled a laugh. "Right." Deke shined the light toward a distant corner filled with rubble, where moonlight leaked in through the building's patchwork roof and cast eerie slashes of light across the cement floor. An animal scurried across the floor.

"It's what I found near the victim." The two moved toward a midsize, worn brown leather bag.

"Looks like a tool kit," Alex said.

"Might be. I'm guessing it belongs to our guy."

Alex knelt and studied the case's weathered exterior. Inside it looked as if it had once held wrenches, screwdrivers, and an assortment of other items but now was empty. Deke wouldn't have mentioned the bag without reason. "Has this been photographed?"

"And dusted for prints."

With a gloved hand, he reached inside the case and, in a side pocket, found a 9mm Beretta. "He stashes the bag and gun in the corner."

"He wasn't expecting trouble, or he had another gun on him that was taken."

Alex glanced back at the charred body. "I'd say trouble found him."

Deke rubbed his chilled hands together, seeming to replay the crime in his head. "Company shoots him. Strips the body and cuts off head, hands, and feet. Sets the torso on fire."

"Nothing to identify the victim." A lot of trouble to go to for a homeless guy.

Deke squatted in front of the bag and shined the light inside. "There's a card tucked in the side pocket. Easy to miss the first time."

Alex fished through the pocket until his fingers brushed the dog-eared card. He pulled it up into Deke's light. The card read DEIDRE JONES, POLICE OFFICER, NASHVILLE POLICE DEPARTMENT. "What the hell."

Deke read the card. "Shit. What's her card doing here?"

"You called me about Jones last week. Wanted me to do some digging. Think she's skimming money. But you gave me her rank as detective. This is an old card. This guy knew her from the past."

"That's my guess."

"Could he have been a confidential informant?"

"Maybe." Deke allowed his gaze to drift. "Keep talking."

"The two had a meet. This guy gets shot and dismembered. You think Jones could have shot him?"

"A cop would know how to make an identification difficult. And this is going to be a difficult identification unless we've got DNA for a cross-check."

Alex had dug only a little into Deidre Jones's past and work life. What he had learned so far was that she was smart. She closed a lot of cases and was well respected.

Deke shifted his stance. "You'd think she'd also have the sense to search the area first. Sanitize it completely."

"Jones has been with the Nashville Police Department for eight years. Top in her class at the academy. Worked as a uniformed officer for four years before being promoted to detective. Impressive closure rate. Good cop by all appearances. But that's skimming the surface." Alex sifted through more Deidre Jones facts. "She's in tremendous shape. Organized a marathon training group. Well liked. I considered joining the group but decided against it. These days when I show up, people clam up. I'm trying to make friends with a member of Jones's running group."

"Make friends?"

"Miracles do happen." Alex's waking hours were spent working, and the one or two folks he called friends dated back to middle school. "She's recently separated from her husband. Divorce wasn't friendly."

Deke grunted. "Which ones are?"

"You should know."

Deke absently rubbed his thumb against his naked ring finger. "Two divorces is my limit."

"You have two strikes already so does that mean you're not getting married again or divorced again?"

"Divorced again." Deke shoved his hand in his pocket. "I asked Rachel to marry me."

"And?"

"She's chewing on it." Deke and defense attorney Rachel Wainwright had been living together for almost a year and a half.

"She's a lawyer. They weigh all the options."

"That's what worries me. On paper, I don't look like a winning horse."

Alex noted the rising and unexpected worry in his brother's voice. "Rachel is the patron saint of lost causes. She'll say yes eventually."

"Saying I'm a lost cause?"

"When it comes to marriage, yes."

"Ass."

Alex shrugged and shifted his focus back to the case. "Deidre did a hell of a job bringing down Ray Murphy. Her case was ironclad, but if she comes up dirty, his defense attorneys are going to have a field day." Ray Murphy was a drug dealer who'd made millions selling meth. Deidre had worked undercover, getting Murphy's girlfriend to flip and wear a wire. It had taken a year, but Deidre had worked the case better than any other cop could have.

"You think Murphy set this little scene up?"

"He's smart enough. I wouldn't put it past him."

Alex studied the bag and then glanced back at the body. "Find anything else?"

"That's it. Ballistics and whatever else forensics finds will have to be sifted through at the lab."

"All right."

Deke stared at the bag, illuminated in the halo of the flashlight. "She's a highly decorated officer. I want whatever facts you can dig up before I talk to her."

Never ask a question without knowing the answer first. They'd learned the lesson in the cradle from their father, the late Buddy Morgan, a legend in the Nashville Police Department Homicide Squad. Most kids got bedtime stories. The Morgan kids heard recaps of homicide cases. Not a surprise all of the Morgan children had gone into law enforcement. Their other brother, Rick, worked homicide with Deke, and baby sister, Georgia, was a forensic technician.

Of all the Morgan children, Deke looked the most like their father. Old-timers said he was a carbon copy. Rick, the next in line, was a slighter version of Deke. Alex shared their dark coloring, but his features were more aquiline and narrow, like their mother's. Georgia, adopted when she was days old, was the outlier when it came to looks. She favored her birth mother's strawberry-blond hair and freckles, though when it came to temperament, she was all Morgan.

Deke and Rick loved homicide and, no doubt, would do the work until the city forced them to take the gold retirement watch. Alex didn't see himself in TBI in the next decade. He made no secret about his political ambitions.

"Okay. I'll keep digging." Alex checked his watch. "I've got to go. Georgia is singing tonight."

Georgia sang on her off nights in Rudy's. Her musical talent had also been a gift from her birth mother. No Morgan brother could have identified a musical key or note, even if presented with a lineup. "I texted her and told her I was here. She understands."

"Right." They might not like it, but they understood the demands of being a cop.

Deke's lips lifted into a rusty grin. "You sure you want to go to Rudy's?" A retired cop owned the bar, which had become a favorite hangout for anyone wearing a badge.

"I told Georgia I'd be there."

"You're going to get hassled."

A smile tipped the edge of his lips. "They can try."

Deke laughed. "I remember when you were a kid. Mom bought you that stupid striped shirt. You were in the fourth grade?"

"Fifth."

"You got all kinds of teasing over that shirt. And instead of trashing it, you wore it every day for two months."

"Became known as my fighting shirt." Alex had never gone looking for a fight, but when one found him, he never backed away. After eight weeks, the shirt had been torn, mended, and bloodied more times than anyone could remember. When it vanished from the wash, his mother had denied responsibility, but they all knew she'd finally thrown it out. Alex could handle the trouble, but their mom could not.

"Georgia also tells me you have a date."

Alex could have asked how his sister knew about the date but didn't bother. She had radar, a fact he'd accepted long ago. "Yep."

"I thought she was joking."

"No."

"So who's the lucky girl?"

"Leah Carson."

"The veterinarian who takes care of Rick's dog?"

Their brother Rick had been a canine officer who'd been allowed to adopt Tracker after the dog had been retired. "Yes."

"How'd you meet?"

"Rick is boarding his dog at the vet's kennel. I told him I'd check on Tracker while he was gone."

"What's special about Leah?"

"She's Deidre's new best friend."

Deke nodded. "You set this up."

"I did."

"How'd you get Rick to board Tracker?"

"Told him I needed an undercover officer with four legs. He liked the idea of his canine working again."

"And now you and Deidre's friend are going on a date?"

"That's right." Digging his phone out of his pocket, he texted Georgia. RUNNING LATE. GIVE MY DATE THE HEADS-UP. BUY HER A DRINK. BE THERE IN TWENTY.

"What do you know about her?"

"Not much. But that's the point of a date. To learn."

"Mixing business with pleasure?"

When it came to catching the bad guys, lying came naturally to Alex. He did what he had to do. In his personal life he never lied. Leah was the first time black and white had muddied to gray.

"Leah's the only personal friend Deidre Jones seems to have these days. Wouldn't hurt to find out what she knows about Deidre." Alex's phone dinged with a text. WILL DO. He slid his phone back into his pocket. "Have you gotten me a rundown on Deidre's recent cases?"

"On my desk. I'll send it tomorrow."

Neither one of them liked the idea of investigating Deidre. But good cops went bad for all variety of reasons, and when they went bad, Alex had the unpleasant job of mopping up the mess. "I'll call you when I have something."

"Talk only to me."

"Understood."

CHAPTER TWO

Saturday, January 14, 8 P.M.

Until death do us part.

The freshly tattooed wedding vow ran along the twenty-six bones of his spine, entwined by a thorny, flowerless vine that coiled around and cut through the neatly scripted letters. A delicate sparrow fluttered above a jagged thorn and the word *Death*.

Each prick of the tattoo artist's needle had been a painful reminder of the love he carried for his sparrow, a lovely wife who, confused and misled by lying friends, didn't understand the true depth of his commitment.

Though she'd left him, he'd never stopped keeping tabs on her, and he'd tracked her to her rented town house near Nashville's West End Park. He'd cried when she'd begun flirting shamelessly with men. When she'd begun sleeping with them, hurt had turned to rage. His little lark had turned into a whore.

Now, he sat in his dark truck parked at the corner of Fourth and Broadway. Across lanes of traffic, he watched her sitting in her car, the engine running. He knew her routine well. When she went out, when she met her new friend for a glass of wine, when she arrived at and left work. No detail was too small. Not one iota missed.

She got out of her car, locked it, and, hands tucked in her pockets with head ducked against a cold wind, and marched up Broadway. She paused at a honky-tonk called Rudy's and, for a moment, stared into the large window, studying the crowd.

A slight smile tweaked the edges of his lips. "Looking for me, babe? Think I'm inside?"

After a pause, another woman approached her, and the two exchanged laughs before she tugged open the front door and they moved inside. He knew the other woman as well. His wife's new best friend.

He shifted forward in his seat, leaning against the steering wheel as he watched her through the window. Rudy's, buffered from the cold and alight with music and laughter, was packed with customers.

His wife pulled her scarf free and opened her jacket as she lingered on the fringe of the crowd. She wore a long-sleeved black turtleneck that accentuated her full breasts. Black hair hung loose around her shoulders. He didn't like the new look. Too dramatic. Bossy. She'd made so many changes, and he hated them all.

She smiled and raised her hand. His gut twisted, imagining the smile for another man. Even with dark hair, she was a pretty woman, and men wanted her. Pretty women like his wife didn't go to bars unless they wanted to find a man. His sweet wife now consorted like a barhopping slut.

Jealousy knifed through anger, allowing the sadness to bleed free as images of those perfect first days of their relationship flashed by. She'd once looked at him with such trust and unfailing devotion, as if only he could make her world better. Her love had empowered him, stroked his ego and washed away the demons of his own troubled past.

Those days had been perfect. And they were gone.

Now, his wife melted into the crowd, no doubt nestling into another man's embrace. Kissing him. Touching him. Whispering seductive words in his ear.

He gripped the edge of the steering wheel and pushed his spine into the seat, grinding hard leather into the fresh tattoo. Pain shot up and down along his spine, firing along all the tender nerves in his back.

"I gave you everything. And you left me."

The men and women who streamed into the bar all had a look. Short hair. Swagger. Frequent glances from left to right before entering. A tug of a jacket over a sidearm. Counting secondary exits. This wasn't an ordinary bar. It was a cop hangout.

Took one to know one.

The badge had attracted her. Her father had died, and she'd been lost and alone. Afraid. She wasn't a badge bunny, looking for a quick lay. She'd needed a man who could take care of her. Be strong. That sweet young girl had needed his protection. And he'd gladly given it, and his love.

Regrets swirled, fluttering like buzzing bees. Maybe he'd held on too tightly. Maybe he'd worried too much about where she went or whom she befriended. He'd always asked, pushed for answers, never satisfied and never noticing how she'd chaffed under his love.

Her abandonment had been devastating and jarring. Anger had receded to desperation and, immediately, he'd set out to prove his love. Flowers, letters, phone calls, visits to her new apartment. All were signs of *his love*. But the harder he held on, the harder she'd pulled away.

Regardless of how long they'd been separated, there'd be no surrender. He would never give up on her. Ever.

"Until death do us part, babe."

Yeah, he'd made mistakes, but the vows they'd spoken had been clear.

"Until death."

CHAPTER THREE

Saturday, January 14, 9:15 P.M.

No should have been the operative word. No, thank you. *Thanks, but no thanks. Maybe another time* would have worked. But Special Agent Alex Morgan had caught Leah Carson off guard when he'd asked her out. With no excuses in her back pocket, she'd fallen into a *yes* before she could think twice.

Leah had sworn she'd never date a cop again, and here she was on the brink. She'd recognized the signs that he was a cop when he'd first entered the vet hospital. The way he moved. His dark, crisp suit. The controlled, careful gaze, always assessing. A cop through and through. She had known. Should have run.

His visits to the clinic all made sense of course. He'd been checking up on his cop brother's retired canine cop dog that was boarding for a couple of days. According to the clinic staff, the Morgan siblings were all cops. A sister worked forensics. Two brothers worked Nashville homicide. And Alex was an agent with the Tennessee Bureau of Investigation.

She inhaled and exhaled. This was a date. Not a relation-ship. Shouldn't be a big deal to go on a date with a cop. Once. But it *was* a big deal. Everyone assumed cops kept you safe, right? They were the good guys, right? Sometimes. Most times. But not always.

"Come along," Alex had challenged. "It'll be fun."

Fun. The word hadn't fit Alex Morgan. Straitlaced. His sharp, assessing gaze devoured details and nuances. And his even, controlled voice gave away nothing. He wasn't a guy who did fun.

She'd been reaching for a quick *no* when he'd tossed in a very disarming smile, and for a split second, she'd been charmed. The *yes* had slipped out through a tiny crack in her carefully constructed barriers.

"Stupid." She curled her fingers over her scarred palms as she glanced around the noisy restaurant. He'd offered to drive her to the bar, but she'd insisted on driving herself. Knowing where she worked was one thing. Knowing where she lived, another.

The energy of the bar, the loud taped music, the buzz of conversation and the clink of glasses swirled. Freezing temperatures had not chased away Rudy's customers. Wall-to-wall mob. A crush. There were a few cowboy hats and men wearing western garb, but the majority had short-cropped hair, long-sleeved shirts, and well-worn jeans. Most had beers and many glanced toward the windows and doors. The ones who sat had their backs to the walls. Made sense that a cop would invite her to a cop function.

When she'd moved back to Nashville, her first stop had been Broadway and a cowboy boot store. She'd bought a midcalf-high boot with a pointed tip, tassels, and a heel tipped in silver. Oddly, she'd not worn the boots until tonight, and only impulse had made her put them on. Now the choice bothered her. The boots had a pay-attention-to-me vibe, made her stick out just a little too much.

A long time ago, in another life, the boots wouldn't have been a concern. A long time ago, she'd been a different person who didn't worry about boots or cop dates. Now, doubts, like the bright neon signs on the strip, flashed. Too much? Too coy? Trying too hard?

Twenty-nine-year-old women should know what normal people did on dates. They were comfortable with men and enjoyed their company.

They. Had. Fun.

Index fingers absently traced the scars on her palms, still rough to the touch. The plastic surgeon had done his best to minimize the scarring, but palms were a tricky stitch job. The wounds had reopened twice and had to be restitched. Never fully fading, the scars always warned that sometimes smiles, even the best ones, hid evil.

Clutching her purse close, she glanced out the front window toward Broadway. The door was opened by a couple and the cold air cut like a whip. If this had been July, the streets would have been teeming with people, but on a cold January night, the sidewalks produced only the occasional group of partygoers burrowed in thick coats and wooly scarves. No one lingered or strolled. All hurried in and out of doorways.

Crowds or near desolation both offered advantages and disadvantages. Crowds offered cover. Empty streets gave her room to run.

A man caught her gaze, but hers quickly flittered away. Before her ex-husband, a stranger's passing glance or a man's seductive smile excited and titillated. Laughter came quickly and easily. *Yes* wasn't to be feared. Thoughts didn't have to be assessed and reassessed.

Philip had changed all that when he'd entered her life. Now, as she had a thousand times before, she wondered how she could have loved him. Married him. How did a smart woman miss the rising tide of suffocating attention and control? Exactly one year after they spoke their marriage vows, his final attack had left her with twenty-three knife wounds, nightmares, and unpredictable panic attacks.

The beat of the honky-tonk music pulsed in Leah's chest, racing alongside her thrumming heart. Twenty feet separated her from the door and a clean getaway.

So easy, fear whispered. *Leave while you can.*

Fear's warnings had stopped her so many times. Too many nights spent huddled behind a closed, triple-locked door. Too many nightmares.

Fear had gifted her with it all.

"You're not quitting," she whispered.

Philip did not have the power to control her. After his attack, he'd vanished. Weeks later, his car had been found in South Carolina at the bottom of a ravine. The car had been badly burned, the body unrecognizable. The authorities had shipped the body and his belongings back to Nashville, and his grandmother had seen to his burial. She hadn't attended the funeral, and had only visited the gravesite once before she'd left for Knoxville. That was to confirm the bastard was in his grave.

The front door opened to herald a few more laughing couples. No Alex.

Still time to leave, fear coaxed.

No, she insisted, *time to stay*. Turning from the cold blast of air, she embraced the warmth, the music, the laughter, and that *before* Leah, who might have been a bit naïve and trusting but who'd been fun. She'd had friends. No fears.

Tonight, she clung to the memories of the *before* Leah and banished warnings and prophecies of doom.

"It's the deep end of the ocean, Leah," she muttered. "Jump or dive?"

A petite redhead, her hair pinned in a loose riot of curls around her face, cut straight through the crowd over to Leah. "Dr. Carson?"

"Yes?"

The woman had a wide, welcoming grin. "I heard my brother Alex invited you tonight. Welcome."

Leah searched her memory for the woman's name, but it lingered out of reach. "Thanks."

Reading Leah's questioning expression, the woman's smile broadened. "Sorry. Right. Forgetting introductions. I'm Georgia Morgan. Youngest of the Morgan clan. My brother Rick speaks highly of you. Loves the way you take care of Tracker."

Tracker. The police canine boarding at her vet hospital. Her nerves relaxed. Dogs were safe, soothing territory. "He's a great dog. We always like seeing him. Your brother Rick wasn't happy about boarding him a few weeks ago."

"It's the first time he's ever boarded the dog. He and his wife are having a great time on their honeymoon, but Jenna knows the dog is not far from Rick's mind."

Honeymoons meant happiness. New beginnings. Love. And on cue, she produced a practiced smile to hide the flicker of worry. "The dog is doing great."

"So I hear."

"Was it Rick's idea to send Alex by every day to check on Tracker?"

Agent Morgan had appeared every day and stayed long enough to take Tracker outside and then speak a few words to her. He always varied his arrival times, a disciple of "trust but verify."

Georgia laughed. "We Morgans keep an eye out for those we love."

Keep an eye out for those we love. The statement should have warmed her heart, but she filed the comment away under *potential threat*. "You're close-knit."

"We are." Glancing toward the bar, she waved toward the bartender, an older man who'd shaved his head bald, sported a thick, bushy mustache, and wore a full, bright Hawaiian shirt that draped a rounded belly.

Leah followed Georgia's gaze. "He looks annoyed."

"That's KC. He owns the place, and he's giving me the stink eye because I'm supposed to be onstage in thirty seconds."

She calculated the distance to the stage. "Thirty seconds. Cutting it close."

Strong fingers with neatly shorn nails waved breezily around Georgia's head. "Well timed, I like to say."

Leah couldn't help grinning. "Don't let me hold you up."

"I hate to give people what they want right away." She lingered, questions dancing in her gaze as she sized up Leah.

"I understand you're a very good singer. I work with a gal at the clinic who's heard you sing a few times. I can't wait to hear you." A bubble of tension grew inside her.

"Thanks. I like to rock the house." She turned, and then paused, as if remembering. "Alex just texted me. He told me to tell you he's running late."

"He could have texted me."

"Didn't get your number. Has the vet number, but not your private cell."

"I must have forgotten to give it to him."

"He won't be much longer. He's sent me five texts in the last half hour, updating me on his status." She leaned closer, as if they were conspirators. "He's communicated more this evening than in the last month."

"I don't picture him texting." In truth, his tardiness gave

her a chance to corral nerves that bucked out of reach despite her positive self-talk.

Maybe he'll be so late you'll miss each other entirely tonight, fear said. *Maybe you'll have a beer, hear some great music, and go home. No harm. No foul.*

Georgia laid her hand on Leah's arm. "If Alex says he'll be here, he will."

"Great." She watched Georgia cut through the crowd, crack jokes with a few of the men and women, and take her place on center stage. The band behind her was comprised of two guitars, a drummer, and a fiddle player. The fiddle player sawed a few chords of "Fire on the Mountain" as Georgia wrapped her fingers around the mic.

Nestling her mouth close to it, Georgia asked, "You boys and girls ready for some trouble tonight?"

The crowd hooped, hollered, and clapped.

The heat in the room rising, Leah moved toward a coatrack and hung her jacket on a peg. Habit had her recounting the exits in the bar. Only two, and neither was easily reached. Tension rippled through her body. What had her therapist said? *Breathe in. Breathe out. You're going to be fine.*

Moving toward an open spot on the bar, she welcomed the task of getting a beer more than the drink itself. Something to hold would make her feel more normal for a second or two. Normal twenty-nine-year-old women held a beer, right? And then, once she got the beer, well, she'd worry about what came next.

As Georgia began a lively tune, a Taylor Swift song about boys and true love, the bartender, KC, caught sight of her almost immediately and lumbered toward her. "What can I get you?"

She smiled because people in lively places like this were

supposed to be having a good time and people having a good time smiled. "A beer."

He picked up a rag from under the bar and wiped the space in front of her. "Bottle or draft?"

"Bottle."

From a cooler below the bar, he pulled out an iced bottled beer. She watched as he popped the top and set it in front of her. As she reached for money, he shook his head. "Alex said he'd cover the tab when he got here."

Was everyone watching her? That should have made her feel protected, right? "How do you know I'm here with Alex?"

"He told me to expect a pretty petite brunette. And I saw you talking to his sister."

He was complimenting her, and compliments prompted smiles. She smiled. "Thanks."

His deep voice cut through the music. "Alex hates to be late. But that's the nature of a cop's job."

"Makes sense. No schedule for crime and all."

As Georgia's voice rose and teased the edges of a high note, KC leaned closer. "He's a hell of a good cop. Great guy. Bit of a control freak. In a good way of course."

She sipped her beer, wondering if there was a good kind of control freak. "Of course."

KC leaned on the bar, in no real rush to move along. "I hear from Georgia that you work at the vet hospital."

The cold beer tasted good. "For about four months now."

Beefy fingers swiped over a thick mustache. "What're you, like a nurse?"

"Like a doctor. I'm a veterinary surgeon."

A dark brow arched, and she sensed he'd checked off another box on a mental list. "A real animal doctor."

Grinning, she raised the bottle to her lips. "I've got the papers to prove it."

"Good for you." A patron at the bar held up an empty glass and called out, but he waved him away. "So how did you and Alex meet?"

"At the clinic. Tracker introduced us."

KC laughed. "Right. Makes sense. That dog gets around." He turned to go, then paused. "You know, there's nothing to be nervous about."

She swallowed a gulp of beer. "I'm not nervous."

He winked. "I used to be a cop. I know nervous when I see it."

A direct gaze, she'd been told, conveyed truth and courage. "I'm not nervous. Must be fatigue. I worked a twelve-hour shift today."

"My mistake." His tone didn't sound apologetic. "Your accent sounds like Nashville."

"Born and raised here. Went to vet school in Knoxville, but as soon as I graduated, I came back home." Maybe, if she tossed the guy a few easy facts, he'd back off.

"Family?" He kept wiping the very clean bar. Most would see a man making conversation, but cops didn't just make conversation.

"Mother and father have passed."

"Sorry to hear that. You got brothers and sisters?"

Smile. Sip the beer. Act normal. "Are you writing a book about me, KC?"

A laugh rumbled in his chest. "Hard to break the cop habits."

"Right." He continued to lean toward her, still waiting for an answer.

Leah nodded toward a couple of women at the end of the bar. "You've got some thirsty gals over there."

KC glanced down the bar at a collection of women raising empty beer mugs. "No rest for the wicked."

No truer words. "So they tell me."

"Back to work."

She tipped the beer bottle's neck toward him. "Good to meet you, KC."

He saluted. "You too, Dr. Leah."

She faced the stage and watched as Georgia sang and swayed to the music. She had the crowd in the palm of her hand, and Leah envied her command of the room.

A tap on her shoulder had her jumping, and she turned to see a tall gal with dark brown hair. She had a full, smiling face and a sharp gaze. Dressed in black, a thick chain around her neck dipped between the hollow of her breasts.

Leah smiled, relaxing. They'd bumped into each other at the front door minutes earlier, but Deidre had made a beeline for the ladies' room. "Deidre."

"I see you're all settled in. Cold night."

"Nice in here."

Leah had met Deidre Jones a couple of months ago at the gym. They'd become friends, and when Deidre had suggested Leah join a marathon training group, she'd agreed. This New Year was about making new choices. Living. Taking full breaths. And having a friend was nice. "What brings you here tonight?"

Deidre grinned. "Got a date tonight."

"A date?"

She winked, like a normal, happy woman would. "Nice to play and not work."

"Still running in the morning?"

"If the date doesn't go too late, I'll be there."

"So is that a yes or a no?" Grinning, she mimicked Deidre's pointed look when Leah waivered on a run date.

Deidre tipped the top of her bottle toward Leah in a touché kind of salute. "It's a yes."

"Good. Always more fun when you're there."

Leah searched around. "Where is this date?"

"In the head. He'll be right back. Just wanted to say hi again."

The familiar face loosened a few knots. "Thanks." A man approached behind Deidre. Tall, blond. "Is that David Westbrook from our running group?"

"Yep." She grinned. "But don't tell anyone in the group. I don't need a lot of shit about it. My soon-to-be ex-husband will just make more trouble."

Deidre had spoken of her divorce to Leah a few times. She hadn't used the word *stalking*, but Leah had recognized the pattern. She'd offered suggestions that Deidre had brushed aside. "Sure."

David grinned as he wrapped an arm around Deidre. "Leah. See you in the morning?"

"I'll be there."

"Great."

"See you." Deidre hooked her arm in David's and the two vanished into the crowd.

"Right." She nudged her back close to the bar and watched as Georgia moved back and forth onstage. The woman had an easy confidence Leah admired.

A man jostled next to her at the bar. When she glanced in his direction, he grinned. "Hey. I'm Max."

She moved back a step. "Hey."

"You here by yourself, little lady?" He had to shout to be heard.

"No."

He made an effort to look around her. "I don't see anybody."

She dug her fingernail into the silver label of her beer

and ripped the paper. Dogs, cats, snakes, even birds she knew. In an animal, she read dangerous fear or childlike joy at a glance, but people, well, Philip had proven that she didn't understand the warning signs. A fight-or-flight impulse tightened her chest. She barely recognized her voice when she heard it. "I'm waiting for Alex Morgan."

Brown eyes narrowed and then widened slightly. "You're dating that ass?"

The mention of Alex's name had several other people shifting their attention to her. So Alex wasn't popular. Interesting. Still, he'd been nice to her, and that fostered an odd kind of loyalty. She sipped her beer. "I only see one ass."

The man's gaze narrowed, but instead of moving toward her, he took a step back, held up a hand in surrender, and melted into the crowd.

As much as Leah would like to think she was a tough customer, small-boned, five foot two and 105 pounds soaking wet, her size didn't scare away much. He hadn't bolted because of her big, bad scary self.

The wall of energy behind her, vibrating and snapping close, had scared him off. Tightening her grip on her beer, she turned to find Alex Morgan standing behind her.

A Saturday night and he wore a dark suit, a white shirt, and a narrow red tie twisted in a Windsor knot. Ink-black hair cut short and brushed off his face stressed a long, narrow face marked with lines around the eyes and mouth. She guessed he'd earned those lines by frowning, not smiling.

"Was he giving you a problem?" Alex's gaze darted past her toward Max before settling back on her.

The tension cranked up a notch. Max was an annoyance. Alex was dangerous. He'd heard the comment, noticed the stares but had not reacted. "He was trying to make conversation."

A muscle in his jaw clenched, released. He shifted his attention away from Max, dismissing him as a non-threat. "I see KC got you a beer." He had to shout over the music.

"He did. Thank you." The music pulsed, making conversation difficult. She guessed she'd been in the bar ten minutes, which put the time at about ten. How long did a date last before it ended?

"Can I get you another beer?"

"No. Just got started on this one." A glance toward the bar found KC twisting the top off a beer bottle and pushing it Alex's way. He scooped up the beer but didn't drink.

Alex turned toward the stage as Georgia finished her song. The crowd cheered, and he raised a beer bottle to her when she looked in his direction. She winked. The band settled into a softer, slower song.

"She's good," Leah said. Maybe talk would burst the anxiety bubble. "Has she always sung?"

"Since she could talk. But she's only been singing in public for a couple of years." He sipped his beer and faced her. "You look pale. Are you okay?"

Lying hadn't always come as naturally as it did now. "I'm fine."

His blue-steel gaze studied her. "You look like you want to bolt."

Normally, a smile and a few fibs deflated questions and concerns. "I spend my days with barking dogs and hissing cats. Haven't been out in a while."

"There's a restaurant across the street. Much quieter and less crowded. We'll go there."

It wasn't a suggestion but a direction. She wasn't sure what scared her more: the pulsing beat of this crowd or being alone with him. The frying pan or the fire?

New Year's resolutions had prompted so many changes

in the last couple of weeks. *Get out. Be a part of humanity.*
It had been an easy enough promise to make on New Year's,
after she'd finished her second glass of champagne, as she'd
watched the televised ball in Times Square drop. "Sure.
Sounds good. Let me get my coat." She set her beer on the
bar and grabbed her coat. He took it from her and held it
out. Not controlling but the move of a gentleman, she reminded herself.

A smile flicking the edges of her lips, she turned and
lowered her arms into the coat. He raised the coat up to her
neck, his fingertips barely brushing the back of her hair.
The physical touch constricted her lungs.

Smiling, always smiling, she turned and faced Alex.

A dark brow arched. "You okay?"

"Great."

She moved out toward the door, threading her body
around the growing crowd. He trailed close behind, and she
caught several angry gazes directed at Alex and her. Outside, the snap of cold air redirected her attention from
worry. "Where to?"

"Right across the street." He moved beside her and
gently placed his hand in the small of her back, guiding
her. Gently. Not all touch equaled pain. No worries.

The restaurant specialized in barbecue and was outfitted
with clean but dinged-up booths. The floor had once been
a black-and-white tile, but years of wear and tear had worn
away the crisp lines, leaving it a shadowy blend of dark and
light. Behind the counter, a hot grill butted against the wall
where a tall man wearing a white apron over a white shirt
ladled barbecue sauce on dozens of sizzling chicken wings
and thighs. The sweet, spicy scents were welcoming.

They settled in a seat by the front window and she
shrugged off her jacket, refusing to be nervous. This was

a date. Nothing more. Dates were fun. And she wasn't a crazy woman. She could go on a date with a guy. She could.

Alex ordered a couple more beers and reached for the laminated menus stuck between the napkin holder and the salt-and-pepper shakers. "Place might not look like much, but the barbecue is great." He unfolded his menu. "Vets eat meat, don't they?"

"I do. Love barbecue." She wouldn't eat much, but she could push the food around and make a show of it. Their beers arrived, and he asked if he could place their order. She agreed, but instantly second-guessed herself, wondering if giving him any kind of control was a smart thing.

She sipped her beer and realized she hadn't eaten much that day. She'd worked late and her appetite was off due to nerves and fatigue. When the waiter set biscuits on the table, she took one and broke off a piece.

"Rick says you're a popular vet with dogs."

"I love what I do, so it's easy." She took a sip of beer. "He says you're a great agent."

Alex traced the label on his bottle. "He didn't say that."

"Maybe not in so many words. But my receptionist got him talking the last time he was in, and she said he had nice things to say about you."

He studied the menu. "So you and your receptionist were talking about me?"

Color rushed to her cheeks. "I suppose we were. We take care of several of the police canines, and we generally talk about them and their families."

He closed the menu and looked up. "Good to know. So you must have a dog?"

"No. No dogs for me. I work long hours. Maybe one day." Since Philip, she'd feared loving anything too much in case it would be taken away.

"I picture you with a houseful of cats and dogs. The homespun type."

"You're making fun of me."

"Not at all. Making an observation."

Homespun jabbed, conjuring rocking chairs, shawls, and, well, old. "You're not the animal type."

"I like Tracker. But I'm not a dog or a cat guy. I'm on the go too much."

"Which begs the question, why did you ask me out?"

He sat back in the booth and tugged his coat jacket in place. "You're different. Interesting."

"In a homespun sort of way?"

"In a multilayered sort of way."

She sensed he had lots of questions, but there would be no peeking behind the curtain where she hid her secrets. "I vaccinate dogs and cats all day. Most interesting thing I've done lately is joining a running group."

"With Deidre Jones? She told me a vet had joined the group."

"I didn't realize you knew Deidre."

"She works with my brother at the Nashville Police Department. We cross paths occasionally. How's the running going?"

"I'm the slowest in the group. And that's not false modesty. It's the truth."

"Tortoise and the hare. Stick with it."

"Maybe." She sipped her beer. "You don't seem to have a lot of friends at Rudy's."

"No."

"Why?"

"I investigate cops. Doesn't win me many points with the rank and file."

She traced the rim of her cup. Ah, that explained the man's comment in the bar. "Does that bother you?"

"No."

His attention shifted to her palm and the scar slashing across it. She closed her fingers, resisting the urge to explain. Whatever she told him would be a lie. She never told the truth about her past, which still shamed her. How could she explain that she was a smart woman who had stayed with an abusive and, ultimately, murderous man? The less said, the better.

"Seems they'd want to weed out the bad apples."

Alex's expression didn't change, but somewhere inside him she thought she saw a door close and lock. "You would think."

They both hid behind walls. Guarded secrets. Good. *You leave mine alone, and I won't dig into yours.* "So, we're two very simple people."

The corner of his lip tipped into that grin. The ice melted for a moment, and that unfamiliar pull of desire flowered again. Some would have embraced it. Leah likened desire to a tiger's dangerous beauty.

"I think we're two people who're fairly bad at dating and don't like to talk about ourselves," Alex said.

His directness charmed her. And that scared her. Being charmed led to liking, which led to desire, which equaled vulnerability. Her nerves stretched tighter and tighter. "Then why're we here?"

A shrug. "I was curious about you. And Tracker likes you. He's a good judge of character."

Secrets, sadness, and shame banged on the wall so carefully built. She sipped her beer, which now tasted flat and lifeless. "Ah."

"So what about you?"

"I'm fairly straightforward. Raised in Nashville. Both my parents have passed. Got my vet degree in Knoxville at the University of Tennessee. Enjoying the single life."

He leaned forward, as if a bullshit meter had clanged in his head. "How did you get the scars on your hands?"

Cut to the chase. This guy didn't waste time or mince words. No need to look down to see the deep slashes that crossed both palms. "Are you this nosy on most first dates?"

"No." No apology. "They look like defensive wounds."

"Nothing so dramatic," she lied.

No adult had ever asked about the scars on her palms, or the ones on her arms. They might have stared, but they hadn't asked. Once a little girl in a grocery store had asked her about them. She'd looked as if she'd believed in fairy tales, Santa Claus, and the tooth fairy. Monsters under her bed could be chased away with a mother's kiss. Leah couldn't bring herself to tell the girl real monsters walked among them. "It was an accident."

"Okay." Alex tapped a finger on the table, as if forcing back more questions that, eventually, he'd ask. "I didn't mean to upset you."

She kept her hand on her beer glass, refusing to tuck it in her lap. "I'm not upset."

"You're pale now."

She moistened her lips. "Just been a long day."

"It's my job to be nosy." That smile appeared again. "Sometimes it's hard to shut off."

"No worries."

Alex Morgan was the kind of guy who'd unearth all her carefully buried secrets. And when he did, what would he think of her? What kind of woman, what kind of fool, would willingly lay down with a monster? The idea that he'd see her as less or weak scraped the underside of her scars.

Her phone buzzed, startling her. With a grateful heart she dug her phone from her purse and read the message. "It's from my clinic. I've got to go by the kennel to check on one of the dogs."

Alex looked more curious and disappointed. If his job was to sniff out lies, then he surely knew this was no fib. Their clinic took emergency calls, and this was her night on call. "You can't eat first?"

"No." She gathered her coat, anxious to step into the cold and slide behind the wheel of her car.

He tossed a couple of twenties on the table and rose. "I'll walk you to your car."

She gathered up her purse and coat. "You don't have to. I'm right across the street."

"I'll walk you." He helped her on with her coat, opened the front door, and waited for her to pass through before allowing it to swing closed behind them. Across the street, the door to Rudy's opened and closed. In a rush of music and flashing light, Deidre and her date sauntered out arm in arm.

Leah envied the couple's easy manner. Her back stiff, she started toward her car, her pace brisk as she fished her keys from her pocket and pushed the unlock button on the key fob. She opened the door, and he lingered back an extra half step. For a tense moment she thought he might kiss her. Normal women on first dates kissed their dates, right? A kiss, a touch, vulnerability, pain, and death.

Alex held back a couple of steps. He watched her. Seemed to see fear and accept it as a fact to be filed away under *Leah Carson*. "Drive safe."

"I'm sorry."

"For what?"

"I've been a real lousy date, Alex. I'm sorry. I'm way out of practice."

A small shrug. "No worries, Leah. See you soon?"

"You don't have to check up on Tracker every day."

"But I will." The patience humming under his tone coaxed her out of her shell a little further. "You want to go out with me again?"

Fear hovered around her like a ghost. *Stay behind the walls.* But something she could not put into words challenged her to reach for more. Elbowing aside gnawing butterflies, she nodded. "I'd like that."

"Great. We'll figure it out."

"Perfect." She drove off, wondering if she'd lost her mind, all the while daring herself not to look in the rearview mirror, knowing he was watching.

He sat and watched as his wife stood by her car and spoke to her date. The guy had dark hair and a trim build. A gust of wind had caught, blown back his jacket, and for a split second, the edge of a gun resting on his hip caught the moonlight before the guy tugged the coat's edge back into place.

This man was not a beat cop like he'd been. He had the look of a detective. "Moving up in the world, babe. The uniform isn't good enough for you anymore."

Embers of rage, always warm and glowing, flared and flickered into a hot flame. His wife and the guy lingered, staring at each other. A smile flashed on her face, and he knew they'd be seeing each other again.

"She's my wife, dick."

This close he could see dick's face. Keen interest sharpened the man's gaze. No doubt he was thinking about getting into his wife's pants.

Irritated, he tore his gaze away and focused on the mission. He studied the text he'd just sent Leah: EMERGENCY AT THE CLINIC. CAN YOU COME INTO WORK?

"I might be a regular cop, but I found her number and I'm going to win this chess game, dick."

She slid into the front seat, started the engine, and rolled down her window. She glanced up, smiling, nodding, and drove off. Dick got into his car and drove off.

He started his truck and shifted into first gear. Slowly, he turned onto Broadway and followed it until it branched right and turned into West End Avenue.

The drive back to his wife's town house took ten minutes, but of course he knew the way. He'd been watching the house since he'd arrived in Nashville a week before. Many a night in the last couple of weeks, he'd sat in the parking lot across the street and watched her town house. He'd gotten to know all her new habits.

His wife arrived an hour later and parked in her reserved spot under the street lamp. She hurried from her car up the brick front steps of the town house, unlocked the door, and vanished inside. Lights clicked on, and though she'd already drawn the drapes, he could see her figure pass in front of the sliding glass door before the lights in her bedroom clicked on.

He imagined her in that bedroom, stripping off her shirt, her full breasts spilling over the top of her bra. It had been too long since he'd kissed those breasts, but he remembered how soft they felt. He remembered her lips tasted like her cherry lipstick. He remembered those lush lips kissing him along his belly, teasing him to the brink of insanity. He remembered every single detail of their life together.

But she wasn't thinking about him as she stripped off her clothes. A different man lingered in her thoughts. How many men had she fucked since him?

It took all his willpower not to scream as he removed a switchblade from his pocket and flicked it open. Moonlight glinted off the sharp blade as he gouged it into the truck's seat. He sliced through leather, imagining it was flesh.

He leaned back against the seat. Her shadow passed back into the living room, and the light of a television glowed as her silhouette lowered on the couch.

In the last few weeks, he'd learned all her new patterns and all her secrets, tracking her and listening via the bug he'd planted in her house. "No one knows you better than me, babe. No one."

After an hour in the parking lot, the cold had numbed his toes and the tips of his fingers. He would have stayed all night, watching her sit on her couch in front of the television, but there were enough people coming and going at this time of night to get him noticed. He drove off, knowing she was alone in her town house, unable to sleep and thinking about him.

Until death do us part.

The words hummed in the back of his throat. So poignant, and yet their meaning appealed to him.

Until death do us part.

His little bird flew free right now, but soon he'd catch her and pluck off her wings. She belonged to him and no one else.

Until death do us part.

CHAPTER FOUR

Sunday, January 15, 6 A.M.

Keys. Where were the damn car keys? Leah brushed her fingers a second time over and then around the lopsided ceramic blue bowl always by the back door and felt for her keys. A quirky yet unbreakable habit, she always put them by the back door in the exact same place. It was a reasonable habit. Made sense. Saved her time. And it worked so well.

But the keys weren't there. She glanced at the clock on her cell and knew she only had a half hour to meet up with the running group. They started at exactly 6:30 A.M., and if she weren't there, they left without her.

"Where're my keys?" Confirming they weren't in the bowl, she checked her purse, rattled it, turned it upside down. No keys. What had she been doing last night?

Ah, the date. It had been a long day, she'd been tired, but she'd agreed to a date with Alex. He was tall, good-looking, and an ambitious agent. He was the kind of guy most women wanted to date.

She'd wanted to like him, should have liked him, but trust was going to take more than a New Year's resolution.

She moved toward the large couch where she'd eaten dinner, reheated Chinese leftovers, after her return to the town house. She pulled out the cushions. Nothing. Irritated and a bit desperate, she ran her hands along the creases of the couch. Her fingers brushed metal and she pulled out her keys, half relieved yet puzzled that she'd lost them.

Leah had her faults, but she was painfully precise. How could a date have thrown off her routine so completely? Maybe it wasn't the date but the text that had proved to be a false alarm? Was her steady, even life so fragile that she couldn't handle any deviation?

Damn.

She snatched up the keys and hurried to her car. The morning chill cleared her head, but she questioned again this resolve to get fit. She turned on the ignition and switched the window defroster on high as she watched the frost on the windshield slowly melt. "Crazy people run marathons. They're insane. Misguided fools. Sane people are asleep in bed right now."

The ice on the windshield yielded a large enough hole for her to see well enough so she could drive. She threw the car in gear and made a run for it.

As she made her way down the dark streets, the lost keys jangled in her mind. Before Philip had died, missing keys would have totally freaked her out. She'd have panicked and called the cops, certain he was behind the mishap. She'd have called her aunt, hysterical.

Her heart raced. "Philip is gone." He was dead. Buried right here in Nashville.

He wasn't messing with her. She'd simply misplaced her damn keys.

Leah released the breath caught in her throat as she wove her way through town toward Centennial Park. She'd joined the running group when Deidre had reached out to her. She'd already decided to give up smoking as a New Year's resolution, so how much worse could it be to add running? Famous last words. Moments like this, she questioned her sanity. Later, after the run and a hot shower, she'd feel a boost of pride and hope, two unfamiliar emotions that had become so addictive.

She spotted the line of ten cars parked at the park entrance. Most people still remained in their cars, staying close to the heat as long as possible. She parked, checked her watch, and realized she had only seconds to spare. She reached for her water bottle and discovered she'd forgotten it. Left it by the back door. The missing keys had distracted her. Thrown her off-track. Damn.

She pulled her ignition key from the ring, tucked the remaining keys under her mat, and got out of the car. The morning blast of cold air hit her hard and she reminded herself yet again that physical fitness was a good thing. She locked her car, unlocked it, locked it again, and checked the door handle to make sure it was secure.

She moved toward the park bench where the runners all assembled. Today was a short run. Five miles. They were all slowly building up their distance. For the best runners in the group, five miles was easy, so they focused on time. She focused on finishing, surviving.

"Leah!"

Leah turned toward the familiar female voice and smiled.

Leah, for the most part, still didn't reach out to a lot of people. When Philip had been at his worst, he'd terrorized her as well as the people around her. She'd learned to keep her distance. During the last four years, she should have felt free to make new friends, but she hadn't. She'd focused on school and work. She'd kept her life as small as possible, not wanting to attract any unwanted attention. Logically, she understood Philip was forever out of her life. She shouldn't worry. But fear and apprehension would not release their grip.

"Deidre." Leah rubbed her gloved hands together, anxious to get started.

"Week three of training and you're hanging tough." Deidre grinned as she stretched her arms.

"Keep telling me why I'm doing this." The cold air transformed her breath into visible puffs of air.

"Oh, you love it."

"You keep saying that, but I'm still waiting on the love."

Deidre laughed. "As I remember, it didn't take much to convince you."

Leah smiled as the other members of the group assembled around them. There were about a dozen today. The day after the New Year, the group had boasted over twenty, but some of the resolutions had drifted away in the following days.

"How did your date go last night?" Deidre asked.

Leah shrugged. "Okay, I guess." Time to breathe a little life into her nonexistent love life. "I'm out of practice, and it showed. It was all I could do to carry on a conversation."

"Why?" Deidre looked puzzled. "You're smart. You have a wicked sense of humor."

"Not the best dater, I guess."

"Why?"

A weight settled in Leah's chest, just as it always did when anyone mentioned her love life. Most times, she could crack a joke or change the subject, but Deidre had a keen eye for details not so easily brushed aside. "I had a bad marriage. A while ago."

Deidre's expression sobered. "I'm sorry."

"Nothing to be sorry about. It's over and done."

"How long ago?"

This was the part when Leah would sound odd. "Four years."

"Must have been really bad."

Leah shrugged.

Deidre rolled her neck from side to side, and for a moment the veil hooding her bright gaze dropped. "I've told you a little about my divorce. Like I said, it isn't pretty. Worse than I've really let on to most people." She released a sigh. "I keep wondering when I'll see the light at the end of the tunnel."

Leah had constructed an impregnable wall around herself that kept her safe but alone. "I'm sure you'll see better days soon."

Deidre leaned against her car and stretched her hamstrings. "How long did it take *you* to recover from it?"

"It's a work in progress. But I'm getting closer."

A frown furrowed Deidre's brow. "Sounds like it was really rough." She let the words dangle, a fish hook in choppy water.

Leah tugged on her gloves, hating the sudden chill racing up her spine. "He tried to kill me."

Deidre's face paled, and she leaned in a fraction. "What? God, Leah, I'm sorry."

"You have nothing to be sorry about." Talk of her marriage created the sensation of standing on the edge of a cliff. She didn't want to fall into the past.

"Where is he?"

"He vanished after the attack but crashed his car in South Carolina a few weeks later. He's dead."

Deidre's eyes widened. "Shit."

Leah's smile held no joy. "Karma's a bitch. I don't dwell."

That wasn't true. The past had a tight hold on her. She still kept the journal she'd started when Philip had stalked her. The journal had been a necessary evil in those days. In fact, it had been her entries that had got her the restraining order. No reason to keep it any longer, but she did.

"My ex-to-be is having trouble with the divorce," Deidre said. She pointed to a long, deep groove keyed into the side of her car.

Leah frowned, remembering the flat tires she'd dealt with during the months after she and Philip separated. "You okay?"

"Nothing I can't handle, but I'll be glad when we sign the papers in a couple of days."

"Stay strong." The platitude buzzed false in her ears.

The coach blew a whistle and the group huddled close. She explained the course, called out projected times for each one of them, and wished them all a good run. Leah knew the course, which would help her with her pace. She wasn't the fastest runner and had been dropped a few times. Deidre would run with Leah for the first half mile, but as soon as her muscles warmed up she would break away.

As the group got under way, beginning to move at a slow pace down the dirt pathway, she focused on her form and breathing. Running made it difficult to worry about anything else. When she ran, Philip receded to the back of her mind.

As they rounded a wooded corner, the color red flashed in her side vision. She turned toward the woods and saw a man standing amid the trees, staring at the group. The runners got lots of stares from the few early morning walkers. A few drivers even honked when they passed a road. The flash of red wasn't out of the ordinary.

But something about this man held her attention. His

hoodie covered his face, making it impossible to get a good look at him. He was tall, muscled, and he dug his hands into his pockets like Philip did when he stalked her.

Philip. Philip was dead.

She'd held his blackened wedding and signet rings in her hands.

She missed a step and had to take a couple of quick strides to keep from falling.

"You okay?" Deidre asked, glancing back.

"Yeah, yeah, I'm fine." She looked back toward the woods; the man with the red hoodie was gone.

"You sure? You look like you've seen a ghost."

Leah smiled, pushing aside the panic that always rose when she allowed herself to think about Philip. "I'm fine. Aren't you supposed to be keeping up with the fast group?"

"I can hang back." Deidre's sharp gaze saw far too much.

It took extra effort to fool her. "Go. I'm good. I won't be far behind."

Deidre hesitated. "I'll wait for you at the cars."

Even as she wished she would stay, Leah said, "See you soon."

Deidre tossed her a thumbs-up and kicked her run into a higher gear. Leah would like to have been able to keep pace, but she couldn't. Another memento of Philip. He'd stabbed her chest and punctured her lung, which had collapsed. It was back functioning, but she didn't have the aerobic capacity she'd once had.

Her pace slow but steady, Leah kept running, and for the next half hour pushed straining muscles and burning lungs. Though she couldn't keep pace with the main group, she would continue to progress if she remained patient.

When she arrived back at the car, Deidre and David

were talking. He was laughing and she smiling. Breathless, Leah paused, pushed her hand into a side stitch, and then slowly walked toward the couple.

David smiled at Leah. "Looks like you're running faster."

"That's the plan. Though I'm not holding out hope that I'll get any sports scholarships or make any Olympic teams."

Deidre smiled. "Use it or lose it. You're doing fine."

David chuckled. "Amen."

Leah dug the key from her pocket. "Well, it would be nice not to be dead last in my age group when I race this spring. Maybe second to last."

David grinned, and she saw his eyes warm with an appreciation that hinted of sexual desire. She should have been flattered. He was a nice guy, and liked to flirt, but old alarm bells rang.

"You two have a nice day," Leah said. "I've got patients to see today."

"We're going to run a few more miles," Deidre said, "and then call it a day."

"Great."

"Want to get coffee this week?" Deidre asked.

"Call me. I've got evenings and days this week, but I'm flexible."

"Great."

"See you."

She tossed a glance at David that she hoped looked relaxed and not a deer caught in the headlights and hurried to her car. She glanced in the backseat and, sure it was empty, slid behind the wheel. Locking the doors, she turned the ignition and waited as the heater warmed and began to blow out hot air. As she put the car into reverse, she looked behind her, spotting again a flash of red. The man she'd seen earlier. He wasn't looking at her, but, instead, leaned against a tree and stared back down the jogging path. Her heart kicked into high gear and her hands tightened on the steering wheel. *It's just a guy, Leah. Let it go.*

Fifteen minutes later, she pulled into her town house driveway. Hesitating, she scanned the bushes around the front door. They were taller than she liked. Tall enough to hide a man standing in wait.

Leah shut off the engine and, key in hand, hurried to unlock the door. She quickly opened and closed it behind her, flipping the dead bolt immediately. She twisted the lock open and then closed it again. She tugged on the door handle to confirm it was really locked.

Leaning against the front door, her heart raced as had did four years before. She turned, flipped the dead bolt open. Flipped it closed again. She did it three times before she was satisfied it was locked.

She drew in a breath and hurried to her purse, where she kept her journal. Filled with fresh pages, it would hold so many notes. How long would it take her to fill this one? A month? Six months? She turned to the third page in the book and wrote down the date and time she'd noticed her keys missing, as well as the time she'd spotted the man in the park.

She stared at her precise handwriting and then slowly began to thumb through the older entries. Ten days ago: the nightmare. Eight days ago: saw man at the mall and remembered Philip. Seven days ago: heard a sound outside her window. Neighbor introduced herself as Julia, but she kept her distance.

Absently, she traced the scar that ran along her collarbone. Philip had aimed for her throat, but that strike had missed when she twisted and skimmed off her collarbone.

Carefully, she closed the journal and released the breath she'd been holding.

He's gone. He can't hurt you. You're safe.

Alex stood at the edge of the park, watching Deidre's SUV. He'd arrived an hour before the group and had run the route through the woods, as he'd done hundreds of times before, in the dark. He liked running in the dark. The peace.

Today his gaze had been drawn to Leah. She hadn't seen his face, of that he was sure, but somehow she sensed him watching. It had rattled her, and she nearly lost her step. Her wild gaze had scanned the woods as she struggled to catch her breath. But she hadn't given up. She fisted her gloved hands tighter, turned her sights on the path, and kept running.

Her scars weren't from an accident. She'd been attacked, and those cuts had been defensive wounds. Normally, unless the job demanded it, he didn't care about a person's secrets or past. But he cared about hers. Liked her. He could dig up her skeletons, but he wouldn't. Her secrets were for her to tell when she was ready.

He jogged up the hill to his car and slid behind the wheel. He was parked on the other side of the lot but still had a clear view of the park and Deidre's car.

Deidre ran daily, sometimes twice, as if her own demons chased her. He understood the need to run. To burn the endless energy that rarely gave his mind a chance to rest. To melt the ice and glimpse life on the other side of detachment.

He sat in his car, the engine running, and reached for the coffee cup. A sip produced only a few cold drops. Irritated, he crushed the cup in his hand and tossed the remains on the floor of the rental car, irritated that he'd run out.

Deidre and the blond guy from the bar last night emerged from the woods, running at a good clip. Clearly, both were very fit. They ran up to her SUV and paused briefly for a few words. He leaned in and kissed her. She smiled and kissed him back before sliding behind the wheel of her car.

As she backed out of her space, she glanced over in Alex's direction, but he turned his face and backed his car out of the parking spot.

He drove across the lot at a steady pace, glancing toward Deidre in the rearview mirror. She was staring in his direction so he ducked his head, letting the hoodie cover his face. Deidre was a good cop. And he didn't need her realizing he'd been there.

Alex glanced toward the empty paths that snaked into the woods. So many good places to lurk and hide. But that was for another day. Not today.

Now, it was time to get more coffee, maybe a bagel. The running group would be back here tomorrow, and he'd be ready and waiting.

CHAPTER FIVE

Sunday, January 15, 10:00 A.M.

Leah arrived at the Nashville Animal Hospital just after ten. The clinic didn't have official office hours on Sundays, but boarding patients recovering from surgery had to be checked, fed, and walked. The third Sunday of the month was also the day her boss, Dr. Nelson, donated his time to the animal shelter. On these Sundays, the two doctors spent several hours spaying and neutering strays.

When she'd graduated from vet school, she'd seen the listing for a veterinarian position in Nashville. Though the job had excited her, the move back to her hometown had given her pause. This was where she'd lived with Philip. Where he'd almost killed her. She'd been anxious to put distance between herself, Philip, and their marriage, but the pay was good and this was *her* hometown, too.

When she closed and locked the front door behind her, Dr. Nelson called out, "Leah, that you?"

"It's me, Dr. Nelson." She paused and, before stepping away from the door, rattled the knob a couple of times to make sure it was locked. "Here to help. Does Tracker need to be walked?"

"No. Just took him out."

"Great." She moved to the back room, where they held the boarded animals in large, spacious enclosures. Tracker lay on a blue blanket brought from home. When she peeked in, he looked at her, yawned, and went back to sleep.

"We've got six cats today," Dr. Nelson said.

She pulled off her coat as she moved through the reception area into the back. "Male or female?"

"Half and half."

She slid on a white lab coat and met the doctor in the surgery. He stood over a large, hissing orange male tabby. The feline had a bent ear and an open wound on his right side. Dr. Nelson lifted the tabby by the scruff of the neck. The cat hissed and spit, but with practiced ease, the doctor lifted a syringe.

"That guy looks like he got into a fight." Leah grabbed a handful of flesh behind the cat's neck and watched as the doctor injected the sedative. Within seconds, the cat turned to dead weight.

"Judging by the scars, he's had a rough go of it."

She scratched the cat between the ears and smiled as his eyes closed. "We'll get you patched right up."

She washed her hands, donned rubber gloves, and laid out instrument trays she'd prepped the day before. The procedures promised to be quick, and if all went according to plan, they'd be done in a few hours.

The cat would be out for two hours, plenty of time to clean and stitch the wound on his side and complete his neutering.

Without thinking, she pushed up her sleeves.

Dr. Nelson adjusted the exam light above the table so he had a better view of the wound. "How'd you get that scar on your arm, Leah?"

She glanced down at the thin white scar expertly stitched by the plastic surgeon. Quickly, she lowered her sleeve and summoned the smile she always used when questions arose. During the winter, turtlenecks and long sleeves kept the questions at bay, but summer shorts and sleeveless blouses meant lots of questions and plenty of opportunities to perfect her story. "Car accident. Happened when I was in college."

"Must have been bad."

"Swerved to miss a dog that had gotten off his leash. Hit a tree." The lie came tripping easily over her lips. For simplicity's sake, she always stuck to the same story.

He glanced at her over his half glasses as she handed him a threaded suture needle. "An animal lover to the bone."

"I suppose so." Some of the twenty-three scars were short and small, barely scratches, while others had been deep and gaping. The one in her belly had been the most damaging. He'd plunged the knife into her gut, lacerating her intestines.

"Gail tells me you had a date last night."

Leah glanced up, a bit surprised that they'd been talking about her. "Funny thing about the date. I got a text from the hospital telling me there was an emergency. But when I got here, the place was dark. I started to think maybe the text was stuck in the airways."

Dr. Nelson shook his head as he sewed. "I didn't send it. Frankly, I'm not sure if I'd know how. Could Gail have sent it?"

"I called, but she hasn't gotten back to me yet."

He shrugged. "I don't know what to tell you. A quirk. Either way, Gail will know."

"Maybe." She hadn't questioned the text too closely at

first because it had rescued her from the date and her growing panic attack. But now, she wondered.

The front bell of the clinic rang. Dr. Nelson glanced up at the clock. "Tracker's uncle. Never misses a visit."

Alex.

"It's Sunday."

"I don't think the day of the week matters to him. Would you mind getting it while I finish up our little friend here?"

Her nerves tightened. "Sure."

Leah moved through the hallway toward the main door, and when she pushed open the door to reception saw Alex standing on the other side of the glass door. He wore a dark suit, a white shirt, and a red tie, leaving her to wonder if the man owned any other type of clothing.

She turned the dead bolt and pushed open the door. "I didn't think you'd come today."

"I said I would check on Tracker daily."

"I guess I thought you'd take Sunday off."

"No. Dr. Nelson said he had surgery today and a visit would be fine."

She stepped aside and allowed him to enter. Once he was in the lobby, she locked the dead bolt behind him, resisting the urge to click it open and then close it again. "It's not a problem. Tracker's sleeping in the back."

A quick nod, and he followed her down the hallway to the holding room. When he entered, Tracker raised his head and his tail thumped. Alex moved toward the cage and opened it. The dog pushed himself up to standing and leaned into Alex's hand while he rubbed him behind the ears and told him he'd be going home soon.

"So did you get your emergency squared away last night?"

She leaned on the doorjamb, her arms folded. Here she

was relaxed, in her element. "Turns out it was a false alarm. I got here and the place was dark and locked up tight."

A frown creased his brow as she glanced up. "That happen often?"

"Never. Odd. I've got a call in to my assistant to find out if she sent the text. No answer yet."

Alex dug a chew stick from his coat pocket and handed it to Tracker. The dog immediately took it and retreated to the corner of his crate, where he greedily started chewing. Alex quietly closed the door and locked it.

He faced her, looking in command of the space even as he seemed so out of place there. "Want to try a second date?"

She pushed away from the door, a quick and sharp tension banding her muscles. "Are you sure about that?"

"Yes."

No maybe. No gray. Black and white. "Okay."

"Later this week."

"I'm off evenings later in the week."

His head tipped slightly to the right. "You said you were out of practice dating. I'm trying to figure out why."

"Busy with school, I suppose."

He shook his head. "That's not it."

"Really?"

"You've pulled yourself off the market. Why?"

Smile. Fold arms. Relax. "I don't think I know you that well."

He shrugged. "We'll fix that on our next date."

"I'm a hard case, Alex. More work than you probably can devote. You sure you want to bother?"

He crossed the room and stood within inches of her. He didn't touch her, but the heat and energy of his body zapped around her like an electrical current. "I'm sure. I'll call you soon, Leah."

He moved past her in a rush of determined energy. The front door opened and she followed. He strode across the parking lot toward a black SUV as she reached for the lock and clicked it closed. Nervous energy buzzed, and she waited for him to drive off before she clicked the lock open. Closed. Open and finally, well and truly, closed.

Detective Deidre Jones arrived at the Nashville Police Department offices just after four. She hadn't wanted to come in today, but she had to take care of business.

As she walked up to the glass-front door and caught her reflection, she paused and studied her features. Some might consider what she'd done wrong, but if they understood that survival and love had prompted her actions, they'd understand. She'd had two choices, both bad, and she'd sacked up and made a decision. Good, bad, or indifferent, she was in this game until the end. Walk a mile in her shoes and then you could judge.

She made her way to the evidence room and smiled at the officer on duty. She pulled her badge from her jacket and flipped it open. "Detective Deidre Jones."

The young officer had a fresh-faced look that Deidre knew she'd once had. When she'd first become a cop, it had all been about catching bad guys. She'd wanted to rid the world of evil, like she was fucking Wonder Woman. The world was black and white. Good versus evil. But in a flash, the black and white had blurred. She still caught bad guys. Still considered herself one of the good ones. But she understood now that life just wasn't as clear-cut as it once had been.

What she'd done bothered her, given her some sleepless nights. But what upset her as much as the dirty deed was that she'd confessed her secret in a moment of weakness to her soon-to-be ex-husband. At one time they'd been so close. They'd met almost four years earlier right after she'd taken the detective job with Nashville Vice. Tyler Radcliff had been working as a deputy in a small town near Nashville, and they'd met at some cop fund-raiser. It had all been wine and roses.

Loving Tyler had been so easy and perfect in those early days of their marriage. His strength had made her feel protected in a world that felt as if it were crumbling. Complete trust had gone hand in hand with love. That trust, combined with a little too much Jim Beam, had coaxed the secret loose.

When their marriage really soured she couldn't exactly say. But the demands of her job took a toll. He certainly blamed the growing distance on her job. How many times had he said that she loved the work more than him? At first, she'd denied the accusations. Of course she loved him more. But each time he correctly pointed to yet another night he'd sat waiting for her at a restaurant or bar while she'd been finishing up a stakeout or meeting with the medical examiner.

As the weeks, months, and accusations accumulated, she'd wondered if he didn't see a truth she denied. She did love her job. Distance grew between them, even as her case-closure rate soared. Nothing, including great sex, revved her up more than catching a piece of scum like Ray Murphy.

Tyler had grown increasingly angry, and several times last fall, when she'd dragged in the back door dog-ass tired, he'd gotten in her face and accused her of sleeping around. She hadn't been screwing around. She'd been working, and it hurt like hell to realize he didn't trust her. Finally, one night after a bad fight, she'd stopped crying and gotten pissed. Five months ago, she'd packed up a suitcase full of clothes and moved out.

Initially, the guilt had chewed on her. He'd begged her to return. Said he loved her. But as much as he pleaded, she understood their marriage was over. There were moments, generally after she'd reached the bottom of her fourth or fifth beer, when she could admit she still loved Tyler. But the next morning, when she woke sober and clear-eyed, she realized the decision to leave had been the right one.

Then he'd started following her. Calling her. Sending flowers. Coming by the station. Generosity gave way to desperation. More than anything, she just wanted him to leave her alone. Stop with the late-night calls. Stop sending her e-mails laced with profanity and threats.

Six weeks ago, he'd completely stepped over the line. He'd approached her while she was in the produce aisle of the grocery store. He'd come up behind her as she filled a plastic bag with apples. He'd scared the shit out of her, and she'd dropped the apples, sending them rolling over the tile floor. When she'd told him to back off, he'd threatened to expose her secret. He had no reason to remain loyal if she didn't. He'd stalked off, leaving her to pick up the bruised fruit. She'd known then what needed to be done. Tyler would bring her career tumbling down. The threats had to be nullified.

Talking to Leah had hit a nerve. They were more alike than she'd ever want to admit. Yes, she was a cop who wasn't afraid to go balls to the wall when chasing a suspect, but right now, her world, as Leah's had been, was a house of cards.

She hated using Leah, but, deep in her gut, she believed

that one day she would look at her and know in her heart she'd done the woman solid.

One day. If this little game of Russian roulette didn't backfire. "Damn."

She signed the evidence log and grinned at the officer. "Cold enough for you out there?"

"I'm not a fan of winter. I dream of floating down the Cumberland in an inner tube and drinking beer."

"Oh, man, don't tease me with those images. I think it'll be July before I thaw."

He laughed. "Heard about the bust you did. Ray Murphy is a Grade A bad guy. Nice work."

"I love what I do."

"It gets noticed."

"Nice to know."

She made her way along the rows of file boxes until she found the one she needed. From her purse, she pulled out an envelope full of worn twenties, tens, and fives and tucked it into the familiar file box. She'd sold her wedding bands and all her mother's jewelry to raise the cash, and though it stung parting with her mother's pieces, making the box whole, paying back the money she'd *borrowed* last week, had been a necessary first step. The second, a more critical step, would come tonight.

She closed the box, locked it, and walked toward the officer as if she didn't have the sword of Damocles hanging over her head. She dug her keys from her purse. "Here's to inner tubes and beer."

"Amen." He rose and nervously tugged on his belt, glancing around to make sure they were alone. "Someone was checking behind you last week."

She tightened her grip on her keys. "That so?"

He cleared his throat. "I could get busted if anyone knew this came from me."

Deidre shook her head slowly, wondering why he placed trust so easily. "No one will ever know."

"Alex Morgan was poking around."

"The TBI agent." Leah's date.

"That's right." The officer wrinkled his nose. "Didn't say a word, just scanned the times you checked in and out of Evidence."

A knot clenched in her gut, but she smiled as if she were floating down the Cumberland sipping a cold one. "Ah, he's just on a fishing expedition. He does that from time to time. Likes to keep people guessing. He say anything?"

"Nope. Quiet as a statue. Kinda unnerving."

"Thanks for the heads-up."

"Sure."

She waved and left the evidence locker. She got in her car and sat for a long moment as she considered this latest twist. What the hell did Alex Morgan want? He was tenacious when on the scent. Never got emotionally attached. Didn't care who he pissed off.

She started her car and, instead of driving home, drove in the opposite direction, across the Memorial Bridge toward the Tennessee Bureau of Investigation offices.

A few male officers had said she had big balls, and she'd always taken that as a compliment. Now she hoped she could summon those balls.

At the front window, she found a thin older man with graying hair and thick glasses sitting behind the thick glass reception window. She leaned toward the speaker. "I'm here to see Alex Morgan."

The man nodded. "I'll call him down."

"Thanks." She moved away toward a bank of chairs. She

wasn't sure what Morgan thought he knew, but she needed to figure it out. He was one sharp son of a bitch, and if he smelled trouble, it was only a matter of time before he dug it up.

She considered sitting on the lobby couch but found she was too wired. The ten-mile run this morning should have taken some of the edge off, but she was juggling too many swords right now.

A door opened and closed, and she glanced up to see Agent Morgan exiting an elevator. A subtle tension snaked up her spine as he approached.

A tall, lean man, who moved with a precision some de-scribed as robotic. Every muscle twitch, word, or turn was judiciously chosen and parceled with machinelike efficiency.

Morgan wore his dark hair brushed back off his lean face, accentuating blue eyes that reflected a keen intelli-gence. Dressed in his dark suit, he had the look of the per-fect agent. Crisp. Buttoned up. And a legacy from a family of cops. Poster boy for the TBI, she'd once joked.

No doubt he had no pang of conscience, nor did he worry about what it took to get the job done. His world was black and white, and he didn't worry if the ends justified the means.

He rarely smiled and could be a humorless son of a bitch. Nice enough when it suited him, he could easily turn ruthless as a snake when the situation demanded. She'd gotten a glimpse of his coldness when he'd arrested a cop three weeks earlier. Officer Jim Fellows had been selling drugs. Alex had accumulated the evidence he'd needed and gone in for the arrest a few days after Christmas. She'd heard that Fellows, just months from retirement, had pan-icked and taken a swing. Alex had ducked, grabbed the man by the hand, and jerked back his wrist until the cop had dropped to his knees. He'd never raised his voice, never sworn, but he'd brought the hulking man down in front of his peers.

Fellows had not only lost his pension but also faced serious jail time. She shuddered when she thought about a cop caged behind bars. Fellows wasn't a choirboy but, all in all, he'd been a really good cop. That had to count, right?

Time to grab the bull by the horns. "Agent Morgan."

His gaze shifted toward her. "Detective Jones. What brings you here?"

"I hear you've been asking around about me."

Most would have reacted to the bold move. There'd have been some tell to tip their hand. Alex's face only registered mild interest and curiosity. "Who told you that?"

"Doesn't really matter, does it? I know you're gunning for me, and I want to know why."

He cocked his head and looked almost amused. "I'm not gunning for you, Detective. Though I've heard you've been distracted lately. Forgot to issue a subpoena and missed a qualifying test at the shooting range last week. What's that about?"

Who the fuck had been talking to Morgan about her? "Minor mistakes happen."

"Not to you. At least not until about five weeks ago."

The video cameras recorded a visual image but, if she kept her voice low, the audio wouldn't pick up. She pressed harder. "I saw you at Rudy's last night with Leah."

He didn't respond.

"She's a friend of mine."

Silence.

Last night, when she'd seen them talking at Rudy's, she hadn't thought too hard about it. But after the evidence officer's comment, she realized it was a critical piece of the puzzle.

He wasn't going to jump to any bait. And the more she talked, the deeper a trench she dug. "Like I said, doesn't matter." She enunciated each word as if she had a right to be outraged. "My point is simple. Dig all you want, but I'm clean."

"Good to know."

She rested her hands on her hips. "I know how you operate."

"How's that?"

"You've got a thing for tearing into good cops. You're too afraid to work the streets, so you lurk in the shadows and find problems where none exists so you can justify your existence."

His dark gaze glinted. "That so?"

"You're not going to ruin my career. You're not. I'm a good cop."

"Then you have nothing to worry about." He waited, as if he expected her to lose her temper and spill her guts. Stupid people spilled their guts. And she sure as shit wasn't stupid. This ass was not going to ruin her life.

He glanced at the burn phone and pulled up the new text message. Attached was a picture of Leah. She was talking to a man. Laughing. This wasn't the first text with pictures of Leah attached. They'd started four weeks ago and arrived several times a week. She was always smiling or laughing. In the gym. Enjoying a glass of wine. At the clinic. The message was clear. Her spirit had not been broken.

This not-so-subtle trail of bread crumbs from Officer Deidre Jones was designed to lure and eventually trap.

But traps were tricky. If the trapper wasn't careful, the coil could spring closed unexpectedly and snare the wrong person.

He slid behind the wheel of his truck and lowered the sun visor. Attached to the visor was a picture of his wife. He unclipped it and studied the image, taken on their wedding day. His wife had a bright smile and a spark in her blue gaze.

God, she'd been so damn pretty that day. He traced the line of the white wedding dress that hugged her curves and skimmed her thighs. They'd been through a lot. Weathered a lot of storms. A part of him really wanted to renew their vows and wish all the past darkness away. Start fresh.

He typed a simple message. YOU'VE GOT MY ATTENTION. WHERE'RE YOU?

IN TOWN.

He barely hesitated before he typed. I WANT TO SEE YOU.

WHY?

OLD TIMES' SAKE.

Deidre's visit and her connection to John Doe weighed on Alex's mind as he entered Exam Room Two for the autopsy of the John Doe found last night in the warehouse.

Standing at the head of the table was Dr. Miriam Heller, a pathologist with the state medical examiner's office. Tall, thin, she wore scrubs and athletic shoes and her dark hair skimmed back in a smooth ponytail.

As she pulled on rubber gloves, she glanced up. "Agent Morgan," she said. "It's been a while since I had the pleasure."

"Dr. Heller." Both his brothers had worked with the doctor on multiple homicides, and they respected her work.

"I hear you've joined the dark side. Working a homicide."

"Never a dull moment." He removed his suit jacket, neatly folded it, and carefully laid it over a chair. He then rolled up his sleeves and donned a gown and rubber gloves.

"And your partner in crime, where is he?"

"Deke's on his way."

She moved to the head of the stainless-steel table where the body lay under a white sheet. Dr. Heller's assistant, a short woman with brown, curly hair, approached the table with a sterile instrument tray and set it on a stand to the doctor's right. Dr. Heller switched on the overhead light and tugged a hanging microphone closer to her mouth just as Deke pushed through the doors. "Ah, now we can start the party."

Deke threw off an overcoat and tossed it over a chair. "We've got to stop meeting like this, Dr. Heller. People talk."

She laughed. "Good. Nothing like a little gossip to get us all through this long winter."

He donned a gown and gloves and joined Alex at the table.

Dr. Heller cleared her throat and switched on the mike. "This is Dr. Miriam Heller, and I'm with Detective Deke Morgan and TBI Agent Alex Morgan. I'm autopsying a John Doe found last night in a warehouse on the East Side of town on the Cumberland River."

Her assistant picked up a digital camera from the stainless-steel workbench and readied herself to take pictures as Dr. Heller pulled off the sheet.

In the clear light of day, the body took on a grotesqueness that last night's shadows had softened. The peeling skin was charred black, and what remained of the extremities had curled inward.

Alex took a mental step back from the carnage lying

before him and focused on evidence and facts. "Let's see what he can tell us."

Dr. Heller winked. "I'm sure he has a few secrets to share."

She began with a Y incision in the chest cavity and began a step-by-step analysis of the internal organs. She declared all healthy and of normal size until her fingers brushed the heart. As she lifted the enlarged organ from the body, even a layman could see the fatal bullet had shredded the heart. She laid the heart down and carefully dissected it until she exposed the bullet. She grabbed it with a pair of forceps and dropped it in a metal pan.

"This is a male subject who appears to be anywhere from late twenties to late forties. Cause of death was a bullet wound to the heart, which sliced through his left coronary artery. Other than the damage from the bullet, I do notice that several arteries are blocked, which leads me to correct my first assessment of age. I'd say the victim was well into his late thirties and likely older. Lungs indicate he was a heavy smoker." Her catalogue of his major organs complete, she moved to his arms. She noted the hands had been severed, but the cuts had not been clean. Dismembering had taken several chops to remove the right and then the left hand. The scenario mirrored the removal of the feet and the head.

"Was there a lot of blood at the scene?" Dr. Heller asked.

"No," Deke said.

"So he was killed and dismembered elsewhere?" she asked.

"Yes," Deke said. "*Where* is the million-dollar question."

With the help of her assistant, Dr. Heller rotated the body on its side and photographed the back, which was covered with tattoos. The fire had so damaged the skin, the images were nearly unrecognizable.

"He liked the ink," Dr. Heller said. "We might be able to analyze the photos and come up with a tattoo that can be identified, but that will take time."

Deke frowned. "Whatever you can give us will help." He glanced at Alex. "See any connections yet?"

Alex thought again about Deidre's visit today. She'd played it cool, but he'd sensed her nerves jumping. She was hiding something. "Not yet. But I will. Do what you can to reclaim any of the tattoos. They might help identify the victim."

When Deidre arrived at home, it was dark and cold. She was tired, ready for a glass of wine and an evening with David. A good roll in the sack would take the edge off the nerves banding her neck and shoulders. But sex and wine would have to wait. The nerves humming in her body needed to remain sharp.

As she fished her keys out of her purse, she stepped inside her darkened town house and flipped on an entry light. She dumped her purse and keys on the table and then carefully stepped out of her shoes, avoiding a glance in the hallway mirror that would toss back too many recriminations. Soon, she'd be able to look herself in the eye again.

On the table sat a framed picture of two young girls. The picture of Deidre and her younger sister had been taken over twenty years earlier. When she'd left Tyler, this photograph, along with her computer and clothes, had been the one personal item she'd taken with her. A second image, which she'd brought from the office, sat next to the first. It featured her surrounded by a half-dozen guys. They were all grinning and standing in front of three million dollars of seized cocaine. That had been one hell of a day.

The pictures reminded her of her priorities. Family and the job.

Moving into the kitchen, she reached for a bottle of wine and then stopped herself. Instead, she filled a glass with tap water and took a liberal sip. Wished it were stronger, but knew it wasn't about what she wanted but what she needed.

Pressing the glass to her temple, she tried to imagine Morgan's face if she were to explain her plan. He would not approve of the methods, but he would like the end result. Maybe after it was all said and done, she'd tell him. That startled a laugh from her. *Likely not.*

She'd learned the hard way to keep her own counsel. No exceptions, ever.

Glass in hand, she backtracked into the entryway and reached in her purse for her cell. She dialed Leah's number. David would have to wait.

Leah answered on the third ring. "Leah, this is Deidre. Wondering if you'd like to grab some dinner tonight?"

"That sounds so nice. But I'm running on empty. That run today plus work wiped me out."

Deidre glanced at her short fingernails. "You're not getting soft on me, are you?"

"Ha! I'm the least alpha of the group. Safe to say I'm not *getting* soft. I *am* soft."

A chuckle rumbled in her throat. "I'd like to get together this week to talk. I kind of touched on my divorce stuff and, well, I just got the sense that you understand."

A heavy silence crackled. "Better than I wish. What's going on?"

Deidre didn't have to dig deep on this one. "My soon-to-be ex-husband made me sign over the house to him or he said he wouldn't sign the divorce papers. I know I'll never live there again, but it hurts to have it taken away."

"You don't want to fight for it?" Irritation edged Leah's voice.

"I want my freedom more. We sign the final papers in two and a half days." She dangled the bait, hating it as she reminded herself that the end justified the means.

"What's a fight going to cost you?"

She held up the glass, turning it, watching the water weep down the sides of the glass. "More than I have."

"Freedom is a good thing, Deidre, and not to be taken lightly. As much as my first reaction is to fight, I know that surviving is best. Maybe it's better to walk away."

Deidre sipped her water, wondering how much it would take to wash down the bitterness. "Yeah. I suppose." Walking away wasn't her style.

"How about dinner tomorrow? We can meet at that burger place that serves those million-calorie burgers. Maybe we can even split a milkshake."

Laughing, Deidre rolled her neck from side to side. She didn't want to like Leah, but she did. "I'd like that."

"Are you okay for now?"

"I'm fine. I'm always fine. And touching base with you helped."

"My ear is here for the bending. Always."

Deidre heard the conviction underscoring Leah's words. "Thanks, Leah. Text you a time and place tomorrow?"

"Perfect."

She ended the call and strolled across the living room toward the overstuffed couch in her den. She'd moved into the place a couple of weeks before, finally deciding to give up the rented hotel suite for a more permanent address. Walking away from a marriage with no possessions and no money made furnishing the place tough, so she'd opted for a partially furnished place. Already she looked forward to the day when she could decorate the place with her own stuff. Other than her clothes, computer, and a few kitchen necessities, nothing here belonged to her.

She took another big sip of water. The price of freedom.

A clang of the trash cans outside had her turning back to the French doors that led out onto a patio. The heavy sheers over the windowpanes blocked out most of the backyard view of the woods. She rose, set down her glass, and removed her gun from her purse. She edged toward the doors, checking her watch. As she reached for the door handle, she spotted the note taped to the outside windowpane. Written in a thick magic marker, the note simply read, *I see you*.

As she glared at the note, a quick test of the door handle found it locked. Quickly, she unlocked the door, snatched the note, and relocked it. She studied the lined yellow paper. *I see you*.

"Where?" Her first thought was Tyler. This felt like more of his bullshit. "Damn you."

She crumpled the note in her hand and turned away from the door, moving back toward her purse. She set her sidearm down, grabbed her cell phone again, and dialed his number. It rang once. Twice. On the third ring, the call went to his voice mail. "This is Deputy Tyler Radcliff. Leave a message."

A litany of oaths crossed her mind as she looked at the crumpled note. There'd be no proving he left it there, but she recognized his handwriting. She could run fingerprints. His might appear. But he was clever and would argue she'd stolen the legal pad he always kept on his desk. A frame-up, he'd say.

She swallowed the oaths and ended the call, tossing the phone onto the table as she shoved the note in her pants pocket. They were scheduled to meet with the judge on Tuesday, and she didn't need to hear her voice ranting to his voice mail on the phone. And in two days all her troubles would be gone.

"I'll put the screws to you in court." A second phone in her purse dinged, signaling a text. It was the burn phone she'd purchased with cash a few weeks before.

I'M HERE.

Tyler quickly forgotten, she put down her personal cell. Her heart rate jumped. All this time and planning and he was here. This time, if he wanted his money or more information, he'd have to face her. *So close to taking the bait. So close to ending this nightmare.*

WHERE?

OUTSIDE.

NOW? WE MEET TOMORROW.

I WANT TO MEET NOW. IMPORTANT.

Sliding her shoes on and with gun in hand, she moved toward the back door. This wasn't the endgame she'd imagined, but it would work. She'd dealt with her share of bad guys in her ten years with the Nashville Police Department. An expert shot, she wasn't afraid to pull the trigger.

The heating system hummed as it blew a fresh burst of warm air from the floorboards. Deidre paused in the hallway, steady, listening and waiting. Adrenaline raced through her. "We're a little old for games, don't you think?"

Again, her answer was the steady hum of the furnace. Slowly, she lowered her weapon and released the breath she'd been holding.

In the kitchen, she flipped on all the lights and searched the nearly bare space. No kitchen table, no canisters on the polished granite countertops, no pictures on the walls. The two glasses and bowls she'd left in the sink last night remained.

Her fingers hesitated over the dead bolt as she thought through what she was going to say. She'd made promises of more money. More information. *Just get in my car.*

Out the back door, the cold stung her face and hands and cut through her silk blouse. Shivering, she looked to the small patch of grass that ringed the back row of town houses. Her small yard backed up to thick dark woods that stood silent. Moonlight caught the bare branches and remnants of snow still clustered on the frozen ground. Her breath froze into white puffs as she searched for any sign of movement. One minute. Two. Three. Nothing.

He wasn't here. He was screwing with her. Typical.

She retreated back inside to the warmth and closed the door behind her. She clicked the dead bolt in place. Safe. Secure.

And still her nerves hummed with worry.

The burn phone buzzed in her pocket, signaling a text. She hurried toward the phone and saw the message from the unknown caller.

I'M HERE!

Eyes narrowing, she held her gun as she reread the message. Had he taken the bait? Had he returned?

She typed back, WHERE?

OUTSIDE. NEAR THE WOODS.

Frowning, she typed, I DIDN'T SEE YOU.

LOOK AGAIN.

She held her gun, eyes on the back door, confident she had the upper hand. *Come to me, baby, come to me.*

Her phone buzzed. EMERGENCY!

As she lowered her head to text back, quick, determined

footsteps moved across the carpeted hallway behind her and into the kitchen. The first knife slashed into her back shoulder blade. She'd been playing chess and her opponent had mated her with one swift blow. As she whirled, he stabbed her again in the shoulder, and she dropped her gun and the burn phone. A man stood in the center of her kitchen dressed in a lightweight hazmat suit. Protective goggles covered his eyes. The fingers of his right hand gripped the handle of a seven-inch knife. She didn't need to see his face to make an ID.

Staggering, she clutched her arm close to her body. "You planned this."

"For weeks."

"Why?"

"You started it. I'm finishing it."

For a big man, he lunged fast, slicing the knife across her neck, destroying her vocal cords and spraying blood on the white walls. Falling to her knees, her hands went to her neck. Warm blood oozed between her fingers. She searched for the burn phone and spotted it by the stove.

She collapsed, her shoulder hitting the floor, and rolled on her back. Her killer's eyes danced with satisfaction.

Deidre struggled to keep her mind clear, knowing she had only seconds. If she could just reach the gun . . .

As if reading her thoughts, her killer shook his head and kicked the gun across the floor. "You'll never reach it. Too bad."

Her vision blurred.

"Windows, Deidre. You should always check your windows."

As the blade sliced at her arms, she raised her hands. *Grab the knife. Grab the knife.* The blade cut across her palm.

The next strike hit her torso. Adrenaline faded, giving

free rein to the pain, which pinched and burned every fiber and sinew in her body. The knife blade kept jabbing, cutting, slicing.

Finally, the cutting stopped. Liquid life drained as quickly as an open tap, while her blurred gaze focused on him picking up the burn phone. This morning she'd thought she'd tamed her past and would soon control it completely. She hadn't. It had caught up to her.

He stood over her, his blood pumping in his veins as hers pooled around his feet. Weeks of planning, and in less than two minutes it was over. Adrenaline surged, but he dreaded the inevitable crash.

Kneeling, he touched her face, smoothing his gloved fingertips over pale parted lips. "You always underestimated me, babe. Always."

He reached in her pocket and pulled out the crumpled note. With one final glance at Deidre, he rose and left through the back door. He made his way into the woods and, under the moonless sky, stripped off his blood-soaked suit and gloves and shoved them all in a trash bag he'd stashed earlier. The cops would be hard-pressed to find any clues linking him to this.

The cops would spend days chasing their tails looking for Deidre Jones's killer, and by the time they were finished, he'd have finished his mission and killed Leah Carson.

Leah's phone was ringing when she turned from the stove and the omelet she was cooking. Wiping her hands on a dishtowel, she lowered the heat on the burner and answered without glancing at the console. Remembering her conversation with Deidre fifteen minutes earlier, she just assumed it was her friend. "Hello?"

"Leah Carson?"

"That's right." Her voice snapped with impatience. "Who is this?"

"This is First National Bank Credit Card Services. We have some questions about your account."

"Okay."

After they asked for the appropriate identifying information, the operator asked, "We're seeing expenses that show you're in Madrid, Spain?"

She turned down the burner. "Excuse me?"

"We have charges that show you were in Madrid yesterday and London the day before that. Did you make those charges?"

"No, I didn't." Immediately, her thoughts tripped back to when and where she'd used her credit card. She fished her card out of her wallet. "What card number are you referring to?"

The operator rattled off the number that matched her card perfectly. "Is that the correct number?"

"Yes, it is." She pressed the back of her hand to her head. "So what do we do now?"

"We've closed the card and issued you a new one. It should arrive at your home in five business days."

She thought through the days. "That's the week after next."

"Yes, ma'am. We suggest you use any backup cards you have."

She blew out a breath. She didn't have a backup card. Damn. "Okay. I'll deal. But I just swiped the card at the grocery store today. That's a legit expense." She spent the next five minutes going through the charges and confirming and disavowing them. "Thanks for calling."

She hung up the phone and pressed her fingertips to her eyes. She checked her wallet and counted thirty-nine dollars in cash. If she brown-bagged it this week and watched her gas mileage, she might not have to go to the bank for cash until the end of the week.

Leah fumbled through her purse and pulled out her journal. She opened the well-worn book and smoothed the newest page flat before carefully documenting the call: the time and details of the incident. Pen poised over the page, she reread the entries of the day, fearing she'd find a pattern.

Keys. Man in the woods. And now the credit card.

Most people wouldn't have paid much notice to any of these incidents. Keys went missing all the time. Men were allowed in public parks. And a hacked credit card was a terrible annoyance but, in the end, wouldn't cost her a dime.

She stared at the list and absently raised her fingertips to the scar along her collarbone. *These are just three very random events. Stuff happens to regular people. Don't need to freak out. One. Two. Three. I don't need to freak.*

She moved toward the front door and clicked the lock back and forth until she was certain it was secure. She moved from window to window, checking the locks. Finally satisfied the place was safe, she released the breath she'd been holding and whispered, "I don't need to freak."

The mantra would have calmed any normal, rational woman.

Normal. Rational. Woman.

Philip's knife blade had left scars, worries, and a stupid journal filled with nonsensical entries.

CHAPTER SIX

Monday, January 16, 10:20 A.M.

The air cut and bit as Alex got out of his SUV and stared at the flashing blue lights of the cop cars ringed in the cul-de-sac of the town house community. He burrowed gloved hands in his coat pockets and moved across the yard, wondering why his brother had summoned him to another crime scene in less than forty-eight hours.

He nodded to a couple of uniformed officers who scowled and folded their arms over their chests. Irritated by the childish behavior, he didn't ask for approval as he ducked under the yellow crime scene tape. Without thinking, he swapped the warm leather gloves for black plastic ones. Pausing at the threshold, he noticed that the front door lock had not been pried open, nor did there seem to be any other signs of forced entry.

As he stepped forward, a uniformed officer blocked his path. The tall man's frame was well muscled like that of a much younger man, but it was his well-worn eyes and lined mouth that gave him away as a couple of decades older.

"Orders are not to let anyone inside," the officer said.

Alex looked up, knowing his gaze reflected restrained

annoyance. "Detective Deke Morgan sent for me. I'm Agent Alex Morgan."

The officer shifted his stance and met Alex's gaze. "I got orders to keep everyone out but essential personnel."

"You telling me I've got to call Detective Morgan and have him come out here? He called me." This bullshit was getting old.

The lines in the officer's face deepened with defiance but he had the sense to step aside.

Alex brushed past him, tired and more annoyed than usual. He'd spent most of the night reading through Deidre Jones's case files. So far, no red flags. She was one hell of a cop.

Instead of quizzing the officer about the victim's identity, he opted to wait for Deke's explanation. He paused in the entryway and noted that the victim had left a purse on a long slim table. Beside the purse sat a ring of keys. Above the table hung a mirror, clean and sparkling and perfectly aligned. Whatever had happened to her, it hadn't been here.

Alex's gaze settled on the picture of two young girls, who were clearly sisters. Smiling, arms wrapped around each other, the girls appeared to be separated in age by about ten years. The older sister had dark brown hair and wore hoop earrings and a peasant top and the younger one sported a Mickey Mouse T-shirt and a gap-toothed smile.

Beside the first picture was another one of a group of people. Six men and one woman clustered around the court-house sign. All were grinning. He remembered the picture. The task force had caught a major cocaine dealer who'd later been sentenced to life in prison. He scanned the collection of blunt haircuts, practical shoes, and holstered guns until he settled on Deidre Jones. He allowed another look at the sensible black purse that couldn't have cost more than twenty-five bucks. No gun.

Drawing in a breath, he distanced himself from the waiting crime scene. He'd learned distance when he'd been eleven. Against his mother's orders, he'd decided to be the first of the Morgan boys to climb Miller's Falls. He'd been inches from the top, feeling mighty proud of himself, when a rock under his right hand had given way. He'd fallen fast and hit hard.

When he'd awoken, stars twinkled in the sky and he'd been perched on a ledge, his arm twisted and broken. Pain had sliced through him and his heart pounded like a fist. He'd tried to sit up, desperate to get away from the edge, when a portion of the ledge crumbled under him. He'd realized if he kept moving or panicked, he'd die. So he'd closed his eyes and stepped back from the fear. He'd called for help until his voice was raw, finally, he'd stopped. He'd slowed his breathing and steadied his heartbeat. In the quiet of his mind, he'd found a refuge away from fear.

He'd lain on that rock for nearly three days, never moving as the crows circled, rain drizzled, and bugs crawled over him. When he'd been rescued, he'd been so calm the searchers had thought he was in shock. Later, when he'd faced his first crime scene, he'd stepped back again and returned to the emotionless place that allowed him to see clues that others, overcome with emotion, missed. This talent, honed to cutting sharpness, resisted corralling more and more. In recent years, personal relationships had suffered. He'd lost touch with too many. And worse, he didn't care.

"Iceman. Ice on the outside. Ice in his heart," Georgia had declared at the most recent family Christmas celebration. A few glasses of wine in her, she'd bemoaned the trials of love. Stone sober, he'd suggested she overrated love. That comment had earned him the "Iceman" moniker.

"Alex." Deke's voice rushed across the sparsely furnished living room.

"Yeah." He turned from the pictures to see Deke standing in the doorway, backlit by the bright sunlight shining in from the kitchen.

"The victim is Deidre Jones, isn't it?" Alex asked.

"Yes."

Yesterday, he'd smelled the lies on her like overdone perfume when she'd challenged him at the TBI offices. He knew he'd hit some kind of nerve with his questions, and she was hiding something big. He'd been right but didn't relish the victory. "What happened?"

"She was stabbed multiple times. She's in the kitchen."

Dozens of questions rattled in his brain, but he silenced them all. *Look first. Then ask.* His old man had said that a million times. *Don't let anyone else's analysis cloud your perspective.*

He moved past a couch and a coffee table. On the table sat a half glass of water, red lipstick on the rim. No furniture beyond the couch, other than a television and a small end table with a lamp on top.

He imagined Deidre had clicked on the light and sipped her water when cop radar prompted a return to her purse to retrieve her gun. Had it been a knock at one of the doors?

Alex shifted his attention to the kitchen and moved carefully past the breakfast bar. He saw his sister, Georgia, dressed in a Tyvek suit and booties, her red hair tucked into a surgical cap as she leaned over the body, snapping photos. Blood pooled around the body and under Georgia's feet. Judging by Georgia's equipment and grim face, she had been here several hours documenting the scene.

He knew this because she would never have stepped into the blood and disturbed the evidence until it was well documented.

Georgia's body blocked a full view of Deidre, but he caught a glimpse of one pale arm, slashed and cut. The upturned palm, gashed and gaping, conjured images of Deidre blocking the blade with her arms and grabbing the knife's edge. She was a tough woman. Could hold her own against most men. How had this killer gotten close enough to stab her?

Georgia rose up, moistened dry lips, and turned from the body. A glance up at Alex revealed anger mingling with sadness.

Refusing to acknowledge the liquid emotion in Georgia's eyes, he took his first hard look at the body.

Deidre lay on her back, her arms and feet splayed. She was fully dressed in the pantsuit he'd seen her wearing when she'd faced him in the lobby at TBI. Knife cuts had slashed the white silk top, cutting into flesh and soaking the delicate fabric with the dark ruddy brown of blood. Knife wounds slashed through her pants, cutting deep into flesh.

Who the hell would do this to her? What the hell had she gotten herself into?

Sympathy warmed in the pit of his belly. She might not have been totally clean, but she'd done good work as a cop, and that counted in the big scheme. Loyalty for a fallen comrade threatened to melt the ice before he summoned cold winds to burn it away. Later, after the killer had been caught, he'd allow anger. Outrage. But not now.

Alex turned from Deidre's body and faced his brother. "Who found her?"

"Leah Carson."

"What?" He was rarely caught off guard. "Leah Carson?"

An open notebook in one hand, Deke clicked the end of a pen in the other. "Yeah, ain't that something? Your date found the body."

He'd seen her at the clinic yesterday. What was the time? Four? "Why was she here?"

"Deidre missed running practice this morning, and when she didn't answer her phone, Ms. Carson came by to check on her."

He'd been at the park this morning, watching the group run. He'd noted Deidre's absence but hadn't worried too much. She'd missed before. Cops always missed because of the job. But this morning he'd been drawn to Leah and her dogged determination to keep up with the group. Even when it was clear she'd finish dead last, she'd kept moving.

Alex folded his arms. "Continue."

"She saw her purse inside through the front window. Front door was locked so she walked around to the back. It was ajar."

Georgia met his gaze. "Did you know they ran together?"

"Yes."

Georgia eyed him closely, shooting him a demanding look.

Alex disregarded the silent demand. "How's Ms. Carson doing?"

Deke shrugged. "She's rattled. Siting in the back of a squad car."

An urge to go to Leah surprised Alex. And the struggle to refrain surprised him more. The case first. "What happened?"

Georgia stepped out of the blood pool onto a tarp, where she rolled her head from side to side. Crime scenes like this one could take days to process. So much data to be collected and sorted, and Georgia wouldn't leave until she'd found every trace. "Leah apparently came into the house through the back door, saw the victim in the kitchen, and then ran to the bathroom, where she threw up. She called nine-one-one from her cell outside."

The image of her fragile frame, pale and drawn, chipped at the ice. More pity flickered. Another struggle to contain.

Lines of worry etched deep in Deke's face. "No signs of forced entry. Nothing appears to have been taken from the town house, but we've got a call in to her sister. She's coming in from California and won't be here until very late tonight. Gun, money, credit cards all appear to be in her purse."

"Where's her husband?" Alex asked.

"Haven't contacted him yet," Deke said. "You said they were getting a divorce? Not friendly, correct?"

"That's what I've heard. I don't have details."

Hands resting on his hips, Deke shook his head, as if trying to clear his thoughts. "I know her husband. He's a sheriff in a small town about twenty miles north of Nashville. Given the basic facts, he's at the top of my suspect list."

"That's a logical conclusion." When a woman was murdered, statistics proved it was someone she knew and at one time loved.

"Signs of sexual assault?" Deke asked Georgia.

"None from what I can tell," Georgia said. "The medical examiner will have to make the last call on that."

"The bedrooms weren't disturbed, but there's a window in the back bedroom that's slightly open. My guess is the killer came in through the window and surprised her."

"Deidre was no fool," Alex said.

"Whoever did this was smart," Georgia said. "I've found very little forensic data."

Alex tugged at his cuffs. "I want to hear every detail, but first, I'd like to talk to Leah Carson."

Brow arched, Deke slid his hand into his pocket and rattled the loose change. "I'd like you involved in this case."

Georgia raised her gaze to her brother's. This was an unusual request from Deke, and one he wouldn't make lightly. Her gaze narrowed, suspecting there was more but knowing other officers were within earshot, stayed silent. The questions would come later.

Alex leveled a cool gaze on his older brother. "I want lead."

The Morgan family could be surly and, behind closed doors, could fight like cats and dogs. In public, they banded together into a united front. "You'll need to keep me posted. Daily."

"Done."

Alex turned and left, passing several uniformed officers. He paused at the door and turned to the guard-dog officer who'd stopped him initially. "What car is the witness in?"

"The one in the back, next to the ambulance."

Alex stripped off his rubber gloves and tossed them in a medical waste disposal bin before making his way toward the squad car where Leah sat. The crisp, cold air felt good as it sizzled through his skin to his molten core. Anger could do that. Boil the blood. He'd now use his anger as fuel. It could drive him for days without much sleep or much food.

He moved toward the squad car, keeping his steps purposeful and steady. It never did well to rush in front of others. Rushing telegraphed a lack of control or fear. He never showed either.

As he approached the backseat, he noticed Leah was staring sightlessly toward the row of town houses and the ring of onlookers who'd braved the morning cold to watch the scene unfold.

Her hair was dark, though, judging by the faint blond roots, not her natural color. The other night her hair had been swept just above her shoulders, but today it was pulled back in a messy ponytail. She wore a black jogging suit and clutched run gloves and a knit hat in her hands. A thick scarf, loosened into a long loop, hung around her neck. Her breath was slow and steady, but he sensed she counted each inhale and exhale.

He lightly rapped on the glass to serve warning before he opened the door, but the sound of knuckles against glass made her jump. She turned toward him, her green gaze wide with shock and bloodshot. She smoothed her hands over her running pants and straightened her shoulders, as if mentally collecting the threads of her composure.

He opened the door, the rush of the car's heater reaching out to him. "Leah."

"Alex. What're you doing here?"

He rapped on the barrier separating the back and front seats, and when the officer glanced in the rearview mirror, Alex motioned for him to leave. Scowling, the officer got out of the car.

When the door slammed, Alex said, "Investigating the case."

Fingers twisted around the black gloves. "She was Nashville Police."

"I investigate cops."

"You were investigating Deidre?"

"I'll be investigating her murder."

"I don't understand."

"Can we talk?" He inclined his head toward the seat, as if waiting for her permission to enter.

She scooted to the far side of the car. "Sure."

He slid inside, adjusted the folds of his overcoat, and closed the door behind him. His frame was lean, and though he wasn't as muscular as Deke, he stood several inches taller at six foot three. The long body was not a comfortable fit in any backseat, but the wire barrier walling off the back from the front made the space feel all the smaller. "Can I get you anything?"

"No, thanks. The officer already asked." She swiped a dark wisp from her face.

"Can I ask you about this morning?" He always led polite, even though it scraped against a natural instinct to badger. Witnesses, even suspects, responded better to soft tones.

She eyed him as if reconciling this politeness to her overly direct date on Saturday. "Deidre and I run together." She allowed a breath to shudder over her lips. "She never misses a run. Last night we spoke on the phone, and she said she'd go running this morning. When she didn't show, I got worried. I called her on her home and cell phones a couple of times but there was no answer."

"Do you always check up on people who miss a training session?"

"No. But Deidre is different. I texted her and she didn't respond. She always would text back. I just got a bad feeling."

"So you came by the house?"

She twisted her gloves in her hands before releasing them and flattening her palms on her thighs. "I don't live all that far from here, and I had the morning off so I thought I'd check."

"How did you meet Deidre?" Her nails were cut short but were neat and polished. She wasn't wearing perfume, but there was a faint hint of soap that blended with the fresh air from her run.

"The gym. She mentioned the running group. I joined in just after the first of the year. It became kind of a New Year's resolution for me. Fresh start."

"Why did you need a fresh start?"

Her gaze rose abruptly, as if she hadn't realized what she'd said. "Doesn't everyone start over at the new year?"

"I suppose they try."

She arched a brow. "I was doing more than trying. I even quit smoking."

"I don't picture you as a smoker."

"Nervous habit."

Around the animals she was relaxed. That smile she'd tossed Tracker had melted some of the ice. But she'd been a different person in the restaurant. Nervous. Jumpy. As if she expected trouble. He did that to people. Set them on edge. And he might have taken her reaction personally if not for the scars marring her hands. Defensive wounds.

Alex relaxed back against the seat. "I heard Deidre had been an avid runner for years. Apparently, she was always talking about the races she ran. She started this group last fall."

That tweaked a small smile. "She was trying to convert me, but I'm not such a good recruit."

"You look like you're in good shape."

"Not really. I needed a goal. I'm tackling a half marathon."

"Why the half marathon?"

"Just because I want to know I can, I suppose." Her cheeks flushed a pale pink.

A small lift of her shoulders reminded him of a defiant child's. She was a grown woman. Why summon defiance? "How has the training been going?"

A slight shake of her head negated her words. "It's going. I'll never win a race, but the plan is to finish, not win."

"So Deidre didn't show up for practice and you came by the house?"

Some of the hard-gained luster in her cheeks faded. "The front door was locked, but the back door was ajar."

"It was?"

"Yes. I pushed it completely open and called out to Deidre. When she didn't answer, I peeked inside and saw her laying on the floor." She pressed trembling fingers to her lips and drew in several calming breaths. "I got sick."

"I heard."

She shook her head, clearly embarrassed they'd been discussing her. "And then I called the police."

"Did you see anyone leaving the property?"

"No. When I saw her, I kinda got tunnel vision. After I got sick, I ran out of the house. I don't even remember talking to the police."

"Do you know if Deidre was having trouble with anyone?"

"She said she was going through a divorce. She told me her ex-husband was giving her a hard time. She thought he keyed her car. She also said he made her sign over their property to him or he wouldn't sign the final decree. She was angry. And, I think, embarrassed by it all."

Alex knew of Deidre's husband, Tyler Radcliff. Good reputation. But putting a best foot forward in public did not ensure a happy home life. "No one in the group had an issue with her?"

"No. No one." She smoothed a small hand over her ponytail, and he noticed the small scar on her palm. Healed, but too reminiscent of Deidre's.

The other night he'd asked Leah about the scars and she'd blamed it on an accident. He'd save the scar for another day. "You and Deidre see each other outside of the running group?"

"We did. I visited her at her hotel, and once here."

"Hotel?"

"It was temporary, she said. Until she found something more permanent. She'd just signed a six-month lease on this place."

"Do you know where the hotel was?"

"Yeah. Germantown." She reached into her pocket, pulled out her phone, and scrolled through the contacts. She rattled off the address. When he didn't move, she asked, "Aren't you going to write it down?".

"I'll remember it."

"You've got a great memory?"

"When I want to remember, I never forget." The scars on Leah's palms, her wrist, and the hair color change: details like that stuck with him.

"Look, do you mind if I go home? I've been here for hours and I'm exhausted. I gave my contact information to the officers."

Alex hesitated, not wanting to let her off the hook so easily. "I may have more questions."

"You've got my number."

"At the clinic. Do you have a cell number?"

Hesitation, and then she rattled off the number.

He keyed it into his phone. "Thanks."

"Sure."

He knocked on the window, and the officer came around and opened the door, which only opened from the outside. Once out, Alex walked around the car and opened Leah's door. She rose, glancing back at the town house one last time and then tensing. "There was so much blood."

"There was." He watched her closely, wondering what other questions hovered behind those troubled eyes.

Her breath hitched. "She was stabbed, right?"

"Yes."

For a moment she swayed, and he thought she'd fall down. "Right."

He sensed weakness and wanted to push just to see what she'd do. Reactions under stress revealed so much. "Multiple times. Lots of defensive wounds. Hands, arms, chest."

She raised her hands to her mouth and turned, as if she'd be sick again. He waited while she wrangled control of her body.

"Are you all right?" he asked.

"Yes." Her voice was a bare whisper. "I'm fine."

"This is your first crime scene. The stress and nerves are understandable."

"Yes."

If he hadn't been looking at her, he'd have missed how her gaze skittered away for an instant. She was lying. She'd been at another crime scene somewhere. The blood she'd seen inside Deidre's house hadn't been the first time she'd encountered destruction. The scars. Where had they come from? "You've seen this kind of thing before?"

"Seen? No. No. I've never found a dead person."

He believed that. Somewhere along the way, she'd been

the one who had been found. This crime scene—no, this stabbing—had rattled not just her but old memories loose. She'd been stabbed. "Let me get an officer to drive you home."

She cleared her throat. "No. I don't need help."

Leah Carson didn't like taking orders, real or imagined. He couldn't fault her there. He'd never cozied up to direction either.

"Okay. But one of my guys will follow you. You're rattled, and he'll be hovering in the background, keeping an eye on you, just in case."

" Hovering in the background.'" Distaste coated her words.

"Is there a problem?"

"No. No. It's okay."

He held out his hand. "I'm sorry you had to see this, Leah. And thank you for waiting to speak to me."

She took his hand. Her scars scraped against his palm. "Thanks."

Leah turned and, without another word, moved toward her CR-V. For a few beats, she simply sat behind the wheel. Finally, she slowly turned on the ignition and pulled away.

He knocked on the window to alert the officer. "Can you follow that CR-V home? She's my witness and she's rattled."

The officer looked up. He wouldn't dare argue, but there was defiance. "I'll keep a close eye on her. Do you want me to stay outside her house for a while?"

"Maybe an hour. See if she goes back out."

"Sure."

The officer settled sunglasses over his eyes and, closing the window, followed Leah.

Alex stepped back, watching Leah drive carefully down the residential street toward the main road. The uniform stayed close behind.

"So what did you think of her?" Deke asked. His brother moved to his side as the two cars turned the corner.

Alex slid his hands into the pockets of his overcoat. "She's rattled as hell."

"Understandable."

"This struck a major nerve. Somewhere along the way . . ."

"What . . . ?"

"I don't know." In his pocket, he fingered a receipt for the tank of gas he'd bought that morning. "But I'll figure it out."

As the medical examiner's van arrived, Leah Carson shuttled to the edges of his thoughts. The mystery of Leah would have to wait.

Alex and Deke stood outside the town house as the medical examiner's technicians entered the house with the gurney. The crowd of residents ringing the edges of the crime scene tape watched as if they were on the set of a cop show. Out here, it was easy for a bystander to pretend it wasn't all that real.

Twenty minutes later, the technicians rolled out the gurney carrying the body bag. A few startled gasps rose up from the crowd. A couple pointed. One or two took pictures with their cell phones.

Alex moved toward the crowd, wondering if the killer lingered to watch the chaos. At the edge of the tape he caught the gaze of a tall man with a thick stubble of beard, wide-set eyes, and short, dark hair. He wore plaid pajama bottoms, a UT sweatshirt, and a thick sheepskin-lined jacket.

Carefully, Alex pulled out his badge. "Alex Morgan, Tennessee Bureau of Investigation. Mind if I ask you a few questions." A question that didn't sound like a question but an order.

"Sure." The guy lowered his phone and tucked it in his pocket.

"Your name?"

"Tim Rogers."

"You know the resident of that town house?"

"Leggy tall brunette. Liked to run. She just moved in a few weeks ago." He leaned in a fraction. "Is she dead?"

"Yes."

"Shit."

"Seen anyone coming or going from her town house?"

"No."

"But you noticed her."

"I mean, I'd steal a look or two when she jogged. Hot. But I didn't track who came and went."

"Anyone around here who would have noticed?"

"You could ask Carol. She lives next door. She pays attention."

"She here now?"

"No. Likely at work. She's a lawyer."

"Okay. Carol got a last name?"

"Rivers. But I don't know the name of the law firm."

Alex glanced at the town house next to Deidre's and noted the address. "Are all the places here furnished?"

"No. The guy who owns that unit works for a bank. Got transferred to New York or Charlotte. He's renting because he can't sell. Left a few pieces of furniture, hoping it would rent."

"Thanks." He walked back toward Deke, careful to keep all trace of emotion from his face. The less fodder for the news crews and cell phone cameras, the better. They didn't need footage ending up on the Internet or networks.

Only when he turned away from the crowd and stood shoulder to shoulder with Deke did he speak. "I'm going to nail the prick who did this, Deke."

His brother's face resembled chiseled granite, but his eyes sparked. "I'm letting you off the chain on this one, Alex. Good hunting."

After the medical examiner removed the body, Alex took a few minutes to stand in the cold and allow his mind to inventory and process what he'd seen.

None of the furniture, drapes, or carpet appeared to have been disturbed in Deidre's town house. Of course the killer could have taken something, but he had no way of knowing now. No signs of sexual assault. Whoever had come into her home appeared to have come with one goal in mind: kill Deidre and cover his tracks.

He turned and strode back toward Deidre's place. "Have you searched the premises yet?"

Deke nodded. "We've got officers going through her room and the back end of the house, and then they'll move into the living area. Georgia is still working the kitchen. She's dusting for fingerprints now."

Alex imagined Leah's pale face and the very faint scar that ran down her cheek. It had darkened the longer they sat in the car. He hadn't noticed it on their date. No doubt she used a special makeup to hide it. "She's rattled. But she had a good command of the facts."

"Does she have any theories?" Deke asked.

"Deidre told Leah the divorce wasn't easy. Her car was keyed. It won't be hard to find her husband and pay him a visit."

"Regardless of what she did, I want her killer found,"

Deke said. "I want to know what she was doing before all this happened."

"Understood."

Deke eyed Alex. "If I didn't know you, I'd say this didn't affect you at all."

Alex arched a brow. "You're more emotional than I ever was." His voice monotone, he might as well have been reciting the alphabet. "You hide it well, but it's there, boiling below the surface. But for me, emotion has never been a significant factor when I'm on a case. It clouds my judgment."

Deke's eyes blazed darker. "RoboCop has nothing on you, Alex."

"That's the perfect description for Alex since Miller's Falls," Georgia said as she exited the kitchen. She'd stripped off her Tyvek suit and booties and now wore her khakis and a long-sleeved, collared forensics shirt. She still wore rubber gloves. "But my all-time favorite Alex description is 'Iceman.'"

Alex didn't like references to Miller's Falls and refused to acknowledge them. Instead, he flipped through a mental catalogue. "Should we share some of the nicknames we had for you?"

She shrugged. "Carrot top, daywalker, ginger. Give it your best shot, bro. Mine are hair-related. Yours stem from a much deeper place."

If outsiders were eavesdropping on their conversation now, they'd peg them all as heartless and unfeeling. But jokes and jibes at times like this eased the pressure valve on explosively deep emotions.

"You're the only person I know who can take your emotions, put them in a box, and lock them away until you need them. And, I might add, you need them almost never."

"Don't forget agent orange," Alex offered.

Georgia stuck out her tongue.

Alex only tolerated this kind of guff from Georgia. She was a pain in the ass, but, as he and his brothers often noted, she was *their* pain in the ass. "How many knife wounds did you count, Georgia?" Alex asked.

Her lips flattened in a stark line. "At least a dozen, but there could be more."

"I would say this is a case of overkill," Alex said. "It wasn't just enough to stab her once or twice, which would have done the job, but the killer stabbed her at least twenty times. Legs, arms, the face several times. This attack carries all the hallmarks of rage. This killing was personal."

"She's arrested and pissed off a lot of very bad guys over the years."

"And, so far, the killer hasn't left any trace evidence," Georgia said.

"Nothing?" Deke asked.

"If you plan it right, you won't leave evidence," Georgia said. "All cops know about Tyvek suits."

"So it could be Deidre's soon-to-be ex-husband, Tyler Radcliff?" Deke asked.

"Statistics suggest Radcliff, but time and evidence will tell," Georgia said. "There's always something."

"When will you have a report?" Alex asked.

"Need time to sort, bro. Will keep you posted."

"I expect this case closed," Deke said.

"It will be." Alex moved past Georgia into the kitchen to stare at what remained of the blood evidence.

Not only was there blood on the floor but it had also splattered the walls and the ceiling. A thin red spray of blood indicated the killer had struck an artery. And the dots and dashes of blood on the back wall had flicked off his knife as he drew it back before plunging it again.

This killer would have been covered in blood. There'd be no way to escape unmarked. But the blood trail stopped outside the back door. Georgia's theory of a Tyvek suit made sense.

He opened the refrigerator and found it undisturbed. Stocked with three bottles of white wine and one red, cheese, eggs, and a loaf of bread. Its clean, nearly unused surfaces glistened. A check of the cabinets revealed standard inexpensive dishes that might be stocked in a rental. Made sense.

"Georgia, when do you estimate the time of death?"

"About ten last night."

Alex looked out the back door and noticed it backed up to the woods. A killer could easily have come through the brush undetected. Deidre's town house was an end unit, and there was a clear path from the back door, around the unit, and up to the parking lot. Easily accessible.

He moved out the back door and walked down the stairs.

"Footprints?"

"It was blistering cold last night and the ground was rock solid."

"So no footprints?"

"Blood smudges by the back door. I think the killer went toward the woods and stripped off whatever protective gear he was wearing. We've got a scent dog coming."

"Fingerprints?"

"Lots, but I don't know who they belong to. I've checked all around the outside of the door as well as the countertops, the cabinet handles, and the refrigerator door handle. I pulled a few good thumbprints from the counter. But if my suit theory holds true, he'd have been wearing gloves."

"You're going to want to see this," Deke called out from outside the kitchen.

Alex turned and moved into the living room, where a uniformed officer knelt by a coffee table. He watched as the officer, with gloved hands, removed what appeared to be a listening device mounted to the underside of the table.

All the personnel in the room grew quiet as the officer rose and held it out for Georgia to inspect.

She took the small device in her hands and studied it closely. "Someone has been listening to Deidre. This device is wireless and has a range of about a mile. I've heard recordings made by such gadgets, and they emit a crystal-clear sound. Whoever was listening would have clearly heard Deidre in this room."

"Keep your voices down while we need to search the rest of the house," Deke said, lowering his voice. "My first choice would be the bedroom, another favorite spot for creeps who like to listen."

Alex pulled on a fresh set of gloves before crossing to Georgia. He held out his open palm, "May I?"

Raising a brow, she handed it to him, whispering. "So polite."

Alex ignored the comment and inspecting the listening device, said quietly, "This isn't cheap. And it's sophisticated. Can also be purchased on countless Internet sites."

"Stalking made easy," Georgia quipped.

"Soon-to-be ex-husband?"

"Top of my list."

Georgia glanced back at the kitchen as emotion flashed in her eyes. *We've got to figure this out. We've got to.*

Alex laid his hand on her shoulder. "He's already caught. He just doesn't know it yet."

CHAPTER SEVEN

Monday, January 16, 11:45 A.M.

Leah's hands trembled as she tried to insert her key in the front door. She fumbled with her keys and then dropped them. Muttering an oath, she picked them up and finally got the key in the lock. She undid the dead bolt and hurried inside. Without hesitating, she locked the door behind her. Beyond tired, her nerves were shot.

A glance out the front window and she saw the cop car parked across the street. She drew in a steadying breath, trying to break the bands of tension in her chest. The cop would be Alex's doing. She'd been as careful and controlled as she could be when she'd spoken to him, but he'd sensed more lingering in the silence between her careful sentences.

Slowly, she turned from the window and down the hallway. She was halfway to the bathroom when her legs gave out and she lowered herself to the floor and buried her face in her hands.

Sadness and fear. Dear God, Deidre was dead. *Stabbed*.

She groped at the scarf now constricting her neck and jerked it free. She unzipped her jogging jacket so that she could draw in a deep breath.

Leah traced the scar slashed across her palm. It had been a defensive wound, just as Alex had said.

She never remembered grabbing the knife. Even now, the attack only came to her in flashes. A knife slashing, whooshing through the air. The prick of a blade against her throat. The softness of Philip's final words. *I'm sorry.*

What really lingered with her were the emotions of that night. Bone-crushing fear. Pain. Weakness.

She dug her fingers in her hair, limp and stringy from running, crying, and vomiting. She wanted to sleep. Needed to sleep.

Leah rose from the floor and with shaky legs made her way to the bedroom, where the rumpled comforter of her unmade bed waited. She crawled between the cool sheets and curled on her side, pulling the blankets over her head. Was she ever going to feel safe?

She closed her eyes, wanting only to sleep for a few hours to escape the horror of what she'd seen today. *Breathe in. Breathe out.* She reached for the bottle of sleeping pills she hadn't used in months. Taking one now felt akin to failure. She shouldn't need it. But she did. Cutting one in half, she popped it in her mouth. Eventually, her heartbeat slowed, and sleep grabbed hold of her.

She wasn't sure how long she drifted just above the waves of deep sleep. It felt good to drift. Weightless. Light. Not afraid, if only just for a moment.

The whispered song tugged on her and brought her deeper to a sleeping no-man's-land where she couldn't separate reality from the past and the unreal.

The gentlest touch of a finger skimmed across her brow. So soft most would have ignored it. But not her.

Even with her system on overload, alarm bells sounded

a warning in her head. The only person who had ever sung to her had been Philip.

A rush of adrenaline surged through her body. Her eyes popped open, and for a moment her eyes couldn't focus. Groggy, she blinked against the day's dimming light and focused her gaze. Silence. Her eyes adjusted as her heart pounded against her ribs and she restrained her panic. She glanced at the clock on the nightstand: 5:21.

"Damn." She moved to the bathroom, where she stripped off her clothes. She turned on the shower and brushed her teeth as she waited for the spray to heat up before she stepped in and allowed the warmth to wash over her very chilled bones.

Tipping her head back, she allowed the water to slush over her naked breasts, which still bore the scars of the attack. She traced the thin pinkish scar that slid across the top of her left breast. The doctors had said the scars on her chest would be the worst. Thin tissue had been the reason.

"Philip is dead," she muttered. "He can't hurt you."

Shutting off the water, she grabbed a towel. She dried her hair, arms, legs. She swiped the fogged mirror clean and did what she rarely did anymore . . . she stared at the scars, tracking each of the twenty-three with her fingertip. No longer pink and raised, they had whitened over time and faded. Just like her memories should have done, but would not.

Finally, she slipped on a robe before padding into her room. The blinds were closed, just as she always left them. Some sunny days tempted her to let in the bright sunshine, but she never dared, remembering how Philip used to sit outside her apartment and watch her.

Hair dripping, she moved to the small desk in the corner of her room and pulled out a calendar. The days had all been marked off except for today, so she took her red pen and put an X through it. They signified all the days since Philip had died: 1,430 days.

Leah dressed and carefully applied a silicone-based concealer that filled in the indented slash across her cheek. It was a five-minute process that had been a part of her regimen for almost four years. Once the filler had set, she applied a base makeup. As she stared into the mirror, she traced her finger along her cheek, wishing memories could be erased as easily.

According to the emergency room doctors, she'd been lucky. After the surgeon had operated and she was stabilized, a very talented plastic surgeon had been on-site, and he'd carefully stitched up her face. He'd minimized the damage, which could have been disfiguring.

For a long time, she hated the scars. Resented them. But now in an odd sort of way she saw them as a gift. Deidre would never have to worry about scars, fillers or makeup. These scars were now a reminder of how lucky she was to be alive.

God, Deidre, who would do this to you?

If anyone could find the truth, it was Alex Morgan. He had the eyes of a predator, a hunter. The way he'd stared at her had reminded her a little of Philip. Cold, direct, and assessing.

Though Philip's gaze had never been so steady. There'd always been an edge, a fear he was missing out, when he looked at the world. They'd met in a bar on Broadway just as she was finishing up college. He'd been with a group of friends and they'd been laughing. Her father had just died and she'd been feeling lost. She'd needed to feel connected to life and strength.

The instant he'd seen her, he'd picked up his drink and moved toward her. He'd told her she was beautiful, and if she wanted to dance, he'd be waiting for her at the bar.

Her friends had called him cheesy, but she'd been charmed. He appeared to be a man who knew what he wanted. And so a half hour later, she'd gathered the courage and asked him to dance. To this day, she'd remembered the song: "Every Breath You Take" by The Police. How many times had she looked back on that moment and wondered if the universe had been sending her a warning.

Their courtship had been a whirlwind, giving her no time to think or take a step back to see the warning signs.

Leah filled her cup with coffee. Deidre would never have taken that kind of guff from Philip. She'd have tossed away a guy like that in seconds. Philip never would have gotten close enough to Deidre to undermine her as he had Leah.

She sipped slowly. She wanted to keep her past locked away. No good came of anyone knowing, though she feared Alex sensed it. Today, in the squad car, his gaze had been peeling back the layers of her defenses. He knew there was more to her. He sensed a problem. A past. Odds were that he would get to the bottom of it.

What happened to her four years ago had nothing to do with Deidre. Nothing. Philip was dead.

Philip. So smart. So clever. So able to win over anyone.

The muscle at the base of her skull tightened as Leah set down her coffee and moved to the dining table, where she kept her purse. She fished out her wallet and from a deep pocket pulled out an old business card she'd carried with her for years. The edges were dog-eared, the card stock thinned with wear.

The name in the center of the card read ROSEANNE JEFFERS, DETECTIVE, SOUTH CAROLINA STATE POLICE. She flicked the edges of the card. In the early days after Philip's disappearance, she'd called Roseanne often. She'd been too afraid to sleep or eat for fear that Philip might return to kill her. Roseanne had been kind, understanding, at first, but after Leah had made a half-dozen calls to her, her answers had grown more terse. Their last contact had been Leah talking apologetically to Roseanne's voice mail. Leah knew she had to get on with her life. Otherwise, Philip won.

"Philip is dead," she muttered.

She hadn't called Roseanne in three years.

Leah closed her eyes, trying to push an old worry back into the shadows. When the threats had been real, she'd had to beg the police to intervene. But when the threat had been destroyed, she couldn't break the cycle of fear.

She reached for her cell phone and dialed Roseanne's number. Her thumb hovered over the Send button for a second or two and, pulling in a deep breath, pressed it. She put the phone to her ear, her heart thrumming in her chest so hard it was a wonder she didn't hear it.

The phone rang three times and on the fourth ring voice mail picked up. Leah hesitated. "Roseanne, this is Leah Carson. Leah Latimer. We haven't spoken in a few years, but we talked several times about my husband, Philip Latimer. You notified me the day his body was found. Logically, I know I shouldn't have doubts about your findings, but I do. Can you call me back so we can discuss the circumstances surrounding his death again? I know this is odd, but a phone call would help. Thanks." She recited her number and then hung up the phone. Carefully, she replaced the card in her wallet and tucked her phone in the side pocket of her purse.

Leah tipped her head back, trying to ease the tension in her chest. She took several deep breaths, but nothing softened the anxiety.

I'm being foolish. I'm being foolish. Philip is dead.

* * *

He stood in the woods, staring up at Leah's town house. Frigid air wafted around him, chilling his skin even as the idea of the chase warmed his blood. The cop watching her house had left, leaving the two of them alone.

Though the drapes were closed, he could tell the lights were on in the bedroom and living room. He saw a woman's shadow pass in front of the bedroom drape and then appear in the living room. A smile curled the edges of his lips.

He switched on a small device that connected wirelessly to the listening device in Leah's town house. He raised it to his ear and listened to the soft hum of the television and her steady pacing. She might look all pulled together and competent, but when she was alone, the demons came out to play. Kept her awake. Made her pace. Good. He wanted, liked her afraid. Rattled and scared.

Leah had found Deidre today. He'd seen her bolt out the door, panicked and afraid. Her hands had been trembling badly when she'd dialed the cops. She'd paced alone in front of Deidre's place, unmindful of the cold. Three squad cars had rolled up within minutes and she'd immediately waved her arms to flag them down.

The cops had talked to her at length. The TBI had been there, sitting alone with her in the backseat of the car.

He hadn't followed her directly home but had taken an alternate route. He didn't need to get on any cop's radar. Stay in the shadows. Be patient. Too soon to reveal himself. Too soon to strike.

Their final meeting would come on the anniversary of the day she'd nearly died. Perfect symmetry, in his mind.

The ultimate goal was in reach and would soon be his.

CHAPTER EIGHT

Monday, January 16, 3 P.M.

Alex and Deke arrived at the sheriff's office in the center of the small town twenty miles north of Nashville. Tyler Radcliff, Deidre's estranged husband, had been sheriff of the bedroom community for nearly five years and had earned himself a solid reputation as a good lawman. Not much in the way of high crimes happened in affluent New Market, but if anything did, Radcliff was on hand to deal with it.

Alex studied the one-story brick building that housed the sheriff's office. A quick check as they'd driven out revealed this boxy, practical building housed only the sheriff's office, which employed five people, including the sheriff, a few deputies, and a secretary.

Tyler faced a reelection this fall. With a few well-placed questions, Alex had discovered that Tyler expected to easily win reelection. There'd been some talk of another business leader running, but none in the Radcliff camp was concerned.

Alex adjusted his sunglasses as he studied the building.

"So how did Deidre, a Nashville detective, and a local sheriff hook up?"

"Couldn't tell you. I never asked and she never offered," Deke said.

Alex pulled off his sunglasses. "You ever have any kind of conversation with her?"

"I knew her only in passing."

"You don't talk to many people," Alex said.

"We Morgans come by it honestly. And you're one to talk. How many years does it take you to warm up to people?"

"A lot." Outside of his family, he kept his relationships on the surface. It wasn't a matter of what he wanted but out of necessity. He investigated other officers, so any kind of friendly relationship with anyone on the job could lead to a conflict of interest.

Alex shook his head. "We're quite the family."

"We're a hardheaded lot. And some would say not the easiest group of individuals."

Deke spoke plainly, and Alex found the raw honesty refreshing. It had been so long since he'd let his guard down, he wondered now if it were possible. "So I've heard."

"That doesn't bother you?"

"I didn't join the TBI to make friends. And if you joined the Nashville Police Department to make friends, well, you'd better find another job."

"I'm not worried about the job. Shit, I worry about it with Rachel. She says I'm sometimes distant."

"Are you?"

"Most likely, yes. That's the same crap that ended my marriages."

"So talk. She's a defense attorney. She's seen enough not to be put off by the job. And she can keep a secret if you need it kept confidential."

"I know."

"I don't like many people, Deke. But she's okay. Don't ruin it."

"I don't want to."

"Then don't."

"You make it sound easy."

"It is." Alex glanced at Deke, the barest hint of a smile softening his features.

They pushed through the glass front doors and, within steps, stood at the desk of an older woman with graying, short, curly hair, dark-rimmed glasses, and a ruddy complexion. She glanced up and, before Alex or Deke could reach for an ID, asked, "What jurisdiction?"

"TBI," Alex said.

"Nashville Police." Neither mentioned that they were investigating a homicide. Once people knew there'd been a murder, defenses slammed into place.

"What're you boys doing here?" An edge sharpened the words. In an office this small, word of Tyler and Deidre's divorce must have leaked.

"Like to visit with Sheriff Radcliff. Saw his car out front when we arrived," Alex said.

"He's busy."

Local law enforcement didn't always appreciate a visit from a TBI agent, and they sure didn't like seeing Alex Morgan. It was one thing for an agent to show, but Alex's appearance made people nervous or angry.

"He needs to make time. We need to see him now." Alex's voice was steady and controlled, and his gaze didn't waver until the older woman looked away and pushed herself to her feet. She'd been around cops long enough to know that when TBI showed up and said it was important, she needed to be flexible, whether she liked it or not.

The woman knocked on the door behind her and, after a gruff "Enter," disappeared behind it. Seconds later, the door snapped open. The secretary retreated to her desk and Tyler Radcliff appeared at the office door. He had broad shoulders and a tall frame that all but filled the doorway, giving him a menacing air that made weaker men acquiesce and alpha males bristle at the implied challenge. He'd shaved his head bald and sported a thick mustache and a scowl.

Alex wouldn't concede because he had too many questions to ask, but he never challenged unless he thought it would be useful.

Tyler stepped aside so Alex and Deke could enter his office. He extended a large beefy hand to Alex, which he accepted easily. Tyler's grip was strong in an overt and dominating kind of way. Alex understood the pressure points in the palm and where to squeeze so that Tyler released his grip.

"Agent Alex Morgan, TBI. Thanks for seeing us."

Deke extended his hand. "Detective Deke Morgan."

Tyler accepted Deke's hand but found himself matched in strength. Alex found the test amusing.

Tyler stepped back, hands folding over his wide chest. "Did Deidre send you here?"

"Why do you say that?" Alex asked.

Tyler stood in front of his desk, his feet slightly braced, as if he were ready for a fight. "You go after cops. And Deidre works for Nashville Vice. She sent you."

In no rush to answer, Alex let his gaze roam the room, taking in the dozens of framed citations and diplomas. No one questioned Tyler's dedication to the job. But cops who excelled professionally often paid a personal toll. "What makes you say that?"

A bitter smile twisted his lips. He shook his head, as if

he were in no mood to play games. "Oh, come on. She's been complaining about me, hasn't she? She's been doing her best to stick it to me since I canceled our joint credit cards. She'd like nothing better than to screw up my reelection campaign this year."

"Why'd you cancel the credit cards?" Alex asked.

Dark eyes, like the ends of a double-barreled shotgun, shifted to Deke. "Don't play stupid. You know we're getting a divorce. You're here because Deidre's pissed."

Tyler had been in law enforcement for twenty-plus years, and he knew how the system worked. He would choose his words carefully.

"When's the last time you saw her?" Alex asked.

Tyler's frown deepened. "Cut to the chase. What's going on here?"

Alex needed Tyler to understand he wasn't in charge of this conversation. "When's the last time you saw her?"

Tyler shifted his stance. "Last week, at the attorney's office."

"She made a call to you last night at about nine."

"I saw the missed call, but she didn't leave a message. I didn't bother to call her back. Why's this important? Did she or her boyfriend have an issue with me?"

The boyfriend, Alex guessed, was David, the guy from the running group who'd held Deidre close at the track. "Why would they?"

"She was forced to sign an agreement giving me full ownership of the house. I also got the few stocks we had."

Deidre, from what he'd learned, had been a fierce competitor who didn't give up easily. Perhaps she had more to gain with David than to hang on to what she'd had with Tyler. Or maybe Tyler knew what buttons to press to make

Deidre concede. "So you think this is about money and property?"

He shifted his stance and adjusted his belt buckle. "I told Deidre if she didn't walk away from the house, I'd let everyone at the Nashville Police Department know that it was her cheating that ended the marriage."

"Who was she having an affair with?"

"I don't know the guy's name. But I saw them together a couple of times. Kissing." He balled up his fingers into a fist before relaxing them. "Blond. Slick. Pretty boy."

"Are you the one who keyed her car?" Alex's question was a guess, but he delivered it as if it were fact.

Tyler's narrowed gaze confirmed he'd hit a nerve. "That what she told you?"

"Did you key her car?"

Emotion colored his cheeks. "No. Hell no."

"You look pretty mad," Deke added. "Mad can make anyone do stupid things."

"I didn't key her car and I wasn't the one calling her in the middle of the night. She accused me of that as well. I'm pissed by her cheating, but I'm not that desperate."

"She still with this boyfriend?" Deke asked.

"I don't know."

"How'd they meet?"

"That running group she started last fall. Started off as wanting to get in better shape, and I was all for that. Next thing I know, she's packing her clothes and moving out. Needed time to think. That was six months ago."

Tyler had yet to refer to his wife in the past tense. Could be savvy as easily as innocent. He was a cop and knew what to expect from another cop. "Deidre was found dead in her apartment this morning."

Alex watched Tyler closely. Intense moments like this

had a way of forcing down the guard. And when the guard was down, even the best lies unraveled.

Tyler shook his head, closing his eyes for a moment as if he hadn't heard. "What did you say?"

Alex enunciated each word carefully. "She was murdered."

Suspicion darkened his eyes. "How?"

"Stabbed." Deke spoke, hurtling the word toward Tyler like he was delivering a punch. "At least a dozen times."

The color from Tyler's face drained and he stumbled back a step, as if the brutal words came with a physical push. He lowered himself into a chair angled in front of his desk and cradled his head in callused, lined hands. His wedding ring, dulled by time, caught the washed-out light from the ceiling's fluorescent fixture. "Your facts can't be right. Deidre is one tough woman. She can kick ass with the best of them."

"No argument here," Alex said. "She was one hell of a fighter. But whoever got hold of her was tougher, or they caught her off guard."

Tyler raised his watery gaze and locked it on Alex. His lips curled into a scowl that deepened the lines around his mouth. "I didn't kill my wife."

They weren't divorced so *my wife* was technically correct. But Tyler's emphasis on the words suggested possessiveness. "I didn't say you did. You're still her legal husband so I owed you a death notice."

Tyler balled his fingers into tight fists, as if gripping onto his emotions. "Fuck. I can't believe she's dead. Have you told her sister Joy?"

"We put a call in to her. She arrives tonight."

"Damn. She's going to be devastated. She and Deidre were so close." He rubbed his eyes as if they stung.

"You two were involved in a contentious divorce. Your tone and manner suggest you're pretty angry with her."

Tyler swallowed as if his throat had filled with sand. "I'd never have killed her. She didn't deserve that."

Deke rested his hands in the pockets of his overcoat. "Where were you yesterday and last night?"

Tyler glared at Deke, absently rubbing the underside of his wedding band. He clearly didn't like being questioned, especially by a younger officer. "Out. On patrol."

Unmindful or, likely, uncaring of the tension radiating from Tyler, Alex removed a small notebook and pen from his pocket. "By yourself?"

"If you haven't noticed, we're a small department, Agent. It was my turn to make the rounds last night and that's what I did. What do you estimate the time of death?"

Alex, unwilling to be pinned, shrugged. "Not sure yet."

"The medical examiner is having a look at her late today or tomorrow. Do you know a woman by the name of Leah Carson?"

"No. Who is she?"

Alex had been willing to tag team with Deke on this interview until Deke had mentioned Leah's name. "She's in Deidre's running group. They were friends."

"I don't know any of her new friends. Did she meet her in that damn running group as well?"

"I couldn't tell you how they met." Alex doled out the truth as easily as a lie if it suited an investigation.

"I've never met her." He tipped back his head. "There was a time when I knew every detail about Dee's life. But in the last year, she's become a complete stranger to me."

"How'd that make you feel?" Deke asked. "Losing control like that can make a guy angry."

"What're you, my shrink now?" Tyler growled at the younger agent.

Deke's easy humor appeared untarnished. "Answer the question."

"Angry enough to cut Deidre off from our joint assets and angry enough to see that she lost ownership in our house."

"And to key her car?"

"I never said I did that. But I can tell you I wasn't angry enough to stab her. Jesus, she was my wife. I loved her."

"I don't doubt you loved her. But a razor's edge separates love and hate." Forensics suggested this murder had been planned carefully, but Tyler didn't need to know that. "Maybe you went to reason with her one last time and the visit turned into an argument that escalated. How many times in your job have you seen domestic disturbances that got out of control?"

"This wasn't a domestic disturbance, Morgan. My wife was murdered." Pain and seething anger covered the final words.

"I've no doubt you love . . . loved her." He'd seen genuine regret and sadness in a murderer's eyes before.

Tyler ran a callused hand over his head. "Fuck you."

He leaned forward, as if he had more to say and then caught himself. "This is the last thing I expected today."

"I'm sure Deidre would agree," Alex said.

"I didn't kill her!" He shouted the words, stopped himself, and then, in a lower voice said, "I might have been pissed, but I'd been pissed at her before. This isn't the first bad patch we've had and I knew it wouldn't be the last."

"Love and hate," Deke said, raising two crossed fingers, "are both powerful emotions."

Tyler stood. "I'm not talking anymore. I'm calling my lawyer."

Alex studied him. "We haven't made any accusations."

Tyler shook his head. "I'm the estranged spouse. That

puts me at the top of the list. I know how it works. Throw me under the bus and tell everyone you've closed the case."

Alex took a deliberate step into Tyler's space. His voice was low, but his words were as cutting as broken glass. "Sheriff Radcliff, I go by the evidence and only the evidence. I don't care about statistics or the easy way out. If you're innocent, then we're square and you won't see me again." His tone dripped with ice. "But if you're lying to me, Radcliff, I'm going to nail you to the wall."

"I was in law before you got out of high school. Take your best shot."

Alex's even white teeth flashed into a very unfriendly smile. "I will."

Alex thought back to the numbers in Deidre's personal phone, found in her purse. Leah. Sister. Husband. Work. And the name Tracy Donovan.

He pulled up in front of a brick office building located north of the city. Straight lines, neatly trimmed hedges, and a parking lot with sharp right angles; it wasn't a surprise when he glanced at the sign out front, which read HALL ENGINEERING.

He parked and moved inside the building, straight toward the desk of a receptionist. She had frosted blond hair, pale skin, and dark brows that made her round face look a little off balance. She glanced up at Alex, her expression clicking from bored to interested in a blink.

"Can I help you?" She tugged a phone headset from her ears and rose.

"I'm here to see Tracy Donovan. I understand she's an engineer."

"Can I tell her who's here?"

Alex pulled his badge from the breast pocket of his jacket. "Alex Morgan, Tennessee Bureau of Investigation."

Her eyes widened. "Sure. Be right back."

She vanished around a corner, leaving him a moment to pace the carpeted lobby. Within seconds, whispered conversations buzzed as the receptionist wove her way through the maze of cubicles.

A tall woman with short, dark hair appeared in the reception area. She wore no makeup, a black pantsuit with a white shirt, and very sensible flat black shoes.

"Agent Morgan?" Her voice was crisp and sharp, like the lines of the building.

"Yes, ma'am."

"What's this about?"

"Deidre Jones. Is there somewhere private we can talk?"

A frown wrinkled an already stoic face. "There's a conference room right here." Her strides were efficient, no wasted movement, and she twisted the door handle with a sharp flick of the wrist. She flipped on the lights in the room and held the door open for him until he entered, then quietly closed the door behind him.

Alex waited until she sat before taking a seat across from her. "Thank you for your time."

"What's going on with Deidre?"

"When's the last time you saw her?"

The frown deepened. "It's been a few months. We went out for drinks. What's going on?"

He tapped an index finger on the polished wood table. "She was found dead in her apartment this morning."

Tracy's mouth dropped open before she raised fingertips to her mouth. "Dead? That doesn't make any sense at all. What happened?"

"She was murdered."

Tracy leaned back in her chair and squeezed the bridge of her nose. "You've got to have made a mistake. Deidre could take care of herself."

"I agree. She was a top-notch detective. One of the best."

"Who would kill her?"

"That's what I'm trying to find out. Can you tell me anything about her? I've spoken to people who worked with her over the past few years, but no one knew much about her personal life."

Tears glistened, and Tracy had to clear her throat a couple of times before she could speak. "We've been best friends since first grade. Our mothers were friends."

"As I understand it, her parents are dead and she has a sister. Is that right?"

"Yeah. Her sister's name is Joy. Joy Martin."

"She's scheduled to arrive in town this evening."

"Joy and Deidre didn't get along and hadn't spoken in a couple of years."

"Was there bad blood?"

"Joy loved Deidre, but she didn't like Tyler. They got into a bad fight a few years ago. Deidre took Tyler's side." She shoved out a breath. "Lately, Deidre said her work and her friends were her family."

"Was she having trouble with anyone?"

"Her divorce wasn't all that smooth. Tyler wanted to save the marriage. She didn't. We spoke on the phone from time to time but hadn't seen each other because she was consumed by the divorce."

"Why didn't she want to work it out?"

"He resented her work and he wanted kids. Though she'd always said she'd like a couple, she loved her job too much to slow down. He felt cheated when she finally made the decision not to have a baby."

"Did Radcliff make any threats against Deidre?"

"He would call her cell and leave long ranting messages about why they shouldn't divorce. He sent her letters. Would leave cards on her windshield. But he never said anything threatening. I really do believe the guy loved her."

"I didn't find any messages on her phone or letters in her town house."

"She deleted or tossed them all. She figured he'd get tired of bothering her and back off."

"Would you say he was stalking her?"

She considered the question. "He was annoying, but he never threatened her. I heard a couple of the messages and I felt sorry for the guy. He did love Deidre. She loved him but said their priorities shifted."

Had Tyler's desperation to save his marriage turned deadly? "He said she was having an affair."

"Deidre made some unfortunate choices."

"She was seeing David Westbrook?"

"Yes. They met through their running group."

He'd seen David at Rudy's the other night before he'd entered the bar. Deidre had been talking to Leah. David had been hovering. "How long had they been together?"

"Since October. But she was planning to break it off. He's a lot of fun, but she knew it wasn't going anywhere long-term."

"Did David want more of a relationship?"

"No. He's the kind of guy who doesn't form lasting relationships. She did say he wanted to ask out a friend of hers in the running group."

"Leah?"

"Yeah, I think. Deidre was fairly certain Leah wouldn't go out with him."

"Why?"

"Jumpy. Deidre was sure she had some kind of trauma

in her past. And David was too pushy for Leah. You know, she was gun-shy."

Alex had guessed the same about Leah. And yet she'd gone out with him. "Anyone else who might want to hurt Deidre? What about neighbors?"

She wiped away a tear. "She wouldn't have known them that well. She told me over the phone she didn't hang around it much."

Alex pulled out a card. "If you think of anything else, would you call me?"

She accepted the card, glanced at it, and then met his gaze. "How did she die?"

"She was stabbed."

Her face paled as she sat back in the chair. "God. Could this be related to the case she was working? I know the case was putting her under a lot of pressure. She wasn't sleeping well because of it."

"What did she tell you about the case?"

"Said it was a cold case. Said if she could collar this guy it would 'close the hymn book.'"

"She said it just like that."

"Yeah. Just like that."

"I can contact you if I have more questions?"

"Sure. Whatever you need."

Alex waited until nearly six in the evening before he began knocking on Deidre's neighbors' doors. Most would be home from work and, if they weren't settled down for dinner yet, they'd at least have dragged in the door, poured a drink, or marshalled kids to do homework. One way or another, they'd be home.

He knocked on the first door. Inside, he heard classical

music and the bark of a small dog. Seconds later, footsteps and then the rattle of a chain. A tall slim woman with red hair opened the door. "Can I help you?"

"I'm with the Tennessee Bureau of Investigation. Agent Morgan. I have questions about the woman next door."

"I think her name is Deidre."

"That's right. Are you aware that she was killed yesterday?"

A barking pug rushed the front door, forcing her to pick the animal up. "Let me put him in the kitchen. I'll be right back."

She returned to the sound of the dog still yapping. "You said Deidre was dead?"

"Yes, ma'am. She was killed in her town house."

"My God. Do you know who did it?"

"That's what we're trying to determine. Has she had any visitors lately that would have caught your attention?"

"I work long hours, and I think she did as well. We didn't see each other a lot and she's only lived here a couple of weeks. I do remember a tall dark guy ringing her bell a couple of weeks ago, right after she moved into her place. He was on her porch when I came home. He said his name was Philip."

"Last name?"

"I don't know. He looked pretty frustrated. Said she had promised to be there. I noticed he waited in his car for at least an hour before he drove off."

"Did you tell her?"

"No. I honestly forgot about it until this moment."

"Anyone else?"

"I know she's dating a guy. Blond. David somebody."

He showed her a picture of David from the running group. "This him?"

"Yeah. That's him. Nice guy. Very charming. I came home one night and he was standing on her doorstep with flowers." A smile tugged at her lips. "I told him she often worked late. He said he knew but was hoping to catch up with her. Knew she'd worked a long day and wanted to cheer her up. So sweet."

"What did he do?"

"Left the flowers on her porch."

"Do you remember when she got home?"

"A couple of hours later. I never got to ask her about him."

Alex handed his card to the neighbor. "If you think of more, you'll call."

She glanced at the card. "Yeah, sure."

The next neighbor was a mother with three bustling teenage boys who were fighting over a remote control. She was a petite woman with short, mousy-brown hair and large eyes that looked a bit harried. She hadn't met Deidre and hadn't noticed anyone coming or going. As she spoke, a vase crashed to the floor and the boys went silent. She looked at Alex, asking flatly if he'd arrest all three boys.

He showed her a picture of Deidre.

"Oh, yeah, the lady with the gun. My thirteen-year-old noticed her gun holster one day. He couldn't stop talking about it. She was dressed in a suit, white shirt, and I figured she was law enforcement. I asked around and found out she was Nashville PD."

The neighbor across from Deidre's town house was a man in his midfifties with short-cropped hair and a few gold earrings in his left ear. His T-shirt had a ragged, stonewashed look, but the logo suggested he'd paid up for it. Stonewashed jeans and cowboy boots fit the look of someone wanting to make it in the country music world. Nashville was full of wannabes.

Alex showed him Deidre's picture. The guy gave it a glancing look. "Don't know her."

"Have another look."

He dropped his gaze. "I've never met her."

"She lives across from you."

"Okay."

"You see any detail that caught your attention at her place?"

"No, not really. She was playing loud music a couple of weeks ago. Terrible stuff. This hard rock stuff. I was on my way over to complain, but it stopped before I got to her back door so I let it go."

"No other issues with her?"

"No."

"Visitors?"

He frowned. "There was a guy a week or so ago. Standing on the sidewalk, staring."

"You get a good look?"

"Wore a skullcap, sunglasses, and a heavy coat. I asked if I could help and he said no."

"You ask for a name?"

"I think it was Phil or Philip. No last name."

Alex filed the name, thanked the man, and left Deidre's town house with little more than fragments. He'd skimmed the surface of her recent case files and hadn't found a Philip. Maybe it was time to dig deeper into her past.

CHAPTER NINE

Monday, January 16, 7 P.M.

Leah spent the entire afternoon cleaning her house, a ritual to burn energy so sharp her skin felt tight enough to split. By the time she'd finished scouring and scrubbing, her place smelled of pine cleaner and bleach. The floors were vacuumed, the sheets on the bed changed, and the bathrooms glistened. As she put away the last of her cleaning supplies, she moved to the center of her living room and stood, her arms folded. There was no more cleaning to be done. Nothing was out of place or not sparkling. And she wasn't working tomorrow. Yet the energy still pumped in her veins.

Maybe she could read a book or rent a movie? She considered a trip to the mall; the idea of wandering from shop to shop might pass the time, but it wouldn't chase away memories of finding Deidre dead.

She shoved out a breath as she sat down and sagged into the overstuffed couch. She reached for the neat stack of magazines on the coffee table and restacked them, lining them up carefully with the edge of the table.

Jesus, Deidre. Who would do that to you?

As she stared at the neat stack, she remembered Philip was a real stickler for a clean house. He liked order, though not enough to do it himself. He liked her to keep their apartment spotless. He always complimented her when she cleaned.

When they'd first married, she'd wanted to please him and so she'd made the effort to clean their apartment often. When her mother had come to visit, she'd joked that she didn't realize Leah knew how to turn on a vacuum, let alone push one. They'd all had a good laugh at her expense, but Leah remembered feeling pride. She'd considered herself grown-up, and taking care of her grown-up house had felt right.

And then her year of working in the administrative offices of the engineering firm had come to an end and it was time to begin veterinary school. They'd talked about her moving to Knoxville and commuting back when she could, but as the date grew closer, Philip had gotten edgier. He'd become more obsessed with a clean house. Then there'd been snide comments, jokes, jabs and, finally, insults.

Leah had done her best to keep up but found her desire to be around the apartment and Philip dwindling. She could clearly remember the day she'd decided to end her marriage. She'd been up late working on homework for a science class, knowing the extra credit would help her in the fall. She'd overslept that morning and realized she was late for work.

Philip had tried to keep her in bed. "Baby, you still have time."

She pushed his hands away, impatient and annoyed. "I can't believe I slept so late. I set two alarms."

He yawned and laid back on the pillow, not the least bit concerned about her tardiness.

She'd have called him on his callousness if she'd had the time, but she was so focused on pulling on her slacks and sweatshirt and scraping her hair back into a ponytail that she'd swallowed her anger. She'd quickly eaten a bowl of cereal, not thinking about anything other than running to class, left the bowl in the sink, and ran out the door.

Hours later, she'd been pleased with herself when she arrived home. Philip had been waiting for her. He'd been standing by the sink, where the bowl sat filled with warm milk and bits of cereal. "I think you forgot something this morning."

She took off her jacket and hung it on the hook by the door. Carefully, she lowered her backpack to the floor as she studied his calm, almost smiling face. "Sorry? What would I have forgotten?"

"The bowl in the kitchen sink." He sounded almost helpful.

"What bowl?" This morning felt like a lifetime ago.

His smile faltered. "You need to clean it up."

Defiance sparked hot in her gut as she stared at him. "I'll get to it."

"Now."

The heat ignited. "No."

Philip crossed the room in three quick strides and, before she could react, slapped her hard across the face. She dropped to her knees, her head spinning and her jaw throbbing. Shock, humiliation, and anger collided. She'd never been hit like that. Never. For an instant, she questioned what she'd said to him. Had she somehow made him hit her?

She didn't look up at him as she made her way to her feet. When she did meet his gaze, she didn't see anger but sadness. Tears glistened in his eyes.

"I hate hurting you," he said.

A part of her wanted him to embrace her, tell her it would be all right. *Just tell me we're fine.* But another part yelled for her to run. *Get out of there! Grab your bag and go!*

She raised her hand to her jaw, which had already swollen.

"Let me get you some ice," Philip offered. He turned quickly and vanished into the kitchen. "We won't worry about the bowl for now."

The bowl. They were back to the bowl?

Now Leah glanced around at her glistening town house. Furious, she reached down and swiped her hand across the coffee table, sending the magazines splaying to the floor.

She would not stay here.

She would not be afraid.

Deidre's death wasn't linked to her past. Philip was dead. Leah had talked at length with the Detective Roseanne Jeffers in South Carolina, who returned his belongings to her. When they arrived, she held Philip's blackened family ring in her hand, finally accepting he was dead before she gave the entire box to his grandmother.

Alex parked at the medical examiner's office minutes after eight. Deke had stopped at the TBI and promised to meet Alex there within minutes for their scheduled meeting with Miriam Heller to discuss Deidre's autopsy.

He pushed through the glass door, welcoming the rush of heat from the lobby. He unwound the thick dark scarf from around his neck and unbuttoned his overcoat. At the front window, he showed his badge to the receptionist and told her he was there for Dr. Heller.

He fought the urge to pace the lobby, his body a hive of

energy. He'd never been good sitting or waiting, and today was proving to be worse than usual. Just as Dr. Heller appeared at the locked door that led to the exam rooms, the front doors whooshed open to admit Deke.

His brother wore his suit jacket open, clearly unmindful of the cold. He crossed the lobby in long hurried strides.

Dr. Heller made a shivering motion as she looked at him. "How can you stand the cold?"

Deke grinned. "Ice in the blood."

Alex slid off his overcoat and neatly draped it over his arm. He found the exchange frustrating but had learned the value of small talk. It broke the ice, allowed everyone to get their minds around the grim task to come.

Dr. Heller shook her head. "The warm weather is why I moved here. I grew up in Maine, but I never liked the cold. If I ever pick up stakes and move, it'll be farther south." Reading the impatience on Alex's face, she said, "Come on back, gentlemen, to my office. I'm running a little behind today. We had an infant brought in today. I put all work aside when that happens."

Alex couldn't help but ask, "What happened to the baby?"

"SIDS," Dr. Heller said. "She stopped breathing. A tragedy that befell a very nice set of parents."

He'd never imagined himself with children. In fact, none of the Morgan offspring spoke about having children. He wasn't sure if they were late bloomers or simply not destined to be parents.

"You're sure you want to be present?" Dr. Heller asked.

"It's not about what I want," Alex said. He turned to Deke. "But you don't need to be here."

Deke grimaced. "I said I would be, and I will."

"But you worked with her."

"And I'll handle this."

Be careful, Alex wanted to warn. *Click off the emotions once too often and they might not return.* "Okay."

The trio made their way to the entrance of Exam Room Two. Her hand on the door, Dr. Heller paused. "Give me about five minutes. Gown up and meet me inside."

"Sure," Alex said.

Dr. Heller vanished behind the swinging door and both agents donned gowns, gloves, and eye protection.

Deke tugged on the cuff of his surgical gown. "Have you ever attended the autopsy of a fellow officer?"

"No," Alex said.

"Only once before for me. It can't be explained."

"I would imagine you're right." A part of him moved to a deeper corner of his soul. Dangerous to live life at a distance, but it was the only way to do this job. Even if Deidre had been dirty, she'd done good work, and that mattered.

The brothers entered the exam room. Directly in their line of sight was the sheet-draped body of Deidre Jones. A ripple of tension washed over them both. Deke cracked his knuckles and flexed. Alex sunk even deeper into the shadowed places in his mind.

Dr. Heller stood at the head of the stainless-steel table. She wore a gown, gloves, a cap, and clear goggles. Normally, she exposed the entire body so the agents or detectives could view all the injuries. This time, she kept Deidre's face and slashed throat covered and exposed the right arm, marred with five gashes, bloodless and gaping. "She sustained injuries on her right side, as you can see, and her palm has a slice down the center. That's a defensive wound."

Alex pictured Leah's scar. Who the hell had stabbed her?

What had begun as mild curiosity grew stronger each time he saw her or she crossed his mind.

Dr. Heller rolled back the sheet a little farther and then moved the body—not Deidre—to its left side. A deep gash marred the flesh above the kidney. "This was the killing cut. It lacerated her kidney and the inferior vena cava, a major blood vein. She would have bled out in a matter of minutes."

"The cut to her throat wasn't enough to kill her?" Alex asked.

"It was nasty but no; she might have survived that wound."

"How many wounds were there in total?"

"Twenty-three." She laid the body back on its side. "This first blow would have brought her to her knees, then I'm guessing she fell to the floor and rolled on her back. All the remaining cuts came at her from above."

That fit the crime scene.

She covered the arm with the sheet and glanced at an open file on the worktable. "Deidre Jones, age forty-two, appeared to have been in excellent health. Cause of death, as I just showed you, was a knife thrust into her kidneys and through the inferior vena cava. Even if rescue crews had been on hand, there'd have been no saving her."

Alex shifted his stance. "So why the extra wounds?"

She shrugged. "Several of the wounds on her arms and legs don't appear to have bled much, which leads me to believe her heart had already stopped pumping." She pulled off her glasses. "The killer overkilled, for lack of a better word."

"Anger, rage, drugs could all be factors," Deke said.

She moved her magnifying glass closer to the body and, with tweezers, plucked several blond hairs from one of the wounds. She dropped the hair in a bag and handed it to

Alex. He held it up to the light, examining the strands of hair. "Get these to Forensics."

"Maybe you got lucky."

"Maybe."

The external exam and mapping of the wounds continued as both officers stood back and observed. Several times Deke looked away, his frown deepening, though he was still listening.

Alex understood. He didn't like standing there witnessing this final indignity either.

Dr. Heller quietly made the Y incision into the victim's chest, working steadily and professionally as she catalogued her findings. An hour later, as her assistant stitched up the incision, the doctor faced the men. "Before you arrived, I did a preliminary exam and can tell you there were no signs of sexual assault. No vaginal bruising. No tearing. She'd had sex in the last forty-eight hours of her life, but that appears to have been consensual."

"You'll get me a DNA sample?" Alex asked.

"Of course."

"By the way, gentlemen, I have an update on the John Doe."

She turned toward a computer screen and, pulling off her gloves, punched a few keys. "After some of my magic tricks, I discovered that one of his tattoos was an eagle and the other was a woman's face, though that part of the body was so badly burned I could only make out an outline." She scrolled down the page. "There were needle marks on the arms. I've run toxicology screens, but they won't be back for a couple of weeks. I've also pulled DNA and have plugged it into the system. Maybe we'll get lucky and get a hit."

The men thanked the doctor and walked out into the

hallway, where they stripped off the disposable gowns and gloves and dumped them in a bin.

"One stab to the back is effective, even lethal, but not very dramatic," Deke said. "Twenty-three cuts would be unforgettable. What the hell do the two victims have in common?"

"It will come together soon. Just let it play out."

He sat in the coffee shop in front of a steaming cup of coffee and a half-eaten Danish on a paper plate. Flecks of white powdered sugar dusted the faux wood tabletop and his jeans. He took a sip, savoring the heat as he leaned back in his chair. It felt good to be off his feet and out of the cold morning.

He tapped his toe on the brown tile floor as he reached in his pocket for his phone. He typed in the four-digit security code and chose the photo app. He took another bite of the Danish and scrolled through the images until he found the ones of his wife. He smiled. She was such a pretty woman. How had a guy like him ended up with such a lovely, smart woman? Going places, his old man had said. From the moment she'd first kissed him, he'd known he'd be devastated if she'd walked out of his life.

He scrolled through more pictures of her. Running. Shopping for shoes. Laughing with a friend over coffee. Cooking in the kitchen.

He couldn't get enough of her. He thought about her every waking moment and dreamed about her in his sleep.

His little bird had balked at his endless attention, and the harder he squeezed, the farther and farther from him she'd grown. She'd tried to tell him he was too much. That he needed to relax. But he couldn't.

He traced her face with the tip of a callused finger. Tears welled in his eyes. She'd betrayed him, left him, and God help him, he still loved her. *Why do you make me hurt you? You know how much I hate to hurt you.*

The thin sliver of moon did little to cut the night's inky black that shrouded Leah as she arrived at the old Victorian-style home. It had been hard finding street parking, and she'd been forced to circle the block a few times before she'd found a spot across the street. By the time she climbed the wide brick front steps, the cold air stung her lungs and nipped at her face.

She reached for the brass doorknob and pushed open the heavy door. Warm air greeted her, and she allowed its embrace to envelope her as she shrugged off her jacket. She smiled to the receptionist, a redhead in her late forties with ruddy cheeks and freckles.

"Hi, Frances," Leah said.

Frances stood, hands on her wide hips. "It's been a few weeks."

"I was busy at work. I kept meaning to come, but I could never get my act together."

"Hey, no worries. We're here all the time, ready to help whether you need us or not."

Leah had joined a support group days after moving back to Nashville. The people in this group had survived an attack from a loved one. When she'd been here last, she'd spoken with such confidence to her counselor. "I've finally taken a giant step toward getting on with my life." But since finding Deidre, all the hard-won territory had surrendered to fear. "Group still tonight?"

"Six P.M. like always. Go on in; they haven't started yet."

Leah slid open the pocket doors that led to what must have been a formal parlor when this house had originally been built as a private home. A circle of chairs, half full, were in the center of what was now a meeting room. A coffeepot on a side table gurgled beside a plate of chocolate chip cookies. There were a few cooks in the group who brought baked goods when they'd had a bad week. Many apologized for the confections, saying cooking was preferable to sitting and worrying. Judging by the spread, it had been a rough week.

She draped her coat over an empty chair and set her purse on it before moving to the refreshment table. She filled a cup with coffee and took a seat nearby. She always chose a chair that faced the back wall and gave her a clear view of the door. Nervous habit.

As Leah sipped her coffee, she scanned the group and realized she didn't recognize the women. They ranged in age from late teens to early sixties. A couple of the older women looked as if they had money. A few others looked middle income. They came from all walks of life.

The facilitator, Sierra, was a short woman in her early thirties. She had a round face, olive skin, and salt-and-pepper hair that brushed her shoulders. She carried a mug that read Number One Mom. Sierra had a master's in psychology and had opened her counseling center, Homestead, ten years before, after she'd nearly died in a car accident caused by her ex-husband.

"Welcome, Leah," Sierra said as she sat down next to her. "How's it been going?"

"Crazy at work. But all good." She'd uttered the last statement from reflex. It hadn't been all good. In fact, not good one bit.

Sierra nodded, sipping her own coffee. She recognized the not-ready-to-talk smile but let it pass. "Cold night."

"I can't wait for spring."

Sierra's gaze roamed the room. "I see familiar faces and some new ones. We always begin the meeting with introductions." She nodded to a slim woman who wore an expensive dark sweater, jeans, and her thick silver hair twisted into a chignon.

The woman grinned. "My name is Ester. I joined the group seven years ago. I haven't been here in a while, but I joined because I was in a plane crash eight years ago. My husband and son were killed. My husband was the pilot, and he intentionally crashed the plane because he knew I wanted a divorce."

Heads nodded before Sierra turned to the next woman. In all, there were six, a few joining after the meeting started. All had different experiences. One woman had been beaten nearly to death by a boyfriend. Another had survived a car accident caused by a lover. Another a near drowning.

"Want to finish up the introductions, Leah?" Sierra asked.

Leah glanced at Sierra, knowing the counselor had called her out on purpose. Leah had a bad habit of hiding, allowing the conversations to swirl around her. "My name is Leah. I was nearly stabbed to death by my ex-husband four years ago."

A hush ran through the room. They'd all suffered violence at the hand of a loved one.

"Leah, you also have an anniversary coming up, correct?"

Leah had only shared her details once, a few months earlier. It had been a spur-of-the-moment decision that had left her feeling stripped bare and vulnerable. Since then, when she came, she spoke little, but it seemed tonight Sierra wasn't going to let her ride for free.

"I used to be very outgoing and happy," Leah said. "Now, I'm a bit of a mess. Especially this time of year. January twenty-fifth was our wedding anniversary, and I always get extra nervous this time of year." She wasn't sure if she could talk about finding Deidre this morning without crying so she opted to keep that information to herself. Maybe one day she would talk about it, but she didn't think she could do it today.

"Why?" Sierra asked.

"My ex-husband attacked me on our anniversary."

Since the attack, Leah had felt isolated from most people who'd never endured what she had. Hearing about evil versus experiencing it were very different things. Theirs was a sisterhood of the broken. Here, she didn't feel so alone.

A young woman with dark brown hair shared the story of a boyfriend who'd nearly strangled her to death. He was in jail now, awaiting his trial. "So, what's it like knowing he died and you never got justice?"

Leah dug her fingernail into the side of her cup. "I can't think about that. It would eat me alive."

"Are you still journaling?" Sierra asked.

"Yes." She glanced into the black depths of her coffee, knowing the caffeine would ensure she wouldn't sleep well tonight. "For those of you who don't know me, I'm a little obsessive about the journaling. I sit down each night and make detailed notes on my day. It goes back to when my husband was stalking me. The police said they could prove the case if they had evidence of a pattern."

"But he's dead," the young woman said.

Leah nodded. "I know. It's a little OCD on my part. But I can't seem to stop. Perhaps it's therapeutic."

"So what happened to bring you here tonight?" Sierra asked.

A knot in Leah's chest wouldn't let her draw in a full breath. "A friend of mine was killed last night. I found her this morning. She'd been murdered."

A gasp swept the room. All eyes focused on Leah, and she knew there was no going back. "She was stabbed. Like me."

The silver-haired woman rose and came up behind Leah. She wrapped her arms around her shoulders and hugged her close. "I'm sorry, honey."

Leah closed her eyes and allowed the embrace. "Thanks."

The woman patted Leah on the shoulder and returned to her seat.

"Finding your friend made you relive your attack?" Sierra asked.

"Made me wonder if I'd been earlier, could I have helped her. The cop who arrived in time to stop my attack had been a military paramedic. He stopped some of the bleeding or I'm not sure I'd have made it. If he hadn't been there, I'd have been Deidre."

"You don't blame yourself, I hope. Replaying the scene with different scenarios never works."

"I know. I do."

"But . . ."

Leah shrugged. "It's hard not to wonder where I'd be or where she'd be if the timing had been just a little different."

A sigh leaked over her clenched teeth. "My life can be divided into before and after the attack. Before I had friends. Most scattered after the attack. My roommate moved all her stuff out of our apartment. I never saw her again. That made me angry for a long time, but I realize now she was scared."

"People are scared of us," a young woman said. "It's almost as if we were at fault."

"I lost a lot of friends while my ex-husband was stalking me," another woman said. "And when he was finally arrested, he couldn't stop apologizing. Said he didn't want to hurt me. Said he hated it. Said I made him hurt me." Bitterness twisted around the last words.

A heavy silence settled over the room, and for a moment no one spoke. Finally, Sierra broke the silence. "You said your husband is dead?"

"He got away from the cops the night of the attack and made it as far as South Carolina. He was in a car accident. His ID was found at the scene and the body identified." Her hold on her coffee cup tightened. "Since I found my friend, my ex-husband is all I can think about."

"So do they have a suspect in your friend's murder?" Sierra asked.

"If the police do, they're not telling me."

"Did you tell them about your past?"

"No," Leah said. "If my ex-husband were alive, I'd have said something. Philip never did like it when I had friends, and it would be like him to target one. But he's gone." She picked at a thread on her pants. "I called the detective who oversaw the identification of his body. Left her a voice mail, and I'm pretty sure she thinks I'm crazy, calling after all this time."

"Why'd you call?" Sierra asked.

Nervous laughter bubbled in Leah. "Maybe because I never saw his body. I never anchored his death in my mind. When his grandmother had the funeral I was still too banged up to travel. I've only visited his grave once."

"When's the last time you called the detective?" Sierra asked.

"On our anniversary three years ago. For whatever reason, I had a little panic attack and needed to call. She was nice. Again, I sounded a little insane. Logically, I know he's dead, but a part of me always doubts."

A young girl with red hair and glasses, who had been the victim of a shooting, snorted. "I don't trust anything or anyone. The system does screw up. I had my husband arrested for beating me and then, when the cops released him, they didn't warn me. Twelve hours after he got out, he tracked me down and shot me. Three days after the shooting, I was recovering in the hospital, tubes stuck out of every end of my body, when the jail called to inform me he had been released."

The women nodded. Several murmured warnings.

"I'm here tonight so you all can talk me off the ledge," Leah said, smiling as if it would lighten the fear. She shifted her gaze to Sierra. "Not a real ledge. Just the proverbial ledge. I'm so tired of being afraid. I'm so tired of fearing every corner or odd sound I hear at night. I thought I was past it, but it's all rushing back now."

Sierra smiled. "Leah, you're doing just fine. Give yourself a break. You suffered a terrible trauma. Give yourself time to absorb it."

"So, you think that's all it is?"

"You found a friend murdered. Give yourself a break. That's a hell of an ordeal."

"I need to give it time," Leah said automatically.

"Yes," Sierra said. "And if the police talk to you again, tell them what happened to you. They might cut you a little slack."

"I know."

Sierra recognized the evasion humming below the surface. "Talking to the cops will make you feel better. You'll at least have them on your side."

"Philip was a cop." This was a detail she'd never shared before.

Sierra leaned forward a fraction. "Come again?"

"He was a cop. That's how he was able to talk himself out of so many spots with me. Trust is kind of an issue for me."

"You can't judge all cops by him," Sierra said. "There are a lot of good ones."

"I know. I know. A good one saved me. If not for him, I'd have bled to death." She ran nervous fingers through her hair. "I even had a date the other night, the first one in years, with a cop."

"He a nice guy?"

"Seems to be." A shrug and a smile, meant to soften the absolute panic, fell flat. "Though I kinda freaked out on the date. A little panic attack."

"It was your first date."

"I know. I've been thrown and I need to get back up on the horse." God, how many times had she heard that analogy and thought it bogus?

Other women shared their stories, and though Leah tried to focus, their voices faded to the background. Philip wasn't alive. And Deidre's death was a terrible coincidence.

By the time the meeting ended, Leah's worries lingered, but she didn't feel so alone. As she walked to her car, her cell phone rang. She didn't recognize the number.

Let it go to voice mail, fear whispered.

Don't be a baby. Her grip tightening, she counted the rings. One. Two. Three. On the fourth ring, she answered. "Hello."

Silence answered her. Long tense seconds passed. She gripped the phone harder.

"Hello?"

No answer.

Her heart kicking into high gear and annoyed, she ended the call. *Get a grip.*

Still gripping the phone tight, she hurried to her car, slid behind the wheel, and locked the doors. The cold leather seat chilled her bones as she studied the still shadows for monsters.

Starting the engine, she glared at the phone. "If that's meant to be a joke, Karma, it's really not very funny," She said out loud. Her heart raced a little faster. "Shit. I don't need hang-ups on a good day."

Distracted, she pulled out into traffic as a horn blared behind her coming from her blind spot. She hit the brakes, realizing she'd nearly driven into a tow truck. *Damn.*

Sweating, white-knuckled the wheel. The phone rang again, and she jumped. Glaring at the display, she watched the same number flash again. This time she let it ring, gritting her teeth until the phone finally went silent. Without checking for a message, she deleted the call from her phone.

Philip is dead. He is dead.

CHAPTER TEN

Tuesday, January 17, 8 A.M.

Tyler Radcliff dreamed of Deidre. She wasn't laughing or smiling. She wasn't wearing that red bikini he'd liked so much when they'd been in Aruba. Instead, she wore that damn black suit that had never been flattering, and her angled face was pale, gaunt, and bloodless. She'd moved toward him, her long arms extended as she reached for him. He'd tried to jerk away, but those ice-cold fingers connected with his brow, sending shivers through his body. She traced the ridge of his brow and with her lips hovering close to his ear said, "I loved you so much once. What went wrong?"

He jerked awake, his hands trembling and his body drenched in sweat. He rolled on his back and stared at the play of shadows across his bedroom as his hand slid to the side of the bed that had been Deidre's. The sheets were ice cold. He rolled on his side and imagined her lying there, sleeping, a slight smile on her face.

He smoothed his hand over her pillow, hating that the down was plump and missing the subtle imprint of her head. *Dee, how did it turn to shit between us?*

With a groan, he rolled out of bed and tugged on a pair

of jeans. Grabbing a T-shirt from the floor, he pulled it over his head and padded into the living room, where a half-full bottle of bourbon sat on the coffee table. Pushing an old pizza box off the couch and tossing it on the floor, he reached for the bottle as he dug the remote out of the sofa and turned on the television to CNN Sports.

He drank from the bottle as he glanced down at the wedding album sitting on the coffee table next to an empty bag of potato chips. The book was open to the last shot, taken just before they'd taken off for Aruba. Deidre was wearing a slim-fitting green dress she'd slipped on after the reception and he wore khakis, a white shirt, and a red tie. Handfuls of birdseed flew in the air above them and both had huddled close as they waited for the seeds to drop. Tracing Deidre's smiling face with a callused fingertip, he drank, savoring the burn of the bourbon as it rolled down his throat.

What the hell had gone so wrong between them?

Their wedding day had been simple but beautiful. No fancy churches or reception halls for them. A small, intimate ceremony had suited them just fine.

He flipped several pages back to the picture taken before she'd walked across the grassy field toward him and the preacher. Curls peeked out from under her white veil, and she'd been so damn pretty he'd thought himself the luckiest man in the world. Later, at the reception, his hands had trembled just a little when he'd reached up under her skirt and removed the blue garter, which he'd tossed toward the single guys. In those days, he could barely keep his hands off her.

Hell, he'd never tired of Deidre in bed. She was wild and didn't mind keeping it fresh and fun. Even right up until last fall, when he'd found the emails to the other guy, he was hot for her.

But the emails had struck him right in the face, like a sucker punch. Initially, he hadn't been able to breathe, too shocked to think. Then slowly, as he reread the emails through the night, his frozen emotions had warmed to sadness and then heated to anger and rage.

If she'd walked in the door that day, he'd have killed her right then. No questions asked. For hours, he'd clenched and unclenched his fist as he imagined what it would feel like to wrap his hands around her neck.

He hadn't told her he'd found the emails at first. Instead, he'd become obsessed with finding out the name of her lover. He'd taken to following her until the late fall day when he'd seen her dart into a trendy café in Franklin and sit down with a cup of coffee. She'd only been at the table a few minutes before a man had entered the shop. She'd risen immediately, and when he approached her, she had hugged him warmly.

Deidre had once hugged Tyler with that kind of passion.

Shit. He reached for the bourbon bottle and drank heavily. He set the bottle down.

The TBI agent had mentioned Leah Carson, Deidre's new friend. He'd known the two had grown close but now wondered what secrets Deidre had shared with her. He didn't need her feeding the cops stories about his troubles with Deidre. Still, as a cop he understood it was better to keep his distance from her. Better to let TBI do its thing and let the whole deal play out.

Better.

Smarter.

But the man didn't want to hear the cop's advice. If Deidre had been here, she'd have talked him out of what he wanted to do. But Deidre wasn't here.

He staggered to his feet and made his way across the living room, littered with dirty laundry, and sat down at his computer. He'd bought it a few years back so he could log into the office and work from home if need be. No one would have expected an old rusty guy like him to take to the computer, but he had discovered a natural talent for all things cyber. He wiped the back of his hand over his mouth and picked up the phone.

He dialed a familiar number, a contact of his in the Nashville Police Department. The phone rang twice before he heard a gruff, "Officer Gilroy."

"Gus, this is Tyler Radcliff."

"Tyler." His tone carried a heaviness that told Tyler that word of Deidre's death had made its way through the department. Made sense. Cops talked, and the loss of an officer hit everyone hard. "How the hell are you doing, man?"

"I'm hanging tough. It's not easy, but I'm keeping it together."

"That's about all you can do, I guess." He and Gus had attended the academy together twenty years ago. They'd had their share of fun, tearing up the bars on Broadway, and chasing their share of skirts. Gus had been one of the groomsmen at his wedding.

"I need a favor."

"Sure, man. Name it."

"I'm going to need pallbearers. Could you help me out?"

"Shit. Sure, anything you want. When's the funeral?"

"I don't know," he said honestly. He was still Deidre's legal husband, and seeing as her parents were dead and her sister was a real flake, the funeral duty would fall to him. Despite all their problems, Tyler had loved Deidre and would see her properly buried. "Deidre is still with the medical examiner." The idea of her lying on a cold slab, her naked body exposed for all to see, bothered him. He should have reveled in her postmortem humiliation, but he didn't. There'd been a time when he'd imagined they'd grow old together, die quietly in their bed.

He'd never imagined her cut up like a cheap piece of deli meat.

"Is there anything else I can do?"

The sincerity in his buddy's voice tightened Tyler's throat. Times like this you discovered your friends. "I don't know, man. I'm figuring this out as I go. TBI came by and asked a lot of questions. It's surreal."

"I heard Alex Morgan was working the case."

"Yeah."

"I don't like the guy, but he's good. He'll figure this out."

"I hope so."

"He said a friend of Deidre's found her."

"Yeah. Carson was the name. A veterinarian."

"Right. She and Deidre were friends." He nestled closer to the phone. "Was Alex looking into Deidre before this?"

A full silence lingered. "Yeah. Word is she might have taken money."

"Shit. Deidre was a good cop."

"I know. I know."

"Okay." He released a heavy sigh. "Thanks, Gus."

"When you've scheduled the funeral, would you find a way to let me know? I can help with arrangements. Get more pallbearers. Whatever you need."

"Yeah, yeah, sure." He stood, swaying a little as the weight of the bottle of bourbon hit him. His thoughts quickly shifted from the funeral and skipped ahead to Leah Carson.

"Thanks. This means a lot." Impatience nipped at him.

He hung up, swayed a little more. The bourbon wasn't good if he wanted to think straight. He needed coffee, lots of black coffee, so he could drive and think clearly.

He needed to have his game face on when he faced the funeral home and made the final arrangements for Deidre. Once that was settled, next on his list would be Leah Carson. He would find out exactly what she knew about Deidre.

CHAPTER ELEVEN

Wednesday, January 18, 5:45 A.M.

It was raining. And cold. Leah expected winter to be cold, but this unending frigid snap made life tough. Hot coffee steaming from the cup holder beside her seat, she drove to the spot where the running group was scheduled to meet today, all the while wishing away the morning run. Before, she'd have hated the weather, but she'd always known Deidre would be waiting. Deidre was always waiting.

Images flashed of her friend lying faceup, skin sliced, sightless eyes staring, blood pooling in a thick dark puddle.

Tears welled in Leah's eyes. So easy to turn the car around, crawl back into bed, and pull the covers over her eyes. It was so tempting.

"No," she whispered. "You aren't going to quit on Deidre or yourself." She'd sworn when she moved to Nashville she wouldn't be frightened. She wouldn't hide from life.

The downpour grew heavier, as if someone had turned the tap on full. She glared at the dark gray sky. *Really? You can't cut me a little slack here?* Thunder clapped. *Right.*

Headlights cut through the rain, and as she rounded the corner into the parking lot, the lights illuminated a half-dozen cars, all of which she recognized. These runners were the heart and soul of the group. They never missed. And they'd certainly not miss today. Pride flickered. Many hadn't braved the weather, but she had.

Leah parked behind a black SUV and reached for her running gloves, which she tugged on. Pulling her skullcap down around her ears, she muttered an oath and got out of the car. Within seconds, her jacket was damp and the cold leaked into her bones.

She jogged up to the ring of runners who, when they saw her, nodded approval. She barely glanced at the half-dozen men and women as they clasped hands and formed a circle. They all bowed their heads in silence.

After a moment, David lifted his head. He liked to lead. Liked directing others. He clapped his hands. "Let's make this a great run!"

She joined the group in a cheer that vibrated in her chest and resonated energy that followed her into the first half mile of her run and kept her going in her typical, if not so fast, fairly steady pace down the rain-soaked, muddied path. When the adrenaline faded, she huffed in a deeper icy breath and imagined herself moving faster even as the group soon broke away, leaving her alone on the trail with her thoughts. On a normal day, there were always stragglers within shouting distance so she never minded getting dropped by the larger group. But today, those slower runners had skipped the run, leaving her alone to bring up the rear.

The rain pelted her face, and whatever heat she'd generated from the run quickly dissipated. The trees along the path grew taller, darker, but she didn't dare a glance into the shadows.

"Just keep moving," she whispered. "Five miles feels like forever, but it's not. You can do this."

Over the next few miles, she fell farther behind, and the stand of trees flanking the path felt like it was closing in around her. Several times, she thought she heard footsteps crushing twigs and leaves as heavy footsteps raced through the woods near her. Her breath huffed faster, more urgent. Gritting her teeth, she kept putting one foot in front of the other until finally the rain stopped as she rounded the final corner of the course and emerged into the clearing back at the parking lot. She'd made it.

Most of the cars of the other runners were gone but two remained. One belonged to David, but she didn't recognize the other. She dashed to her car, raising her hand toward David, and slid behind the wheel. She grabbed a towel she'd stowed on the passenger seat and quickly turned on the car and the heat. Her skin tingled as hot air warmed her near-frozen flesh. As she dried her face, she promised herself a stop at the doughnut shop before work. She earned it.

David honked his horn and tossed her a wave. She waved again and watched as he drove off. The guy could be pompous and irritating, but he'd waited for her. Nice. David had never lingered before unless it was to see Deidre alone. Deidre's loss must have had an impact on him.

Leah tossed her towel aside and put her car in reverse. As she backed up, the second, unfamiliar car lingered across the lot. The engine was running, the driver behind the wheel, head tucked, the windows fogged. Even with distance and fog blurring her vision, she knew it was a man sitting behind the wheel.

Eyes narrowing, she stared into her rearview mirror, straining to make out his features. Who else had waited for her? She didn't recognize the car, and as she ran through the list of the people she'd seen today, she couldn't match the runners with the vehicle.

Who was that guy?

No answer came, and the nothingness sent a chill slithering up her spine, one vertebrae at a time. She quickly backed out of her space. As she crossed the empty parking lot, she glanced in the rearview mirror, wondering and fearing if he'd follow. However, the car remained in its spot, the driver's face still obscured.

As the distance between Leah and the unknown driver grew, the tension snapped her nerves, even as she attempted to summon calm. *Lots of people run in the park.*

There weren't a lot of dedicated runners on days like today. But there were some. A stranger didn't necessarily mean trouble.

Alex sat in his car, leaning back just far enough in his seat so Leah couldn't see his face. He'd wondered if she'd show today. Wondered who else in the running group would show. He'd arrived just as the group had set out on the footpath. He'd waited ten minutes before he'd followed. Good to be close, but not too close.

Leah had fallen behind, and several times he'd had to slow his pace so he didn't overtake her. He could hear her breathing, knew she was struggling, but she kept running. Kept moving.

She was an odd mix. Loved animals, even lowered her guard around them, but with people, she was always on guard. Somewhere along the way, she'd been broken.

Toward the end of the run he'd cut down the side path and turned on the juice, his long legs eating up the space so that he arrived ahead of her. He'd seen David's car in the lot, waiting. Was he being gallant or was he lurking? Stalking?

He'd gotten into his car, stripped off his wet jacket, hat, and gloves. He turned on the engine and heater, soaking up the warmth.

Blowing into chilled hands, he waited and watched the woods for Leah to emerge. Another ten minutes had passed and he'd been on the verge of heading back down the muddy path when she'd appeared, soaked to the skin but still running. One foot in front of the other.

Most would have been put off by Leah's odd juxtaposition of personality traits. She certainly was everything he didn't need. But he liked her quirks. Her spirit. Her. He'd never understood the concept of love at first sight. Thought it was for fools. The weak. Not logical. But in this moment, the idea had merit.

Leah drove home, all the while checking her rearview mirror for any signs of the car. Nothing. No one was behind her. False alarm.

At a stoplight, Leah slumped back in her seat and swiped a hand over her damp hair. *I'm losing it. A man in the park. This has nothing to do with me. Philip is buried in the ground.*

In the days when Philip had been stalking her, she'd learned to vary her routine. Never take the same route twice. Instead of turning onto her street as she normally did, she circled the block once and then twice, all the while looking in her rearview mirror to confirm no one had followed. Now, distracted, she didn't notice the traffic stopping unexpectedly. When she did, she had to jam her foot on the brakes. Her wheels hydroplaned and she nearly slammed into the car in front of her. Heart pounding, she rubbed her eyes and tried to focus. No one was following her, but if she didn't get her act together, she'd have bigger problems.

Rattled, she drove directly to her town house and parked in front of it. A glance at the clock, and she realized she'd not only almost wrecked her car but she was late. Damn. No time for doughnuts. She dashed inside, locked the doors behind her, and hurried to the shower.

As she stood under the spray, the heat of the water teased a shudder from her chilled bones. She quickly washed her hair and then soaped her body. Fingertips grazed the uneven scars on her forearms and belly, lingering on the thick raised scar on her left side. Not Philip's first cut, but his most lethal. This had been the cut that nearly ended her life.

Leah flexed her fingers, rinsed off the remainder of the soap, and shut off the tap. As she toweled off, she looked toward the long full mirror, thickly clouded with condensation. Wrapping the towel around her, she wiped clean a section and exposed only her face so that she didn't have to see all her scars. The two on her face ran along her right chin. The plastic surgeon had worked long and hard to repair the damage.

She dried her hair and applied the special makeup designed to cover birthmarks and scars. Once it was applied, her skin looked almost normal. A half hour later, she emerged from her town house, coffee in hand, dressed in a dark turtleneck, jeans, and black walking shoes.

The rain had cleared out, but the January morning jealously gripped the cold. Her purse slung over her shoulder, she hurried to her car, set her cup in the holder beside the early morning's stale one. She started the engine, welcomed the heat, and was reaching for the gearshift when her phone rang. She glanced at the number. A local area code. Because she didn't recognize it, she let voice mail pick up the call and drove into the office.

She arrived at the clinic by eight. Flipping on the front lights in reception, she immediately locked the main door behind her. She made a habit of always locking the doors when she was there alone. Gail would arrive at eight thirty, and from then on the doors would be open.

Most mornings, she had about half an hour to check on the overnight patients and review the morning schedule before the first round of appointments arrived. Only two overnight guests were housed in the kennel at the moment. Tracker and a tomcat who'd gotten into a fight. She'd stitched up the cat yesterday and given him a strong sedative so he would sleep through the night. Now he was awake and glaring at the cage bars as he scratched at the white cone-shaped collar around his neck.

Tracker rose, silent, his gaze alert as the cat hissed. Normally, the shepherd was a quiet dog. Not one to bark but always paying attention as he waited. Friendly enough, he never wagged his tail until Alex arrived to check on him. Tracker understood Alex was part of his pack.

"Going home today, Tracker." She checked her watch. "Your dad should be here by lunch."

She opened Tracker's cage as the cat batted his cage. The shepherd eased out of his crate, his joints stiff from age and years of police work.

As she hooked Tracker's leash and led him toward the back door, the tomcat hissed loud and clear. She laughed. "Don't complain to me, mister. You're the one who likes to duke it out on the mean streets. You're lucky you didn't lose a foot. I'll feed you in a minute."

Outside, Tracker raised his nose and sniffed the air, as if

savoring the cold. They walked around the parking lot and toward the ring of woods that surrounded the lot. As much as she didn't like the cold, she didn't rush Tracker. Fifteen minutes later, the two were back inside and she was loading fresh food and water into his bowls. The dog ate happily.

Leah cleaned the cat's litter box and then filled his bowls. He dove into the food, growling as he gobbled. She went to the break room and put a pot of coffee on to brew before heading to her office.

Her room was a small space, barely large enough for the desk, a chair for her, and another for anyone else who needed to sit. Bookshelves lined the walls behind her, but other than a few of her veterinary textbooks, most of the space was filled with books that had belonged to the former vet. Her diploma hung on the wall, but she had no personal photos or mementos for the shelves. Maybe, over time, she'd make memories and her own mark.

The front door opened and closed, and she recognized Dr. Nelson's slow, steady footsteps. She always relaxed a fraction when he or Gail arrived and she was no longer alone.

"Leah," Dr. Nelson said, leaning on her door frame. "Did you have a chance to walk our overnight guest?"

"I did."

"Thank you. I was worried because I was running late. I had a power outage last night and overslept."

She smiled. "You can always text me."

"I had my wife call and she left a voice-mail message."

Leah reached in her purse for her phone and noted the number. "I'll put her name and number in my contact book so I recognize her the next time. Sorry about that."

He rubbed his cold hands together. "No problem. Nice to know I have good help."

She rose and slid on her white jacket. "We got a lot of icy rain last night. Did that damage your power lines?"

"My wife's got a call in to the electric company. But we're the only house without juice."

A distant alarm bell clanged in her head. It was easy to cut the power to a house. It took so little effort to totally ruin another's day.

"So what's on the agenda?" she asked, clearing her throat.

"Full morning of appointments. The usual. Shots. Check-ups and a case of mange. The rest I'm not so sure about. Routine."

"I like routine."

She filled her coffee cup in the break room and headed out toward reception, where she found Gail logging onto her computer. She had short, curly hair that framed a round face, wore a scrubs top over her jeans. She had been with the clinic at least two years. Young and full of energy, she talked often about becoming a vet tech but hadn't done much about looking into programs. Still, the clients loved her because she knew every pet's name and history.

Leah and Dr. Nelson began the morning round of appointments and she soon lost track of the time. By the time she took a break, it was after eleven.

She handed the last of the morning files to Gail. "Busy morning."

"You just missed Tracker. His owner got him."

She checked her watch. "He's early."

"I couldn't tell who was happier to see who." Gail grinned. "He said to say thank you."

Tracker was gone. That meant no more visits from Alex. "Glad to help."

Gail reached for a large arrangement of flowers. "We just got a delivery," she said, her eyes bright with excitement. The crystal vase, filled with purple irises, caught the fluorescent light and somehow made the arrangement even more beautiful. The display of freshly cut flowers was stunning.

Leah took a small step back. Irises. She'd carried a bouquet of irises at her wedding. At the time she'd loved the delicate soft petals. She'd bought extra that day because the flowers had been on sale. Later, she'd discovered they'd been on their last legs and had died almost immediately.

With her soon-to-die flowers and wearing her modest white dress, she'd smiled up at Philip moments before she was to walk down the aisle.

Philip had frowned. "You look sad."

Jitters made sense on a wedding day, but her feelings had strayed toward sadness and worry. "I wish my mom could be here. Doesn't seem right."

He draped a large arm around her shoulders and pulled her into a tight hold. "She'll come around. You'll see. Just give her time."

"I don't know. The fight we had the other night was pretty bad."

A hint of a smile flickered over his eyes and passed so quickly that she decided she'd imagined it. "You've got me." He pulled a blossom from her bouquet and carefully tucked it behind her ear.

Now, as Leah stared at the flowers, tension, regret, and guilt collided. As quickly as those flowers had withered, so had her hopes for her marriage. How could she have been so blind? So foolish? She was a smart woman with very poor judgment.

"You okay?" Gail asked.

Moistening now-dry lips, Leah injected a false lightness into her voice. "I'm fine. Who're they for?"

Gail beamed and plucked out a small white card nestled in the blossoms. "You."

"Me?" Fear sliced through the nerves in her body. "Who would send me flowers?"

Gail arched a brow. "What, a girl like you doesn't have some boys hanging around?"

"No. None."

Gail shook her head as she wistfully stared at the bouquet. "Maybe it's a secret admirer."

Confidence cracked under her like thin ice. "You make that sound like a good thing."

"Honey, it is. I'd love to have one."

"Be careful what you wish for."

Gail's gaze, caught by Leah's tone, rose. "You look like someone walked over your grave."

Leah's eyes slid to the flowers, an explosion of purples and whites. When she finally spoke, her voice sounded distant and tense. "I'm fine."

"You don't look fine. You look like you're going to pass out."

Dr. Nelson appeared. "What's going on?"

"Someone sent Leah flowers and it's spooked her bad," Gail said.

Dr. Nelson took the card from Gail. "You want me to open it?"

"No," she whispered. She wanted to be brave and prove the past was behind her, but she couldn't. They were just flowers. "I just wasn't expecting flowers."

"Do you mind if I open the card?" Dr. Nelson asked.

Leah grabbed the card from his hand and stared at the

handwriting on the outside of the envelope. Her name was written in blue ink. The L ended and began with a loop, and the h rose with a high upward swipe. The handwriting was female. Not male. Not Philip.

Gritting her teeth, she pushed her neatly shorn thumbnail under the envelope flap and tore the paper.

"You sure you don't want me to do it?" Dr. Nelson asked.

Nervous laughter bubbled and fizzled. "I should be able to open an envelope."

"You look like you're going to be sick," he cautioned.

A not-so-genuine smile tugged the edges of her lips. "I'm not a fan of cut flowers. I like plants."

Gail shook her head. "Honey, what girl doesn't like flowers?"

"I'm more of a candy girl, I guess." The attempt at humor fell flat as the two stared at her. "Chocolate wins my heart." She pinched the top of the card and pulled it from the envelope. *Don't be such a child. They're cut flowers, for God's sake.*

Logic soothed her nerves enough for her to pull the card free and glance down at the handwriting. However, all sense of peace and calm shattered with a glance. The card read, *Happy Anniversary.*

She staggered back a half step as she dropped the card and watched it flutter to the floor. Her chest tightened.

Dr. Nelson picked up the card and read it. He frowned, more out of curiosity than concern. " Happy Anniversary.' What anniversary?"

A past she'd locked tightly in a box rattled against the confines of its enclosure. She hadn't reconnected with past friends and she hadn't told new ones about Philip.

"I was married when I was just out of college. It didn't end well."

He frowned. "Do you think your ex-husband sent this?"

"No, he couldn't have. He's dead."

"Dead?" Gail asked. "That's horrible."

Leah rubbed her fingertips over the tense muscles now banding across her forehead. "We were divorced when he died." A lie. "But still terrible." A bigger lie.

"Who would send the flowers?" Gail asked.

Her rising gaze met Gail's, filled with anger and worry. Instantly, she was sorry she'd said anything. Philip had systematically isolated her from her friends with threats and violence, and she refused to allow him to do it again from the grave.

"Did either of you two surprise me with the flowers to celebrate my four-month anniversary at the clinic?"

Both shook their heads.

She forced a laugh that almost rang genuine. "Then it has to be some kind of mistake." Funny how easily she lied.

As she traced the edge of the card with her finger, she wondered. What if he weren't dead? What if the cops had made a mistake and didn't even realize it?

There'd been too many oddities that had popped up in her life in too short a period of time. The man in the park. Phone calls. Deidre's death.

As tempted as she was now to lock herself in her office and dial the South Carolina detective's number again, she wouldn't. She didn't want Dr. Nelson or Gail to think this was more than a minor jolt. She didn't want them to know she'd married a true monster.

"Gail, why don't you keep the flowers out here in reception? They really are lovely and it would be a shame not to share them." She slid the card in her pocket. "You know what this is? I'll bet my late husband's grandmother sent the flowers. She was always so sweet to me and she does have dementia." More lies. Soon, they'd weave around her like a spiderweb and choke her alive.

Leah moved into her office and closed the door. She picked up the receiver as she glanced at the card. The flowers had been sent from a store called Nathan's. She dialed the number. Five rings later, her call went to voice mail. She cleared her throat. "This is Leah Carson. I'm calling about an order of irises I just received. Maybe you can help me solve a mystery. I can't figure out who would have sent me such a lovely arrangement." She left her number and hung up.

Leaning over, she put her hands on her knees and allowed herself deep even breaths. She straightened and dialed the South Carolina detective's number. Again, she was routed to voice mail. Again, she left a message.

If she didn't hear back from the detective really damn soon, she'd drive to the office in Greenville and park on somebody's doorstep until she did receive answers.

Tyler waited in the lobby of the funeral home, sitting on the edge of a fancy couch. Soothing music hummed overhead and the faint scent of gardenias hovered in the air. The double sliding oak doors opened, and he glanced up to see a tall woman. She wore a navy-blue dress and had pulled back long, blond hair into a bun. Hints of makeup accentuated her eyes and full lips. She crossed the room, her sensible shoes barely making a sound on the hardwood floor, and extended her hand to him. "Sheriff Radcliff?"

He rose, gripping the brim of his sheriff's hat. He could have come in civilian clothes today, but somehow wearing his uniform gave him comfort, maybe even a little distance from what was about to happen. "Yes, ma'am."

"I'm Jessie Dupree. I've been assigned to your wife."

"Yes, ma'am." He extended his hand. "I brought a set of clothes for her. It's a dress. She didn't love the dress, but it was one of my favorites. Made her look so pretty."

"I'm sure it will be lovely."

"You had no problem with the state medical examiner's office?"

"Not a bit. Once you gave them our name, the process was quite smooth. We just received Mrs. Radcliff from the medical examiner's office." She had a firm grip and her gaze held steady. "I understand you'd like to see your wife."

He'd seen his share of dead bodies and had rarely been troubled by them. They were evidence. But the idea of seeing Deidre's lifeless face rattled every sinew and bone in his body. The side door opened, and a tall, slim woman wearing a lab coat approached him. "Yes?"

"We've not finished, and I would recommend that you wait. Our makeup artist is very talented and will be able to showcase her natural beauty."

"I'm sure. And that will be fine for the funeral. But for now, I'd like to see her just as she is."

A neatly plucked brow arched. "If that's your wish."

"Yes."

"Follow me."

He trailed behind her down a long carpeted hallway past several sets of double doors that led into parlors. A couple were marked IN USE. Tyler had the sense of walking down a dark tunnel. The deeper he moved down that tunnel, the tighter his grip on his emotions grew. He would not cry. He would not lose his shit in front of the doctor.

At the end of the hallway they pushed through another

wooden door, this one leading to a tiled room filled with a collection of drawers stacked neatly one above another. In the center of the room was a stainless-steel table, and beside it a collection of face paints and fillers. She moved to a drawer in the middle of the wall and laid her hand on the silver handle. "You're sure?"

Hell no, he wasn't sure. "Yes."

She twisted the handle and the door swung open. Inside lay a draped body. She pulled out the slab until the body jutted out several feet. As she gripped the edges of the sheet, he thought her hands were just as pale as the thick fabric and wondered how someone came to have a job like this. Slowly, she pulled back the sheet.

For a moment, his breath caught in his throat as he got his first full look at Deidre since her death. There were angry bloodless gashes on her face. One across the cheek. The other across her chin. Color had abandoned her skin and her pale lips were parted slightly, as if she needed to whisper something to him in his ear.

Tears burned the back of his eyes and his throat tightened with emotions he'd never imagined.

Even in death, she possessed a terrible beauty that still drew him. He'd loved her for so long, he wondered what would fill the space in his heart that she'd carved out for herself. Whatever lay before him now might look like his wife, but he understood that his Deidre was dead and gone forever.

Carefully, he leaned forward and kissed her softly on the forehead. Cold to the touch, her skin didn't feel like Deidre's. Despite all the bitter problems that had eaten away at their marriage, he took satisfaction in knowing the last lips she'd ever feel against her skin would forever and always be his.

* * *

The phone cradled under his chin, Alex dialed Deke's number as he made his way through traffic. His brother answered on the second ring. "Yeah."

"Any more information on the listening device found at Deidre's town house?"

The sound of Deke shuffling through papers echoed through the phone line. "Can be ordered from a hundred different Internet sites. Has a listening radius of a couple of miles."

"Who was listening in on Deidre's life?"

"Controlling soon-to-be ex-husband and secret lover aside, I think this could also have something to do with her work. Have you reviewed her case files lately? She's put away a couple of really bad drug dealers."

"Who's top of the list?"

"Top three is more like it. Ray Murphy, Tyrone Willis, and Sammy King. All three of them are hurting because of her undercover work."

"Which cases would have moved forward without her testimony?"

"They're all solid cases. She did a hell of a job and she's the one who triggered their downfall. We both know Ray has one bad temper. But the other two could be just as guilty. Killing a cop sends one hell of a message."

Anger strained under his even tone. "Have you dug into their alibis for Sunday night/early Monday morning?"

"As a matter of fact . . ." More papers shuffled. "Tyrone was in jail. Picked up in a prostitution sting. Sammy can prove he was in Memphis. And Ray is wearing an ankle bracelet. All have good alibis, but all could have hired someone."

Alex considered the answer and rejected it. "This killing wasn't done by a hired third party."

"There's very little evidence. This killer knew what he was doing. He was a pro."

"Agreed. But if this was a hit, why not just shoot her and leave?"

"Violence sends a message."

"It does. But this killing feels personal. The killer would have been looking into Deidre's eyes as he'd stabbed."

"Locking a guy away can feel really personal."

He couldn't dismiss the logic. "Which of the three has the biggest ego?"

"Ray Murphy. Guy thinks he's invincible. Has never worried about jail time. Always has a smug look on his face, like he can beat the rap."

"But you said if he killed Deidre the case would continue."

"Provided her death didn't intimidate the other witnesses. If he can kill a top cop, he can kill anyone."

Alex conjured up the last minutes of Deidre's life. "Deidre opens the back door; before she can react, the killer plunges a knife in her and she hits the floor. Rolls onto her back. He keeps stabbing as she watches."

"But he keeps stabbing."

"Because he's pissed or trying to send a message."

"I think this killer wasn't angry as much as sending a message."

"To the other witnesses?"

He came to a stop at a stop sign, looked both ways, and turned left. "I don't know."

Another voice hummed over the line, as if someone had entered Deke's office. After a hesitation, a door closed.

"Why not take the listening device after he killed her?"

"He had to be covered in blood even if he were wearing a Tyvek suit. It takes time to strip off the suit and cross into the living room. And if she screamed, he'd have been worried that someone called the cops. Leave the untraceable listening device and get out of there."

"It still could be Ray. He's lying low and armed to the teeth with lawyers. Getting through to him isn't going to be easy."

"Keep working on it. I want to find out if there were any glitches in Ray's monitoring device. I'm on my way to David's office. Time he and I had a chat."

"You think he has the stones to kill Deidre?"

"Everyone has the potential. Just depends on whether you dial up the right combination."

"Right."

Alex pulled into the parking lot of a tall glass building. He got out, showed his badge to reception, and, within minutes, was in David Westbrook's office. He worked for a law firm service that specialized in corporate matters such as insurance fraud and corporate espionage.

Dressed in his suit, David looked quite different from when he ran in the morning. On the track, each runner was judged by athletic skill. But elsewhere, the pecking order shifted to money. David rose and came around the side of his desk. "Agent Morgan, correct?"

Alex extended his hand. "That's right. I'm here to talk to you about Deidre Jones."

The handsome, smooth features lost their luster. "We're all still stunned."

"Was there anyone bothering her?" Alex asked.

"I never saw anyone creepy hanging around the track. I know her ex wasn't thrilled with her. I think he keyed her car. I asked her about it, but she wouldn't say. I think she was kind of embarrassed."

Alex didn't like David. The guy was a salesman; he sold

whatever bill of goods suited him. Deidre was an adult and made her own choices, but David was the kind of guy who would have smelled her weakness and played on it. "You two were dating."

"For about a month. Nothing serious. We were just having fun. But I liked her. I liked her a lot."

"You two spend much time together?"

"We hooked up a few times a week. Her job kept her busy. Not unusual for her to cancel on me." He shook his head. "Was this related to her job?"

Alex purposefully softened his expression with what he assumed looked like a sad smile. An icy stare didn't foster trust in a witness. "That's one of the theories."

David leaned in. "Who found her?"

"A woman from your running group," he said. "Leah Carson."

"Leah? What was she doing at Deidre's?"

"Trying to find out why she missed the morning run."

David ran long fingers through his hair. "God."

Alex studied him closely. "Did Deidre ever mention anything that made you think there was trouble in her life? Was she worried? Did she ever think anyone was following her?"

"No. No. She never wanted to talk about much when we were together. She liked a good laugh. And she liked the bedroom. Beyond that, we rarely had much to say." He paused a moment. "That ex of hers might have been trouble."

"You said she wasn't worried about him."

"She said she could handle him." He slid his hand into his pocket. "Do you think it was him?"

Alex glanced past David to a credenza covered with photographs. One stood out. David standing with a pretty blonde. "Who's that?"

David drew in a breath. "My wife."

"Your wife? She know about Deidre?"

David shifted in his chair, tugged on the cuffs of his hand-tailored shirt. "We're separated right now, but we're trying to work things out."

"What's her name?"

"Alicia." David glanced at Alex and very quickly added, "But she wouldn't hurt anyone. She's sweet. Maybe too sweet. But I love her. And besides, she's been in New York the last month, visiting family. There's no need to talk to her."

"Not now." Alex held his ground. "What do you know about Leah Carson?"

"Leah? She's about the worst runner there is. I was shocked when Deidre invited her to the group. Why ask about her?"

"She and Deidre were friends."

"Not exactly. I think Deidre kind of felt sorry for her. Leah is an odd duck. Keeps to herself. Beyond me why Deidre kept trying to take Leah under her wing. And it figures she'd check on Deidre. She's a worrier."

"Why's that unusual?"

"Deidre doesn't have . . . didn't have a lot of patience for weakness. It's why she left her husband. His drinking got to be too much. It's why she'd have dumped me sooner than later. Leah had that wounded-bird kind of vibe. She told me Leah's neighbors called the cops right after she moved in. Seems Leah was screaming. Told cops it was a nightmare."

Nightmares. Defensive stab wounds. "She say anything else about Leah?"

"I asked her once what gives with Leah, but she said something about the sins of the past."

"Sins of the past?"

"I know, it makes no sense. They only just met. But that's what she said."

"You didn't press."

"No. She had a way of distracting my thoughts." He grinned.

Alex's face turned to stone. "She strike you as the type that would bend the law?"

"Deidre? I don't think she'd like it, but if push came to shove, sure, I think she'd do it."

"She ever talk about doing anything shady?"

His spine stiffened, raising him up an inch or two. "No. She never talked to me about work or anything illegal. Shit, the last thing I need is to be an accessory after the fact."

"All right." Made sense that Deidre wouldn't tell David about her work, or any off-the-books work. Made sense he wouldn't push, unless he thought the information would be of use.

Alex handed David his card. "Let me know if you think of anything."

"Sure."

Outside, Alex pulled Ray-Ban sunglasses from his breast pocket and put them on. Deidre had alluded to sins of the past when Leah's name was mentioned. What the hell did that mean?

CHAPTER TWELVE

Wednesday, January 18, 4 P.M.

There had been no surgeries today and no afternoon appointments so Dr. Nelson told Leah to go home early. "No sense in both of us sitting around here," he'd said.

She'd volunteered to stay, but he'd insisted she leave, promising her there'd be times in the future when she'd wish for the time off.

And so she gathered her purse and slid on her coat. Keys in hand, she headed toward her car. She'd just reached the car door when she heard the crunch of footsteps. Leah reached in her pocket for the Mace she always kept close as she whirled around. Alex Morgan didn't flinch, but his gaze dropped to her hand, as if assessing the threat. She eased her thumb away from the Mace's trigger.

"So how're you holding up?" He waited for her gaze to meet his.

"Alex. What're you doing here? You know Rick picked up Tracker today."

Alex was silent for a moment. "I know. He texted. You always this jumpy?"

She scrambled through her basket of ready lies. "I'm the nervous sort."

He moved slowly toward her, as if approaching a skittish animal. "You're relaxed around the animals."

"I understand them. It's always black and white with animals."

"But not with people."

She arched a brow. "And you think people are black and white?"

He shook his head. "I know they're not."

She spoke metaphorically, universally, the way he was talking about her. He saw the grays and shadows that swirled around her like a second skin.

"I get the impression there's a lot more to you than meets the eye."

"I can promise you, I'm very boring."

"You're not boring." He moved within inches of her, standing so close she could smell the scent of his aftershave mingling with cold fresh air.

She curled her fingers into fists tight enough to hide her scars. "What're you doing here?"

A hand slid in his pocket, enough to push his jacket back and reveal the badge and gun behind it. "I did a little digging on you."

She tightened her hold on her purse strap. "That so?"

"Your neighbors called the cops last month. They said you were screaming."

She shook her head, remembering the cops pounding on her door. There'd been an officer to the right of the door, a hand on his gun, and two at the bottom of the steps. Another had been in the parking lot. "I have nightmares. They can be pretty bad."

"Nightmares."

"Nothing I talk about. I was in my kitchen eating ice

cream when the cops arrived. It was embarrassing. I let them search the place because it was clear they were on edge when they arrived."

"Nightmares." He spoke the word again, as if he were dropping it into a file cabinet.

"Yeah."

He waited a beat, but when she didn't expand on the comment, he asked, "So what brought you back to Nashville? I don't think we covered that on our . . . date."

It hadn't been a real date. She'd been on the verge of a panic attack when the text arrived. "I'm from Nashville. Went to vet school in Knoxville. Moved back for the job."

"You always wanted to be a vet?"

"Yeah. I like animals. Trust them. Like you said, they relax me."

"As opposed to people."

"I didn't say that."

He folded his arms as he shook his head. "How'd you get the scars on your palms, Leah? You go out of your way to hide them."

She resisted the urge to glance at her palms that were now in fists. "I told you. An accident."

"What kind?"

"You like to push, don't you?" The crack of temper was a surprise.

A flicker of amusement warmed his eyes for a brief second. "I do. I do indeed."

Her temper simmered. "Sorry. I'm not worth worrying over."

"You are. Even if you and Deidre weren't friends I'd be interested in you."

"Why?" She'd always wondered what Philip had seen in her. Was it a weakness? A vulnerability? Some men liked that sort of thing.

"You've got grit. You found Deidre's body, but you held it together. That kind of thing would have forced some people to take a few days off. And yet you're back at work."

"What was I supposed to do? Stay at home? I'm better off working."

A rattle of change in his pocket signaled a shift in mood from somewhat light to dark. His blue gaze catalogued everything about her: breathing, a shift of the shoulders, a moistening of her lips.

"Have you ever met or spoken to Deidre's husband?"

"No. I know next to nothing about the man. And what I thought I knew, I told you."

"But she did tell you she was getting a divorce."

"We talked about it several times. I told you: she said he had a hard time letting go." This all cut a little too close to home. What had her friends and neighbors said about her after the stabbing? "This feels like a violation of Deidre's privacy. I know you need answers, but I feel as if I owe her that."

"Deidre's privacy is irrelevant. I'm trying to find out who killed her, Leah. Anything you can tell me would be of help."

Her privacy had been irrelevant after her stabbing. All her mistakes and foolish choices had been laid bare. She didn't want to do that to Deidre, who had been nothing but kind to her; she didn't want to repay that by gossiping about her. "Did you talk to David?"

"I did."

With the car pressed behind her and Alex directly in front of her, she felt boxed in, trapped. "Why did Deidre confide in you when she told no one else other than David?"

"I don't know. That last day when she spoke about the

divorce, I told her I'd been divorced. Maybe she sensed we were kindred souls."

Divorce. Another word clanged into the file, like an old penny falling into a piggybank. "Nasty divorce?"

Not a path she wished to travel with anyone, especially him. "You could say that."

"Where's your ex-husband now?"

"He's dead. Car accident near Greenville, South Carolina. Four years ago."

She could tell Alex she'd dropped to her knees and thanked God when she'd learned her ex-husband was dead. But statements like that opened the door to more questions, and she couldn't bear to have him look at her with piteous, distrustful eyes, as so many had after the stabbing.

"What was his name?"

"Why do you care?"

"What was his name?"

"Philip Latimer."

Blue eyes narrowed, and she sensed a shuffling through more old files tucked in his memory. "Did you and Deidre get together often?"

"We went out for drinks a few times. She had me over to her place once or twice. I liked Deidre. She reached out to me when I joined the gym. She was nice."

"You liked her well enough to check up on her when she didn't show up to the running group."

And so they circled back to the murder. "She'd said she'd be running on Monday. We challenged each other to be there. Deidre didn't back down from a challenge. I saw it in the group enough times."

"Explain."

"There are a couple of gals who run as well as Deidre.

Several times they got into sprint challenges. Deidre went all out each time. She never lost."

His gaze flickered over her frame. "I'd think you'd be a good runner."

She had been in high school. But she'd never fully recovered from the stabbing. "Nope. Not fast at all."

His hands slid from his pockets as he straightened his shoulders a fraction. "Do you ever remember Deidre being afraid?"

He liked to switch back and forth, keep her off balance. "No. Frustrated and angry once or twice but never afraid."

"What upset her?"

"Her divorce. That last day we ran, she mentioned it. I told you she thought he'd keyed her car."

"You never saw him around?"

She frowned. "You keep asking me the same questions. I guess that's part of a cop's Jedi mind-trick kind of thing, but it's not gonna work on me. I've told you all I know."

Like a striking match, his eyes burned with humor for a split second. "Notice any men hanging around when you were with her?"

A search of her memory produced a memorable detail. "There's been a black truck at the track a couple of times. You think it was him?"

"That black truck was me."

"You? This morning, that was you?"

"Yes."

"Why?"

"Curious to see who would show after her death."

"Were you in the woods?"

"I was."

Relief collided with anger. "Then why ask about my running? If you were there, you know I suck."

"You've got sand, I'll give you that."

She wasn't sure if she should be charmed or pissed by his honesty. "You kinda freaked me out."

"You didn't look freaked out."

"Never let them see you sweat."

A brow cocked. "I'll keep that in mind."

"Have you found anything at the crime scene to help find the killer? I thought you had all the latest in forensics."

"We're going through all the evidence. We'll find out who did this. I promise you that."

He was a methodical, careful hunter, not driven by passion or rage but logic. In her mind, that made him far more dangerous. "Do you know when her funeral is going to be held?"

"No date set yet."

"The running group wants to be there. I want to be there."

"I'll be in touch with you."

"Right." She fumbled through her keys until she had the fob in her hand.

Alex stood there as she unlocked the door, slid behind the wheel, and started the engine. "See you soon."

With him standing there, she resisted the urge to check the backseat. She drove, not daring a peek into the rearview mirror, sensing his gaze and remembering exactly what it felt like to be in a predator's sights.

Alex picked up Deke at the Nashville Police Department offices just after six. The sun had set and the rolling land around the offices was dark on this moonless night.

"So did you get a lead on Ray?"

"I did." Deke stretched out his long legs and relaxed

back against the seat. Deke, like Alex, lowered his guard just a little when it was just family. "He's been staying out of sight, but that ankle bracelet makes it easy to find him."

"Where's he staying?"

"His house is about twenty miles north of the city. He's in a gated community."

"Gated. Fancy. Crime pays."

Deke snorted. "It's going to be a short-term investment when he goes to prison."

Alex shifted in his seat. He'd seen enough guys like Ray elude justice to assume the case pending was a slam dunk. "You said, according to his bracelet, he was at home."

"Makes more sense that he'd send someone to do his dirty work."

Deke shook his head as he folded his arms over his chest. "That's the thing with Ray. He *likes* to do the dirty work. If he wanted Deidre dead, he'd do it himself."

"With all his troubles, it makes sense for him to hire out the job."

"Read the interviews with Ray Murphy," Deke said, flicking lint from his pants.

"Give me the CliffsNotes."

"They revealed a psychology that teeters on psychotic. He loves to create fantasy worlds. Guy wears a black goatee sculpted into a long point. Thinks it makes him look like a devil. His sideburns were also trimmed into sharp edges. Wears hints of dark makeup around his eyes." Deke shook his head. "I'd have laughed if not for the pictures taken at the raid of his competition's warehouse. The raiding crew found six men strung up by their feet. Their bodies had been scorched nearly to the bone."

Scorched. Like the warehouse victim? "The more, the better."

"It's high entertainment for this sick bastard."

"So stabbing Deidre isn't out of his realm."

"Not at all."

They arrived at the mansion, a very traditional brick Colonial with a large circular driveway and a white expanse of steps that led to black lacquer double front doors.

Alex reached for a brass door knocker shaped like a dragon's head. "He's in to dragons."

"I'd heard that."

The door opened to a tall, muscular man who wore a Glock at his side. Behind him were two other men, also armed.

Alex and Deke held up their badges. "We're here to see Ray."

The man glanced at the badges and turned to one of the other guards, who vanished behind a pair of pocket doors. "Please come in."

The entryway wall was covered with a large, intricate mural of a young man fighting a legion of dragons. The dragons were painted in tremendous detail, including scaly faces, fanged teeth, and red eyes that all but jumped off the wall.

They didn't have to wait long before Ray Murphy appeared. He wore his trademark goatee and sideburns, a purple silk shirt, and pants that lay over the bulge of his ankle bracelet. Barefooted, he moved toward them with a wide grin on his face and his hand extended. "I haven't had the law here in a couple of days. Agent Morgan and Detective Morgan." He studied them. "Must be brothers."

Deke ignored the comment. "We have a few questions."

Ray moved into a side parlor decorated in deep purples and with pictures of dragons and wizards. In a large stone hearth, a fire blazed. Ray sat on a large, plush chair, resting his arms along the back. "What brings you out here today? It's an unexpected surprise."

"Just came to ask you about Sunday."

"What about it?" He looked amused by the question as he relaxed back in his seat.

"Where were you?"

Ray laughed as he jerked up his pant leg. The thick tracking device was strapped to his ankle. "Church."

"And after church?"

"Pull up the data on my bracelet."

"I'm asking you."

"I was here."

"Mind if Agent Morgan checks your anklet?"

"Have at it." Ray wiggled his toes but didn't bother to rise.

Alex shook his head. "Stand up. Put your foot up on a chair."

Ray grinned. "Don't want to kneel before the dragon lord?"

Alex's expression remained stoic.

With a shrug, Ray rose from the chair, settled his foot on an ottoman, and lifted his silk pants leg. Alex moved forward and inspected the monitoring device. "It looks intact." He stepped back. "No signs of tampering."

"Mind telling me why you're checking?" Ray settled back against the chair cushions.

"Don't you have a girlfriend, Ray? I think her name is Kendra?" Deke asked.

Eyes darkened with suspicion. "Kendra. Why do you want to know about Kendra?"

"Where is she?"

"New York. Shopping for my birthday present." He rolled his shoulders, muscles flexing with a portion of an elaborate tiger tattoo. "No, wait. She's in protective custody. That cop got her and she flipped on me."

"Funny you should mention that detective. She was killed Sunday."

Ray tsked as he glanced at buffed fingernails. "Damn, that's too bad. What was her name again?"

"Deidre Jones. From what I hear, Deidre got Kendra to wear a wire. Those tapes are what got you in trouble."

A smile quirked his lips. "My lawyer isn't so sure about that. This case is no slam dunk for the cops."

"That's not what I heard. I also heard you were pissed and threatened to kill Detective Jones and anyone who talked to her."

"I don't recall anything like that." Ray's smile widened and a gold tooth flashed. "And last I heard, Kendra is alive and well. Besides, I have no hard feelings for Kendra." He touched his fingertips to his breastbone. "I love her."

Deke shook his head. "Kendra's lucky a guy like you is so forgiving."

"That's what I told her," Ray said.

"You forgive the cop that got her to wear the wire?"

Dark eyes glinted before he smiled. "Deidre Jones is nothing to me."

"If we can believe that anklet, you didn't kill her, but maybe you sent someone to do your dirty work. Maybe you told your guy to mess her up bad . . . send a message to Kendra."

"I don't care about a damn detective. And Kendra and I've gone our separate ways. Alive or dead, she makes no difference to me. You said she was messed up. How was it done? How was she killed?"

Deke's tone deepened. "Stabbed."

Ray shook his head. "That's got to hurt. Hell of a way to go."

Alex kept his voice low, even. "You like knives, don't you, Ray?"

He nodded, shrugged. "I do like them. But I didn't kill your detective. And I don't know who did."

Deke's headlights shone bright on the rental car parked in the lot by the running trail. He pulled up beside the four door and checked his watch. "Hell of a place and time to meet."

"She and Deidre talked about this place. She knew Deidre loved it here. She wanted to see it and I didn't want another night to pass without talking to her."

Deke pointed toward a bench where a lone woman sat, staring at the park. "Deidre's sister, Joy?"

"That would be my guess."

Neither liked rehashing the details of the detective's death, and interviewing loved ones who'd lost family always left a sour taste. "Let's do this."

They found Joy Martin sitting on the bench, her hands resting in her lap as she stared down the path. It was as if she were trying to picture Deidre's last steps on the path. She wore a midweight overcoat suitable for California but not nearly adequate for the cold nights here. Long hair draped her narrow shoulders. Silver rings decorated long fingers. She tapped a nervous high-heeled foot.

Alex pulled his badge from his pocket. "Ms. Martin."

Joy looked up with brittle green eyes that reminded him of Deidre. "You must be Agent Morgan."

He tucked the badge back in his breast pocket. "Yes, ma'am. We spoke on the phone. This is Detective Deke Morgan. He's with Nashville Homicide."

"Two Morgans?"

"We're brothers, ma'am."

"Ah." Nodding, she turned her gaze back to the woods. "She mentioned you both a few times. Frankly, I don't think she liked either of you."

"I'm not the most likable guy," Alex said. "And neither is Deke." He kept his tone soft.

Deke nodded. "We won't win any popularity contests."

Joy looked up at Deke, a wistful expression in her gaze. "She said you were one of the best detectives she ever worked with. She respected you."

He moved toward the bench but didn't sit, as if he were breaching a hallowed space. "I'm trying to find out what happened." He avoided using the words *killed* or *died*. The words triggered hard emotions that muddied clear thinking.

She rose and stood almost as tall as Deidre. Her shoulders weren't as wide, but her body was equally lean. "You know she was getting a divorce."

"Yes."

"It wasn't friendly." She slid her hands into her pockets. "Tyler didn't want to let go."

"She didn't talk about her personal life. But I've since learned the divorce was rough."

"No, she wouldn't want anyone at the office to know. She loved her job and never wanted anything to tarnish her reputation." She turned from the path in the woods. "She was dating again. A guy named David. I met David once. Struck me as lots of fun and no substance, but a step up from Tyler."

"I understand you and Tyler weren't close."

"No, we're not. In fact, Deidre and I had grown distant because of him. I don't like him. She was too good for him. It was only after they separated that we reconnected."

"Anything unusual going on with your sister that you know of?"

She twisted a silver ring on her index finger. "She was really rattled the last time we spoke. I asked her what was going on, but she wouldn't tell me. Said it had to do with a case."

"She mention anything about the case?" Deke asked.

"She just said she'd made a mistake and now she was going to have to fix the problem so that she could move on with her life."

"A mistake?" Alex asked. *Sins of the past*; David's words echoed.

The sister nodded. Tears filled her eyes and a few escaped down her cheek. She swiped them away. "I think it had to do with me."

"You?"

"I got into trouble five years ago, when I was in college in Nashville. I was arrested for dealing. I was holding a lot when they caught me. Enough that I faced felony charges. I was in a panic. The arresting officer told me I could go to prison for twenty years. I called my sister as soon as they offered me a phone. Deidre had just made detective in Vice."

Good cops went bad for a lot of reasons. Sometimes it was money or greed. Sometimes the motivations were cold and calculating. "You told Deidre about the dealing?"

"Yes. I told her I was scared. I told her the local cops had evidence that would put me away for years. I cried. Deidre didn't say anything for a long, long time. She then asked if I'd be willing to go to rehab if she helped me."

"Did you agree?" Alex asked.

"I swore I would. Of course I'd sworn before, but in that moment, I really meant it."

Tension banded in Alex's chest as he wondered what he'd do to help a sibling.

"Deidre said she would help me. She asked for the arresting officer's name. And I gave it to her."

"What happened?"

Joy threaded her fingers together. "She told me to sit tight. She'd call me soon."

"And she came through?" Alex asked.

"Yeah. She came through. About five hours later, she told me the evidence was gone. I was free. She drove me straight to rehab and I stayed for sixty days." She raised her chin. "I haven't used since."

"Why do you think this relates to her death?" Deke asked.

"Like I said, Deidre was upset when we were talking on the phone. She was actually afraid of a past mistake. I asked her about it, and when she wouldn't answer, I knew it had to do with my arrest. She was so by the book. She wouldn't have bent the rules, except for me."

"And she told you she was going to fix this problem?" Alex asked.

"Yes. I asked Deidre how, but she told me not to worry about it. I asked her if there were anything I could do, and she said she'd figure it out. Said not to worry. She was gonna kill two birds with one stone. Said not to worry."

"Do you know what that means?"

"I don't know. I wish I did. I might have been able to save her." She glanced toward the park, as if wondering where her sister would be if she'd taken a different path.

Did it all go back to Joy's case and the missing evidence? "Do you remember the name of the arresting officer?"

"Yeah. I'll never forget it. Philip Latimer."

Alex had returned to his office immediately and done a search on Philip Latimer. It couldn't be a coincidence that

Latimer had been married to Leah, and Deidre had sought Leah out. Pieces of the puzzle didn't quite connect, but they had moved closer.

It didn't take much digging for Latimer's name to pop. He'd been a cop in Nashville for eight years, and he'd served with distinction. He'd also been disciplined after his estranged wife had filed stalking charges against him. According to statements, Latimer had sworn he'd lay off the wife. Tensions had appeared to ease, and then Latimer had broken into his wife's apartment and tried to stab her to death. He'd eluded the cops and gotten out of Tennessee. He'd died in a car accident three weeks later in South Carolina.

How had Latimer gotten out of town? Did he have help?

Deidre had said she'd clean up her sister's legal mess. Had she'd figured she'd approach Latimer and ask for a favor?

Alex had no proof that Deidre had ever contacted Latimer, but a connection was logical. Another puzzle piece.

Several calls to the Nashville Police Department earned him the files that detailed Leah's stabbing. Within an hour, he was staring at the graphic images of her bedroom sprayed bright red with her blood. It could have been Deidre's crime scene.

Leah. Nervous around people. No damn wonder.

He had seen his share of Philip Latimers in the world. Fucked-up bullies who preyed on the vulnerable. Manipulation began with guilt, then harsh words, physical abuse and, all too often, murder.

He was sorry the guy had died in the car accident. It would have been a pleasure to deal with him personally.

He dialed dispatch and left word for the officer who'd responded to Leah's attack to call back. He wanted to talk. An hour later, Alex's phone rang.

"Officer Boyle," Alex said. He reached across his desk

and pulled over a legal-size pad for notes. "What can you tell me about the Leah Carson Latimer case? It was a domestic violence attack. Four years ago. The attacker was a Nashville cop. Philip Latimer."

"Shit. That was a long time ago, but I don't think I'll ever forget it." He sighed. "The husband worked for the county as a patrol officer. I even crossed paths with him a few times. Seemed like a good guy."

"When did the stalking start?"

"Right after they separated."

"According to her complaints, it was unrelenting."

"It was. And she filed for a restraining order against him. Of course we'd been notified, but when Latimer's boss talked to him, he swore he'd back off. And he did for a few days." Another sigh full of regrets. "We shouldn't have believed him. She'd made such a good case with her journaling. Great eye for detail. Never had a victim keep such detailed records." A chair squeaked in the background, as if he leaned back. "I heard Latimer died in a car accident."

"That's what his wife told me."

"So why the call?"

"His name came up in another case. Apparently, he crossed paths with Deidre Jones a few years ago."

"The detective who was stabbed?"

"Yeah."

"That doesn't make sense. Like I said, he's dead."

"Did Latimer have any friends or family that would have resented Leah Carson for filing charges?"

"There were some officers in his department who didn't believe her. Latimer did a good job of painting her as hysterical and unstable. But when he stabbed her, well, there was little to argue. All his support was immediately withdrawn after that."

"You sure he didn't have any faithful followers?"

"None that hit my radar. I can ask around. Where's Leah Latimer—I mean, Carson?"

"She's back in Nashville. Works as a vet."

"How's she doing?"

"She's doing well."

A heavy silence lingered. "That's good. She was a mess after the attack. Hell of a lot of rehab. But from what I heard, she was pretty determined to get on with her life."

He thought about her running through the park in the early morning rain. One foot in front of the other. "Is there anyone who knew her then that I could talk to? Anyone who would have known her or Philip during that time?"

"You've got my files. I don't remember names, but there was an adviser at school who went out of her way to help her."

Alex rustled through the case file. "Dr. Susan Miller was her adviser. That her?"

"She's the one. Give her a call."

Alex hung up and dialed Dr. Miller's cell. On the third ring, there was a breathless, "Hello."

"Dr. Miller?"

"Yes."

"This is Agent Alex Morgan with the Tennessee Bureau of Investigation."

"It's after ten, Agent Morgan."

"I'm sorry for the late hour." He explained the reason for the call.

"Leah Carson." In the background, he could hear pots and pans rattling and water running. The water turned off and the pots stilled. "She was one of my favorite students. Smart. Great with animals. Is this about her ex-husband?"

"Yes."

"Why're you asking? God, he made her life awful. I hope he's burning in hell."

Fury had him sitting straighter. "What was she like before the troubles?"

"Lots of fun, outgoing. She had to delay leaving for Knoxville for a year so she took a couple of courses here. After the attack, she changed. Became very guarded and withdrawn. But you have to understand, she endured a brutal attack. Post-traumatic stress would be a normal reaction."

"She still has scars. Keeps her journal."

She released a weary sigh. "I went to see her in the hospital after the attack. The plastic surgeon did a great job stitching her up, but she still looked like Frankenstein."

Alex shifted in his seat, trying to connect the woman he'd met a week ago with the woman who'd been so brutally attacked. He'd thought her odd initially, aloof and stand-offish. Now, when he considered the attack, he had nothing but pure respect for her.

"During that last summer school session, after the attack, a boy in class who didn't know her history jumped out and surprised her. She grabbed her textbook and hit him hard in the face. She would have hit him a second time but he fell to the floor."

A smile flickered. "Did he file charges?"

"Not after I explained her history. But he walked one hell of a wide circle around her after that."

"Any other incidents?"

"Not that I saw."

"Thanks, Dr. Miller. I appreciate the insight."

Alex hung up and immediately dialed a contact in South Carolina.

CHAPTER THIRTEEN

Thursday, January 19, 9 A.M.

He arrived at the humane society kennel just as it was opening. The mornings, he learned, could be chaotic there. Dogs being dropped off. Dogs needing feeding and walking. Deliveries. It was a busy time.

He pushed through the front door, wrinkling his nose at the smell of animal urine. Dogs weren't his favorite. They were demanding emotionally and needed lots of care. Cats were more to his taste. They took care of themselves and didn't need constant attention. His wife had always wanted a black Lab and had mentioned it when they'd been together. Of course with their busy lives, there hadn't been time for a dog so he'd refused to allow one.

That had been a mistake. Maybe if he'd said yes to the dog, she'd have been happier, wouldn't have been so discontented. Maybe, maybe, maybe.

The lady behind the counter looked up through horn-rimmed glasses. A rubber band bound dark graying hair in a loose ponytail that allowed wisps of hair to frame a very round face.

"I'd like to look at the dogs," he said. "My wife wants a black Lab."

The woman rose, revealing a blousy peasant top worn over faded jeans that covered a very wide set of hips. He wasn't a fan of overweight figures, and when his wife splurged on ice cream or chocolate, he was always quick to joke about her clothes getting too tight. He'd never teased her out of meanness. He'd only reminded her of what she ate because he knew she was aware of her figure and would have been upset if she'd put on a few pounds.

"You specifically want a black Lab?"

He smiled. "Well, that's the kind of dog she always talked about. She likes to take walks, and I know Labs need a lot of exercise." He extended his hand. "My name is Brian Lawrence."

"Hey, Brian. My name is Betty. I'm the morning manager."

He glanced at the clock. "I know you just opened. I bet you haven't had your coffee yet."

"I'll delay the coffee for a dog."

He rubbed his hands together. "So what do I need to do?"

"Let's have a look at the dogs, and if you see one that might work in your family, we'll talk about the paperwork."

"Sounds like a plan."

He followed her down a tiled hallway. Green hospital walls were covered in a collection of photographs featuring all kinds of dogs and cats. A Lab shepherd mix. A dachshund mix. A tabby cat with a bent ear. A collection of white furry puppies. Happy and upbeat, they made him feel better about his decision to get a dog. He imagined the look on his wife's face when he surprised her with the dog.

Betty pushed through a swinging door and they entered a long room lined with cages on the right and left. Barking dogs and meowing cats filled the sterile room. The floor was tile, easily hosed down, and the walls were painted a mint green. The animal smell was strong.

"So you only want a Lab? Because we have some very cute animals here today. We don't have a Lab, but you might be surprised by the friendly dogs we do have."

He nearly refused, but then reminded himself that he needed to be more flexible. More open-minded. She would've loved any dog. Any animal. "Let's see what you have."

As they moved down the row of cages, Betty paused and spoke lovingly to the dogs. Most rushed to the front of the cage and licked her fingertips, eager for her attention. He smiled at the animals, but his smile wasn't genuine. He found the dogs, especially the puppies, to be a bit annoying and dreaded the idea of coming home to one each day. Still, he kept smiling, even petted a couple of animals so Betty wouldn't think him odd. He was supposed to be an animal lover.

Finally, at the end of the row, he spotted a medium-sized black dog. It didn't rush to the front of the cage but didn't cower in the corner either. It eyed him with an all-seeing gaze that made him stop. He sensed, as the creature looked at him, that it knew his secrets, knew he'd done bad things.

"You like this one?" Betty asked.

He tore his gaze from the dog. "Yeah, I think I do."

"Are you interested in adoption?"

"I think so." He turned away from the cage.

"It's a female. Her name is Charlie. She's nine months old but still needs to be spayed."

"Okay. What does that mean?"

"The Nelson Animal Hospital does our spaying for us. We would drop her off there, and once the surgery is done and she's had time to recover, you could pick her up."

"The Nelson Animal Hospital?"

"It's run by a nice guy and his new associate, Dr. Carson, who's a real charmer."

"Okay. You said something about paperwork?"

"Right out front."

He glanced back at Charlie. She stared at him with those guarded brown eyes, and he found himself growing leery of the animal. She wasn't dumb. She didn't rush up to anyone. She was selective. He knelt down and extended his fingers through the cage. Slowly, she approached and licked his fingers.

He smiled. "I think she likes me. Can I hold her?"

"Sure."

Betty unlatched the cage and allowed the dog out. She moved toward Brian and allowed him to pet her. She ducked her head and wagged her tail before slowly moving closer.

"She trusts me."

"She's a slow one to warm up. I suspect she'll be a one-owner dog. Very loyal."

He scratched the mutt between the ears. "I like that."

Out front, the bells on the door rang, signaling that someone else had entered the shelter. Betty frowned. "I need to check on that."

"Go ahead. Charlie and I are just spending a little quality time together."

"I can't leave you alone with the dogs."

Voices out front grew louder. "Sounds like you might have trouble."

Betty glanced between the front door and him, as if making a decision. He grinned. She smiled back. "I'll be right back."

"We'll be waiting." He rubbed Charlie between the ears. "We'll be waiting, won't we, girl?"

Betty hurried up front, and as she vanished around the corner his gaze faded. "Charlie, I don't know about you, but I want out of this place." Ears back, she licked his face.

He glanced to the back of the hallway and the emergency exit. "What say we get the hell out of here?"

He could hear Betty's voice rising, as did the other two voices. "Don't worry about that. I paid those guys making the noise to make a fuss. We don't need anyone telling us when you can leave with me."

He picked up the dog, which tucked nicely under his arm, and strode toward the back door. No alarm sounded as he opened the door and moved at a steady, even pace, all the while scratching Charlie's head. She was wagging her tail by the time they got to his truck. He settled her on blankets he'd arranged on the front passenger seat and quickly started the car. He drove off, glancing in his rearview mirror and catching the reflection of Betty standing at the emergency door, searching for them.

He started to whistle. "I can't wait for you to meet Leah. She's gonna love you."

Charlie looked up at him and wagged her tail. Her pure love and devotion bolstered him like a tonic. "You're a good girl. And I like you."

She wagged her tail.

"But you've got a job to do, little lady. You've got to make Leah fall in love with you."

She barked, with excitement.

"She's gotta fall for you, hook, line, and sinker and when she does, then I'm gonna test that love, use that love." Gently, he rubbed her between the ears, and when he spoke, his tone was gentle. "I'm counting on the fact that she'll crumble when she sees me holding a knife to your throat."

The dog edged closer to him, and he allowed her to sit beside him. "Yes, ma'am, you're gonna work out just fine."

It took a few phone calls to track down the man who'd last worked with Latimer as a partner. Gary Gilbert was a uniformed officer who, today, had been assigned the East Nashville beat. Alex called his sergeant and arranged to meet the officer in a coffee shop.

When Alex arrived, the officer was sitting in his car outside the shop, the motor running. When he saw Alex he frowned, shut off the engine, and got out.

Alex extended his hand to the man, who reluctantly took it. "Officer Gilbert."

"Agent Morgan." Gilbert appeared to be in his late twenties. His build was slim and his hair dark, but his eyes held the wariness of a man who'd seen more than most. "I understand you have questions about Philip Latimer."

"That's correct. I was told you were his last partner before he tried to kill his wife."

Gilbert rested his hands on his hips. "That's right."

"What can you tell me about the man?"

"I was a rookie when I was partnered with him. He was good to me."

"I'm more concerned with how he treated his wife." Experience kept his tone neutral.

As Gilbert shifted, the leather of his gun belt creaked. "He loved her."

Alex dropped his voice a notch as he clung to the reins of his anger. "He stabbed her twenty-three times. If you've never seen the crime scene photos, I'd be glad to share."

Gilbert paled. "That's not necessary."

"Tell me about Latimer."

The officer glanced from side to side, clearly wrestling with loyalty to a fellow officer and what needed to be said. "After she left him, he couldn't stop talking about her. He became obsessed."

"He stalked her."

"He never talked about that stuff in front of me, but there were plenty of times he'd call her while we were on a lunch or dinner break. His messages never sounded threatening."

"What would he say to her?"

"That he was thinking about her. That he loved her."

"Did you know what he was planning?"

"Shit no." The words blasted out, as if fired from a gun. "He gave me the impression they were gonna renew their vows on their anniversary." He shook his head. "He told me they had a special date planned. He took the night off. Was excited." The officer met Alex's gaze, all traces of annoyance gone. "If I'd have known what he was planning, I would have reported him. I met his wife a couple of times, and I liked her. She was nice. How's she doing?"

"Remarkably well. She's a vet now."

That prompted a smile. "She was planning to go to school before he attacked her. I never heard. Glad to know she's doing well." He tapped an index finger on his belt. "Why all these questions after all this time? Latimer died in a car accident."

"That's what the reports say."

"What's that mean?"

"He was a smart guy, from what I've gathered."

"Yeah, real smart."

"Could he have faked his death?"

Nervous laughter burst from Gilbert. "Yeah, I suppose. Do you think he's still alive?"

"I have no idea." He relaxed his stance, shrugging as if he'd tossed a Hail Mary pass. "Just following up on a long-shot, crazy idea. I follow all the leads, even the odd ones."

Gilbert adjusted his hat. "I attended his funeral. A lot of cops did. We all agreed he'd lost his shit that night when he went after his wife, but he'd been a good cop. He'd saved a couple of guys, made clean busts, was well respected on the streets."

"I never questioned his work as a cop. It was exemplary until his commander threatened him with suspension after Leah Carson filed the restraining order. I'm here about the man, the husband."

A cold wind blew, making the officer turn away from the chill. "He didn't have much family. A grandmother and a cousin, and there was Leah and the force. Losing either Leah or both would have been a hell of a blow."

"And he'd have done anything to keep both."

After a wary hesitation, he nodded. "Yeah."

When Leah got out of surgery it was late in the day, and her back ached. It had been a tough surgery she'd assisted with Dr. Nelson. She checked her phone and noted a missed call and voice mail from Alex. She hit Play as she stretched backward and forward. "Leah, I want to talk to you about the case. I have more questions."

She lowered the phone from her ear and hit Redial, quickly finding herself in his voice mail. "Alex, returning your call. Leah."

"So, what're your plans for tonight?" Gail asked.

"After we close up here, I'm headed home. Hot bath."

"Ordering in?"

"No. I'm not a fan of takeout."

Gail laughed. "Good Lord, why? I would have starved to death years ago if not for the pizza place near me."

"I like to cook." Sort of true, but she really didn't like having delivery people showing up at her front door. Even if she were expecting them, they were strangers, wearing uniforms and ball caps that hid their faces too easily.

"What're you cooking?"

"I went to the market on Sunday. I'll likely make a minestrone soup." She fished her phone out of her purse and saw that David had texted. WOULD LOVE TO SEE YOU. DINNER?

"That isn't a happy expression," Gail said.

"Guy I know from a running group wants to talk to me."

"Think he's the one who sent the flowers? Maybe his card really meant happy one-month anniversary in the group."

"No. He didn't send the flowers. We both knew Deidre, but other than that we're just acquaintances."

"You don't think those flowers are romantic? They were expensive. A guy really likes a girl when he's willing to spend money on her."

"I think sending flowers and not signing the card is creepy." Once, Philip had left a single rose on the driver's seat of her car. She'd always locked the car, and the flower was his way of telling her he could get to her anytime.

"You gonna text him back?"

"Of course."

Her fingertips hesitated over the cell phone keys.

"Just say you have surgery tonight."

Tempted. "What about tomorrow?"

"You'll be busy then, too. It happens a few times, he'll get the message to back off."

"Assuming he's the kind of guy who operates under normal boundaries."

Gail cocked her head. "Sounds like experience talking. Your late husband wasn't a nice guy?"

Leah sighed. "He wasn't, but you'd never have known it when you first met him. So charming. And then it was either full-on romance or anger. Little in between."

"Was it terrible for you?"

"For a while it was." She shook off the fear. "But I'm not worried about that now." Absently, Leah tugged the edges of her coat over her scars.

"I see you day in and day out. Most days you do a good job of hiding them." Gail frowned. "Did he attack you?"

Shame warmed her face with a flush of color. As kind as Gail had been to her since she'd arrived, she couldn't bring herself to explain her tale.

"I see the scars."

She'd kept the past locked in a box for four years. At times, the past banged and clanged against the box's restraints, as if it were a wild animal. But she'd always kept it contained. Now, after all that fighting, she simply lifted the lid and set it free. "He stabbed me twenty-three times."

"My God, I remember that case. It was in the news."

"Thankfully, the media dropped it quickly." Color rose in Leah's face as embarrassment flooded her. How could she have been so fooled by a monster?

"It's okay, honey," Gail said. "I didn't mean to embarrass you. I've got a big mouth and I can put my nose into business that isn't mine."

"It's fine. It's the past. My husband died in a car accident shortly after the attack. It's over." She glanced down at the phone. She wasn't going to lie to David. She texted back,

I CAN MEET FOR COFFEE IN AN HOUR. She hit Send. "See you tomorrow, Gail."

"Are you okay?"

"Yes. I'm fine." She dug deep for a bright smile, but she couldn't find one. "See you tomorrow."

"Sure thing, honey."

Leah grabbed her purse and coat from her office, and as she exited through the back door, her hand on her Mace, she paused to scan the parking lot. She approached her car carefully, glancing in the backseat.

As she put her key in the lock, she hesitated, the hair on the back of her neck rising. She turned and scanned the parking lot, searching for anyone who might be watching her. There were only Gail and Dr. Nelson's cars in the lot, but across the street, the strip mall was filled with cars. Anyone could be sitting in a car watching the people around the shopping center. And each shop window was large, designed so that customers could gaze inside at the merchandise.

But the windows were also for the monsters who liked to hide in plain sight, day and night, watching their prey.

CHAPTER FOURTEEN

Thursday, January 19, 6:30 P.M.

Leah arrived at the coffee shop just after six thirty. The café had a collection of small tables and, at the far end, a large glass counter filled with sweet and savory pastries. The air was heavy with the scent of coffee, cinnamon, and chocolate.

She moved to the counter and ordered a large coffee and a cheese pizza. Within minutes she'd settled at a table near the back wall. She faced the front door, which allowed her a clear view of everyone who entered. Back to the wall, she faced the door and counted the exits. Maybe one day she wouldn't think so strategically when she entered a store or restaurant, but she doubted that day would come anytime soon.

She bit into her pizza and savored the taste of melted Swiss cheese and the blend of oregano and basil on the warm crust. She hadn't eaten out in a long time. Too many people watching, too exposed. But tonight she didn't want to worry. She wanted to enjoy her life, and maybe she'd add having fun to her growing list of resolutions.

Bells over the front door jingled and a cold blast of air

elbowed its way into the room. Her gaze lifted, careful and wary, until she spotted a couple entering the coffee shop arm in arm, smiling. She noted the woman's relaxed posture and the way she slung her arm casually over the man's. He smiled down at her, and they laughed at a private joke. Envy jabbed at Leah. She doubted she'd ever enjoyed that kind of trust or joy, even in the early days with Philip.

On the heels of the couple, a final blast of cold air shoved David inside. The collar of his overcoat was turned up, and his thick hair had been tossed by the wind. Briefcase in hand, he looked every bit the professional. She'd never seen him dressed for work before, and though he'd always looked sharp working out, now he was distinguished. She waited for the flutter of attraction that would have been a normal response but none came.

He raised a gloved hand, smiled, and moved straight to the counter to place an order.

Coffee cup in hand, he moved toward her. She rose and smiled.

He set his cup down and reached over to hug her. The move was easy, relaxed, meant to be a gesture of friendship. She ordered her muscles to relax and gave him a quick hug, patting his back softly while keeping distance between their bodies. His faint cologne teased her nose. "David. How're you doing?"

Straightening, he pulled off his coat and slung it over a spare chair before sitting. "I'm rattled as hell. How're you doing? I can't stop thinking about Deidre."

"I'm still stunned," Leah said.

"Me too. She was awesome. I really liked her." He reached for two packets of sugar and dumped them in his coffee. "The cop said you found her."

Images of Deidre, dead, upended her calm. "I did."

He sipped his coffee, staring at her as if waiting for her to share details of the crime scene. She hadn't told anyone at the clinic about the murder, and now to discuss it with David smacked of dishonor.

Understanding her hesitation but not ready to surrender, he hurried on to say, "It's just so terrible. The cop came to see me. He had all kinds of questions. It almost felt like I was some kind of suspect."

She reached for a piece of her pizza but realized her appetite had vanished. Many shared David's morbid curiosity. She supposed that didn't make him evil, just human. However, fear whispered, *Smiles and nice clothes don't mean he's good either.*

As if it were an annoying fly, she brushed fear aside. "What kind of questions did they ask?"

"Basically, if I knew of anyone who might have been bothering her. Did I see anything or notice anyone who set off alarm bells?"

What secrets hid behind his beautiful mask of concern? Deidre had said he once joked he was a man of secrets. "Did you?"

He tapped his index finger against his coffee cup. "No. I never saw anything. She never spoke about her ex-husband, but I'm wondering now if he could have been behind this."

"Deidre didn't talk to me about her personal life. If I hadn't seen you two at Rudy's on Saturday night, I'd have never known you were dating."

"I wouldn't say we were dating. Friends. With benefits. But no romance. Just laughs." He sipped his coffee. "Have you heard when the funeral is going to be?"

"No." She hadn't attended Philip's funeral, but months after the attack, when she'd regained some of her strength, she'd visited his grave. Fresh flowers had adorned the site, and she guessed that had been his grandmother's doing. Myrna had adored her grandson. Leah had knelt in front of the stone for a long time, tracing her fingers over the raised letters of his name. She'd barely glanced at the year of his birth, but she'd stared at the date of his death for a long time. She'd thanked God he was dead. "I'll be there."

"Me too."

She traced the rim of her cup. "That last morning you two ran. You ran extra miles that day."

"She wanted to grind out five more miles and I was game. Not many people can keep pace with me, but she could. She challenged me."

"Not every man likes to be challenged."

"I liked it."

A half smile tipped her lips as she weighed his words against his tone. "She was a great athlete." She lifted her cup to her lips and paused. "You didn't see anyone at the park that day?"

He sipped his coffee, sat back, and appraised her with a wary eye. "You sound like a cop."

"Sorry. Most women who're murdered are killed by someone they know." During Philip's stalking, she'd had a therapist suggest her husband could kill her. She'd dismissed the idea as preposterous. Her therapist had leaned forward in his chair, looked her in the eye, and said, "Seventy percent of the time, women are killed by someone who *loved* them."

But David had said he didn't love Deidre. *Friends with benefits.*

"I've called my lawyer," he said.

"Why?"

"I didn't hurt her. I can't help the cops. But I only trust

the system so far. Things get twisted. Evidence gets messed up or misinterpreted. It never hurts to have an attorney."

Until now, her opinion of David had rested on his looks and athletic talent. Now, she decided, she didn't like him very much. He wasn't worried about Deidre. Only himself.

She checked her watch. "David, I really have to get going. It's been a long day."

"Yeah, sure. But you haven't eaten."

She pushed her plate away, her stomach knotting. "I'm not hungry."

"Can I have it? God, I'm starved."

"Yeah, sure. Help yourself." She rose and pulled her coat off the back of her chair. He moved to stand, but she stopped him. "It's okay. See you soon."

She left him eating her pizza. Bells jingled overhead as she tugged open the door. An icy brace of air stung her face. As she zipped up her coat, she glanced back into the coffee shop. David, smiling now, had his head bowed as he typed into his cell phone. *Deidre, what did you see in that guy?*

She burrowed her hands into her coat pockets and moved down the street toward her car. As she walked along the cold, nearly deserted streets, her senses tingled, as if someone was watching her. The feeling grew so acute, she stopped and looked back, half-expecting to see someone there. But the street was empty. No sound of footsteps. No lingering shadows.

A chill rushed up her spine as she hurried to her car. She glanced in the darkened backseat and, satisfied it was empty, unlocked the door and slid behind the wheel. Immediately, she locked the doors. The drive home took less than fifteen minutes, and she was grateful to pull the door to her town home behind her and lock it. She reached for the dead bolt, clicked it open and then clicked it closed again. Three times. Locked. Safe.

Shrugging off her coat, she'd pulled her hair into a ponytail and changed into sweats and a T-shirt. She scrubbed her face clean of makeup. Without makeup, under the soft glow of the bathroom lights, her scars brightened. Gently, she traced the jagged line across her chin.

Next, she allowed her gaze to drop to the scars she so often ignored. Carefully, she fingered the slash above her left breast and the short, jagged scar along her collarbone. The scars, like memories of her marriage, had faded but were not forgotten. And as hard as she worked to deny them, in the end they were always lurking, waiting to be unmasked.

When she turned from the mirror, she wasn't upset or troubled by her scars. Like DNA, the scars were an undeniable part of her. A readiness to move forward washed over her. Time to abandon the past's lonely road. Life brought enough darkness without her stirring up what had passed.

She dressed in pajamas and moved into the living room. There, she flipped through the day's mail, which was mostly bills. The last envelope was light purple and hand-addressed, clearly personal. She turned over the envelope and saw her aunt's return address. They spoke from time to time. Her aunt had slipped into the spot her mother had once filled. But the handwriting didn't quite match her aunt's.

Carefully, she tore open the end of the envelope and removed the card. On the cover was an adorable black Lab. Touched that her aunt remembered her love of Labs, she flipped open the card. It read, "Thinking of you."

She turned the card over to see if there were any other notes, but the rest of the card was blank. She checked her watch and realized it was early in Oregon so she dialed her aunt's number.

She answered on the third ring. Her voice sounded rough and heavy, as if she suffered from a cold. "Hello."

"Aunt Jane, it's Leah."

"Leah? This is out of the blue. Is everything all right?" In the background, a television hummed with the sounds of a game show.

"Everything is fine. The job is going well and I seem to be settling into the new town house."

"Something must be wrong." Her tone had grown stern.

Leah deserved her aunt's skepticism. She'd called too many times, terrified and scared, in moments when she'd imagined Philip lurking in the back booth of a café or hovering at the edge of an alley. The shrink had said it was PTSD, post-traumatic stress disorder. He'd given her tranquilizers, which she'd never taken. "No, it's all good. I got your card and wanted to thank you for sending it. I love the Lab puppy on the front."

A silence followed. "Leah, I didn't send you a card."

"The card has your home address on it."

"Leah, I didn't send it."

Her smile flattened to a frown. "Are you sure?"

"Honey, I know when I've sent out a card. You said there's a Lab puppy on the front. What does it say on the inside?"

A tension crept up her back and circled around her throat, constricting her breath. "It says *Thinking of You*."

"Is it signed?"

"No."

"Do you think it's an old card, maybe one that got lost in the mail? I could have sent it last year."

She picked up the envelope and rechecked the return

address. The handwriting was bold and masculine. "It's your new address. The house on Mulberry, so it can't be more than a couple of months ago."

"It didn't come from me, honey." Her aunt spoke carefully, as if fearing Leah would panic.

"Any relatives staying with you who might have sent it?" Leah stared at the card, all traces of goodwill fleeing as she struggled to find logic.

"No, hon. I just got back from my cruise, so no one has stayed with me in a while."

The chill skimming along her skin grew colder. "This doesn't make sense."

"No, it doesn't." Her aunt paused. "But Philip is dead."

"Yes. Of course." Her voice didn't hold the conviction it should have.

"What about the local police? Have you called them?"

Several times in Knoxville, she'd imagined sounds and called the cops. They'd never found signs of any intruder. "A neighbor called them a month ago. I was having one of my nightmares, and they heard my screams. I've made a New Year's resolution not to stress about sounds and noises." She wanted to tell her aunt about Deidre, but that remained too painful.

"My word, I think the earth just stopped spinning."

Her aunt's dry tone coaxed a half laugh. "There's life on the other side."

"Yes, there is. And it's good to hear you laugh, Leah. I've missed hearing you laugh."

Leah traced the edges of the pup's face on the card. "Aunt Jane, I'm not going to worry about this card. It's some kind of odd mistake."

"Of course it is. I wouldn't worry, honey. I know, given your history, it's natural to be worried and upset. But my guess is that the card is some kind of advertisement or mistake."

Logic refused to listen to fear's rants. "The envelope has your address and mine. Whoever sent this knows where we both live." She glanced toward the front door and resisted the urge to test the lock. "Yesterday someone sent me flowers at work. They were addressed to me, and the card said *Happy Anniversary*."

"Your wedding anniversary is a few days away. Could they've been for some other kind of celebration?"

"I don't think so."

"Leah, have you seen anyone around your town house?"

"No."

"Has anyone been bothering you?"

"No."

"What about odd phone calls?"

"Those are all the kind of things Philip did."

"I know." It wasn't any one event but the *drip, drip, drip* of all those little things that coalesced into a flood.

"Did you call that South Carolina detective?"

"I left a voice mail. She hasn't called me back yet. She probably thinks I'm back in crazy town."

"You were never crazy. Never forget what happened was all Philip's doing. How many days has it been since you called?"

"A few."

"Why don't you call her again tomorrow? Be polite and ask her about Philip. Just double-check. It will make you feel better. Do you think it could be Philip's grandmother? She always took his side."

An unspoken tension hummed between them. "His grandmother passed last year, but I know he had cousins and a half brother." She moved toward the front door, peered past the drawn drapes at the dark parking lot. She double-checked the dead bolt on the door. Locked. "He also had friends who weren't happy with me. They could have sent them."

"How would they know our new addresses?"

"Philip was clever. No one ever questioned his intelligence. For all we know, there could be others in his family or at his old job just as clever."

"Only a monster would support something like that." Her aunt spoke carefully, as if speaking to a wild horse ready to spook. "Just call the detective tomorrow and save the card, like you had to do in the old days."

Leah moved to her purse and pulled out her journal. "I'm sorry we can't ever have a real conversation. I'm sorry there's always a problem."

"You didn't deserve this. It was never your fault. And I'm happy to talk to you any time."

"I insisted on dating Philip. Mom was against it, and we argued a few times about it."

A sigh shuddered through the phone. "Maybe one day I'll share with you some of the boneheaded things I did when I was young. And a few things your mother did as well."

A mental picture of two mature women, neatly put together, didn't jive with the confession. "You two couldn't have been that bad."

"You might be surprised. Just do me a favor and don't let this throw you into a tailspin. Stay away from the cigarettes and keep going to your group meetings. You're still going, aren't you?"

"Yes. I went yesterday." As much as Leah wanted to talk about Deidre, she didn't dare. She'd brought more than enough trouble to her aunt's doorstep and didn't need to bring anymore.

"Are you going to be okay?"

She pulled a pen from her purse. "I'll be fine. Sorry to bother you, Aunt Jane."

"Don't worry about it. I love you."

"Love you, too."

"Call me when you figure this out."

"I will." She ended the call and immediately began to write about the incident in her journal.

Alex arrived at the state medical examiner's office minutes after eight, a newly acquired file tucked under his arm. He approached reception, showed his badge, and stated he had an appointment with Dr. Heller. He'd only had minutes to wait before she appeared at the side door. Dark slacks and a chestnut-brown turtleneck accentuated her long frame. She wore her hair pinned up in a tight bun at the base of her neck. Reading glasses perched on her head.

She crossed the lobby, smiling. "Alex, what can I do for you?"

"I have a file I'd like you to review."

"Sure. Come on back." She scanned her card at the door and it clicked open, and the two moved to a small conference room off the lobby. She sat at the head of the table and he took the seat to her left. "What do you have for me?"

"It's an autopsy report. Done by a coroner in South Carolina."

"Okay."

He pushed the file toward her. "Read it and let me know what you think. It's only a couple of pages."

She perched her glasses on her nose and leaned forward as she opened the file. She read the first page and frowned.

The second page deepened that frown, and by the time she'd reached the third page, she looked puzzled.

"What do you think?"

"I think it's rather incomplete. The body was badly burned in the car accident, but there was no DNA testing done, nor were dental records pulled. The identification was made solely on a charred wallet at the scene, a ring on the victim's finger, and hearsay from several witnesses."

"If you were going to fake a death . . ."

"I'd pick a jurisdiction like this. It's rural, the county coroner isn't a medical professional by trade, and it would be a place where identification mistakes are likely. That's not to say they didn't ID the right guy. They may have, but I'd want more evidence to make a ruling."

He sat back in his chair, almost sorry his instincts were proving correct. "Right."

"Why pull this file?" She glanced at the name on the file again. "Why care about Philip Latimer? It's way out of your jurisdiction. Why care about a guy who died in South Carolina four years ago?"

"Latimer was a police officer in Nashville until four years ago. His boss disciplined him when his estranged wife filed stalking charges against him. Latimer ended up trying to kill her."

Frown lines appeared as she tapped a finger on the file. "I think I remember that case. She survived."

"She did." Alex mentally traced the scars on Leah's palm, remembering their roughness. "Latimer stabbed his wife twenty-three times."

Dr. Heller yanked off her glasses. "Deidre Jones was stabbed twenty-three times."

"Yes, she was."

"Are you suggesting a connection to the Deidre Jones case?"

"I am."

She wrapped her index finger around a thin gold cross hanging from a chain around her neck and absently slid it back and forth. "How'd you come up with this guy's name?"

"The woman who found Deidre's body was Leah Carson. Also known as Leah Latimer. She was the wife Latimer stabbed twenty-three times. Deidre's sister also got into serious trouble five years ago. Drugs. The arresting officer was Philip Latimer, and the key evidence in the case vanished."

"What're you saying?"

"I have no hard evidence, only a theory. I think Deidre approached Philip for a favor, and he helped her out. Then, a couple of months later, when he was on the run after nearly killing his wife, he called in Deidre's favor. She helped him get out of town."

A deep frown furrowed her brow. "And fake his death?"

"I don't know. But you're not happy with the quality of the report. And given the manner of Deidre's death— twenty-three stab wounds—I'm wondering if Latimer might be alive."

"Why come back after all this time?"

"Money. Deke had a suspicion Deidre was skimming money from some of her cases. Up until a month ago she worked hard at her job, and there were no whispers of scandal. Then money started vanishing. Maybe she got tired of paying and Latimer killed her." That didn't explain the John Doe at the warehouse, or how Deidre's business card had ended up in a bag nearby. He didn't have all the pieces but he would.

"You really think Deidre helped him?"

He always relied strongly on instinct. "I do."

She closed the file, absently tapping her index finger on the folder. "Have there been any signs that Latimer is alive? Has anyone seen him?"

"If they have, they haven't said." Maybe the charred body was an unlucky bastard who spotted Latimer. But it begged the question: if Latimer were alive, why had he left Leah alone these past four years? Why hide out and not go after her again?

"Has his ex-wife noticed anything that would suggest she's being stalked?"

"Not that she's told me. And I think if Latimer is alive, and he did kill Deidre, he would have to lay low, stay out of sight."

"What's he waiting for?"

"Their anniversary. According to the files, he stabbed her on their wedding anniversary."

She leaned back and pulled off her glasses. "That's one heck of a theory, Agent."

Hints of doubt rang clear. "I've asked Georgia to cross-check the fingerprints and DNA found at the murder scene against Latimer's."

"I would consider that one hell of a connection if you can make it."

"If I'm right, we only have a few days before Latimer makes a move on his ex-wife."

He sat in his car, just a half block down the street from Leah's house, shelling peanuts and popping them in his mouth. The shells littered his lap and the floor mat around him. Charlie slept wrapped in a warm blanket on the seat beside him.

A small speaker sat by him on the passenger seat, and he listened as Leah moved around her house, restless and unable to sleep. She'd called her aunt. Worried about the card. Good. Worry. Guess. "I did send the card. I know all there is to know about you."

Charlie glanced up at the sound of his voice and he rubbed her between the ears and gently tucked the blanket around her.

"Lack of sleep is going to impair Leah's judgment," he said softly. "A canceled credit card is going to make life a challenge. That's all good."

The dog thumped her tail under the blanket.

As he rubbed the dog's head, he closed his eyes, remembering Deidre's face when he'd stabbed her. After the first plunge of the knife, terror had flashed in her eyes and reason had deserted him. He'd felt empowered. Aroused. Vindicated. When he'd stepped away from her lifeless body, blood had dripped from his face and hands. A lesser man would have crumpled, but his training and weeks of practice had taken over. Outside, he'd stripped off his Tyvek suit, shoved it in a garbage bag, and left the scene. The bag had landed in an incinerator. No trace evidence. Only memories remained.

He opened his eyes and looked at the dog. This savage side of himself was a surprise. Monsters stabbed women. Monsters raped and killed. He was no monster of course, so where had this streak of violence come from?

He'd been raised well. Had wanted a traditional life, including a wife and children. He didn't want this kind of mayhem and violence stalking him. He wanted to be free of it. He was a victim.

Later, as he'd watched the flames devour the bag filled with the blood-soaked suit, he'd promised himself to have more control the next time. Lack of control led to mistakes. And if he didn't make sloppy mistakes, it would all work out in the end.

He reached into the paper bag and pulled out another peanut, cracking the shell in his palm. Charlie looked at him, her ears perked. From his pocket he dug out a dog treat and handed it to her. She took it, greedily chewing the soft beefy strip.

He would be careful around Leah. He wouldn't let it get out of hand. He wouldn't strike until he was ready.

He reached for his tablet and found the Web site dedicated to Leah. It wasn't live yet because the story wasn't finished, but that was simply a matter of time.

ALL ABOUT LEAH

The Web site wouldn't pass as professional, but it wasn't bad. Leah's picture was front and center. The first tab revealed thousands of older pictures. Many had been taken with a phone when she'd been a senior in college. Racing across campus with her backpack slung over her shoulder. Standing in line at the sandwich shop.

He'd created a new tab for photos taken in the last few months. Leah at the clinic, walking a dog. At her running group, warming up as the sun rose. On a date with David, the blond con man, who poached other men's wives. He zeroed in on one image. She'd been at the park and he'd called out her name. He'd startled her, and she'd turned with only the barest hint of panic in her gaze. He loved the combination of the sun, her hair, and the way her panic brightened her blue gaze.

Watching her, trailing her was intoxicating. Distance was key right now, but a couple of weeks ago he'd bumped her shoulder as she'd passed him on a crowded street. He'd smelled her perfume, heard her soft intake of breath and her quick footsteps behind him. He'd vanished into the crowd, excited that he'd touched her.

Hunting juiced him.

He touched another tab. This one was marked FRIENDS. He opened the tab and searched the faces of David, Alex Morgan, and of course Deidre. Many of the pictures he'd taken as the trio had been running. Parks were an easy place to hide, or so he'd thought. Deidre had spotted him, though. He'd tried to turn away, but she'd caught the sunlight glinting off the lens of his camera. He'd feared her conscience would get the better of her and she'd confess all. Though he'd been thinking about killing her for weeks, in that moment he'd known she had to die that night.

Charlie still chewed her treat. "Be right back, girl."

He got out of his truck and, glancing sideways to ensure he was alone, approached Leah's car. He flicked open the blade of a pocketknife and knelt by the tire. Though tempted to slice the tire, he wasn't ready to leave solid proof. Better to keep them all guessing until it was too late. He unscrewed the cap on the air valve and pressed the tip of the knife into the valve. Air hissed out and conjured memories of the air gurgling from Deidre's lungs as she'd gasped her last breaths.

Killing Deidre had been more thrilling than he'd imagined. The plunge of the knife into her skin. The tear of her flesh. The warm, sticky blood on the tip of the knife. He wondered if killing Leah would offer the same level of excitement. A few more days and he would know.

CHAPTER FIFTEEN

Friday, January 20, 6 A.M.

Leah had plenty of excuses not to run this morning. Plenty of reasons to roll over and grab an extra hour of sleep. She hadn't fallen asleep until after one in the morning, and it was going to be a long day at the clinic. Plenty of excuses.

But that all rang hollow. They all suggested she'd be a wimp if she listened to one of them. And Deidre . . . well, Deidre wouldn't have bit on any of those excuses. She'd have shot Leah the look.

And so she'd rubbed her dry eyes, pulled on her cold-weather gear, and with a hot cup of coffee in hand, headed to her car. She was feet away when she noticed the back right tire was flat.

What the hell? She moved to the tire, kneeling and rubbing gloved hands over the rubber, searching for slices or cuts. Philip had sliced her tires when he'd been stalking her. In those days, she'd known he'd done the deed, but she could never prove it. Those flat tires always happened when she had to be at work early for something important or drive to Knoxville in final prep for the move.

Finding no slices or gouges, she wondered if this was more bad luck. The exposed skin on her face tingled in an icy breeze as she dug her cell out of her pocket and checked the time. Still a half hour before the running group met. AAA would never make it here in time for her to run this morning.

Gritting her teeth, she put her coffee in the car's cup holder and popped the trunk. If being stalked had a positive side, it was learning to be independent. She could change a tire, rub out scratches, fix a slashed screened window, and even glaze a broken window. Thanks to Philip, she'd acquired an odd collection of skills.

She reached for the jack in the trunk and popped off the hubcap. Putting the jack under the body's frame, she cranked the jack until it was supporting but not lifting the car. She loosened each of the lug nuts and then raised the flat tire off the ground. The flattened tire removed and tossed in the trunk, she grabbed the smaller spare. She seated it on the hub, hand-tightened the lug nuts, and then lowering the car to the ground finished each off with a hard turn of the tire iron.

She slid behind the wheel, cold and irritated. A glance at the clock showed she still had time to make the run. Heater blasting, she drove the few miles to the track, where a collection of cars waited, lights on, exhaust wafting. The black SUV was in the spot closest to the running course. Alex would be there. Little seemed to dissuade him from anything.

She shut off the engine and, sipping the last of the lukewarm coffee, got out of the car, wincing as the icy air whipped.

At exactly six thirty, Alex got out of his SUV. He glanced in her direction and looked almost surprised to see her. That look alone was enough to make her happy she'd made the trek. She might be the slowest in the group, but she was no quitter. She jogged to the track along with the other runners.

David glanced at Alex, frowned, but said nothing as he checked his watch. "We'll do a five-mile run today. Check your watches. Let's see what you can shave off your time."

Leah checked her watch, knowing a personal best today would be finishing. She stretched along with the others, grateful Alex kept his distance from her. The less said, the better.

The first half mile of the run was rough. Her muscles complained about the work and her lungs stung each time she pulled in cold air. But she kept putting one step in front of the other and slowly her body warmed and found its steady rhythm. Days ago, she could have looked to the front of the group and seen Deidre's long lean body eating up the distance with ease. But today it was Alex alone, running ahead of everyone. He moved from the track down the small trail cutting through the woods. Seconds later, he was out of sight.

The woods around her grew thicker with each pace, but as long as she could hear the foot strikes of the others she was fine. She sensed Alex was always close.

Managing a decent pace today, she never fell so far behind that she couldn't hear the other runners. She was improving.

Alex had run point so that he could scan the woods for anyone that might be waiting or watching Leah. When he finished his run easily in forty minutes, he stopped at the mouth of the trail, waiting as each runner emerged.

There'd been a total of eleven today. David was first to emerge and then several other men. A few women reached the end five minutes later, and after another twenty minutes all were out except Leah. Nothing to be alarmed about. She ran slowly. Hell, when he thought about the medical records he'd read yesterday, it was a wonder she ran at all.

David walked up to him. "Leah is always the last one out."

"Right."

He hitched his hands on his hips. "Deidre always had a thing about waiting for her. Didn't like leaving her alone in the woods. Since . . . well, since Deidre's death, I figured I'd wait for Leah."

"You don't have to wait. I got this." He cupped his gloved hands close to his mouth and blew hot air out to warm his fingertips.

"Any leads on Deidre's killer?"

"Working on it." He studied the still, quiet entrance to the path, very tempted to jog into the woods and check on her.

"She wouldn't like that," David said.

"What?"

"Deidre went in after her once. When I saw Deidre come out of the woods, I asked her about Leah. She said Leah was polite but not really happy. She didn't like being babysat."

Alex checked his watch. Whether she liked it or not, she had two more minutes before he went in after her.

"She'll be here soon," David said. "She's slow as hell."

"Never quits."

"Yeah, I guess that should mean something. But let's face it, they don't hand out trophies for last place."

"Right."

"She's odd."

"Really?"

"I offered to pick her up before a run session, but she came up with a reason to meet me here. Seemed kinda nervous that I knew where she lived."

"You run with her, but that doesn't mean you know her or she knows you."

David shrugged. "I just wanted to give her a ride to the group. Trying to be a gentleman."

"Right."

"I haven't heard about a funeral date yet," David said.

"No news yet."

"God, I hope you catch the creep."

"I will." He stared at the woods, his internal clock ticking. She had one more minute and then he was going in to find her.

"She's a veterinarian, you know?"

"I'd heard that."

"Got to be smart to pull that off."

"So I hear."

He leaned in, as if they were conspirators. "A couple of weeks ago, I touched her on the shoulder and she froze up like I'd done something terrible. She shrugged and stepped away. Lots of issues with that one. And you've seen the scars."

"Yes."

"Leah and Deidre were pals. Have you asked Leah where she was the night Deidre was stabbed? She's just weird enough, and it doesn't take much to wield a knife."

"Really?"

Color warmed his face. "Look, I'm not trying to lay blame on Leah."

"I didn't say you were."

"But you came by my office asking questions."

"I'm asking a lot of people questions."

"Just so you know, Deidre and I'd planned to take a break from each other."

"You said that."

"It was all hot and heavy last summer, but things really cooled off in the last couple of months. I think I was the excuse she needed to leave her husband. It was never a long-term thing with her."

"Did that piss you off?"

"No. Deidre and I had fun. That was enough for me." He nodded toward the entrance to the park as Leah emerged. "Besides, my wife and I are talking again. We might work it out."

"Good." He took a step toward the woods as he saw Leah jog down the path and up toward the parking lot. Relief jabbed like a pesky bug.

"Leah's a good-looking woman."

He agreed. "You think she's odd."

"A man can deal with a lot of quirks when a woman is attractive."

Alex rubbed his hands together. He wondered just how hard David was working on his marriage. "Better get going."

David opened the door to his car. "Keep me posted on Deidre's funeral."

His gaze didn't waver from Leah. "Sure."

When Leah came out of the woods, all the other runners had left. Even David was nowhere to be seen. The lone car in the lot was the black SUV, where Alex stood waiting, his arms crossed.

He'd been waiting for her. Her throat tightened with emotion as she made the final push across the field to the parking lot. When she stopped running, her breath was quick and ragged and a stitch pinched her side.

Alex moved toward her, his steps slow and easy. Already,

the cold air chilled her skin, whereas he seemed to barely notice the cold. "You need to get warm. Get in my car."

She glanced toward the SUV. Imagining herself alone with him in the car, she hesitated before she caught herself. "Sounds great."

He walked beside her, shortening his long strides so he didn't outpace her. He opened the passenger door, and a rush of warm air greeted her. She slid onto the leather seat. He closed the door and, head ducked to the wind, crossed the front of the car.

The car was neat, well organized, and looked as if it had been freshly vacuumed. Her car wasn't so pristine. She'd transported a couple of dogs from the shelter to the clinic last week, and they'd left paw and nose prints on her back-seat windows and seats. Her cup holder held today's coffee and yesterday's, along with a couple of empty water bottles littered the floor.

He opened the door and slid behind the wheel. The interior of the car shrank as his broad shoulders filled the space. "Thirsty?"

"Yeah."

He reached in the backseat and grabbed a couple of water bottles. He handed her one. "What's going on with your tire? I can see it's a spare."

She'd forgotten all about the earlier frustration. "Flat."

"What happened?"

"I don't know. These are new tires. Maybe there's a problem with the valve. Maybe I picked up a nail." The excuse sounded good but didn't quite ring true even to her. "I had to change it before I could get here."

Alex's gaze warmed. "Aren't you handy."

She twisted off the top of the bottle and drank. "Jack of all trades."

"Anything else happen out of the ordinary?"

She tossed him a nervous look. "Why do you ask?"

He hesitated. "Just asking."

The card from her aunt had thrown her off base, but that hardly seemed worth mentioning. "No."

He studied her. Again, peeling back layers. "Keep me posted on anything odd that happens."

Unspoken words hummed between them. "Do you know something about Deidre that I should know?"

"No definitive word yet on her case. I'm running theories. As soon as I'm sure, I'll have questions."

She frowned. "Mysterious."

"Not meant to be. I like my facts in good order before I present them."

She sipped her water. "I suppose her husband will make the funeral arrangements."

His brow rose. Had he picked up on the bitterness? "Does that bother you?"

She shrugged. "Just seems wrong he'd be the one."

"Her sister is back in town. She'll be involved. But Radcliff is still her legal husband."

"I know." A smile flickered, halfhearted. "And it's really not my business."

"But it bothers you."

"I suppose it does. But in the eyes of the law my feelings don't really stack up."

"No."

He studied her face, churning up a wave of self-consciousness. Was her scar showing? "I thought you weren't coming today."

"Takes more than a flat."

Blue eyes sharpened. "You had a good run time today. I hear the time was probably your best yet."

"Maybe one day I'll approach the glory days of high school when I ran cross-country."

"You ran cross country?"

She laughed. "It was a small school, and I liked to run."

"Must have been some team."

"Hey, I'll have you know I ran a seven-minute mile in those days."

"You ran a seven-minute mile? Amazing."

She didn't explain a stab wound left her with diminished lung capacity that derailed her time. "I hardly remember those days."

"High school is a million miles away for me." His darkening gaze conjured questions about what he really knew about her. He wouldn't have to dig too deep to uncover her past. The idea of him poking around the shadows annoyed her. "I bet you were a straight A student."

He shook his head. "Did what I thought I needed to do and no more."

"I pegged you for the classic overachiever."

"That bug didn't catch me until I joined TBI. What about you?"

"Classic A student. Cheerleader. Whole nine yards. Both my parents were still alive and healthy. Good times."

She glanced at the clock. "So what brought you here today?"

"Checking out the running group."

"Again? They all know you're a cop."

He shrugged. "Never know what you'll learn."

She sipped. "If you're looking to catch people when their reserves are low, we're doing intervals tomorrow. That workout always kills."

That unpracticed smile flickered. "Are you trying to chase me away?"

"No. Not at all. As fast as you run, I doubt it will be a challenge." He stared at her, not responding. Nudged by the heavy silence, she said, "Thanks for being my body-guard and for giving me the water, but I've got to get to work."

"Sure." As she reached for the handle, he asked, "David ever talk about Deidre?"

She paused. "He invited me out for coffee last night. I think he's worried. Doesn't like being associated with murder. But then, who does?"

"He say anything about Deidre?"

"Only reiterated that they were friends with benefits. No passion. No reason to kill." She cocked her head. "Is there a problem with him?"

"Why would there be?"

"You're TBI. Deidre is dead. And you have questions about him."

"I'm asking questions about everyone in the running group."

"Even me?"

"Yes."

"Fair enough."

"Deidre ever talk about her past?"

"Like what?"

"Anything."

"Other than her marriage, no."

"What about work?"

"Never talked about work, but I got the sense she loved it."

"Okay."

"That's it?"

"For now."

She opened the door. "Thanks again for waiting."

"See you soon."

"Right." Leah trotted across the lot to her car, glanced in the backseat, and then slid behind the wheel. She turned on the heat, promising never to complain about summer again. The SUV waited until she put her car in reverse, backed up, and waved. He nodded and followed.

As she pictured Alex waiting for her at the top of the hill, attraction snapped. The sensation was odd, something she hadn't felt in a very long time. She'd been too nervous on their so-called date to feel anything other than nervous, but she felt something now.

Energy hummed in her veins. Her skin warmed. As much as she wanted to embrace the unexpected feelings, she feared them. She'd once been attracted to Philip.

The two men appeared to be similar, powerful and in charge, but she could see now that Philip was weak compared to Alex. Power, not fear, radiated from Alex, and the way he looked at her made her a little weak.

Getting close was a dangerous, risky thing to do. She'd promised herself she'd try dating this year. But she'd made no resolutions about starting a relationship, especially not with a man as dangerous as Alex.

Leah finished up the morning appointments just before two. Normally, the morning didn't go so long, but there'd been a couple of emergencies, including an old cat having seizures and a dog that had been hit by a car. The cat had been stabilized and the dog, with a shattered back leg, had gone into surgery immediately. It had taken her over an hour and a half to set the pin in the dog's hind leg, stitch it up, and build a cast. The half hound/half mutt named Maisey was in her cage. She was sleeping peacefully now, but when she woke in the next hour she was going to be sore and an unhappy camper with her cast and the cone around her neck.

Leah stood outside, behind the vet hospital, leaning against the brick wall. The afternoon sun hit this spot and it warmed the brick. It felt good to be in the fresh air. Instinctively, she reached in her pocket for a pack of cigarettes. Her fingers brushed dog treats and a rumpled pack of gum. She considered hopping in her car and making the five-minute drive to the drugstore, where she could pick up a pack of cigarettes. She'd only smoke one, she reasoned, and then she would throw out the rest of the pack.

"Damn," she muttered. "You're not going to do that."

She opened her eyes and pushed away from the wall, her gaze catching sight of the spare tire on her car.

The image stirred the tension in her gut. She'd dropped the flat tire off at the garage that morning and the mechanic had promised to have it ready for her by the end of the day.

Her skin prickled, as if a thousand spiders crawled over it. *It's just a tire. No big deal.*

Remembering her promise to call the South Carolina detective, she fished her cell from her pocket and checked. To her surprise, there were ten messages in her voice-mail box. She didn't recognize any of the numbers. *What the hell?*

She played back the messages. Several from the local American Red Cross about a blood drive, one regarding real estate properties in Franklin, one from the Democratic Party and the other from the Republican Party. There was also one missed call with no message. Was someone giving out her phone number?

Frowning, she dialed the South Carolina number and waited as it rang. On the fourth ring, voice mail picked up again. "This is Leah Carson, former Leah Latimer. I called you a couple of days ago, checking on the status of an old case. Philip Latimer. He was my ex-husband, and his body was found in your county. Could you call me? I have a few questions." She rattled off her number and hung up.

She turned to head back inside when she caught a shift in the shadows. She hesitated, gripping the phone in her hand. A tall man dressed in jeans, a collared shirt, a thick leather jacket, and cowboy boots stepped in her path. He had thick, dark hair, peppered with gray, and a thick mustache. He wore a cowboy hat.

"If you're looking for the clinic, the front entrance is around the corner."

His stare lingered on her long enough to ignite all the alarm bells in her head. "You Leah Carson?"

"Who're you?"

"I'm Tyler Radcliff."

"Deidre's husband."

"That's right. You must be Leah."

"What do you want, Mr. Radcliff?"

A smile twitched the edges of his lips. "Seems kinda strange for you to be calling me mister anything. I mean, with you and Deidre being friends, I bet you discussed all kinds of details about our crumbling marriage."

"Deidre was very private," Leah said. "We didn't talk about you." That wasn't true.

"She didn't have a lot of close friends. We were each other's best friends."

When Philip had been very angry, his voice could be so soft, his words sound so reasonable. In the early days, she'd tried to reason with him. But no matter what she said, the cord holding back his temper always snapped and his words lashed.

"You're not talking."

She took a step back. "I can't help you, Mr. Radcliff."

"Of course you can help me! You were Deidre's friend. Christ, you're the one who found her body."

The image of Deidre lying facedown in her own blood flashed in her mind, and she grimaced. "I've got to get back inside."

"You're done with the morning appointments. I already spoke to the receptionist."

"When did you call her?"

"This morning. I wanted to catch you alone so we could talk." He checked his watch. "You're late. You should have been finished a couple of hours ago. Must have been that hound. She was wrapped in a blue blanket and her owner was holding him close. Looked panicked. Hit by a car?"

The idea that he had been watching the clinic both scared and irritated her. "You were watching the clinic."

"I wanted to talk to you. And you didn't answer your phone."

"You were the unidentified number. You didn't leave a message."

"What I need to say is better said face-to-face."

"I'm not talking to you." Her anger rose as she pulled her phone from her pocket. Philip would have pulled a stunt like this. "I'm going back inside."

He blocked her path. "Not before we talk."

"I don't have anything to say to you." She glanced at the phone and typed in 9-1-1.

"She ripped my heart from my chest."

The agony-laced words also reminded her of Philip. He could make her feel so guilty for not loving him. "I don't know what to say."

His eyes glistened. "You have to know! She was your friend, and I know how women talk."

"We didn't talk."

"That's not true. That's not true."

"I can't help you, Mr. Radcliff."

Large hands fisted and unfisted. "Like hell you can't."

So much for politeness. "I'm calling the cops."

He snarled, "I *am* the cops."

Her gaze rose, her finger suspended over the Send button. Memories of Philip talking and joking with the police after she called leered out from the shadows.

"No one is going to believe you. I'm a good cop with a great record."

"I guess I'll just have to try real hard to convince them you aren't such a good guy."

He advanced toward her. "You'll look like a fool."

"You really think I'm afraid of that?" Ghosts of being stabbed stirred her anger. She wouldn't be bullied by Tyler Radcliff.

As if he read the conviction etched on her face, he doubled down. "They won't believe you."

"Yes, they will."

"Who's gonna take your word over mine?"

Gravel crunched behind Tyler. "Me."

Leah looked past Tyler to see Alex Morgan. Dressed in a dark suit, polished shoes, and a dark overcoat that accentuated broad shoulders. His hands in his pockets, his badge and gun caught the afternoon sunlight.

Tyler turned around. "Morgan, this has nothing to do with you."

"What're you doing here, Radcliff?" His feet planted, he wasn't going anywhere.

"I came to talk to Leah about Deidre. I want to find the bastard who killed my wife."

"It's not your place to talk to Leah or anyone else attached to this case. That's my job."

"No way will I be staying on the sidelines. Deidre was my wife. We might have had our problems, but I'm sure, in the end, we would have worked it out."

Leah studied the tall, broad-shouldered man, wondering if he were lying or simply delusional.

Alex shook his head. "Are you armed?"

"Sure. I always carry."

Alex's hand settled on his gun. The holster strap was unclipped. "Step away now. Let me handle Leah."

"No way, Morgan. Deidre's murderer is my responsibility. I'm her husband."

"If you don't start moving now, I'll lock you up. And that's not going to do anyone any good. I know you've got a tough reelection coming this fall, and I sure would hate to see you lose your job."

"You'd really arrest me?"

"Yes, I would." Conviction strengthened the words as Alex nodded to the gun holstered at Tyler's side.

Tyler clenched and unclenched his hands. "I'm trying to find out who killed my wife."

"I got people working on Deidre's case around the clock. Go home, Tyler. Do yourself a favor and let me handle this. Go home *now*."

Tyler glanced back at Leah, his gaze narrowing. "She knows more than she's saying. I can feel it in my gut."

Leah held Tyler's gaze, her anger over this entire situation rising. "You don't know anything about me."

"Leave," Alex ordered.

Tyler looked back at Alex. "I'll be checking in with you."

"Looking forward to it."

Alex stood his ground, watching as Tyler got in his pickup truck and drove away, the wheels squealing as he accelerated.

She glanced at her phone and the 9-1-1 call she'd never put through. "He told you he had a gun. He told you he's on some kind of hunt. You just let him go."

Alex faced her. "I did."

Emotions burned hotter, and her voice was louder and angrier than she'd intended. "He could have killed Deidre."

He seemed to chew on unspoken words, wondering if he should share his thoughts with her, before he rejected the notion. "I'm not here to talk about Tyler. I'm here to talk about you."

His noncommittal response didn't dampen her temper. She'd guarded her emotions so closely for so long, and now her anger threatened to spill over. "What's that mean?"

"It means I know about your past. I know what Philip Latimer did to you."

Her temper reared, pulled at the leash. "Wow, Deidre's husband is tracking me down and you've dug into my past. That's the kind of thing Philip would have done."

He shoved a hand in his pocket, seeming to chew on a few more less-pleasant words. "I didn't do it out of morbid curiosity. I spoke to Deidre's sister. In our conversation, Philip Latimer's name came up."

"What? She must be wrong. How would Deidre know Philip?"

"Deidre's been a cop with the Nashville Police Department for twelve years."

"I know." Pieces she'd never thought to connect scurried together and locked into place. She thought back to when they'd first met. Deidre had approached her. Deidre had invited her out to coffee. Into the running group. She'd initiated it all. Nausea had her stomach contracting. "She worked with Philip."

"She didn't work with him, but they knew each other."

His tone remained even, unstirred by emotion. "She ever ask about what happened to you four years ago?"

"No. We didn't talk about the past." She rubbed her right thumb over the rough scar on her left palm. Deidre had opened the door to the past a couple of times during a few conversations, but she'd never passed through it. "What do you know?"

"I don't have the whole picture of Deidre's past, but I'm putting it together."

"What do you know about Philip and me?"

"About the attack? I've read everything on record."

"When?"

"Yesterday."

She pressed a trembling finger to her temple. "Why should their past connection matter? Philip was killed in a car crash in South Carolina."

Alex studied her, and she sensed him digging in his heels. "Have you ever read Philip's autopsy report?"

"No. Why would I do that?"

"I've read it. I even had the medical examiner in Nashville review it. I'm not convinced the body was Philip's."

For a split second her head spun. This worst-case scenario moment still invaded her dreams and could bring her out of a sound sleep screaming. "What?"

"I'm not sure he's dead."

Missing keys. Strange charges on her credit card. The flowers. A flat tire. All the random events lined up into a pattern. She clamored to hang on to control and not panic. "I spoke to the officer in South Carolina several times. She told me he was dead."

Alex's cool demeanor didn't waver. "I'd like to have his body exhumed."

"What?" Opening that grave was akin to opening a

wound that had never healed. She feared what unseen poison festered there.

"I want to test the DNA. I'm not convinced it's Latimer in the grave."

Panic gripped her chest. This couldn't be happening. Had she been fooling herself for the last four years? Had he been there all along, watching from the shadows?

"You're his legal wife." His rough tone grated against the words. "You can give me permission."

Tears streamed from her eyes as she shook her head. "I'm *not* his wife."

"Legally, you are."

"He *is* dead."

"Maybe. Maybe not. I could get a court order, but that would take time we don't have. Your anniversary is approaching."

She raised trembling fingers to her forehead. "Do you think he's alive?"

"I don't know. But I know Deidre and Philip worked together. I know he helped her lose evidence in a case involving her sister. Weeks ago she started skimming money. And she was stabbed to death."

"Oh, God. Why kill her?"

"She knew him. Might have helped him escape. Maybe, after all this time, she decided to turn him in to the cops and clear her conscience."

All Deidre's smiles and nice words flashed. Was it all false? Could Deidre have been using her? God, this was her worst nightmare. "I don't want to open Philip's grave. I want this nightmare to go away."

His tone warmed, softened. "Pretending and hoping doesn't fix anything."

She glared at him but heard the truth. Before, she'd prayed he'd stop, but of course he never had considered ending his cruel campaign. Hiding wouldn't stop someone like Philip, who fed on fear. "I'll sign whatever you want me to sign."

"Good." He reached in his pocket and pulled out a neatly folded piece of paper. "Sign this and I'll submit it to the judge."

She took the paper from him and dug a pen from her jacket pocket. Without reading it, she scrawled her name, Leah Carson, the tip of her pen digging deeper into the paper on the last few letters.

He accepted the paper and studied the signature. "Did you change your name back to Carson legally?"

"I did. But of course I had his death certificate. Do you want me to write Latimer?"

He frowned and folded the paper, creasing the edges to sharp points with his fingertips. "No. This should do."

"I pray you're wrong."

"So do I."

She reached for the door handle, anxious to be within the safety of the clinic walls. "Did you know about Deidre's connection to Philip when you asked me out?"

"I knew Deidre was skimming money. I was investigating her. And I knew you were her new best friend. I suspected something but didn't know for sure."

"I thought you just came to check on Tracker."

"My brother Rick agreed to board Tracker here for a few days so I had a reason to meet you."

"I see." She rubbed the scar on her palm. She had to give Alex points for honesty, even if the words cut. "Rick said he hated the idea of boarding the dog."

"He only did it because I asked him to."

As much as she hated truth's bite, she preferred it to Philip's lies. Deidre's lies.

"This bothers you."

"Hurts a little to learn this was part of your job. Took a lot for me to agree to a date."

"I like you. Admire you. That's the truth."

"Truth? Excuse me if I'm skeptical. My people-reading skills are the worst."

"I've never lied to you."

"Just didn't tell me the whole truth."

"When I asked you about the scars, you said it was an accident."

"My past is no one's business."

"And neither are the details of my job. Keeping secrets is a necessity."

Her hand rested on the door handle. "You're right about that." She yanked open the door, disappointment chasing her, as she vanished inside, letting the door slam hard on Alex.

Inside, she leaned against the cold metal door, tense and waiting. She half-expected Alex to bang on the door or circle around and enter through the clinic's front door to say something else to her. He didn't knock or call her name, and that fostered an odd and very troubling sense of loss.

He was a man who liked to win. And she was a piece on the chessboard. Stupid to get attached.

Inside the clinic, a phone rang and a dog barked, but she stayed close to the door until she heard what she thought was the crunch of his footsteps against the gravel. Her breath burning in her chest, she waited longer and then, finally, when she heard the engine, exhaled slowly and carefully.

She wanted Deidre's killer to be found. She wanted the questions about Philip silenced and, God help her, she'd wanted a relationship with Alex.

Life had taught her that wanting didn't always coincide with receiving.

CHAPTER SIXTEEN

Friday, January 20, 4 P.M.

Disappointed with himself, Alex closed the car door and jammed his keys into the ignition. That wasn't the way he'd envisioned this conversation with Leah. He'd known his theories would upset her, but he'd hoped they'd find a way to work together. And he found the pain etched in her features troubling.

Damn. He started the car. He hadn't spun this damn web of lies. That had been Deidre and, perhaps, Philip's doing. His job was to untangle it all.

Alex gripped the wheel. If his theories were correct, he needed to stay on point to protect Leah. Philip Latimer had attacked her, and if he were alive, he would do so again, of that Alex was certain.

God knows, Leah had no reason to trust him, but he wanted her trust. He was on her side. And when he picked a side, like it or not, he was all in.

Leah didn't realize that. She considered talk cheap. Words carried little weight with her. One way or another, he would show her that he was on her side.

He drove to the Nashville Police Department to meet with

Georgia and Deke. The three were to discuss the findings from Deidre's crime scene.

He found Georgia in her lab, her red hair twisted into a topknot as she leaned over a black cotton shirt laid out on a light table. She peered through a magnifying lens suspended over the table with an adjustable arm. With a pair of tweezers, she plucked a hair sample from the shirt's collar and carefully placed it in an evidence bag.

"Is this a bad time?" Alex asked.

Georgia glanced up and smiled. "No. Your timing is perfect, as always. I was just wrapping up with this piece." She carefully refolded the shirt and placed it back in a large evidence bag.

"What's that from?"

"A homicide on the East Side. Looks like a drug buy gone bad. This shirt is from the shooter."

When it came to everyday life, his sister could be scattered, but when it came to work, her focus was laser sharp. "Got time to talk about Deidre's crime scene?"

She pulled off rubber gloves. "I do. We worked that crime scene for two full days, dusting and collecting in the kitchen as well as the entire house."

"So give me what you have." He hitched his hip on the corner of a metal desk.

"As the blood splatter suggested, it all went down in the kitchen." She reviewed the details of the killing.

"So this guy must have been covered in blood."

"Yes. There were bloody footsteps that led to the back door and down the three back porch stairs, but they ended at the grass. Like I said at the crime scene, I'm guessing he was wearing some kind of protective gear."

"This wasn't a random attack."

"Not in my professional opinion. No other signs of blood

or disturbance anywhere else in the area. Though I did find traces of hair on her body, which I've sent off for DNA testing. I can't imagine our killer would go to so much trouble to hide trace evidence and then drop hair, but you never know. I also found semen on her bedsheets that were less than twenty-four hours old. Again, testing for DNA."

"The medical examiner's final report said she had consensual sex within twenty-four hours of dying."

"Fits."

"When will you have the DNA?"

Her cheeks puffed and she blew out a breath. "Couple of weeks, and that's putting a rush on the tests. Then we've got to run it through the databases and see if there's a match."

"Can you test the DNA against one particular individual?"

"The boyfriend or husband?"

"Both. And I'd also like it tested against a guy by the name of Philip Latimer. He was a cop in Nashville who worked with Deidre."

"Where'd you come up with that name?"

"He was Leah Carson's husband." Though they might be legally married, he considered Latimer an ex-husband in every sense of the word when it came to Leah.

Georgia raised an index finger. "I remember that case. He nearly killed his wife. Stabbed her. Many were shocked because he was a decorated officer."

Alex nodded. "Latimer stabbed Leah twenty-three times."

"Like Deidre."

"So it would appear."

Absently, she tugged on a loose strand of hair. "I thought he was dead."

"Supposedly, he died four years ago. And he might very well be dead. I could be wrong."

That coaxed a smile. "I should get that on tape."

He stared at her.

"Brother, you're not wrong. You figure stuff the rest of us don't."

"DNA will move this theory to fact."

"I'll see what can be rushed." She glanced at her case file. "I also found a footprint by the back door in the grass. He must have stopped to remove his protective suit and booties. Shifting weight to one leg left the imprint."

"What kind of shoe?"

"A sports shoe. Judging by the tread, a cross trainer. Men's size thirteen."

"A big guy." Like Philip. But also like Tyler and David. Deke entered the room, his face darkened by a scowl.

"Georgia was just getting me up to speed on the evidence in Deidre's case," Alex said.

"Have you heard our brother's crazy theory?" Georgia asked.

Deke sighed. "Which one?"

Georgia gave him the rundown.

Deke shook his head, but he didn't laugh off the explanation. "Deidre's connection to Philip would explain the missing money. Back from the dead, he no doubt needed money, and what better source than Deidre. Might also explain Deidre's old business card, which we found near the John Doe."

Alex held up a hand. "Let Georgia run her DNA, then we'll get into how crazy this sounds. Leah has also signed a consent form so I can open Latimer's grave."

"That's going to take time."

"I know. But I filed the papers."

"Fair enough." He opened the manila folder in his hand. "I just received Deidre's cell and home phone information.

It came in late last night, and instead of sending it over, I decided to just go through it."

Alex struggled with a jab of annoyance. Big brother taking command again. It had been an argument they'd had before, but now wasn't the time to revive it. "And what did you find?"

"Deidre's burner phone received a dozen calls from three different numbers that lasted anywhere from three to five minutes. The calls started about six weeks ago. All from burners."

"Three different people?"

"Maybe. Maybe it was one person who didn't want to be traced."

"Like a dead guy."

"That would fit."

The skin on the back of Alex's neck tingled. DNA or no, he was right about Latimer. "What about her official cell phone? Any calls on that show up as unusual?"

"An interesting calling pattern there as well. Over the last months, she received two dozen calls from pay phones. All at random times. No patterns. None of the calls lasted more than a few seconds."

"Someone was harassing her or keeping tabs on her?"

"One or the other. The calls stopped abruptly about four weeks ago."

"What about Radcliff's number? I caught him harassing Leah Carson today. Stands to reason he'd be harassing a soon-to-be ex-wife. Did his number show up on her records?"

"Several times, but all the calls were made during normal business hours. Any attorney could argue they were reasonable."

"Radcliff's smart enough not to leave an electronic trail.

He's got that reelection campaign this year, and he doesn't want to screw it up with stalking charges."

Deke closed his file, his scowl darkening. "Why the hell would Radcliff go after Leah?"

"Leah knew Deidre from the running group, and the two had a budding friendship. Radcliff thinks Leah knows more about Deidre's personal life than she's letting on."

"Does she?"

"I think she's told us what she knows about her."

Georgia folded her arms over her chest. "I hear a *but* in there."

Alex rose, shifting his stance. "No but. She's open about Deidre. It's her own past she guards closely."

"Do you blame her?" Georgia challenged. "She was married to a monster. She's likely carrying some guilt and shame."

"Why?"

Georgia flicked a loose strand of hair from her eyes as if it were an annoying bug. "How long were they married?"

"Not very long."

"My guess is that Latimer didn't go postal on her all at once. I bet he slowly turned up the heat and she kept taking it. She's ashamed she kept taking it. I know I would be."

Deke nodded. "I saw the scars on her hands."

Georgia drummed her fingers against her arms. "She was stabbed, and then she finds a friend stabbed. God, she must be freaking out at the idea that Latimer is still alive."

"She was spooked." Alex rarely second-guessed himself, but he again wondered if he should have dumped such explosive theories in her lap and simply left.

"My attacker was killed two years ago," Georgia said. "I still have nightmares, and I sure don't like to talk about it. I can't imagine what she's feeling."

Deke seared his sister with his gaze. "You're sharing all your worries with your therapist, right?"

Georgia wrinkled her nose. "I don't like her."

Alex faced his sister. "I don't like a lot of things, but that doesn't mean I don't do them. You still seeing her?"

A sigh leaked through clenched teeth. "Yes. I see her. I just don't like it."

Deke studied her a beat longer, clearly determining if he should believe her. "So, when are you going to share with us?"

She laughed. "Never."

Alex twisted his gold cuff link. "Why not?"

"You two aren't the warm and fuzzy types."

"Would you tell Rachel?" Deke asked. Rachel had lived the nightmare with Georgia, nearly died with her, and, in the end, saved her.

Georgia shrugged. "She and I talk."

Deke's gaze softened. "I didn't know that."

"Exactly. By the way, I think she wants to marry you. She's scared of giving up her independence, but if you ask again, I bet she says yes."

Deke's gaze sharpened. "How do you know?"

She shot him a look.

"Right. Thanks."

"Anytime. But don't screw this one up, Deke. I like Rachel."

Deke grunted. "So do I."

Georgia snapped her fingers, as if suddenly remembering. "That John Doe who was shot and burned. Ballistics just came back. The bullet that killed him was fired from the nine-millimeter Beretta you found at the scene."

Alex rubbed a thumb and index finger together as he thought. "Left the murder weapon at the site. Why?"

Georgia shrugged. "That's your gig, bro."

Deke looked at Alex. "I'm calling the lab and doing some leaning regarding the DNA on that victim as well."

"Lean away, brother," Alex said.

"Show them who's boss, bro," Georgia coaxed.

"Smart-ass." Clutching his file, Deke left.

Georgia leveled her gaze on Alex. "I thought you kinda liked Leah."

Alex studied his sister, unwilling to admit to any feelings. "What makes you say that?"

"I know you well enough. You wouldn't have asked her out just for a case."

He didn't answer.

She shook her head. "Alex, I've no doubt you can lock away the emotions and do your job, but you need to be careful. One day you're going to look for the key to those emotions and you won't be able to find it."

Thoughts of Philip stalked Leah all afternoon as she finished her afternoon appointments by five. She moved to the front desk, where a large tabby cat named Felix lounged. He was Dr. Nelson's cat and visited from time to time.

Leah scratched Felix between the ears and handed the last chart to Gail as an elderly couple with a fifteen-year-old terrier left through the back door. Glancing out the window, she searched the lot for any signs of a car that didn't belong or a person who stood a little too long in one spot. She saw nothing.

Gail accepted the chart. "How is Misty doing?"

Leah could almost hear the wheels in her head screeching and groaned as she forced her thoughts to change direction.

"Surprisingly well. The Smiths are committed to giving her insulin shots each day and keeping her on a modified diet."

"They do love that dog. I've been here ten years and remember when they brought her in as a puppy. They lost their son last year and I think losing Misty is just too much for them right now."

"I can't imagine losing a child." She smoothed her hand to her flat belly. Philip had talked about having a baby often. Though she hadn't had the strength to leave at first, she'd known for damn certain bringing a child into the mix would be dead wrong.

As the Smiths drove off, she spotted a black truck parked in the lot of the strip mall across the street. The windows were tinted, making it impossible for her to see inside. Had the truck she'd seen at the park have tinted windows? That was the kind of thing she should remember. Details were important when she documented her days in her journal.

Gail's dark brows rose and she rested a hand on her full hip. "You've never had a pet?"

Leah pulled her gaze from the truck. "I had a black Lab as a kid. She was a great dog. She died right before I left for college."

"That's a long time ago. I'd think by now you'd be ready for another dog. You know Dr. Nelson would be fine with you bringing it to work."

"I know. And maybe I will one day." She'd avoided pets since Philip. She'd feared what he'd do to it if she had one. And now Alex thought Philip could be alive. Shit. She couldn't dare risk loving anything now.

"A few new kittens arrived. All strays. Six or seven weeks and very cute. They're in the kennel in the back."

Knowing she wouldn't take any of them, she said, "I'll check them out."

"While you're back there, have a look at the post-op cases. We have the broken leg, two neuters, and a female Dr. Nelson is going to spay in the morning. The owner dropped the dog off while you were in surgery. She's sweet, and I know she could use a walk."

"Sure. I'll have a look." Leah headed back to the kennel, where she found her patients. Most were still dazed from surgery and lying in the corners of their cages. The dog, however, saw her, barked, and tucked its tail.

Leah moved to the cage and, taking a leash from the wall, opened the cage and took it from the wall. She checked the dog's chart. "Charlie, how're you doing?"

The dog's tail relaxed at the sound of her name but she kept barking. Laughing, Leah hooked the leash to the dog's collar and took her out the back door. "You don't have anything to worry about, Charlie."

The afternoon air was warmer, the sun bright, but a snap of cold in the air triggered a shiver. She led the dog to a patch of grass behind the clinic. The dog sniffed and calmly looked up at her.

Leah shivered. "Come on, girl, let's get the job done. I'm not wearing a fur coat."

The dog wagged her tail and then dropped on her hind legs to pee.

"Bless you."

To give the dog extra exercise, she led her around the front of the building. She glanced toward the parking lot and noticed that the black truck was gone. "It was a damn truck in a parking lot. You don't need to freak out because it had tinted windows. Alex is wrong. Philip is dead."

The dog looked up at her and wagged her tail.

Leah shrugged. "Dog, if you got to know me better, you'd realize I worry about everything. I write down all the crazy details of my day because I can't stop worrying."

The dog cocked her head.

She knelt down and rubbed the dog between the ears. The dog licked her face and she laughed. Moments like this, she'd give anything to cut Philip from her past. She wished she could go back in time and be distracted just long enough so that their first meeting never took place. She wished.

Leah rose and guided the dog back in the front door, welcoming the heat. She took Charlie back to her crate, filled her food and water bowls, and patted her on the head before she closed the crate.

She spent the next half hour examining the other patients, who were all recovering nicely.

It was after six by the end of her shift. Gail had closed the front office, shut off the lights, and locked the front door. Alone in the clinic, Leah shoved aside a feeling of unease. Her skin prickled and her belly tightened, as if someone was staring at her. Watching from the shadows, like Philip used to do.

She went into her office, checked her cell phone, and immediately noticed she'd received a voice mail from the South Carolina detective. Her nerves jangled as she checked the message. "Mrs. Latimer." The moniker had her gritting her teeth. "I've been traveling and just got your voice mail message today. Your husband's death investigation was an open-and-shut case. We have no reason to reopen it. I received an inquiry from a TBI agent and forwarded my files to him. Again, we ruled this an open-and-shut case."

Leah waited, expecting a "Call me if you need more information" or "I'm here to answer your questions." Neither came. Clearly, the detective had better things to do than answer her questions.

Leah sat down in her darkened office and replayed the message. Nervous energy snapped through her as she tried to imagine, if Philip were alive, where he would be. If he'd been alive these last four years, she'd had no sign of him, or any real hint that he was out there stalking her. The creepy, tingling kind of feeling she used to get when he stalked her had returned a couple of weeks ago, but she'd chalked it up to nerves, a new home, even the New Year's resolutions that forced her out of her comfort zone. There'd been plenty of reasons for it not to be Philip.

Unable to sit, she rose and grabbed her coat and purse. Keys in hand, she left by the back door, which locked behind her. She crossed the parking lot, glancing into the deep, dark shadows and the backseat of her car before she slid inside, and immediately locked the doors. She switched on the ignition and started driving. The idea of going home to darkness and solitude triggered more tension, so she opted to drive to the mall, full of bright lights and people.

She parked in a well-lit spot and hurried through the cold. She entered through the food court and was immediately drawn to a table of teenage girls who were laughing over a pizza and Cokes. Near them, a mother fed her two toddlers chicken nuggets, while several tables over, an elderly couple ate Chinese food.

The normalcy of it all surprised her. These people appeared to be going on with their lives, unaware that monsters like Philip Latimer lived in their world. A part of her wanted to scream a warning to them all. Philip had done a good job of toying with her sanity and making her question every creak, shadow, and bump in the night. But to behave like a crazy person now would do her no good. She held her silence.

She moved to a vendor and ordered a hot tea and a cookie. After paying for both, she chose a seat backed up against a wall in the center of the food court. She sipped her tea, watching a young couple saunter past. Their hands were linked, and the girl leaned into the boy as if she drew energy from him. She found herself searching the young girl's bare arms, neck, and face for bruises. When she saw none, her utter cynicism struck her. She'd been hoping for a new way of living and thinking, and in the blink of one conversation, she'd regressed four years.

She reached in her purse and pulled out her journal. Carefully, she began to detail the day. She recorded the incident with Tyler Radcliff and Alex, and of course the latter's theory about Philip. The craving for a cigarette rose up in her, so sharp and strong she wondered if there was a drugstore nearby. She caught herself before she went hunting for one.

Philip, you're not going to keep ruining my life. You're not.

Curling and flexing her fingers, she reached for her phone and dialed the South Carolina detective's number. Yep, she was officially a nag when it came to the whereabouts of Philip Latimer, but she figured she'd earned the right. Though the one-hour time difference between Nashville and Greenville ensured she wouldn't reach a live person, she made the call regardless. Ranting at a voice mail would work for tonight. After the phone rang and she waited for the away message and the beep, she said, "This is Leah Carson. I dropped the Latimer name years ago. I would like a call back in the morning regarding Philip Latimer's case. I would like to discuss the details of his accident. So give me the courtesy of a return call in the morning or I'll be contacting your supervisor." She hung up, her face flushed with frustration and a bit of worry over her tone.

Leah rose, slung her purse over her shoulder, and grabbed her tea and cookie. But instead of heading home right away, she headed toward the crowds.

"Leah Carson."

Leah stiffened just for a moment at the sound of the voice. She turned to find Alex Morgan standing just feet from her. "Alex."

"What brings you here?"

"Just grabbing a bite to eat." She found herself smiling. "I wasn't interested in going home. You don't strike me as a mall rat."

"God, no. I come here only when I must." He held up a bag from a sports store. "I needed new running shoes."

"Plausible, but I don't buy it."

"Why not?"

"I've been stalked before. I'm not the most trusting person."

His gaze held steady. "Shoes really don't last long when you're training. A few months at best." He leaned forward a fraction. "No more signs of Tyler Radcliff?"

"No. No signs. I'm hoping he was just venting his anger and grief."

"Anything else catch your attention?"

"You mean like my dead husband coming back to stalk me?"

"Exactly."

If she weren't so scared, she'd laugh. "No. And he wouldn't be that careless. He was clever and knew how to turn up the heat without it blowing back on him."

Alex frowned. "Why do you think he'd lay low for four years?"

"He was scared. Found someone else to stalk. Was bored. I don't pretend to understand him."

"If you had to pin one reason down?"

"He'd hate the idea of prison. He might still want me dead, but he wouldn't want to pay the price." She shook her head, running a trembling hand over her head. "And I think he might have been fine to leave me be as long as I stayed in the shadows. My life was fairly isolated in Knoxville. Now I'm back in Nashville. I have a good job. Friends. And I had a date; just one, but a date. He would hate that. Hate it."

"You think another date would upset him?"

"It would."

"Then let's have dinner."

She studied him. "This business or pleasure, Agent?"

He smiled. "Pleasure. But I won't lie. If I can catch a bad guy, that's icing on the cake."

"You're honest, I'll give you that. I'll take you up on the date after this is over. Then we'll know for sure it's pleasure."

He nodded. "Do you have my phone number in your phone?"

"I do."

"Good. Don't hesitate to call."

"You'll get the first call if a crazed man with a knife appears." The morbid joke undercut some of the fear.

"You have a ride to the running group tomorrow?"

"I can drive myself." She rose. "So, are you going to follow me around until Philip's status is resolved?"

He stood and moved closer until she could feel the energy radiating from his body. "Yes."

She studied him, trying to gauge the depth of his

commitment. One thing to say you'd help, it's another to do it. "If you've done your digging, you know our anniversary is January twenty-fifth."

"Yes."

"He'd see a certain symmetry in killing me on our wedding anniversary."

"I know."

"So what do we do?"

"For the next few days either I or one of my men will shadow you."

"This is the part where I tell you not to worry about me. I'm supposed to declare I can take care of myself. But I'm not going to do that. Follow me all you want."

He took her arm with his hand and gently tugged her toward him until only a sliver of space separated them. He leaned his head forward to kiss her. Fear and excitement gripped her, but she held steady. Despite everything, she wanted this. Wanted to know what he tasted like.

He tilted his head and pressed his lips to hers. She raised her hand to his arm, and her fingers gripped the folds of his jacket. The kiss, tentative at first, grew a bit more insistent. She rose on her tiptoes but resisted the urge to wrap her arm around his neck. In the distance, she heard young girls giggling at their display. That thought led to another . . . was Philip watching?

She pulled back, moistening her lips with her tongue. For an instant, her voice seemed to have fluttered away and she couldn't speak. She cleared her throat. "Was that business, too?"

Alex traced the line of her lip with his thumb before allowing his hand to drop possessively to her shoulder. His touch sent shivers through her body. "Definitely pleasure."

* * *

He wasn't a fan of the mall. He didn't like the crowds or the noise. So much going on that it could overwhelm the senses. But Leah was here, so he followed. While she ate her cookie, he treated himself to a hamburger and fries across from her. A group of giggling girls at the table beside him had him remembering the first time he'd seen his wife.

She'd been with a group of her friends, and though some of the other girls were pretty, his gal had stood out to him like a beacon. He'd known from the moment he'd seen her that he wanted her. And so he'd set about following her. Not in a creepy, malicious way. He didn't want to scare her. But he'd made a point of figuring out the places she liked, and he managed to be there. Soon he'd had her schedule down pat, so it became only a matter of time before they bumped into each other.

Now, as he watched Leah kiss this man, old memories soured. Leah, like Deidre, was a fickle creature. They were users. One marriage ended and they moved on to the next.

He balled up his napkin and threw it on the remnants of the burger and fries. As tempted as he was to attack her tonight, he quieted the desire. *Move with patience and care. Slow and steady wins the race.*

She'd have seen the dog by now. No way she couldn't love that damn dog. Hell, he almost missed the mutt who'd stared at him with dopey, adoring eyes.

He rose and spotted another couple talking. The man clearly was attracted to the woman and the woman, though tentative, clearly liked him, too. A stab of envy sliced through him, and he knew, despite his slow and steady mantra, he'd get a pound of someone's flesh soon.

CHAPTER SEVENTEEN

Saturday, January 21, 8 A.M.

A flat tire was the last thing David needed. He rushed out of his apartment across the lot, and when he spotted the tire he swore.

David was running late for work. The morning run had gone long and he'd lingered at the coffee shop after that, flirting with the redhead who worked behind the bar. And now the damn tire was flat and he not only had briefs to file that morning, he had to make an appearance in court. With the cops asking him questions, he didn't need any more trouble.

He fished his cell out of his pocket, ready to call AAA, when he saw the truck pull up behind him and the driver roll down the window. "You need a hand?"

David nodded, praising his dumb luck. "Hell yes, man. There's fifty bucks in it for you."

Grinning, the man leaned on the steering wheel. Rolled-up sleeves revealed tattooed forearms. "I'll have it changed for you in ten minutes."

"That's great," David said. "This flat was such bad timing."

"Isn't it always?"

The driver got out and moved to the back of his truck.

From a built-in silver toolbox, he removed a jack and a tire iron. "You look like you're in a rush."

David glanced up from his cell, already distracted, and reminded himself to be nice. He needed this guy. "I am. So much to get done, and now this. I'm lucky you happened along."

"Lucky is right. I'd just finished my shift and was headed home."

David's halfhearted interest in conversation hummed behind his need for quick help with the tire. "You live in this area?"

"Not too far from here." The driver jacked up the car and quickly and easily removed the lug nuts. Soon, the flat tire was off and the spare from the trunk seated on the hub.

Be friendly. Make conversation. He didn't have time for AAA. "Do you think I picked up a nail?"

"Naw, man. Someone sliced the tire."

"What?"

The driver ran a finger along a neat, clean slice. "Right here. You must have pissed someone off."

That had him sliding the phone back in his pocket. "Why do you say that?"

A grin tugged at his full lips. "You see any other flat tires in the lot?"

David glanced around and realized he was the only one with the issue. Shit. *Had* he pissed someone off? If not for Deidre's death, he'd never have clung to worry. A first glance at the driver's badge gave him a name: Brian. Brian was his only ally on this cold, shitty morning.

"Brian, I appreciate the help."

Strong, callused hands screwed on the lug nuts before he reached for the tire iron. "No worries, man."

"You from Nashville?"

"I'm new to Nashville. Been here a few weeks. How about you? You been here long?"

"All my life." He watched as Brian finished. A little more small talk. "I'm an attorney."

"I figured you were some kind of hotshot. Nice suit."

David caught the man's grin, his tone more teasing. He fished fifty bucks from his pocket as Brian lowered the jack. When David opened the trunk, Brian loaded the flat tire in the trunk bed.

Closing the trunk with a hard slam, Brian took a rag from his back pocket and wiped the grease from his hands and the trunk hood. "You're good to go."

David handed over the cash. "Thanks, man. I really do appreciate it."

Brian pocketed the money. "The extra cash will come in handy. Just bought a necklace for my wife and spent a little more than I should've." He grinned. "Happy wife, happy life."

"No truer words, Brian."

"You got a wife?"

"We're separated. Trying to work it out."

A slow, thoughtful nod conveyed understanding. "That's rough. My wife and I are separated, too. But we're getting back together. Made it through the fire, so to speak."

David had no desire to rekindle the flame with his wife. He liked being single. Playing the field. "Nothing better than a solid marriage."

"Ain't that a fact."

The tire change complete, David's interest skittered back to the office. He opened his car door. "Thanks again, man. I appreciate the help."

Brian flashed a wide grin. "Glad I could help."

* * *

He watched David drive away, proud of himself for not killing him. Today, at least. It would have been easy to jab a knife in his gut, watch him fall to his knees, and bleed out in the parking lot. It sure had been easy enough to slice his tire.

Sliding his hands in his pockets, he fingered the pocketknife he'd jabbed in the tire hours ago. But killing David wasn't part of the plan. Yet.

Minutes past eight, Deke made his way down the narrow, rocky path that led to the river and the two forensic technicians working the scene. Georgia was on the job today, wearing a thick black skullcap, heavy coveralls that read FORENSICS on the back, and thick, steel-toed boots. She held a digital camera to her eye and focused on a numbered yellow cone placed next to what looked like a severed hand. The other tech, Brad Holcombe, was a tall slim guy with blond hair. He also wore a thick black skullcap. Dark plastic gloves covered his hands.

"Georgia," he said.

"Give me a minute, Deke." She snapped a couple more rapid-fire photos and then turned to Brad, who held a clipboard in his hand. "You got that marked on your area map?"

He was in his early thirties, but all traces of the fresh-faced guy who'd joined the force five years earlier had vanished. The job had aged him. "I do."

"Great. Take five. Drink hot coffee. I'll finish up here."

Brad tossed Georgia a grateful grin. "Thanks."

She faced Deke. Her nose glowed red from the cold. "Great way to start a day."

He thought about the warm bed he'd left, in which he'd been nestled close to Rachel. She'd accepted his ring last night, and he'd been filled with hope and joy. He'd had very different plans for this morning, but the job had its own ideas. "I can think of better."

"Join the club."

"I see a hand."

She nodded and pointed. "A hand there. Near the river's edge a foot, and a few yards west is another hand. And there's no torso or head. But then, I hear you found a torso a few days ago."

"Stands to reason we have a matched set, but we shall see. Any idea who the guy might be?"

She sniffed, her nose runny from the cold. "Not a clue. But these cold-as-hell temperatures have kept the remains intact, and I was able to pull a clean print from the index finger. Who knows, our guy might have prints on file."

"Anything you can tell me about him?"

"He had calluses on his palms, and the foot was still encased in sneakers. Nothing remarkable about the shoe. The thumb looked as if it had been broken a long time ago."

"Any idea how he was killed?"

"Not a clue. That's for the lovely Dr. Heller to decipher."

"If he's a match to our John Doe in the morgue, it was a gunshot to the chest."

"That will do it."

Deke moved down the edge of the river and studied the yellow cone that marked the spot where the other hand lay. Even in the cold it had already degraded and could easily have been overlooked as not human. "Was he in the water?"

"I'd say so. My guess is the parts were first tossed into a bag and then into the river. Everyone thinks the river will keep their secrets, but it doesn't take much for the bag to tear and its contents to float to the top. Head is likely out there somewhere."

"If these parts connect to my body, why leave it exposed in one location and dump the hands and feet in the river?"

She shrugged. "Maybe our killer likes a puzzle."

The torso. The bag with Deidre's card. Now the hands and a foot. Felt more like a trail of bread crumbs.

"How long has he been out here?"

"That's hard to say. Cold distorts everything. Maybe the prints will match a missing persons report."

He grinned. "Thanks for the tip."

"Always here to help, bro."

He rose, his joints creaking as he straightened. "Don't know what I'd do without you."

She raised a gloved hand and gave him a thumbs-up. "Keep me posted on what the medical examiner says. This one is a curiosity."

"Will do."

Leah didn't sleep well the night before. Alex had followed her home from the mall, and as he pulled away, a police cruiser had parked in front of her town house. Two hours later, when she saw another set of headlights flash through her window, she'd risen and peeked through the curtain. Another cop car arrived, the officers spoke, and then the first car drove away, leaving the new guy to babysit.

Fatigue itched her eyes as she arrived at the clinic early to walk the dogs. She and Dr. Nelson traded shifts, and today was her day on. They had three patients in the kennel: a cat that had been injured in a fight, the dog that had been hit by the car, and the black dog, the spay from yesterday.

The black dog, the healthiest of the three, barked and wagged her tail when Leah entered the kennel. The cat meowed and the dog with the broken leg looked up at her, then went back to sleep. Dr. Nelson had told her the dog remained on heavy painkillers and would be slow for a few more days. The good news was, he was going home today.

She moved to the black dog's cage, smiling as she got closer. The dog, Charlie, barked, clearly excited to see her. She grabbed a leash from the rack by the back door and opened the dog's crate. The young dog bounded out of the cage and into Leah's arms. Laughing, she quickly slipped a collar and leash around its neck and led her out back. Despite the cold, the dog barked and jumped, grateful to be free. She quickly took care of her business. Leah, pleased with the dog's quick recovery, took her around the parking lot, letting her sniff and dig in the dirt before the cold forced her back inside.

While Charlie watched, she cleaned out the dog's crate and set fresh food and water in there for her. The dog eagerly went back into the crate and ate.

Leah closed the crate door and checked the dog's chart. No complications. No issues. So why hadn't the owner returned for her?

By the time Leah had cleaned out the cages and fed the other animals, Gail arrived.

"So what's with the Lab?" Leah couldn't hide her interest. "Where's the owner?"

"I don't know. I called three times yesterday and never got an answer. I don't know if there's a problem, or maybe he decided the bill was too much for him."

Leah frowned. This dog wouldn't be the first abandoned at the vet when a bill couldn't be paid. "That's too bad."

"From what Dr. Nelson said, the guy was a little odd. On the way in and out, he kept looking around the clinic, as if he were searching for something."

"Like what?" Vet clinics had to be careful of drug thefts; many of the meds they used were stored on-site.

"I don't know. But I double-checked the medicine supply room and made sure it was locked before I left each day."

"Give me his number and I'll call him."

Gail moved to the front office and dug the number from a file in the active clients bin.

Leah took the phone and dialed. The phone rang once, twice, and then, on the third ring, she got a message: "This is Brian. I can't take your call right now, but leave a number. I'll call back."

Leah listened to the deep voice, half-searching for traces of Philip's voice, but found none. "Brian, this is Dr. Carson at the Nelson Animal Hospital. We have your dog here and she's ready to go home. Would you come by today, or better yet, call us this morning so we'll know when to expect you." She rattled off the number and hung up. "We'll see if that gets results."

"Like I said, I left three messages for the guy and he's yet to call me back."

"Just seems odd." Black dogs were common but this one reminded her of a dog she once wanted when she was married to Philip. The owner vanishes. Dogs and cats were abandoned by pet owners all the time. But none of this felt ordinary.

As Leah left the voice-mail message, he sat in front of his computer, watching a live feed of her standing in the office of the vet hospital. She'd washed her hair and dried it, leaving it to hang loose and full around her face. He'd always loved the touch of her hair after it had been freshly washed and dried. So soft. He wondered if Leah's hair smelled of roses or honeysuckle.

He replayed the message on his cell phone and listened

to her voice. She was sexy. Hot. And he couldn't wait until they stood face-to-face.

It's just a matter of time before you take that dog. A matter of time. I picked her because I knew you'd want her. Take the dog, Leah; you know you want it.

He glanced at the calendar. Their anniversary was in four days and he'd bring this little adventure to an end. He touched his fingertip to the screen and traced it over the curve of her jaw and along the column of her neck.

He rose from the desk and moved to the closet, where a simple white dress hung. She'd left it behind when she'd left him, but he'd kept it, savoring and hating the memories they'd shared.

He heard footsteps and glanced at the ceiling above. Shutting off the screen, he climbed the stairs and padded to the back bedroom, where a naked woman searched for her clothes.

"Leaving so soon?" he asked.

She turned and smiled. "Got work this morning, baby."

Dark mascara smudged under her eyes and her cheeks looked hollow, her skin sallow in the morning light. Last night, in the bar, she'd reminded him of Leah just a little.

Still, seeing her naked, with the sound of Leah's voice still echoing in his head, he got hard. Smiling, he moved toward her and traced a hand along her collarbone. He'd sliced his knife along Deidre's collarbone exactly there just days ago.

"You have a few minutes, don't you?"

She smiled. "You never told me your name."

"It's Brian." He laid his palm at the base of her throat. So easy to cut into the tender flesh of the neck.

She took his hand in hers and led him toward the bed. And soon he was inside her. As he moved, he closed his eyes and pictured Leah. So small. So petite and, soon, all his once again.

CHAPTER EIGHTEEN

Saturday, January 21, 3 P.M.

Leah finished her shift at three. Before leaving, she went into the kennel to check on the black dog, who immediately sat up and wagged her tail. The cat had been picked up, and so had the dog hit by the car. All had been happy, tearful reunions that had made her smile.

But there'd been no call from Charlie's owner today, and she'd begun to wonder if he was returning. People faced with a vet bill did abandon their animals at the clinic. She stared at the dog. The dog stared back, doleful eyes, wagging tail.

She threaded her fingers through the bars and let the dog lick her fingers. Something inside her softened. Released. Taking the dog was a huge risk. So much could happen. "When you look at me, you know you're breaking my heart." No one wanted to take Charlie to the shelter, and Gail was talking about placing an ad.

"You're a sweet girl, Charlie." The dog barked and wagged her tail faster.

More ice melted and fell away from her heart. Warmth spread, and the sensation scared the hell out of her. Unshed tears stung the back of her eyes. She'd be wise to keep her distance from the dog. Better for everyone. Too easy for her to love and too easy for Philip to destroy.

The dog licked Leah's hand and wagged her tail. Ignoring her better judgment, she opened the cage, and the dog bounded up to her, nuzzling close. The dog smelled musty and would need a bath when her stitches healed, but that was easily done. She imagined all the supplies she'd need for a dog.

Suddenly, the idea of returning to a solitary home saddened her. Half-living, her aunt had once said. Her husband's knife blade had nearly taken her life, and fear tried to steal it now.

Defiance burned bright. "Charlie. I like the name Charlie even though you are a girl. Do you think you want to stick with that?" The dog nudged her fingers. "I can't make you any promises, but we could try one night. How's that? Your owner might call, or you just might hate living with me. I'm a bit of a neurotic."

The dog barked.

She went to a wall of collars and chose a red one that might be the right size and slipped it around Charlie's neck. The dog barked with excitment. *This can't be a good idea.*

She hooked a leash on the dog's collar, and with her purse slung over her shoulder, the two headed out the back door. After a quick spin around the parking lot, she loaded up on a few basic supplies to get them through the night and they got in her car. Charlie settled in the passenger seat, clearly staking a claim.

Because of her early morning call, she'd missed her run, and as tempted as she was to go to the gym, she understood it really wouldn't be possible tonight with Charlie. The dog would need her full attention tonight. As they drove through the city streets, she detailed all the reasons why this was such a bad idea. Expense. Time. Commitment. Philip.

To hell with Philip.

Brave words and a promise of one night with Charlie didn't erase four years of fear and hiding. Suddenly, doubt elbowed past the newfound confidence, and she scrambled for second guesses.

Instead of driving home, she drove to the counseling center. Maybe Sierra would be there.

With Charlie in tow, she climbed the concrete stairs and entered the front door. The dog jumped and barked. She knelt to calm her. "You're going to have to learn a few things about manners, Charlie. No barking."

The dog cocked her head and then licked Leah's face.

And in that moment, her heart was gone, taken by a dopey expression and a wet kiss.

Footsteps sounded, and Leah looked up to see Sierra peeking out of an office door. "Leah, what're you doing here?" She saw the dog and grinned. "And who's this?"

"This is my big mistake. Charlie."

Sierra watched Charlie lick Leah's face. "Why's this your big mistake?"

Leah scrambled for reasons. "I'm not being fair to the dog."

Sierra knelt in front of Charlie and rubbed her between the ears. The dog fell to the ground and rolled to her back. "She's sweet."

Leah held tight to the leash as she assembled logical reasons. "Caring is a very dangerous thing."

"Why's that?"

"Caring led to a lot of pain and suffering the last time I really opened my heart." Emotion tightened her throat. "And I'm terrified of making that kind of mistake again."

Sierra laughed when the dog's tail thumped with pleasure. "This is a dog. Not a husband."

"I worked hard to build the brick wall around me. Real hard." Fear caught her voice in her throat. "And now it's crumbling around my feet. And I'm really afraid that Philip might be back."

Sierra kept her gaze on the dog. "Why do you think that?"

"Someone sent me flowers and wished me happy anniversary. I had a flat tire the other day. My credit card got messed up." She shook her head. "And a TBI agent thinks Philip might be alive."

A frown wrinkled Sierra's brow as she scratched the dog between the ears again. "Does he have proof of that?"

"Not yet. But I wouldn't bet against it."

"Why?"

"Apparently, the identification wasn't as ironclad as I thought."

"You're sure?"

"I'm not sure of anything, but the cops want to exhume his body. I signed a release form. They want to make sure the man in the grave is Philip."

Sierra rose, adjusting the bracelets on her wrist. "How do you feel about this?"

"Terrified. And angry. I want answers."

A smile quirked her lips. "You sound like you want to face this head-on. That's good. When are they going to do the exhumation?"

"A judge has to sign the order. It could be days. Long after our anniversary." She tipped her head back so that the blooming tears wouldn't spill. As brave as she tried to sound, she was scared.

Sierra twisted a silver ring on her index finger. "The cops could be wrong."

Leah shook her head. She didn't need hard evidence to know the truth. "They think Philip might have killed Deidre."

"What?"

"She was stabbed twenty-three times. Like me."

"Leah, why would he go after her?"

"She knew Philip from before. They had some kind of connection." She rubbed her palms together, the rough scars scraping against each other. For the better part of the day, her skin had itched and crawled, as if someone was standing over her shoulder. "He's so clever."

Sierra didn't say anything.

"You and I both know cops can drop the ball. Men get released from prison, return to a city, and no one tells the victim. Mistakes are made in small localities. Easy to misidentify a badly burned body. Whatever the mistake, the stalker kills the victim and then everyone wonders how it all could have gone so wrong. I don't want to be the one people talk about one day and say 'If we'd only known.'"

Sierra cleared her throat. "So you're going to live in fear for the rest of your life?"

The challenge irritated her. "I didn't say that."

"What *are* you saying?"

"I want to live my life."

Sierra smiled. "You've got a dog. I bet this little lady will alert you if anyone gets close to your house."

Leah rubbed the dog on the head. "I haven't decided whether I'm going to keep her."

"You might not have decided, but Charlie has."

CHAPTER NINETEEN

Sunday, January 22, 5 A.M.

Charlie had a surprisingly good night with Leah, making it all the way until five A.M. until she needed a walk. Leah pulled on sweats, a thick T-shirt, sheepskinned boots, and a heavy coat as Charlie barked. "I'm coming. I'm coming."

Her neighbor, a short woman with long, brown hair, waved. The woman owned a pug, but her name escaped Leah. She waved back. Charlie barked.

As she walked the dog toward the corner, she noticed the police car parked across the street. It was there for her protection, but it was a reminder of Philip and the dangerous days ahead.

After the walk, she was energized and ready for a morning run, but when she thought of leaving Charlie alone in her house while she ran, she considered the consequences. "A new dog alone in a town house is a recipe for chewed shoes," she said as she cupped the dog's face. "Or maybe I'll find a shredded comforter." The dog licked her face and wagged its tail.

"I know you look all innocent now, but I trust you as far as I can throw you. We're buying a crate today."

While Charlie chewed on a toy she'd scavenged from the clinic, Leah quickly showered and dressed. Breakfast was a toasted bagel while Charlie munched on dry food. By seven thirty the two were headed out the front door back to the clinic. Charlie, unaccustomed to walking on a leash, pulled her all the way across the lawn and, when they reached her car, circled her several times, wrapping the leash around her legs. Laughing, Leah unlocked the car and carefully unwound the leash. She picked up the dog and settled her on the front seat. Charlie barked, clearly excited about a ride in the car. Another patrolman waited across the street, and she knew this couldn't go on forever. One day the protection detail would have to stop.

As Leah drove toward work, the tension gripped and then ebbed each time she glanced at the dog. The pup looked up at her with trusting eyes, and a few more bricks vanished from the wall.

When the two entered through the back entrance of the clinic, Gail laughed. "I almost sounded the alarm when I saw the black dog was gone, then decided to wait until you arrived."

Disappointment tugged. "Did the owner call?"

"No."

She rubbed Charlie on the head. "His loss, my gain."

"I don't hear disappointment in your voice."

"If he really wants her back, it's not for me to stand in his way."

"Bull."

"What?"

Gail laughed. "You're not giving that dog up."

Leah shrugged. "I could if I had to."

Gail studied the dog, clearly happy to be at Leah's side. "I suppose she'll be the newest vet pet."

"I'll keep up with her. I might need a bit of help if I'm in surgery."

"Doc Nelson brings in Spike. As long as they get along, we should be fine, and Spike's a softy. We also have a spare crate and food to get you started."

She rubbed Charlie's head. "Thanks."

"So why the change of heart? A few days ago, you were against a dog."

Not a dog. Bringing someone into her life and closer to harm. She was tired of being afraid. "We all evolve."

Charlie settled on the couch in the reception room, behind Gail, and Leah began her morning routine of seeing patients. The worries of the last couple of weeks eased, and it seemed as if the stresses melted. Here, she felt safe.

Leah was doing a routine physical on a female pit bull when Gail poked her head in the exam room door. "Got a minute?"

"I'll be right there."

"Better come now. Your neighbor is on the phone."

Leah finished the injection with the dog and looked at the client. "I'll be right back."

She hurried to reception and picked up the phone. "This is Leah."

"Leah, this is Julia."

"Julia?"

"I live next door. You gave me advice about a sick pug right before Christmas. I waved to you this morning."

The woman's face didn't come to mind but she remembered the dog. "Right. Julia. What's up?" She hesitated and then recalled the dog's name. "Roscoe not feeling well again?"

"He's fine. I was just wondering. Are you moving?"

"What? No, I'm not moving."

"I didn't think so, but there's a moving van in front of

your town house. I told the guy you aren't moving, but he has a signed work order to move out your furniture."

Leah imagined the floor wobbling under her feet. "What! I'm not moving."

"The movers are loading boxes as I speak."

Leah gripped the phone, leaning into the receiver as if it would convey more desperation. "Julia, do me a favor and call the cops. I'm headed home right now."

"Will do."

Leah explained the situation to Gail and then, grabbing her coat, hurried to her car. She drove home, running more than a couple of yellow lights. When she pulled up in front of her town house, a yellow Ace moving van was parked in her driveway. The back of the truck was open, the ramp lowered to the ground. Three large-muscled men stood in front of her door talking to two uniformed cops.

Leah parked in front of the house and ran up to her door. "What's going on here?"

A tall uniformed officer broke away from the movers and came closer to her. "Are you Leah Carson?"

"That's Leah," Julia said.

The officer ignored her neighbor. "Are you Leah Carson?"

"I am. What's going on here?"

"Do you have identification?"

"This is my house!"

"Ma'am, we need to be sure."

With trembling hands, she dug into her purse and fished out her wallet. She plucked out her newly minted Tennessee driver's license with her Nashville address and handed it to him. He studied her name. "Would you mind waiting right here?"

"Why?"

"Just need to check out a few things."

She folded her arms over her chest, irritated that she had

to go to such lengths to get people off her property. But as much as she wanted to rant and rail, logic called and told her to calm down. "Sure. Go ahead."

She glanced at her neighbor and the movers, who looked confused and annoyed. As the officer slid behind the wheel of his car with her license and typed into his computer, she looked at the movers. "Who sent you here?"

The tallest, a dark-skinned man with broad shoulders and flecks of gray at his temples, said, "The work order came in two days ago."

"Who put in the work order?"

"I don't know. All I know is that we were supposed to pack the whole place up and move it."

"Move it where?" The tone of her voice spiked with anger and fear.

He glanced at his work order. "A storage facility north of town. There's a unit waiting to take the furniture into storage."

"Can I see your work order?"

"Sure." He lifted the clipboard at his side and pulled off the top sheet. "This is what I had in my assignment box last night."

She read over the order, keying in on the vital information. It was her name, address, even her phone number. Paid in full. Her gaze skipped to the last line. She wanted to know who had issued the order. The name was Leah Carson.

She gripped the strap of her purse as if it were her lifeline. "This doesn't make sense. I didn't order this move."

He flipped through the pages and held up a paper with her name and the last four digits of her credit card number. "Your name is on the credit card receipt."

The order had been placed last week. Before the bank

had shut down this account. "I didn't order any of this!" she said, louder than she'd intended.

She took the receipt, her stomach tightening with nausea. The bank hadn't called her about this expense, but then, why would they? It was a local buy and not extravagant, and it had been made before they'd issued a new card. She'd have picked up on it when her credit card statement came in at the end of the month, but that would have been too late to stop today's fiasco.

A black SUV pulled up behind the police car, and she instantly recognized Alex Morgan as he got out. The folds of his overcoat caught in the wind, revealing his badge and gun as he strode toward her.

She was glad to see him in an odd sort of way. The officer got out of his car and Alex spoke to him for several minutes. His gaze locked on Leah, and he strode toward her in long confident strides.

"Want to tell me what's going on?"

His calm frustrated her. She wanted him to be upset and screaming. "I don't know. I got a call from my neighbor asking me why I was moving."

"Why're you moving?"

"I'm not moving! I didn't order this." She held the now-crumpled work order in her fist. "My name is on the form, but I didn't authorize it."

"She paid for it," the mover said.

"I didn't pay for it willingly." She looked at Alex. "Someone skimmed my credit card and used it for the purchase. This is so classic Philip!"

Alex turned toward the officer. "I think we can establish that this is a mistake."

The officer nodded. "Sounds like it."

The lack of conviction in his voice irritated her, as if he

was suggesting that she was lying. She glared at the officer as Alex stepped between them. He turned to the movers. "Whatever you took out, put it back."

"I got to call my boss."

"You can do that right after you put what you removed back." Steel coated each syllable.

The movers glanced at each other, then headed toward the back of the truck. They spent the next fifteen minutes moving boxes back into the house. Leah noticed most were marked KITCHEN.

When her belongings had been put back in the house, she walked up to the mover. "I want the name of your supervisor."

He handed her a card and her house key.

She studied the new key. "Where did you get this?"

"Under the mat, just like you said."

"I don't leave keys under the mat. *Ever!*"

He sighed, not sure how to handle her. "Lady, it's what I was told."

"Sure. Thanks." She watched as he and his coworker got in the truck and drove off.

Leah turned to her neighbor and tried to smile. "Julia, thank you for calling. I don't know what I would have done if I came home and everything was gone."

Julia glanced from Leah to Alex. "Sure, Leah. Glad to help."

Leah watched her walk away, so tempted to call out and say, "I didn't do this! I'm not crazy!"

But she kept her silence, aware that when doubt had been sewn into another's mind, shouting only reinforced it. She moved into her house to survey the damage. Most of the furniture was in place, but her pictures had been re-moved from the walls and wrapped in brown paper. Her kitchen had been stripped and packed away in the boxes that now stood in the center of the room. It would take her hours to unpack.

The front door closed softly behind her. She turned to see Alex surveying the house.

"I wasn't moving," she said.

"I know."

God, how she wanted to believe it was a mistake. She wanted to ferret out a reason that would offer any explanation other than the actual one. Philip. "He's playing with me."

"Why would he bother with this kind of game?"

"Because he knows it will ruin my day. He'll be all I think about. He had a knack for messing up my days with just a phone call or the click of a mouse."

He drew in a breath. "Have you seen any sign of him?"

Hands on hips, she thumbed her index finger. "None. But that's part of his thing. He never shows his face."

He tugged his cuffs down over his thick wrists. "Okay."

"He was always so good at messing with me. He could make me feel like I was going insane." She raised fists to her temples and turned. "When I left him, he was furious. He stalked me for months."

"Tell me what happened the night he stabbed you."

The hard edge had softened. "You've read the reports."

"You tell me."

The story had been bottled up for years; she'd shared only bits and pieces with a very few people. "He broke into my apartment. When I woke up, he was standing in the corner of my room. I called nine-one-one, but we both knew I'd be dead before the cops arrived." She shoved out a sigh, as if some poison had been trapped in her lungs. "After the first plunge of the knife, adrenaline exploded in me. I forgot about the pain. I assumed he would kill me, but I refused to go easy."

A weight lifted from her shoulders. Alex had dug into her past without asking, but as they stood there together, she sensed some of her burden had shifted to his shoulders. She liked Alex. Appreciated his intelligence. But she couldn't say whether she fully trusted him. She nearly laughed. He was here, listening, and beggars couldn't be choosers.

"Anything else happen since we spoke?"

"Someone abandoned a dog at the clinic."

"That happens, doesn't it?"

"This would be the kind of thing Philip would do. He'd give me something he knew I'd care about and then take it away so I'd suffer."

Alex stared at Leah's flushed face and the unshed tears that glistened. She glanced at her hands twisting her thumb and index finger over an invisible wedding ring. "I was raised in a good home. I'm smart. I should've figured out this guy was trouble. But I missed all the warning signs."

"How old were you when you met him?"

"Twenty-two."

"You were a kid."

"I should have known better." She wrapped her arms around her chest.

"You know better now."

She stared into his stoic gaze, feeling a connection. "You're not exactly the most open person. You keep secrets. You can be cold. And yet I've got a thing for you. What does that say about me?"

"You have good taste."

The deadpan answer coaxed a laugh. "Right. Or I'm just insane."

"You're one of the sanest people I know, Leah."

His words tugged at her heart as if it were a kite and he the flyer. "I've got to get back to work. I have patients this afternoon."

"I'll check around here and call you."

"How're you going to find him? He's been a step ahead of us."

"What was the name of the florist that sent you the flowers?"

"It was Nathan's on Broadway. I called them, but they couldn't tell me much."

"They'll talk to me."

Alex was en route to Nathan's when he got a call from Deke. "What do you have?"

"I've been going through Deidre's financials, just looking to see if anything popped."

"And?"

"Two listening devices were charged to her credit card. The make and model match the one we found in her town house the day she was murdered."

"The exact same model?"

"Yeah. Exact. What we found, she most likely put there."

"So why would she bug her own place?" Alex turned onto Fourth and found street parking. He shut off the engine but didn't move.

"She was in a tough divorce. Maybe she wanted to get something on Radcliff."

"Maybe." He tapped his fingers on the steering wheel. "If she planted the device, that means the receiver has to be close to her house."

"Within a mile."

"A search of the place revealed nothing that would have recorded conversations."

"She just moved to that place."

"Run down where she used to live and search it. And go over her car carefully. Then get back to me."

"Will do."

Alex got out of the car, bracing against the wind that whipped along the buildings, which acted as a wind tunnel. He walked the half block to Broadway and turned right. Fifteen paces later he was in Nathan's.

A tall slim man in his midforties glanced up from an arrangement of red roses. "Can I help you?"

Alex pulled his badge from his breast pocket. "Had a question about an order placed here a few days ago."

The man raised a brow and laid down the rose he'd been trimming. "I'll help if I can."

"It was an order of irises, sent to a Leah Carson."

"Name doesn't ring a bell, but let me have a look." He shifted a few feet to the right to his computer. A few taps of the keys and he was nodding. "We had one order for her. *Happy Anniversary.*"

"That's right. Who sent them?"

"The buyer's name was Brian Lawrence."

"Did he give an address or phone number?"

"Phone number." The clerk rattled off the number. "I think I got a call from Ms. Carson asking about the flowers."

Alex jotted down the number. "Do you have a credit card number?"

"Sure." He glanced at the computer and shook his head. "He paid cash. Did Ms. Carson call you?"

"I've spoken to her. The flowers weren't welcome."

The florist frowned. "I saw the arrangement myself. It was stunning."

"They were sent by a man who we believe is stalking her."

"Oh. I had no idea."

"Do you have security cameras?"

"No. But the bar next door does. That camera might have picked him up."

"Thanks."

Alex left his business card with the florist and moved next door to the bar. This early in the evening the place was empty, except for a few patrons who sat at the bar. A tall, muscled man wore a black T-shirt. The guy took one look at Alex and frowned. "Cop."

Alex pulled out his badge. "TBI. I'm looking for security footage."

"From when?" No shock. No surprise. He knew the drill.

"Wednesday, January eighteenth. I'm looking for a guy who went into the florist shop about ten in the morning that day."

"I can't help you, but my tech guy shows up in an hour. I can have him pull it for you."

Alex handed him a card. "I'd appreciate that."

The bouncer flicked the edge of the card with his thumb. "Guy bought flowers?"

"Among other things."

All afternoon, every noise, every ringing phone, every footstep in the hallway, set her nerves on edge. Her stomach churned and she found it harder and harder to concentrate as the minutes ticked by. When Gail locked the front door for the evening, she breathed a sigh of relief.

"Are you okay?" Gail asked as she slid on her winter jacket.

Leah's smile was a throwback to the days when she smiled all the time to conceal her fears. "I'm fine."

"Haven't had a chance to ask, but what was going on

with your neighbor? She sounded pretty upset. Something about a moving van in front of your house."

"It was a mix-up. The moving company parked at my house when they should have been a few houses down. It took just a second to clear up the problem."

"So everything is fine?"

"Of course. Why wouldn't it be?"

"You just seem a little rattled."

"I'm fine." She widened her grin just a fraction, knowing overdoing it could set off red flags. Didn't want to look desperate. She'd made that mistake with her roommate when Philip had been stalking her, and when her roommate had pressed, Leah had cried and confessed her troubles. She didn't want to cry now, or give Philip the satisfaction of knowing she was rattled. "Really."

Gail's gaze settled on her an extra beat before she nodded. "By the way, when you were in your last appointment, I ran Charlie outside so she's ready to go home."

She teetered, feeling touched at the gesture and fear for the dog she'd be taking home to a house that had been violated that morning. "Thanks. That's so sweet."

"You two get on. It's been a long day."

"I hear ya." She moved into her office, where she found Charlie sleeping on a dog bed by her desk. Gail's doing, no doubt. The dog looked up at her and wagged her tail. Her gaze still had a bit of a panicked look, as if she didn't know where she was going. Too many homes in too short a time.

Leah reached for the leash, and the dog began to wag her tail faster. As she petted Charlie on the head and fastened her collar, she worried aloud. "Let's get home and hope it's still there."

The dog sprang to her feet and barked.

"That's right. Home. For better or worse, you're with me."

On the drive home she detoured into a strip mall. First a stop at the ATM for cash, and then she and Charlie went into the pet store, where she picked out a proper collar and leash, and also made an ID charm from the machine. She bought dog food, a bed, and chew treats. By the time she left the store, she was a couple of hundred bucks lighter and sure that she had fallen in love with this dog.

When she pulled up in front of her house, it was dark. Normally, she left lights on so she never returned home to the dark, but today, in the rush to close up the house after the movers had gone, she must have turned off the lights.

"What the hell happened today?" She gripped the steering wheel as she stared at the dark house.

The sound of her voice had Charlie barking again, pulling her away from her thoughts. She took the dog with her to the front door and let her inside. Leaving the main door open and the screen door closed, she returned to her car to gather her purchases. Once she had carried all her purchases inside, she closed the exterior door and flipped the dead bolt closed. Charlie barked and sniffed the purchases. Leah wanted to smile, but first she had to check her town house. Keys in hand, she moved from room to room, turning on lights and checking the windows. With each click of a light switch she flinched a little, half-expecting to see Philip standing in a darkened shadow.

When she determined the house was clear, she allowed herself a smile. "Good. We're in the clear tonight."

She took Charlie with her into the kitchen, where the packed moving boxes stood, a loud reminder of the day's chaos. She wasn't in the clear. Not even close.

"You did this to me, didn't you, Philip? I know it was you." The dog whimpered, clearly picking up on the tension in her voice. She smiled at the dog and rubbed her on the head. With Charlie in tow, she again checked the bedrooms and all the closets, and only when she was sure the house was indeed empty did she begin to wash out the bowls and then fill one with dried food and the other with water. She placed both on a new doggie place mat.

As Charlie ate, Leah rolled her head from side to side, realizing her back was a knot of tension. She opened the fridge and pulled out a wedge of cheese and a half full wine bottle. Turning, she reached in the cabinet to get a glass and realized it had been packed. *Damn.*

She studied the boxes and searched for any that might say glassware, but they were all marked simply KITCHEN. She grabbed her keys from her coat pocket and cut through the tape that held each box closed. She found her wineglasses in the fourth box. Carefully, she unwrapped a glass, rinsed it in the sink, and filled it with wine. She took a long healthy sip, savoring the cool flavor as it rolled down her throat. As much as she wanted to settle and relax in front of a movie on television, she couldn't bear the idea of waking up to these boxes, a reminder of today's nightmare. She turned on the television, soothed by the hum of the evening news, which gave her the sense she wasn't alone.

She set up the dog bed for Charlie and gave her a chew stick and then set about unpacking the twelve moving boxes that had contained her kitchen. It took nearly two hours to unpack, unwrap, wash, and replace every item. Finally, just before nine, she was able to break down the last of the boxes and put them out by her back door by the recycling bins. Next, she moved into the living room and spent another half hour rehanging the pictures the movers had wrapped. More paper, more trash out by the back door. By ten she'd put her house back together, retrieved her journal, and was seated with Charlie on the couch, the television humming in the background.

She turned to the last blank page and detailed the day's event. She began with the call from her neighbor, the movers, the credit card, the boxes, and Alex Morgan.

As she wrote the last words, she found the journaling this time did nothing to ease her worries. She'd been afraid to look back over the last couple of months and see if there were any patterns. Hesitant to fear the facts. Facts were power, and after today, she could no longer ignore the fact that Philip was finding ways to reach her.

It took her less than fifteen minutes of reading to realize just how close Philip was. The missing house keys. The flowers. The flat tire. The man at the park. The movers.

She'd been rattled by all of these incidents but she'd been determined not to freak out and call the cops. Each incident didn't mean much, but all together they told her very clearly that someone was stalking her.

She closed her eyes, absently rubbing the scars on her palms. *How am I going to do this? How am I going to battle him again?*

An overwhelming weight settled on her shoulders. As much as she wanted to think Alex would help, she knew cops did what they could but often it was a case of too little, too late.

Charlie jumped up on the couch and nestled her nose in Leah's lap.

She looked at the dog, rubbing her between the ears. "You were dropped off at the clinic and left. You're black, like the dog I once wanted. He would have known that. Known I'd fall in love with you right away."

A wave of nausea rose up in her throat as tears welled in her eyes. "He wants me to care so he can take you away, or worse, hurt you. Charlie, I'm afraid we've both fallen into a trap."

There would have been a time when she'd have wept and worried and hidden. But not anymore.

Leah rose and moved to her computer and logged on. She looked up locksmiths and found a twenty-four-hour service. It would cost her a fortune, but there'd be no way she could sleep tonight knowing someone had copied her house key.

Phone in hand, she dialed the number of the locksmith. A man answered on the third ring, his voice gruff and a bit irritated. "Watts Locksmith."

She glanced at the front door and wondered if she'd locked it. "Can you change the locks on my house tonight?"

"Tonight?"

"Yes. I had a break-in today and I think someone has a key to my house."

"Sure, I can change the lock. It's overtime rates, though."

"Do you take checks?"

"Cash or credit."

"All I have is a check. My credit card was skimmed and I'm waiting on the new one." Philip had boxed her in. "I'll pay double if you take a check."

"How do I know it's good? I've been stiffed before."

"I've never bounced a check in my life."

"Right."

"I'm a vet. I can give you my work address, and you'll know where I live. I wouldn't be pressing if I weren't scared. He's gotten in at least once before."

"He?"

The words stuck in her throat. "My ex-husband."

A sigh shuddered through the line. "Give me your address."

She rattled off her home address and he promised to be

at her place within the hour. As she waited, she moved from window to window in the house, checking and rechecking the locks. Charlie followed her from room to room, carrying her chew stick. She sat patiently as Leah went from room to room.

When she'd moved in, she'd taken a hammer and nails and secured each window in place with a single nail. It was a simple but effective trick she'd learned after Philip's last attack.

By the time she'd checked the windows, her doorbell rang. Charlie barked, the fur on the back of her neck rising. Most dogs would be excited by a visitor, but this dog, like Leah, associated strangers with trouble.

She looked through the peephole and saw an elderly man wearing a white work shirt. The name Mike had been stitched over the right breast pocket. He carried a well-worn toolbox, and beyond him was a van that read LOCKSMITH.

"Ms. Carson," he said. "It's Mike Watts."

Holding Charlie's collar, she opened the door. "Mr. Watts, thank you for coming so late."

He glanced at the puppy, a grin tipping his lips. "Mighty tough dog you got there."

She picked up Charlie. "I've only had her a couple of days, but she owns the place."

He laughed. "The best dogs always do. My dog Buster has me wrapped around his paw." He nodded to the lock. "Any other doors in the house?"

"Off the kitchen there's another door. Just the two doors."

"Well, then, it shouldn't be too hard." He inspected the lock and then jabbed his thumb toward his van. "Let me grab a couple of locks. Be right back."

She and Charlie waited as he moved slowly and easily to his van and opened the back. He rattled around there for several minutes. As she watched, she glanced around the darkened street, searching for a car or a person, anything that was there that didn't belong. There was nothing out of the ordinary on the street, and yet the hair on the back of her neck rose, as if invisible fingers stroked her skin.

Mr. Watts reappeared with two locks and a work blanket, which he laid in front of the door. He knelt and got to work on the lock. He had it removed and replaced in twenty minutes. He moved through the house and opened the back door, noticing the collection of broken-down boxes.

"Getting ready to move?"

"No," she said. There'd been a time when she'd have chatted about her day and told him about the mix-up. Instead, she stayed silent, holding Charlie close as Mr. Watts changed out the lock.

With a grunt, he rose. He locked and unlocked the door with the key three times before declaring the lock sound. "You're good to go, Ms. Carson."

"Thanks." No sense of relief because she knew this was only the beginning of a new chapter, which she thought had ended four years ago in South Carolina.

Leah walked Mr. Watts to the front door, where she dug out her checkbook. She wrote the check for double the rate, wincing at the financial hit. "Thanks again."

He reviewed her check, folded it, and tucked it in his pocket. "Glad to help."

By the time he'd left it was nearly midnight. Charlie was asleep in her arms and her body ached with fatigue and tension.

She locked the doors, once, twice, three times, and then put the keys in her jacket pocket before taking Charlie into the bedroom with her. She climbed in her bed, slid under the covers fully dressed, and lay back against the pillows. She might be safe for now, but now didn't last very long.

The locksmith was a setback he hadn't been expecting. Leah was smarter than he'd anticipated. She wasn't as timid as she appeared.

Kinda sucks, doesn't it, Leah? No friends, always looking over your shoulder, jumping at every sound. If you think this is all I've planned for you, you don't know how motivated I am.

CHAPTER TWENTY

Monday, January 23, 6 A.M.

Leah packed the journal from the last six months into a brown paper bag. She wasn't sure if Alex would be at the running group this morning, but she needed to speak to him and show him what she was up against. She needed him to really understand what kind of monster he was fighting.

She worried about what to do with Charlie, but after an early morning walk, she decided the dog would be safer in the crate she'd put together in the living room. She lined the crate with one of her blankets and put a chew toy inside before scooting the dog inside.

To Leah's relief, Charlie settled down in her crate and began to chew on her toy. She left and made the fifteen-minute trip to the park where the group was meeting today. She was glad to see the collection of cars that lined the parking spaces. However, a wave of disappointment washed over her when she didn't see Alex's SUV. *You would pick today not to show, Agent Morgan. Now I'll have to hunt you down.*

She grabbed her knit hat, pulled it over her ears, and got out of her car. Most mornings she hated these first few minutes. Hated the cold. Hated the tension in her muscles. Today she welcomed it all.

She stretched as the other runners got out of their cars and made their way to the open field that led to the woodland path. She checked her watch, set her timer, and glanced around the field. No place for anyone to hide. Good.

As she was about to start her run, the black SUV pulled up next to her car. *About time, Morgan.*

Feeling the weight on her shoulders ease again, she began to run slowly. The other runners passed her easily, but she didn't mind. After a poor night of sleep, it felt good to move, to breathe full, deep breaths.

The steady thud of footsteps sounded behind her, but she didn't glance back, knowing it was Alex. He came up beside her. She was already breathing hard. He looked almost bored with the pace.

"You doing okay today?"

"I'm hanging in there. I had the locks on my house changed."

"Smart. You might think about an alarm system."

"It's crossed my mind." More money. More expense. The vacation she'd considered taking in the fall was slowly moving out of financial reach.

"I want to talk to you after practice."

"Good." He matched her pace.

"You don't have to babysit me." The words puffed out of her as she struggled to talk and run at the same time.

"I'm happy to take it easy today." He had barely broken a sweat.

"Don't patronize me, Alex. Run."

"You're willing to go the route alone."

"I'll be fine. Anniversary isn't for two more days."

Bravado aside, she was afraid, but she wasn't going to let it ruin the lives of the people around her.

He nodded, as if accepting she needed to do this. "I'll be waiting at your car."

Breathless, she held up a thumb and watched as he easily picked up his pace, his long legs eating up the space as he overtook the other runners. She soon lost sight of him and the others as they dashed down the path.

Workouts could be hard because the exertion chased away the day's thoughts and made room for memories.

Together always, Leah, Philip whispered against her ear.

Leah missed a step and nearly stumbled as she rounded the last corner. "Get out of my head," she whispered.

She increased her pace, pushing her muscles and her lungs, which stung from the cold, beyond what she'd managed since she started the group. The trees thickened around her, and once or twice she imagined the snap of a twig and the rustle of branches. Her breathing grew more rapid, but she kept running, fisting fingernails into the scars on her palm.

When she finished, she checked her time and realized it was her fastest to date. The small victory offered a measure of satisfaction.

Alex waited by her car, two water bottles in his hand. He handed her one as she approached. "Great run. Where're the demons that are chasing you?"

She accepted the water. "It's the same every day, only today they were nipping at my heels. Did you find out anything from the florist? Get a name?"

"Ever heard of Brian Lawrence?"

"No."

"We're tracking him down. The man who bought the flowers used that name."

"Philip isn't going to announce himself until he's ready."

"We need to talk about what happened to you."

"It's more than a five-minute conversation." She sipped her water. "I brought my journal from the last six months. It chronicles anything out of the ordinary."

"Really?"

"I'm very detailed. And I do see now that I've been obsessed. I know I appear crazy."

He studied her. "I'll swing by your town house in a couple of hours and you can show me the journal."

"Let's meet at a neutral place. A coffee shop. Somewhere public. No listening devices."

"You think your house is bugged?"

"I've searched it, haven't found anything, but there are so many hiding places. Until this is over, I'm assuming it is." She ran a hand over her head. "I know, sounds crazy."

His frown deepened as he thought about the device in Deidre's house. "The TBI offices are safe."

"Okay."

"Ten o'clock?"

She twisted off the top of the water bottle and then refastened it. "Sure."

In her car, she turned on the heat, put the water bottle in the drink holder, and drove home. The closer she got, the tenser she became. Until yesterday, it had been a sanctuary. A place away from work and her past. All her own. But yesterday, someone had violated that space. She'd changed the locks, but it was no longer a sanctuary.

Inside the front door, Charlie barked in her crate, jumping up and down. Smiling, Leah let the dog out, fastened her leash, and walked her around the neighborhood. Though she did her best to focus only on the dog and the crisp sky, her gaze roamed constantly for anything out of the ordinary. Cars. People. Nothing jumped out at her, but her nerves remained tied in knots.

Once Charlie had worked out her energy, Leah returned home to shower and dressed for her meeting with Alex. She took time with her hair and makeup, just as she had when things had been so bad with Philip. She'd always thought if she looked pulled together, maybe she could pretend everything would be fine.

Charlie got another walk before she crated her and gave her a chew toy. The dog settled onto her blanket, wagging her tail as Leah promised to be back soon.

The drive to the Tennessee Bureau of Investigation took twenty minutes. The closer she got, the tighter her nerves twisted. What had happened yesterday couldn't be passed off as a fluke or forgetfulness. Philip was stalking her.

The journal in hand, she hurried through the cold toward the large front doors. Inside, a rush of warm air greeted her as she moved toward the security station. She leaned toward an intercom centered on the glass partition separating her from the guard. "I'm Leah Carson. I'm here to see Agent Alex Morgan."

An older man with a receding hairline and large reading glasses studied her for a beat. "He's expecting you?"

"Yes."

With a nod, the guard picked up his phone, dialed, and announced her before hanging up. "He'll be right here."

"Thanks."

She turned away, wishing like hell she didn't have to do this. One stupid mistake in her life and it seemed fate still expected her to pay more. "When is it going to be enough?"

"Excuse me?"

She glanced at the guard, realizing she'd spoken aloud. "Nothing. Sorry."

Minutes later, a side door opened and Alex appeared. As always, he wore a dark suit, a white shirt, and a red tie, and his shoes were polished. Always buttoned down, always on guard. If she felt more comfortable with him, she'd joke about being so pulled together. During his runs, he barely seemed to sweat, and if this had been a different time or place, she'd have joked about his lack of sweat glands.

"Right on time." His gaze flickered over her briefly, taking inventory. A flicker of appreciation warmed his gaze.

"No sense delaying the inevitable."

"You sound like you're heading to a firing squad."

"It feels like it."

The glint in his gaze softened just a little. "Come on up to my office." He reached for her journal. "Would you like me to carry it?"

"No, I have it. I've made it this far; I can make it the rest of the way." She'd been shouldering this burden for over four years, and now releasing it would almost feel awkward. How would she live her life if she weren't worrying?

In the elevator, she was aware of the smallness of the space. When the doors opened, she followed him down a carpeted hallway. Conversations buzzed behind cubicle walls as the fluorescent lights hummed overhead.

Alex opened the door to a conference room and flipped on the lights. "Can I get you coffee?"

She would have loved a cup but feared, given her nerves, she'd spill it. "No. No, I'm fine."

He pulled out a chair for her at the long oak table and watched as she carefully placed her journal on it. She shrugged off her coat, laid it on the chair beside her, and took a seat.

Alex pulled out a chair across from her, adjusted his tie, and waited.

She put a hand on the thick journal. "I told you I kept a journal."

He arched a brow. "That's the journal?"

Color flushed her cheeks as she raised her gaze to his. "Might as well see just how crazy I am."

"I don't think you're crazy."

His words did little to ease the tension banding her chest. "This kind of journaling is crazy."

"Not necessarily." A smile quirked his lips. "I appreciate attention to detail."

That jostled a laugh. "I take it to a whole new level."

"What happened?"

Slowing her breathing calmed her nerves just enough. "Seven years ago, I met a man while I was in college. My father had just died and . . . well, when Philip came into my life, he felt like the steadying influence I was craving." Her throat tightened. "My dad and I were close, and when I lost him . . . it was hard."

Alex's expression softened with empathy. However, he didn't say a word.

"We got closer and closer, and he just kind of took over my life. He asked me to marry him. I shouldn't have said yes. I should have broken it off then, but I was afraid of being alone. My mother was opposed to it, but I thought I knew what I wanted. We got married in a simple ceremony a few days later. It never felt okay. He had a way of making me feel as if I failed him. When I was accepted in vet school, I knew I'd have to move to Knoxville, and I was glad for the break from him. I imagined I'd commute home on the weekends. Philip hated the idea. I didn't really have the money for the first year, so I had to defer my entrance. He was thrilled. I wasn't. I worked as many hours as I could to save for school, and the closer I got to leaving, the meaner he got."

"How much worse did it get?"

"A lot worse. He started hitting me." Her belly twisted with shame and guilt. "And I took it for a while because he'd be so sorry afterward." She shook her head. "My story is a million years old and has been replayed countless times." She smoothed her hand over the journal. "I finally left and got my own apartment. That's when he started following me. Everywhere I was, so was he. I couldn't do anything without Philip watching.

"I filled out a restraining order, which he never honored at all. The cops told me to keep a record of what he was doing so they could consider stalking charges. That's when I started keeping the journal."

"How many pages are in there?"

A bitter smile twisted her lips. "I've never been able to stop journaling."

"How many?"

"Hundreds."

He absorbed the detail with no judgment. "And Latimer fled Nashville after your attack and died just weeks later."

"Yeah, very convenient. He was able to escape my apartment through the window and missed the cops by seconds." She unfurled her hand to reveal the scars. "You were right to know these were defensive wounds."

Alex tipped his head back, seeming to struggle with emotions foreign to him.

"He broke into my apartment and stabbed me. The cops arrived just in time. He ran, thinking I would die."

"But you hung in there."

"The emergency room doctors said if it had been another five minutes I would have died."

His jaw tightened and a muscle pulsed in his cheek. "And you haven't had any sign that he's alive?"

"Nothing."

He traced a long finger over a black journal. "Why have you kept the journal?"

"PTSD, I think. It's my way of coping. If I can look at the day's events, or even events from weeks or months back, and see no patterns of trouble, I feel okay."

"Why didn't you tell me about this before?"

"It never occurred to me that Philip might be alive, or that Deidre knew Philip. It never occurred to me that my past might be linked to her death."

He drummed his fingertips on the table. "I still have no solid link between Deidre and Philip. They worked together, yes, but I can't prove they ever communicated."

"How did she land on your radar?"

"Money went missing from evidence in the Nashville Police Department. My brother asked me to look into it. Her name popped up almost immediately. And then we found one of Deidre's old business cards near the body of a murdered man."

"Who was killed?"

"We still haven't identified him. The killer chopped off his hands, feet, and head and set fire to the body."

She grimaced.

"My plan was to interview Deidre about the body, but she died." He leaned back in his chair. "There was a listening device in her town house. We're not sure who put it there."

"Why aren't you sure?"

"The purchase was charged to Deidre's credit card."

"Why would she want a listening device?"

"I don't know." He drummed his fingers on the table again. "When did you notice things were off?"

"A month ago, I had that nightmare. I dreamt someone was in my house and I woke up screaming. That's when my neighbors called the cops."

"I saw the report."

"A false alarm." She held out a trembling hand. "I never spotted Philip or anyone who resembled him, but I've had a sense I was being watched. Of course that's what Philip wants. He wants me afraid all the time. He can control me without trying."

"He's not in control."

"I wish I could believe that. But I know how life can spin out of control fast, and there's nothing you can do to stop it."

"Leah, I've got this. I'm going to find him."

"How? If he's still alive, he's been avoiding arrest for four years. He's clever."

Unspoken confidence radiated from him. "That's before I got involved. I'll find him."

"You make it sound easy."

"Not easy, but he'll slip up."

"How?"

"I'll make some calls, see if he's popped up on any databases in the last few years. Is there anyone you could stay with in Nashville?"

She shook her head. "No. I'm on my own here. But . . ." She closed her eyes, gathering her worries. "I can stay at my house alone. I changed the locks, and I got a dog."

"A dog?"

"She's a puppy. Not scary, but she makes a lot of noise."

"Sounds terrifying."

She smiled. "Very."

"Let me look into this, Leah. I'll put the pieces together. One way or the other, I'll find him."

She smoothed her hands over the journal. "Do you want me to leave this with you?"

"Yes. Let me read through it. Fresh eyes can make all the difference."

"Sure." She rose. "Thanks."

When Leah arrived home after her meeting with Alex, her nerves were dancing on edge. She took Charlie for a long walk, hoping to calm herself. The afternoon had warmed under a bright sun, but the tension straining her nerves never quite loosened. She found herself searching for Philip, looking behind trees and bushes, even into the open windows of her neighbors' town houses. Each time a car door closed, she flinched. Each time a curtain fluttered, she tensed. Each time she heard footsteps, she expected to see Philip.

Behind the locked doors of her town house, the fear coiled tighter, and she found it impossible to relax. In the kitchen she made a sandwich with chips, and while Charlie chewed her bone, she watched a movie on television. But no matter how hard she tried, she couldn't shake the sense that she was being watched. She felt like a caged animal.

She finished her sandwich, rinsed the plate, and put it in the dishwasher. She leaned against the counter, staring out into the living room. The hair on the back of her neck tingled, and she had the sudden overwhelming sense that someone was listening to her. She couldn't say how she knew, only that she did.

She hadn't found anything out of the ordinary when she'd cleaned, but she knew he was listening. With no motivation other than her paranoia, she began searching for something that might prove she wasn't going crazy.

She turned over the coffee table and skimmed her hand over the bottom. She pulled the cushions off the chairs. She upended her couch and searched the underside. All the while, Charlie sat happily, chewing on her bone as if it were perfectly normal for her owner to be searching for listening devices. "You've landed with a real winner, Charlie."

The dog glanced up when she heard her name and wagged her tail before returning to the chew toy.

After fifteen minutes of searching, Leah sat on the floor, certain she wasn't losing her mind. Philip had left something here. She knew it. As she leaned back against the couch, her gaze drifted to the heating vent by the baseboard. Curious, she retrieved a screwdriver from her kitchen junk drawer and squatted by the vent. She undid the screws, removed the vent cover, and flipped it over, inspecting it carefully for anything that didn't seem to fit. Nothing. She looked in the vent. Nothing.

She replaced the vent cover and moved to the next one in the room. Again nothing. Charlie, thinking she was on the floor playing a game now, trotted over to her and licked her face. She smiled, rubbing the dog's head.

After a half hour of searching and beginning to feel part fool and part lunatic, she sat down on the floor and leaned against the wall. "Maybe I *am* losing my mind."

As she leaned forward to rise, her gaze caught sight of something attached to the underside of the light fixture hanging from the ceiling. It was small, barely larger than a dime. She grabbed a chair, positioned it under the light, and climbed up. Her fingertips skimmed the warm glass until it slid over a small metal object. Heart racing, she plucked the metal disc from the underside.

She held it up to the light, triumph racing through her. It appeared to be a listening device.

For several long seconds, she stared at it, the sound of her heartbeat thudding hard in her ears. *Philip. You bastard.* Slowly, she closed her fingers over the device.

Four years ago, she'd have screamed into the device, telling Philip she *knew* he was listening! She'd have battled hysteria. Cried. And then she would have smashed the device before calling the cops. But not today. Today she was smarter. Afraid, yes, but wiser.

Carefully, she reattached the listening piece to the underside of the light fixture and smiled. Now it was a matter of setting the trap.

CHAPTER TWENTY-ONE

Monday, January 23, 3 P.M.

Deke arrived at the forensics lab office after three. He showed his badge at the front desk and then swiped his access card, allowing him behind the security doors. He found Georgia in the lab, staring into a microscope. Her red hair was twisted into a topknot and a deep frown furrowed her brow.

"From the day Mom and Dad first brought you home, you were frowning," he said.

She glanced up, her green eyes dark with curiosity. "I had three older brothers waiting for me and, genius baby that I was, I knew that meant trouble."

He chuckled. "You were right. It's a wonder Mom didn't equip you with your own sidearm."

"Believe me, I asked more than a few times for a handgun, but she said it wasn't a good idea for a five-year-old to be packing."

"Didn't you ask Santa for a pistol one year?"

She laughed. "No one would give me one, so I went to the man himself."

He rubbed his hand over his head. "Damn, how many little girls ask Santa for a handgun?"

"I think I requested a nine-millimeter Beretta like Dad's."

"Jesus. It's a wonder Santa didn't call child protective services."

"Santa was an off-duty cop making an extra buck. He knew Dad had a houseful of hellions."

"Ah, well." He leaned against the side of the desk. "I understand you have an identification on my victim."

She pushed away from the microscope and shuffled through a stack of files until she found the right one. "The one with parts missing?"

"That would be the one."

"I do." She opened a manila folder and read her scrawled notes. "You read Dr. Heller's report. The victim was dismembered postmortem."

"I did."

"I'm also cross-checking DNA with the John Doe you found in the warehouse. Remember the one without hands, feet, and a head?"

"Stands to reason the two might be one and the same victim."

"We'll see. But I know who owned the hands and feet because I pulled a good clean print from the index finger of the right hand. We can thank the cold weather for that."

Deke reached for his phone to text the findings to Alex. If the victims were one and the same, this case might break. "That's about the only reason to like winter."

"Do you think we'll ever see summer again?"

"I'll remind you of that when it's July and we're sweating buckets at a crime scene."

Smiling, she glanced at her notes. "I ran the victim's prints through AFIS and got a hit. Lucky for us, he was in the military. Served eight years in the army. His name was Brian Lawrence."

The name meant nothing to Deke, but it would give him a possible address, job, and known associates. He texted the update to Alex. "So much for Alex's theory that our guy was Philip Latimer."

"The guy by the river isn't Latimer. I have no conclusive information on the warehouse victim."

"Guy gets out of the military with honors and a year later ends up in pieces on the banks of the Cumberland River."

Deke had learned long ago not to become too closely attached to his victims. Emotions like anger, revenge, and guilt could be a hell of a motivator, but they could turn out to be your worst enemy. "Crossed the path of the wrong guy."

Deke's text on his mind, Alex left work after six intending to drive to Leah's as soon as he swung by his house and got a bite to eat. They had a lot to discuss, but he hadn't eaten in fifteen hours and he was starving. He would be at Leah's by eight.

It was getting dark when he arrived home. The brick colonial was located at the end of a cul-de-sac that backed up to woods. He'd chosen a small rural community north of Nashville to build. Though he'd been in the house two years, he'd furnished only a couple of rooms, and those were sparsely done at best. Georgia had said it needed a woman's touch and had offered. The idea of her pulling out paint cans and adding color to perfectly fine antique white walls made him smile. The house might not have much, but it was simple and quiet. Safe haven.

He pulled into the long gravel drive and shut off the

engine. Out of the car, he fished for his house key on the ring as gravel crunched under the beat of rapid footsteps. Instantly, he tensed, twisted, and reached for his gun, but before he could free it, something hard hit him across the rib cage. He woofed out a breath of agony, rolled to the ground, and scrambled for his gun. He raised it, not even sure what was coming after him, only knowing he was going to kill whatever it was.

He glimpsed a hooded figure wearing a mask. The attacker gripped a baseball bat but, seeing the raised gun, hurled it at Alex and ran. The bat swished by his head, missing him by inches before it clanged and rattled on the pavement.

When he looked, his attacker had vanished.

"Motherfucker," he muttered as he tried to sit up. Pain shot through his midsection. On the heels of the slicing pain, memories of falling off Miller's Falls washed over him. "Damn it." Anger juiced him enough for him to sit up and reach for his cell. He called Deke.

"Detective Morgan."

"It's Alex." He took a breath and tried to step back from the pain. "I just got attacked in front of my house."

"I'll be there in twenty minutes. And I'm calling the local police."

"Right." Alex struggled for breath as he held his gun close and tried to push himself to his feet. However, he quickly discovered the pain in his side robbed him of breath and the will to move. Gritting his teeth, he angled his back toward his car. He wasn't sure how long he sat there, but a chill had settled deep in his bones when, in the distance, sirens finally wailed.

The rescue squad and a sheriff's car pulled up by his car, and when they got out, he shouted, "I'm here."

A paramedic, a young woman with long, brown hair twisted into a knot, ran around and knelt beside him. "What happened?"

Breathing hurt. "I was hit with a bat. The guy threw it at me, so it's around here somewhere. It might have his prints on it."

She didn't bother a glance toward the bat. Her gaze remained on Alex. "Where did he hit you?"

Alex winced, nodded toward the right side of his ribs.

The sheriff's deputy hovered behind the paramedic. "Did you get a good look at the guy?"

"No. Didn't see him coming."

"Can you tell me anything?"

Alex shook his head. "No."

The paramedic pulled on rubber gloves and gently touched his side. He groaned and gripped his gun tighter.

When the paramedic spotted the gun, she sat back. "Can you give that to me or the sheriff?"

"I'm TBI, and I'm keeping it until my brother arrives."

"Badge?" the deputy asked.

"Right breast pocket." He gritted his teeth as pain bolted through him like lightning. "Get it and look for yourself."

The paramedic pulled the badge and handed it to the deputy. "Agent Morgan."

"That's right." Strained, tight words hissed through clenched teeth.

The deputy shifted his stance. "I know you."

Pain cut. "And you hate my guts? Heard it all before."

"Not at all. I admire the work. Bad is bad."

Alex looked up, not sure if the guy was joking, and heard the screech of tires and, seconds later, saw Deke approach, his hand on his gun. He moved with quick, even strides, and his normally solemn expression darkened to murderous.

The paramedic flexed gloved fingers. "That your brother?"

Alex held tight to his gun, as if he expected the paramedic to reach for it. "That's right."

The paramedic sat back on her haunches, resting gloved hands on her thighs. "Give him your gun."

Deke showed his badge to the deputy and squatted beside Alex. "What the hell happened?"

He closed his eyes and eased his grip on control. Pain washed over him. "I was hit with a bat. It's around here somewhere."

"I can't treat him while he's holding a gun," the paramedic said.

Alex's fingers loosened their grip on the gun's handle and Deke gently took it from Alex. "I got your back, Alex. I'll find the bat. Let the paramedic do her job."

His head dropped back against the car. "I can't believe I didn't see it coming."

Deke's grin didn't reach his eyes. "And don't think I'll ever let you forget it, my little piñata."

"You know what Wednesday is?"

"Yes."

"Our anniversary." Philip's hand moved up and down Leah's lower leg. The gentle touch did not mask the restrained power in his fingertips. Those fingertips, those hands, could wield pleasure as well as pain. How many times had he hurt her with those hands?

"We aren't married anymore, Philip. You're dead."

His hand paused on her knee. "But I'm not dead. I'm right here. I've always been close, watching."

"You are dead. You are part of my past, not my present."

"Wrong, Leah. Dead wrong."

Tears welled in her eyes. This close, she could smell the spicy scent of his aftershave and feel the heat of his body. This close, she remembered he stood tall at six foot three and had a muscular frame born of genetics and endless workouts. He liked knowing he could bench press three hundred pounds, and that his fist packed an iron wallop.

This close, she felt small, vulnerable. "No, we're not married."

Like a jackal springing on prey, he pounced, covering her body. Those long, strong fingers wrapped around her throat and began to squeeze. "Say we're married. Say it!"

The breath caught in her throat and quickly grew stale in her lungs. Her heart beat faster. Her skin tingled. Her vision blurred. She shook her head no.

Leah jolted awake and glanced around sightlessly. Seconds ticked by. Her heart pulsed, rapid and hard. And then, finally, she realized she was in her living room, on the couch. Dragging a trembling hand through her hair, she looked at the couch and the remote control in her hand. A sitcom from the eighties was showing on the television. She glanced around the room, jumping to her feet, half-expecting to see Philip.

Charlie glanced up at her, her expression worried. The dog had burrowed under a blanket on the couch and had curled into a tight ball.

As the dregs of the dream faded, she struggled to shake off the fear that gripped and tightened her airway.

She glanced at the clock and realized it was after eleven. She checked her phone, fearing she'd missed a call from Alex. No messages. Whatever he'd said he was going to do, he wasn't coming by here tonight.

She shut off the television and rose, rolling her head

from side to side. She shouldn't be disappointed. He had other cases. Other priorities.

Charlie raised her head and yawned. Leah smiled, and the dog lazily got up off the couch and allowed Leah to click on the leash and guide her to the door. She shrugged on a coat, and the two went out into the dark.

She should be afraid. It made sense that if Philip was out there, he could attack at any moment. But she knew he was waiting for their anniversary. He was waiting for the day they'd exchanged vows. In his mind, that was the day he'd reclaim what he considered his. She had two days and counting before their anniversary. She could run, but he'd follow, and again they'd replay this deadly wait-and-see game until he was ready to end it. No, her best chance was to stay and fight. She understood the depths of his evil and wouldn't allow him to hurt her again.

Her thoughts turned to the listening device.

"I'm not going to be a sitting duck this time, Philip," she whispered. "I'm not helpless."

Rick got the call from Georgia, minutes after eleven, that Alex was in the hospital. He'd received a similar call two years before from Deke, right after Georgia had been admitted to the hospital. Memories of that long night chased him as he strode through the emergency room doors, ignoring the stiffness in his leg.

Georgia paced in the waiting room, her fingers clenched. Stress had drained her face of color, drawing more attention to the splash of freckles across her nose. The freckles made her look young and vulnerable. However, one look at her expression told him to tread carefully. She wanted to hurt someone.

"Is he alive?" Rick asked.

She nodded quickly. "Yes. He's going to be okay."

Relief bolted through Rick, and he had to pause a moment to calm a too-fast heartbeat. "Where is he?"

"He's in X-ray, and those damn nurses won't tell me anything." She glanced around him. "Where's Jenna?"

"Parking the car. She'll be here in a minute. Where's Deke?"

Relief drained most of his anger and worry, but good news hadn't calmed Georgia. "He's picking up Rachel. She wants to be here."

He glanced toward two nurses, both grim-faced and annoyed as they traded stares at Georgia. Baby sister had been on the warpath.

"Let me talk to them."

"They don't speak," she said in a loud voice. "They just tell you to wait. I don't like to wait!"

A couple of the nurses glanced in her direction again, but neither made a comment. They turned back to their charts and monitors.

"No one does. Take a deep breath. I'll handle this." Rick walked to the desk and offered a tight grin, his version of friendly. He pulled out his badge. "I'm Detective Rick Morgan with Nashville Homicide. What can you tell me about Agent Alex Morgan's injuries?"

"Are you family?"

Rick carefully tucked his badge in his back pocket. "Older brother, but consider me here in an official capacity as well."

The nurse, tall, thin, and in her late twenties, glanced from him to Georgia. "She's your sister?"

"Yes."

Her gaze looked both pleading and annoyed. "All I ask is that she be polite."

"Understood." Someone should probably apologize for

Georgia, but he didn't. Whatever had happened with Alex
had shaken them both.

The nurse opened a chart. "Your brother sustained a bad
blow to the ribs, which are going to be real sore for a week
or two. We'll know soon if they're broken."

Behind him, he heard Georgia's loud footsteps as she
paced and released a loud sigh.

The nurse leaned in a fraction and lowered her voice.
"Your sister isn't making this easy."

"The Morgans don't like hospitals. And she's the worst."
He and Georgia had done time in the hospital, as had Alex
when he'd shattered his arm as a kid. All the Morgan siblings would have preferred the operating room to the waiting room. "Know how much longer it will be?"

A brow arched. "He should be in his room any minute."

Rick gently tapped the nurses' station counter, as if
closing a chapter. "Thanks."

Her computer dinged and she glanced at the monitor.
"He's headed to his room now. If you give me a minute or
two to get him settled, he'll be ready to be seen. But you
can't stay long."

"Soon as we know he's fine, we'll clear out."

He moved back toward Georgia. "Just give it a few more
minutes."

She wrapped her arms around her chest. "I hate the
smell of this place."

The elevator doors opened to reveal Deke, Rachel, and
Jenna. The trio of Morgans stepped off the elevator and
moved toward them. Deke looked grim-faced, par for the
course, whereas Rachel's expression was cool and controlled. That was her courtroom, don't-let-the-jury-see-you-
sweat face. Jenna's long hair hung around her shoulders

and over a black V-necked sweater and faded jeans. Seeing his bride smoothed the edginess grating Rick's insides.

He shook Deke's hand. "Hell of a family reunion."

Deke rubbed a callused hand over his dark hair, his relief palpable. "We've never been good at normal. What's the deal with Alex?"

"Maybe broken ribs. He should be in his room any minute and we can ask him. Can you tell me now what the hell happened?"

"Don't know. He called and said he'd been attacked. I didn't ask questions, just bolted. Uniforms were on the scene first."

"Did he get a good look at his attacker?" Rick asked.

"I tried to get a description out of him, but he wasn't able to give me one."

"Did he see a car? Anything that would help us catch this creep?" Jenna's hand rested on his shoulder, halting the rising heat of his temper.

"No."

"This isn't a case, boys," Georgia said. "This is Alex."

"Georgia." Rachel's voice hit a steady, even chord. "Alex is going to be fine."

Georgia glanced at Rachel, her expression sharp. "That's what Deke said when I stood in this very room after Rick got shot. Hell, that's what Mom said when they brought Alex here as a kid."

"And I stood here after you were hurt," Rick said. "It's just our turn to wait on Alex. Shit. It sounds like he doesn't even have a legit injury." The last comment was meant to distract, break her growing panic. "As a kid, he at least had a compound fracture and signs of exposure."

"That's not funny!" Georgia shouted.

Rick shrugged. "Cracked ribs, Georgia. Don't be dramatic."

"We don't know it's just cracked ribs! They might not be telling us the worst."

So that she could fight rather than cry, Rick said, "Alex's old scar and, hell, my scar are a hell of a lot longer and nastier than a few bruises."

Deke, understanding Rick's motive, nodded. "Alex won't even have a scar. Just bruises. This really doesn't even count as an injury."

"I agree," Rick said. "Just like Alex to get a baby injury and then try to hog all the attention."

Jenna and Rachel swallowed smiles when they glanced at Georgia's thunderous expression.

Georgia gritted her teeth. "God, you two are such jerks. Why's it always a competition with you guys?"

"It's no competition when you know you've won, Georgia," Rick said. "He'll be out of here in a day with a handful of aspirin. I had months of rehab."

Georgia's face reddened.

Jenna laid a gentle hand on Georgia's shoulder. "Tell me again why you like having older brothers?"

Tears glistened in Georgia's eyes. "I don't. They're a pain."

Jenna smiled. "I know. But in a good way, right?"

Rachel's pale face revealed her worry far more than her words. "He's going to be fine."

A young doctor wearing green scrubs and a white medical jacket rounded the corner, and Jenna was the first to spot him. "Your answers have arrived."

The five turned and arguments and jokes were silenced.

The doctor had thick, brown hair and dark circles shadowing smiling eyes. "Your brother said to follow the sound of arguing voices. He said when I located the source, I'd find the Morgans. Have I found the Morgans?"

Deke extended his hand. "You found us. And before my sister attacks, how's Alex?"

"He's got bruised ribs. But he'll be fine. He'll be out in the morning."

Deke looked at Georgia. "See?"

She swiped away a tear. "Jerk."

Rick winked at her. "Brat."

Deke grinned. "Can we see him?"

"Room 206. He's awake and ready for visitors. Though I want you to clear out in ten minutes. He needs rest."

The Morgan entourage made their way up in the elevator and then down the hall. Georgia was the first to push into the room and find Alex trying to sit up. Pain and fatigue had paled his angled face, but his gaze remained sharp and alert.

"You're supposed to be resting." Georgia came up behind him and propped his pillows.

"Just the idea makes me want to jump out of my skin," Alex said. "I want out of here."

Jenna and Rachel hovered close to the door of the small room while Deke and Rick moved to the foot of the bed. For a moment, neither spoke as the weight of the evening lessened.

"Get a look at the guy?" Rick asked.

He grunted as he settled against the pillows. "Like I told Deke, fucker came out of nowhere. I think he'd have caved in my skull if I hadn't drawn on him."

"What did you see?" Deke pressed.

"Hoodie. Mask. Tall. Lean. Broad shoulders. Black jeans and tennis shoes. Couldn't tell you more than that, which really pisses me off."

"Okay," Rick said. "Take it easy. This isn't something we're going to figure out tonight."

"The doc says you have to spend the night," Deke said.

Alex pushed to straighten up, winced, and collapsed back against the pillows. "I want out."

"I can stay the night," Georgia said. "Consider me your personal nurse."

"I'm fine," Alex said. "Really."

"I want to stay."

Alex shook his head. "I can't sleep if you're staring at me."

Her sweet smile belied her tenacity. "I won't stare."

"Yes, you will. And you'll fuss. I'm not doing that tonight." A crooked smile meant to soften the honesty fell short. "I mean it."

Georgia smoothed her hand over the rumpled sheet. "You shouldn't be here alone."

Alex closed his eyes. "I need to sleep and get better. Someone is going to pay."

Deke laid a steady hand on Georgia's shoulder. "He'll be fine. You can see him first thing in the morning."

She pointed a finger at Alex, her voice cracking as she spoke. "You scared me."

Alex arched a brow. "You'll survive. Where's my phone?"

"You can't have your phone," Georgia said. "You have to rest."

"Phone, Georgia." Pain honed the words to brittle sharpness.

She rolled her eyes and moved to the closet, where his personal items had been stowed in a plastic bag. She fished out his phone and tossed it in his lap.

He winced. "Brat."

Groaning, she closed her eyes. "Are all my brothers jerks?"

"Yes," Alex said. "Now beat it."

The Morgans left the hospital, each grateful to be away from the antiseptic smells and fluorescent lights. The five hovered near the emergency room doors. Cold wind blew across the lot, forcing them all to burrow deeper into their coats.

Whatever goodwill they'd projected to Alex vanished. Deke glared at Rick. "What're you doing tonight?"

"I'm at the station with you, trying to figure out what the fuck happened to Alex."

Leah arrived at the hospital just before one in the morning. She paused as she entered the emergency room. The last time she'd been there, she'd been on her back, bleeding, pain cutting through her body. The doctors had been talking over her, as if she weren't there. Several times, when her eyes were closed, a few of them had voiced their fear that she would die.

But it was a young nurse who had taken her hand and said, loud enough for everyone to hear, "You hang tough, Leah. We're going to fix this, but you have to stay with us. We need your help."

Leah had opened her eyes and seen the vivid smile. The moment of kindness had been the anchor that had kept her among the living.

At the admitting desk, she cleared her throat, and a clerk gazing at a computer screen looked up at her. "I'm here to see Alex Morgan."

"It's after visiting hours."

"I know. He texted me and told me he was here." The truth wouldn't get her past the gatekeeper. "I've got his medicine. He asked me to bring it."

The clerk's gaze narrowed. "What kind of medicine?"

"I'm not exactly sure. He's a private guy." She fished a bottle of prescription pain meds out of her purse. It was for a canine with a bad hip. When the owner, a longtime client of the clinic, had called in, she'd offered to drop it off. They hadn't been home when she arrived so she'd kept the pills. Pills rattled as she shook it. "I won't be long. Honest."

"I can give it to him."

Her fingers tightened around the bottle. "He was clear I take it to him."

"Let me check."

Frustrated, she turned and waited. The clerk's phone started ringing just as an ambulance crew showed. They had a teenager with alcohol poisoning, the paramedic shouted to a harried doctor. All this offered just enough distraction for her to slip past the desk and down the hallway toward the elevators. She punched the Up button and waited, as if she had every right to be there. The doors opened and she slipped inside.

Seconds later, she approached Alex's door. A television buzzed conversations as the light from the screen flickered and cast shadows on the wall. She knocked gently.

"What?" He sounded angry and annoyed.

She pushed open the door. "Good to hear you're in such a good mood."

Gripping the remote control, he turned from the screen. For a moment, he didn't say anything, as if he wasn't sure she were real.

"Better let me in your room. There's a nurse out there right now paging security to have me thrown out."

He clicked off the television. "Breaking and entering."

She closed the door behind her, moving toward his bed. "That would be correct. The hospital has a thing about visiting hours."

He pushed himself up into a sitting position and winced. Without a word, she came behind him, fluffed his pillows, and settled him in a comfortable position.

She sat on a chair beside his bed, not sure why she'd come to his side. He'd returned her text an hour ago, saying he'd been delayed by a minor injury. "So what happened?"

He tossed the remote control aside. "Someone confused me with a piñata."

Carefully, she set her purse on the floor. "You were hit with a bat?"

"That's correct."

His even tone belied the jolt of panic shooting through her. "Did you see the guy?"

"No. Too quick. That's what I get for not paying attention."

"Do you think it was Philip?"

"That's one guess." His gaze lingered on her face, as if searching. "But I've made more than a few people angry lately."

"Imagine."

A smile flickered. "Why'd you come?"

She shrugged off her coat. "I was worried."

"Why?"

She shook her head. "I don't know."

"You have any trouble?"

"No. But I'm now counting the minutes until Wednesday."

"He's not going to hurt you again." So much confidence. So certain.

She traced a pale finger along the handrail of the bed. "I'll do whatever it takes to catch him. Whatever. You just need to let me know how to help."

"I'll come up with something, Leah. I promise."

Her gaze caught the darkening bruise on his forearm. "I had a bruise like that once. I was blocking a blow."

He frowned. "That's what I was attempting to do."

"Not as easy as it looks in the movies, is it?"

"No."

She reached over and brushed his dark bangs away from his eyes. "Tonight, you sleep. Tonight, you let yourself heal, and tomorrow we'll worry about Philip."

"We?"

"The way I see this, we're in it together."

"Yes, we are."

She laid a hand on his. "Nothing is going to happen tonight. Sleep."

His brow furrowed, as if he were weighing and arguing a dozen points at once. "I'll try if you try."

"Deal."

She rose, leaned forward, and kissed him softly on the lips. His hand came up, resting at the small of her back and coaxing her forward. She deepened the kiss, savoring his taste and the feel of his lips against hers.

Outside, she heard a sharp voice, a nurse, and, grinning, pulled back. She touched her fingertips to her lips. "That would be my exit cue. See you soon, Agent Morgan."

"Count on it."

Music pulsed from the jukebox as he elbowed his way into the crowded all-night diner. He flexed his fingers, still annoyed that he hadn't caved in Alex Morgan's skull. He'd had a clear shot, had moved fast, but the son of a bitch had heard him coming at the last second and whirled out of his way. He'd heard the crack of the bat against bone and the agent's thud to the ground. Before he could take a second swing, Morgan had drawn, and he'd been staring down the barrel of a gun.

He'd underestimated Morgan. Roughing him up should have been an easy job. *Don't think I forgot you, Agent Morgan.*

He spotted the woman sitting at the counter and forced himself to push aside his disappointment. He'd failed with Morgan, but he wouldn't wither. Shrugging off the anger, he straightened his shoulders and adjusted his jacket as he stepped up to the hostess stand. "I see my wife at the bar. You mind if I scoot in the seat beside her?"

The young woman smiled. "Sure."

He moved through the crowd of people and took the seat beside the woman. After ordering a coffee, he grabbed a laminated menu. "What do you recommend?"

He spoke loud enough for her to hear but was careful not to lean toward her or even look at her. A smart predator always moved slowly and carefully until he pounced.

Her gaze flickered toward him, as if she wasn't sure he'd spoken to her.

He smiled, knowing the dimple in his right cheek could charm the hardest of hearts. Carefully, he sipped his coffee as he closed the menu. "I see you like breakfast for dinner."

Grinning, she held his gaze. "It's the cheapest and best dinner there is."

"I hear ya." When the counter waitress came up to him, he handed her the menu. "Whatever she has looks great."

"Two eggs over easy, pancakes, grits, and bacon."

"It's a winner." He liked the taste of fresh eggs. Not the powdered crap most places served these days but cracked fresh from the shell. And he liked bacon crisp with lots of fat. "Do you remember me?"

She leaned back a fraction as she studied his face. "We

met at the church last week. And you dropped Charlie off at the vet."

He produced a sheepish grin. "Gail, right?"

"Good memory. You never came back to get Charlie."

He nodded. "My mom died within an hour of my dropping off Charlie. I only just got back into town. Is she doing all right? You didn't send her back to the shelter, did you? Poor thing hated the place."

Her gaze warmed a degree. "No, we didn't send her back. Fact, one of our vets wants to adopt her."

"Really?" He shook his head. "I was gonna call first thing tomorrow and ask about her."

"Good luck getting her away from Leah."

"Leah?"

"The vet."

"Does she really love the dog?"

"Crazy about her. Crazy in love with that dog."

A smile quirked his lips. "That's good for Charlie. Real good. I need to settle up with the clinic for my bill."

"You gonna take Charlie?"

"This Leah really does love her?"

"Yes. Loves her."

He shook his head, low and slow. "Don't know if I have the right. And I want the dog to be happy."

"She is."

"Tell Leah I'll be by tomorrow to settle up, and if she's really loving that dog, well, she can have her. The pound's got plenty of dogs that need a home."

She leaned in a fraction. "The dog reminds Leah of one she had as a kid."

"That's good. Real good." He set the salt shaker close to the pepper shaker. "It's been a week for losses."

She cocked her head. "You lost your mom."

"Yeah. Sudden." His grin was watery, vulnerable. "Let's talk about something else."

"Like what?"

He shrugged, sensing he'd dropped just the right bait in the water to catch this fish. "I don't know, what's got you eating dinner so late tonight?"

"I work some evenings at the animal hospital. I just got off and I'm starving." She reached for a crispy piece of bacon and carefully snapped it in half.

He'd chosen her. Not because she was pretty or because she was remotely his type. He'd chosen her because she knew Leah. And he wanted to show Leah how close she was to dying.

As the waitress set a black coffee in front of him, he reached for the sugar shaker and dumped in a couple of teaspoons. As he stirred slowly, his spoon clinked against the sides of the mug.

Winning a woman over was one of his strengths. He knew when to smile, when to compliment. Seduction required a certain degree of skill, an artist's touch, if you will. And so he set about winning the fair Gail; charming her, sensing the right things to talk about and to avoid. Within thirty minutes, both had finished their meals and were lingering, laughing.

When she spoke to him, she leaned in just a little as she gently tucked a strand of hair behind her ear. "Want to get out of here?"

"Sure. Where?"

Color warmed her cheeks. "My place is a mess."

He kissed her very gently on the lips. "I don't care."

She kissed him back in an aggressive way he didn't quite enjoy but allowed. When a woman believed she was in control, she'd go just about anywhere with a man.

She drove her car and he drove his truck. Risky to release control for this brief time, so he stayed close on her
bumper, even running a red light to keep her in his sights.

When they arrived at her apartment, he parked directly
beside her and quickly crossed to her door so that he would
be there to escort her inside. Under the glare of the street
lamp, she blushed as he closed her car door. He leaned forward and kissed her very softly on the lips. She ran her
tongue over her teeth and took his hand in hers.

Hand in hand, they climbed the stairs to her apartment,
and as she fumbled to put her key in the lock, he kissed
the nape of her neck. She giggled. When the door closed
behind them, he threaded his fingers through her hair and
pulled her, none too gently, closer to him.

She giggled.

He growled.

Leah arrived home at two thirty in the morning. Fatigue
had drained her body, and her mind refused to stop spinning.
Charlie barked from her crate, and she crossed the room to
let the pup out and took the dog outside for a walk. Back
inside, she changed into sweats and a T-shirt and, with Charlie at her side, settled in front of the television to unwind.

An infomercial playing, she relaxed her head back
against the couch and thought about the listening device
perched feet from her. Philip. She'd wanted to tell Alex
about the device, but one look at his pale, drawn features
and she'd decided the information could wait. If she had
told him, he'd have ignored his body's need for rest and
forced himself out of bed.

At some point she dozed and only started awake when
she heard her cell chime with a text. A glance at the clock

and she realized it was four in the morning. Assuming it was Alex, she imagined he wasn't having much luck sleeping. She reached for her phone, and when she glanced down and saw Gail's number, she grew curious.

She opened the message. Gail was smiling, laughing, her eyes brighter than Leah had ever seen them. The man next to Gail was kissing her on the cheek. His face was turned away from the camera, but there was no missing the strong shoulders and the military-neat, short, dark hair.

Leah was poised to text back a smiley face when she took a second look at the man. Something about him . . . and then she saw his hand and the dark signet ring on his pinky finger. The gold embossed L shined out at her like a warning beacon.

Bile rose in her throat, and she nearly dropped the phone. That was Philip's ring—the same ring that had winked in the moonlight as he'd traced the tip of his knife along her belly.

Silence coiled around her and tightened as she stared at the picture. This was all a game to him. He wanted her to know he was close. Wanted her to know he could reach any of her friends. Wanted her to be afraid. Her bones chilled.

Hands shaking, she texted Gail. Who is this guy?

She waited, one, two, three minutes. But no text came back. She hit the Call button and leaned forward as the phone rang. Four rings and her call went to voice mail. "This is Gail. Leave a message!"

"Gail, this is Leah. Who's that guy? He looks a lot like my ex-husband, Philip. If he's Philip, he's very dangerous. You need to get away from him. Call me."

CHAPTER TWENTY-TWO

Tuesday, January 24, 7 A.M.

Alex struggled as he tried to slide his left arm into his shirt. Pain shot up his arm and across his ribs, and for a moment, his breath caught in his throat as an oath leaked past clenched teeth.

Deke found him cursing when he knocked on the door. "How's it going?"

Cutting pain banded his ribs. He was almost sorry he'd refused the painkillers when a nurse had offered them to him at five that morning. He needed a clear head today. Too many pieces of this puzzle still missing. A fuzzy mind wouldn't get the job done. "I'm fine."

"You don't look fine."

Positive talk didn't temper the pain as he slid the arm into the sleeve and slowly pulled it up to his shoulder, inch by painful inch. The second arm promised to be more difficult. "Looks are deceiving."

Deke came up behind him, set two cups of coffee down on the side table, and lifted the collar of Alex's shirt so that he could insert his arm into the sleeve. The simple task left Alex's heart pounding as he reached for the first button and began to fasten it. Not as painful, but miserably slow-going. "Thanks."

"The doctors said you're supposed to be on pain meds for a few days."

"I'm waiting for the aspirin to kick in." He'd reached for his cuffs and started rolling them up.

"Aspirin? I think something stronger is in order."

"Not today."

"Going to be a tough guy?" Deke sipped his coffee, a grin peeking over the cup.

"You'd be wise not to poke the bear today." Alex left the second cuff unrolled as he accepted the warm cup and took a sip. "Thanks."

Deke's mouth lost its grin but the smile remained in his gaze. "Understood."

"This tastes good. The nurses wouldn't give me coffee this morning."

Deke grunted. "That's just not right on so many levels."

A half smile tweaked his lips. "A few of them barely escaped with their lives."

Deke pulled up a chair, flipped it around, and sat. "I also think the doctors aren't expecting you to leave so soon. Is this a sanctioned escape?"

"No."

"You haven't been cleared?"

"Cleared enough. Bruised ribs, no breaks, and no internal damage. And when the aspirin takes hold, I'll be fine. I just need to get moving."

"I'm guessing they want you to take it easy for a few days."

Alex set down his coffee and rolled up the second sleeve. "It's not about what they want, it's about what I need to do."

Deke sipped his coffee. If any arguments crossed his mind, he kept them to himself. "Any thoughts on who would like to beat the hell out of you? I've theories, but I'm curious about your ideas."

"There's a long list somewhere."

"Any of Ray Murphy's pals? Tyler Radcliff should be at the top. And the mysterious Philip Latimer."

"Radcliff is laying low, from what I've heard. He's taken the week off from work."

"So no one knows if he's passed out drunk at home or wandering the streets with a baseball bat?"

Carefully, Alex tucked in his shirt and considered the theory. "Maybe."

"Do you really think Deidre's plan to bring Philip Latimer to Nashville worked?"

"Someone has been stalking Leah. She keeps a journal like she did when her ex-husband stalked her."

"She still keeps notes?"

"She's the first to admit it's a bit OCD."

"Yeah."

"I read through the journal yesterday. Lots of odd things have been happening to her. Almost as if someone's been slowly turning up the heat. She thought someone was in her house. Hacked credit cards. Flowers wishing her a happy anniversary. Someone set up movers to move all the stuff out of her house."

"You think it's Philip Latimer?"

"If it's not him, it's someone just like him."

"She dated anyone else since him?"

"She says no."

"Crazy neighbors? Odd coworkers? Stalkers come in all shapes and sizes."

"I'd agree, if not for Deidre. She's tied up in this."

"She nailed the stalker, maybe?"

"I don't know."

Deke smoothed out Alex's crumpled red tie and handed it to him. Then he pulled Alex's gun from his waistband. "I hung onto this after they admitted you."

"Thanks." He fastened the cuffs of his shirt and, with Deke's help, eased on his coat. He reached for his wallet, pocket change, and utility knife and slid it in his pockets. He opened his phone and typed in his passcode. The low battery light blinked. One more text from Leah. Maybe she'd scored a few hours of sleep last night.

I RECEIVED A TEXT FROM A FRIEND LAST NIGHT. SHE WAS WITH A MAN. THE MAN'S FACE ISN'T CLEAR BUT HE IS WEARING PHILIP'S RING. I'M FORWARDING THE PICTURE. ALSO FOUND A LISTENING DEVICE IN MY HOME. CALL ME.

Alex studied the picture Leah sent and showed it to Deke as he supplied the backstory.

"A listening device. Like the one found in Deidre's town house. Someone was tracking them both?"

"I'd say so."

"Why play cat and mouse?"

Anger churned as he thought about Leah alone and worried over the texted picture. "Control is part of the thrill, the addiction. He gets a kick out of playing games."

"So who's in the picture with the mystery man?"

"Her name is Gail. She works at the animal hospital with Leah."

"And Leah can't reach her."

"Not as of the last message, which she sent twenty-two minutes ago."

Deke handed Alex his badge. When Alex clipped it on his belt, Deke took his coat and held it up. Alex eased the arm of his injured side into the coat first and carefully followed with his second. Painful, but not as bad as the shirt.

"Want me to get a wheelchair?" Deke asked.

"Hell no."

A nurse swiped back the curtain. She was tall and wore green scrubs and a scowl. She'd tried to convince him to take the pain meds earlier, and when he'd refused, she'd eyed him with suspicion. "I thought you would try to make a break for it."

Alex braced for a fight. "I am."

She shook her head, disapproval furrowing her brow. "I brought you these." She held up a cup with two pills.

"No meds. I need to think."

"They won't make you woozy. Not much stronger than aspirin, but they'll take the edge off better than anything over the counter."

"You sure they won't cloud my head?"

"Positive."

Alex gratefully accepted the pills and tossed them in his mouth. He chased them back with a cup of water from the nurse.

"Try not to get banged up again, Agent Morgan."

"Will do my best."

He took a step forward and saw the waiting wheelchair. "I don't need that."

"If you want out, that's your only ticket. I've met you halfway; now it's your turn."

"Fine." He lowered himself into the chair and was oddly grateful to be sitting again. With the nurse pushing, Deke led the way. As Alex waited with her at the front entrance curbside, Deke got in his car and drove around front. It was a late-model black four-door that looked like it would move if Deke stomped on the accelerator.

Alex slid into the passenger side and very slowly buckled his seat belt.

"Where to, boss?"

"The vet hospital where Leah works."

"Will do."

Alex dialed the hospital and got a recorded message. Halfway into the recording the message stopped and he heard a breathless, "Nelson Animal Hospital."

"This is Agent Alex Morgan. I'm looking for Leah Carson."

"She's in surgery right now. Can I take a message?" Papers shuffled in the background, as if she was searching for a pen.

"Who is this?"

"This is Gail."

"Ms. Carson called me this morning about you."

"Yeah, she looked a little freaked out when I poked my head into surgery a few minutes ago."

"When will she be out of surgery?"

"In about two hours."

"I'll be there in two hours, and I'd also like to talk to you."

"Does it have to do with that guy I went out with last night? I know Leah thinks it's her ex-husband, but that's just crazy. His name was Philip, and this guy's name was Brian Lawrence."

"Brian Lawrence." Shit. That was the guy who ordered flowers for Leah.

"Is something wrong," she asked.

"I'll explain when I get there."

"Yeah, sure."

He hung up. "Leah and Gail are at the clinic."

"Then why do you look angry?"

"Brian Lawrence. Gail went out with the same guy who sent Leah flowers."

Frowning, Deke reached for a notebook and pen. "Are you sure about that name?"

"Yes."

Deke's expression darkened as he rounded a corner and

slowed for a yellow light. "Remember what Dad used to say about coincidence?"

"Yeah. No such thing."

"You hear about those hands and feet we found by the river?"

Alex shook his head. "Vaguely. Didn't pay too close attention."

"That guy's name was Brian Lawrence."

"Gail," Leah said. She hadn't been out of surgery five seconds before she went looking for the receptionist. "What's the deal with texting me that picture last night?"

Gail yawned, not seeming the least concerned. "I didn't text you a picture."

Leah got her phone and showed it to Gail. "You did."

She frowned as she studied the picture. "I don't remember sending this to you. He was the one who suggested taking the picture."

"But that's you. The text came from your phone."

"Yeah, so? What's the big deal? We had a few drinks after we got back to my place. Maybe he sent it." She reached for a patient form and tucked it back in its file. "Again, what's the big deal?"

Leah moved closer to the counter. "Who's the guy?"

Gail looked up, her face flushed with irritation. "I'm sorry if the text bothered you, but why do you care who I spend the evening with?" She dropped her voice a notch. "It's none of your business."

Leah might be stepping over the line, but she couldn't let this go. "He looks like my ex-husband."

Gail cocked her head, as if she expected a punch line. "Really?"

"Yes, really!"

She dropped her gaze and straightened a stack of invoices. "We ran into each other at a diner. It went from there."

Leah could feel the earth shift under her as she struggled to keep her voice calm. "If he's the guy I think he is, he's pure evil."

Shaking her head, Gail held up a hand. "He was very sweet and nice. I haven't had such a good time in forever."

Leah glanced one last time at the picture and then shut off the phone.

Gail leaned back in her chair, regarding Leah with a weary gaze. "You really think this guy is your ex-husband, and he came back from the dead to take me out?"

"I think he faked his death. I think he's been waiting to return." Even as she spoke the words, she understood how crazy she sounded.

"To do what?"

"Wreck my life and everyone I know."

"That sounds pretty weird, don't you think?"

"I don't care if it sounds weird or not." Hands fisted, she clung to control. "We need to assume that Philip is alive and be careful."

Gail folded her arms over her chest. "You sound insane."

She dragged a shaking hand over her hair. "I know. I know. But you have to trust me on this. Philip is a very charming man. He's attractive, and he knows the right things to say to make a woman feel good."

"I think you're losing it. I think the death of your friend Deidre has really upset you, and you're seeing trouble when there is none. Maybe it's like one of those flashbacks, the kind soldiers get when a car backfires. They hear a loud noise and think someone is shooting at them."

"The ring on his hand. It's exactly like Philip's."

Gail flattened her palms on the desk and leaned toward

Leah. "It's a ring, Leah. Give me a break. There must be thousands just like it.

"Philip's grandfather gave him that ring."

"You're stretching things, Leah. I mean, I think your ex-husband did bad things to you, but, really, you think he'd fake his death and then come back just to freak you out?"

"Yes, I do. I'm starting to think Philip had something to do with Deidre's death as well."

Gail shook her head, her eyes darkening with concern. "It's a big stretch, Leah. In fact, I'm kinda worried about you."

"I know what I'm talking about."

"Do you have proof?"

"My credit card was skimmed, someone tried to move my furniture out of my house, and remember the anniversary flowers?"

"When's the last time you saw this guy?"

She rubbed her palms together. The uneven skin of the scars brushed against each other. "It's been four years."

"And he suddenly just shows up with a different name and starts killing and shagging your friends."

If Philip could hear this conversation, he'd be laughing. He loved knowing he could upset her. "But it all feels like Philip."

"Philip. And my date's name wasn't Philip. It was Brian."

"Brian what?"

She hesitated. "Lawrence."

"Brian Lawrence? That's the guy who dropped off Charlie. I called him and left him a message."

"He explained that. Said his mother died. He said he was coming by to settle up the bill with you for Charlie."

Settle up. Shit. That bastard was sending her a message.

"Just because it feels like Philip doesn't mean it *is*

Philip. Maybe you need to take a break." Gail flattened her lips. "Leah, maybe you have PTSD or something?"

"This isn't PTSD, Gail. I know what I'm talking about."

Settle down.

"It's not like I plan to date the guy. It was a fun night."

Not really listening now, Leah glanced toward the couch at Charlie, who stared at her with sad eyes. The dog sensed her fear and agitation. Philip was coming for her, of that she was certain. "Could you keep Charlie tonight?"

"Why?"

"Like you said, my anniversary is tomorrow, and it would be better if she isn't around me until I know for sure if this is Philip or not."

Gail shook her head. "Nothing is going to happen."

Unshed tears burned in her throat. She wasn't crazy. She knew what she was talking about. "Will you take her?"

"Yeah, sure."

"Thanks."

Deke and Alex drove to Brian Lawrence's address, an older home with brick front steps and a wide front porch. The yard appeared to have been kept up. The hedges were trimmed, and the front sidewalk looked as if it had been patched in the last year.

Alex climbed the front steps and rang the bell, which echoed in the house. He rang again and then pounded. No answer.

"I'll have a look around back," Deke said. "Give me a second."

"Thanks."

Deke trotted down the stairs and around the house and returned minutes later. "It's locked up tight. But there's no sign of anyone. Looks like he's got a construction project going. There's quite a bit of lumber stacked in the backyard."

"Let's talk to the neighbors."

They knocked on three different doors before they got an answer. The woman was older, with graying hair and a lined face.

"Ma'am, we're with the Tennessee Bureau of Investigation and the Nashville Police Department. We're looking for Brian Lawrence."

She gathered the folds of her sweater at the nape of her neck in fragile, deeply veined hands. "I haven't seen Brian in a few weeks."

"Does he travel often?"

"Not this time of year. He owns a tow truck, and this is one of his busiest seasons. People are always getting stuck in the ice and snow. Dead batteries. I hate the cold, but he says he smells green when the temperature drops."

"He drives a tow truck?"

"Well, the last couple of weeks it's been his cousin driving the truck. He said Brian had to go home to visit their grandmother. She's sick. And I think that's just so sweet."

"What's his cousin's name?"

She cocked her head for a second. "Funny, I don't know. He must have said it when I introduced myself, but I didn't catch it. Bob maybe?"

Alex showed her the cell picture. "Is this Brian's cousin?"

She smiled. "Face isn't clear, but it must be. I recognize his ring."

"Ring?"

"The one with the L on it. He said their grandfather gave one to him and one to his cousin."

Deke and Alex thanked the woman and walked back to the car.

"Cousin." Deke studied the house. "Brian Lawrence, the real one, was an army vet. Served with distinction and started a towing business. Has a solid reputation. He has no connection to Leah Carson that I could find. Who's the cousin?"

"Care to make a bet? Philip Latimer. He's back in town, and I would bet money he killed Brian and took over his identity."

"If it is Latimer, why has he waited all this time to come after Leah? He's had four years to kill her. Why now?"

"Stalkers can take breaks, but you're right. That's one of the puzzle pieces I haven't placed yet. You check the DNA on the body found at the warehouse?"

"As a matter of fact, I'm having it cross-referenced to the body parts found by the river as we speak."

"Good." Everything pointed to Philip Latimer. Everything. And yet the puzzle was missing a key piece.

Deke studied his brother, reached in his pocket, and pulled out a fresh packet of crackers. "You look like shit."

"Thanks. I feel like a million bucks."

Deke glowered. "Mom had a dry sense of humor like that. Drove Dad crazy."

Alex unwrapped the crackers. "Dad liked the slapstick stuff. Falling-on-banana-peels kind of humor. But considering what he saw on the job, I can't blame him."

"Mom went for subtle humor. Slightly dark. Like you."

Alex bit into the cracker, realizing just how hungry he was. "Since when did you become the mother hen?"

"Since you landed in the hospital with bruised ribs. I'll go back to ignoring you in a day or two."

* * *

Leah arrived home at two. Stressed and unable to concentrate, Dr. Nelson had given her the afternoon off. She had texted Alex a couple of times but hadn't heard back from him and knew she was on her own. Her skin itched with worry and dark anticipation.

Again, she considered stuffing a bag full of clothes and running. Dr. Nelson would give her some time if she explained. Just a few days to buy time.

Time.

Laying low might chase away some of the biting energy that nipped at her now, but it wouldn't solve the problem of Philip in the long run.

Philip would find her, and she had no desire to prolong this evil dance. Better to stay. Face the demon. And if he didn't appear? Or if he were a figment of her imagination? Then she'd begin the long wait until this time next year.

Inside her town house, bright lights waited for her. She shrugged off her coat, dropped her purse on the table by the front door, and hung up the coat. She crossed to the kitchen and made a pot of coffee. Coffee this late in the day would rob her of all sleep, but she didn't care. She wouldn't be sleeping tonight.

Remembering the listening device in the living room, she switched on soft music. She checked all the closets in her town house and under her bed. When she was certain they were all empty, she returned to the front door, double-checked the chain, and then checked every window. All locked. Satisfied, she moved into her bedroom and stripped off her work clothes. She turned on the shower, pinned up her hair, and, when the water was hot, stepped into the spray. The heat felt good against her skin, but she didn't dare linger in the shower. She quickly dressed and moved into the kitchen for her coffee. As she reached for a mug, her front doorbell rang.

She moved slowly toward the front door and looked through the glass. Alex's stern gaze lifted to hers, as if he knew she was there. He looked tired, his features drawn.

She leaned closer to the door, her fingers poised over the dead bolt. "Alex?"

"Yes. And I'm alone."

With a trembling hand, she turned the dead bolt and opened the door.

His gaze roamed over her. "May I come in?"

"Sure." She stepped aside and caught the barest hint of his scent as he passed. "You're looking a little rough."

"It's been a long night and day."

She closed the door and locked it, double-checking the door handle with a twist of her wrist. If Philip was listening now, he'd be furious that she had a man alone in her place. Good. Let him get an earful. "Did you get my text?"

"I did. I spoke to Gail. I just missed you at the clinic. There's not much she can tell me about her guy."

"No. She thinks I'm crazy now for sounding the alarm."

"Better crazy than dead."

"Come on in. Sit down. God, you must be sore. Can I get you something to eat? Coffee?"

Carefully, he tugged off his jacket and hung it on the peg beside hers. His gait was almost even, but she noticed it wasn't as fluid as it was when he ran. "I just made coffee."

"I'd love a cup of coffee."

"I can pop a pizza in the oven."

"That would be great."

She went into the kitchen to put the pizza in the oven and pour him a cup of coffee. "How do you take it?"

"Black's fine."

She handed him his cup and took a seat beside him on the couch. As he sipped, she reached into the side table for a pencil and pad and wrote in clear block letters: REMEMBER, I FOUND A LISTENING DEVICE. SOMEONE IS LISTENING.

Alex read the note as he sipped and nodded. Many men would have been afraid, branded her too much trouble. In a clear voice, he said, "I think Philip Latimer is in Nashville."

To think it could be true was one thing. To hear it from Alex added frightening depth and meaning. "You're sure?"

He settled back on the couch, as if he didn't have a care in the world. He spoke as if they were discussing the recent cold snap. "I think he killed Deidre and a man named Brian Lawrence."

"Brian Lawrence? Gail's date was Brian Lawrence. He's the man who dropped off the dog at the clinic a few days ago and never claimed her. I even called him myself and left him voice-mail messages."

"Really?"

She nodded her head. "The instant I saw Charlie, I remembered a dog I'd had as a kid. Philip would have known I'd fall for that dog right away."

"Where's the dog now?"

"Somewhere safe. I didn't dare bring her home tonight."

"You think he'll strike on the anniversary?"

"I know he will. The date meant a lot to him."

He set his coffee cup down and reached for her hand. Slowly, he turned it over. Tempted as she was to pull her hand away, she held steady and allowed him to trace the tip of his finger along her palm. A dark frown deepened the lines on his face.

He raised her palm to his lips and kissed it. She closed her eyes, savoring the explosion of warmth that spread through her body. "Very, very brave."

"I'm afraid. All the time, I expect him to return. I hate that."

"Philip thinks he's in charge of the game. He's not. You are. I am."

She wanted to believe, but even now, with the two of them alone, they both sensed Philip listening. Lurking.

Having Alex this close gave her a sense of courage. She'd wanted to touch him and kiss him since the first time he'd asked her out. But fear had kept her at bay. No more. She leaned in and kissed him on the lips.

"I told you, it's bugged. He'll hear us," she whispered.

He cupped her face. "I know."

"You know he'll come after you again."

"That's the plan."

For her, what was happening between them was based on need. Need for feeling. Need for pleasure. For revenge. "He'll be enraged," she whispered in his ear.

He kissed her a second time, injecting a passion that surprised and thrilled her. "And he'll make a mistake. And when he does that, I'll be there."

He kissed her hand again and then rose from the couch. She led him to the bedroom, toward the bed. He cupped her face again, kissing her, making her forget everything but him.

When they'd first met, she'd been afraid of him. She'd recognized the intensity in his gaze and mistaken it for Philip's. Alex possessed a darkness, but there was also tenderness in his soul, a need for truth and knowledge.

She leaned in and kissed him, slowly unfastening the buttons on his shirt. When she pushed it over his shoulders, his muscles flinched, and she saw the swath of dark bruises that skimmed along his rib cage. Gently, she touched it with her fingertips. "I'm sorry."

"It's not the first time I've taken a lick." Again, he raised her fingers to his lips and kissed the tips. She stepped back, her gaze locked on his as she pulled off her shirt and exposed her naked scars to his gaze. She tensed as she waited for him to see only the scars, but his gaze settled on her breasts seconds before he cupped them in his hands. "So pretty."

She arched into him, and all the self-consciousness evaporated in the heat of this moment.

He traced the underside of one breast with his finger. Energy shot through her body, and when he gently squeezed her nipple, she sucked in a breath.

She gently touched the bruise on his side, tracing the reds and blues with her fingertip. She knelt down and kissed the bruise.

When she reached for his belt buckle, he hissed in a breath. "Is this business or pleasure?"

He kissed her. "All pleasure."

She unzipped his pants and slid her hand against him. The moan that rumbled in his chest sounded part animal, and she knew under the cool exterior beat a primitive heart.

When she took him in her mouth, he threaded his fingers through her hair. Again he moaned, closing his eyes and dropping back his head. She savored this womanly power.

Soon, both were naked and on her bed. She straddled above him, tracking her fingertips gently over his bruised ribs. He tensed but didn't ask her to stop.

His finger grazed the scar on her belly. Anger flashed

across his gaze, so quickly she wasn't sure if she'd imagined it. He traced his fingers lower, and she forgot about shame or worry. She moaned his name and gave in to the sensation.

He sat in the car, listening to the transponder. His hands gripped the steering wheel as Leah called out another man's name as she climaxed. He'd thought back to when he'd listened to Deidre make love to another man. She'd moaned and cooed like a dog in heat.

He reached for the knife in his pocket, flipped it open, and jabbed the razor-sharp tip into the seat. Leather tore as he slid the blade over the seat cushion. When the blade reached the seatback, he lifted it and drove it into the seat again. As it ripped, he imagined it was skin and muscle.

CHAPTER TWENTY-THREE

Wednesday, January 25, 6 A.M.

When Leah awoke, sunshine streamed in through the windows. Her body was relaxed, liquid, and a strong sense of hope burned inside her. It had been the worst day of her life four years ago, and today it was one of the best.

When she rolled onto her side, she found Alex lying still as a stone on his back. His breathing was slow, but a tension rippling over his muscles suggested he was not asleep.

"What're you thinking?" she asked.

A sigh shuddered through him as he reluctantly surrendered the peace of the moment. "About today." He opened his eyes and wincing rolled on his side to face her. "I've been running through scenarios, trying to figure out what Philip will do. So many unknown variables."

"He's smart. And he's patient. Four years is a long time to plan."

Alex traced a lock of hair away from her face. "He'll make a mistake." Confidence radiated from Alex, which made believing him easy. Of course he was good at what he did.

"Philip won't back down," she said.

He traced his palm down her arm, his fingers skimming

over a scar. "I'm planning on it," he whispered, close against her ear.

She laid a hand on his cheek, wanting to believe that somehow this nightmare with Philip would soon end. She leaned in and kissed him. The kiss quickly deepened, and he rolled on top of her, his erection hard against her. The desire that had overtaken her last night had felt uncontrollable. So much time alone, and then to feel a physical touch—it had been too much to resist. Now, in the light of day, making love to him now felt equally as tantalizing, but it also felt like a choice, not a primal need. She was choosing to be with him. Choosing to allow her heart to open just a little. Choosing to feel.

Having feelings for anyone risked everything as far as she was concerned. And the risk, much like standing on the edge of a cliff, scared her as much as it exhilarated. Caring was dangerous. But the idea of spending the rest of her days alone scared her more. She wanted to feel. To love.

She slid her hands down his back and slowly opened her legs to him. He kissed the hollow of her neck, her breast, as he moved inside her.

She arched, sighed into his touch, and allowed the walls to drop.

Leah stood at the front door, watching Alex drive off, remembering her promises to him to stay here. He had also posted a uniformed officer parked in front of her town house. He wanted her safe while he went hunting.

She'd been alone ten minutes when a text dinged on her phone. The number was Gail's. She opened a picture, an image of Gail, Charlie, and a man with a blurred face sitting on Gail's couch. Gail looked grim-faced and worried. The man appeared to be grinning. The message read: OPEN UP. WE WANT TO COME IN AND PLAY. DON'T CALL LOVER BOY.

The blood rushed from Leah's head as she approached her front door. He'd been a cop. He knew how to be careful. How to approach a house.

A knock sounded on the door. She jumped, heart pounding and fingers sweating as she moved toward the chained door and glanced out the peephole. The man on her doorstep was wearing a cop's uniform, and though he faced the door, his head was tipped slightly so that the brim of his hat shadowed his face. He rapped on the door again. She jumped, not sure if she should laugh with relief or cry with fear as sharp as a razor's edge.

Carefully, she opened the front door. "Yes, Officer?"

The man looked up, and she stood face-to-face with Tyler Radcliff. Feet braced and arms on his hips, he filled the front porch, grinning and alone. "What're you doing here?"

He touched the brim of his hat. "Mind if I come in for a minute? It's about Deidre's funeral."

Her heart twisted with guilt. Of course he'd come about the funeral. Even as she reached for the doorknob, fear tugged at her. *Don't. Deidre was afraid of him. And she'd died.* "Whatever you have to say to me you can say on the porch."

A muscle tightened in his jaw as he summoned another grin. "I know I wasn't at my best the other day, Ms. Carson."

"You're not coming into my home, Sheriff. What do you want?"

Brown eyes darkened to a savage black that robbed her of breath. "I'd think for Gail and Charlie's sake you'd let me inside."

Every thought and feeling in her stilled. "How do you know about them?"

He raised his hand, and the gold signet ring with the letter L winked in the light. Philip's ring. Before she could process it, he pushed his way into the town house, knocking her aside as if she didn't weigh more than an ounce.

She stumbled. "Where are Gail and Charlie?"

"Safe."

"Where? And why would you take them? I told you all I know about finding Deidre. I can't help you find her killer."

Slowly, he removed his hat and traced the brim with his fingers. "I know who killed her."

"What?" She dug fingernails into her scarred palms. "How could you know?"

His gaze rose to hers. "Because I killed her."

Leah took a step back, her thoughts skittering to the officer parked across the street. She ran toward her door, hoping to barrel past him, but he caught her easily, covering her mouth with his hand. "He can't help you anyway. Right about now that coffee I gave him is putting him to sleep. He'll be out for hours."

She struggled and kicked, knowing she'd go to her grave fighting if that was what it took. She angled her head, trapped his finger between her teeth, and bit down hard. Pain rumbled in his body, but instead of letting her go, he slammed her hard against the front door, knocking the wind out of her. "I planned to make your killing quick and easy, but if you piss me off, I'll take my time, just like I did with Deidre."

She squirmed more and tried to scream, but he held her close. He easily lifted her off her feet and carried her to her bedroom, where he tossed her on her bed. Tears filling her eyes, she scrambled to get off the other side, but he caught her leg and jerked her back hard. He easily flipped her on her belly and twisted her hand behind her back, sending a bolt of pain up her arm and robbing her of breath. She screamed, but he pushed her face into the coverlet, muffling the sound. He held her like that, and soon she struggled to breathe.

Hyperventilating, her body quickly became starved for oxygen. She grew light-headed as he kept his knee in her back and her face in the coverlet. Finally, she passed out.

Alex knew he was missing a critical piece of the puzzle. Something was off.

Just as he arrived at his office, his cell buzzed. He glanced, expecting Leah, but found Deke's name on the display. "Deke."

"Preliminary DNA on the warehouse victim has arrived."

"Fast work."

"The body in the warehouse is a match to the hands and feet found by the river."

"Brian Lawrence." He shook his head, processing. "What the hell was he doing with Deidre's card? Did he find out what she'd done for Latimer? Was he bribing her?"

"I don't know. He was deployed when Latimer supposedly died. However, when his grandmother died a couple of years ago, Brian was back in Nashville, and he inherited all her belongings."

Alex's nerves tightened and twisted. "None of this feels right. How the hell does Lawrence fit into this mix?"

"I've got officers in his house right now, going through everything. I want anything that has to do with Latimer."

Alex rested his hand on his hip. "Latimer stabbed Leah

twenty-three times. Clearly, he was driven by rage and desperation when he stabbed her."

"Okay."

"And he stabbed Deidre twenty-three times like Leah," Alex said.

"Right."

"He left plenty of DNA around when he stabbed Leah. But he left none when he killed Deidre."

"He's getting smarter?" Deke said.

"I listened to Leah's nine-one-one call four years ago. She told the cops it was Latimer. I didn't hear anything on the tape that suggested he was worried about discovery. He didn't care who knew he was killing his wife. Then he goes dark for four years. And when he returns, he goes to great lengths to cover up a connection to Deidre's death." Alex tapped his index finger against his belt. "And why stab Deidre? If his aim was to kill her, there are more efficient ways."

"What are you getting at?"

"I'd swear we're dealing with two different assailants."

When Leah regained consciousness, Radcliff was wearing a Tyvek suit and goggles. He had turned her over and she was able to take a full breath of oxygen, vaguely aware of cold metal clinking against her wrists. He'd secured her wrists behind her back. As her eyes drifted open, he was little more than a hazy monster. Not the one she'd feared for so many years but a new one, just as evil and just as dangerous.

"Why?" she whispered. "Why?"

He shook his head. "It was never about you, Leah. It was always about Deidre. Since the day I found out she was cheating on me, I wanted to kill her. I dreamed about killing her. Hell, I could barely sleep with the hate pounding in my head." He shook his head. "But killing is easy. Getting away with it is another story. I'd have been the first guy the cops would have arrested."

Fear rippled through her.

"Deidre told me about Philip. He helped her get that lame sister of hers out of jail. And when he needed to get out of Nashville, she helped him. You didn't get justice because of her."

She'd always wondered how he'd escaped. "Is Philip dead?"

A smile tweaked his lips. "He's dead. Died in South Carolina, just like the reports said. And that suited me just fine. The more I thought about old dead Philip, the more I realized he was the perfect man to frame. The perfect man to kill Deidre and you."

"That was you with Gail."

"It's been me all along." He traced a gloved finger along her cheek. "It didn't take a lot of work to dig into Philip's past. Found his cousin right here in Nashville. He took all Philip's belongings when their grandmother died. There was a computer that had belonged to the grandmother, with so many pictures of you from Philip's stalking days. And then I found his ring. The ring that helped identify his body. Almost too easy."

"I didn't know he had a cousin."

"He's dead now, so it really doesn't matter."

She recoiled. "Brian Lawrence."

"Very smart. Yes. I killed Brian and slipped into his shoes when it was convenient." He took a handful of her hair and curled it around his finger. "I started texting Deidre from a burner phone. *Philip* told her he wasn't dead. Said he needed money and would ruin her career if she didn't help."

Leah scrambled through her memories of Deidre. "Deidre sought me out."

"Philip told her that he wanted her to text him pictures of you. And Deidre got herself a burner and started sending him pictures." He shook his head. "But she wasn't one to lie down and take it. She was planning to kill Philip when he finally faced her. If he were really dead, she'd be in the clear. But she wasn't expecting me."

"Sins of the past. That's what Deidre said."

"Yes."

"Who planted the listening devices?"

"I did. Used Deidre's credit card to buy them. As you know by now, I'm good at skimming credit cards." He nodded his head.

"You did that?"

"And I let the air out of your tires. Did all kinds of annoying things, just like Philip would have." He grinned, pleased with himself. "I listened as she buddied up to you. She wasn't your friend, you know. She was using you."

Deidre had used her. Yet that last morning at the track had been a real moment. Deidre knew Tyler was dangerous, and she'd said she could handle him. As the image of Deidre, bleeding and slashed, flashed in her mind, she couldn't summon anger.

Tyler reached in the pocket of his pants and pulled out a small box. The back hinge creaked as he opened the top. Inside was her wedding band, which she'd left at the apartment she'd shared with Philip. "We can thank Brian for being a pack rat." He moved behind her and bent down as he took her left hand in his. She fisted her fingers, but he easily peeled them back. She winced in pain as he shoved the ring on her finger.

The ring felt tight. "You don't have to kill me. You don't. There's nothing between us."

"Your death will keep me out of jail. You're going to be killed by your husband, who's risen from the dead. He killed Deidre, your friend and a threat to his freedom, just like he tried to kill you. Killing you is my perfect alibi." From another pocket, he pulled out a knife and traced it between her breasts. "Happy Anniversary, Leah."

She didn't speak as tears choked her throat. She remembered the last time those words had been whispered to her at knifepoint.

He cupped her face with rough, callused hands, holding her chin just a little too tight in his grip. "Deidre didn't understand the meaning of our wedding vows. I meant it when I said until death do us part. Did you mean it when you said your vows?"

"I did. I did mean them."

"Then why did you break them?"

"I never broke my vows."

"You left your husband."

"Because he hurt me." She tugged hard against the cuffs. "He betrayed me when he hit me!"

"There was never another man?"

"No."

"There's Alex Morgan."

She stilled at the sound of Alex's name. "Alex has nothing to do with this."

"Of course he does. Do you think Philip would let him live after what you two did last night?"

"He's not part of this."

"Where's your cell phone?"

She didn't speak, accepting that she would die protecting Alex.

"Tell me, or you'll watch me slice parts off of Gail and Charlie, bit by bit." He closed his eyes. "The sound of a dog howling in pain is just awful. Pitiful."

Tears fell down her cheeks.

"And I'll make Gail scream. She'll be begging me to kill her."

"Please, don't."

"Where's your cell?"

He would kill Gail and Charlie. He would make them suffer. In so many ways, he was worse than Philip. "In the front hallway, by the door in my purse."

He would have to leave the room to find her purse. With him out of the room, she twisted her left hand in the cuffs, scraping skin against metal. Skin burned and tore as her wrist rose a fraction.

Before she could free herself, Tyler returned. "We're calling Alex Morgan."

"Leave him alone, please."

"Alex has another strike against him. He's too damn smart. He could be the one person to put the pieces together, and I can't have that."

"I'm not going to call him."

Tyler held up the display on his phone, a photo of Gail, tied up and crying. "She and the dog are in the trunk of my car. Right outside."

"She has nothing to do with this. Charlie doesn't deserve this."

"I like Charlie. She's a good dog. Loyal." He dialed Alex's number. "I'm going to hold the phone up to your mouth. You warn him and I promise you'll die after you watch me butcher Gail and Charlie."

Tears streamed down her face.

"Do we have a deal?"

She nodded.

"Good." He hit Send and held the phone to her mouth. Alex answered on the second ring. "Leah."

She cleared her throat. "Alex, can you come back by the house?"

"Is something wrong?" Tension rippled in his voice.

"No." She cleared her throat again as she stared into Tyler's dark gaze. "I need to see you. It's important."

"Sure." He paused for a moment. "I'll be right over."

A warning scream rattled silent in her throat, begging for release. But before she could voice the warning, Tyler ended the call.

Alex heard the fear ripping in Leah's voice. Her tone had been clipped, and there'd been an edge. He grabbed his jacket and pushing past the pain burning through his muscles hurried out of his office toward his car.

On the road, his mind grappled with the facts at hand. Logical to assume it was Philip. All the signs pointed to his return. But had he returned, killed his cousin, and reclaimed his possessions? Possibly, but why the four-year gap? Why leave Leah alone when he'd savagely attacked her and left her for dead four years ago? It didn't make sense.

Alex called the officer on duty in front of Leah's house. The phone rang six times, but with no answer, the call went to voice mail. Swearing, he dialed Deke's number. "Leah is in trouble. She just called me, but something's wrong. I'm en route."

"I'm calling for backup."

"Have them come in quiet and stop short of entering Leah's block. They need to keep their distance. I'm afraid the sight of cops might get Leah killed. I'll go in alone."

"And then you'll get killed."

"Not today."

"If this is Philip, killing you will be top of his list. I'm on my way."

"Deke, no."

"Yes, Alex. I'll park down the block. But I'm coming."

Alex rang off and punched the accelerator. Ten minutes later, he pulled into Leah's driveway. Her car was parked at the top. Ignoring the pain in his ribs, he moved toward the marked police car and found the officer unconscious.

He climbed the front steps. Blood pumped in his veins. His muscles burned. He tested the doorknob and found it unlocked. Gun drawn, he opened the door slowly and moved inside, seeing Leah immediately. She was sitting in a chair, her hands tied together. Standing behind her was Tyler Radcliff. He had a knife in his hand and was tracing her jawline with it.

"Radcliff." Shock quickly gave way to understanding. He was the common denominator that connected several sections of the puzzle.

"He killed Deidre," Leah said. "And he's going to kill us and make it look like Philip did it."

Tyler traced the knife along Leah's neck. "Put the gun down, Agent," Tyler said. "Or I'll slice her throat."

Leah's watery gaze sharpened. "Don't, Alex. He'll kill you, and then he's going to kill Gail and Charlie."

"Where are they?" Alex asked.

"Somewhere safe," Tyler said.

"Where are they?" Alex demanded.

"In his trunk," Leah said.

"You should be worried about yourself, Leah. Not them." Tyler gently twisted the tip of the knife below Leah's eye. "The gun, Alex."

Alex lowered his body to a crouch and put the gun on the floor.

"Now toss me the backup gun. All cops carry one."

Alex stilled and then slowly removed the gun from his ankle holster.

"Kick the guns toward me."

Alex's jaw tightened. Tyler sliced a deep nick into Leah's neck. Blood flowed down her white skin. He complied. "Why am I here?"

"Because you butted into Philip's marriage when you didn't have a right. To keep this looking real, I have to act like the outraged Philip would."

"This was all about killing Deidre, wasn't it? She left you and you couldn't take it."

"We promised each other forever. I kept my word. She lied."

"I guess you just weren't man enough to keep her. I mean, what kind of man stalks a woman? Keys her car. Plants listening devices in her house. Fuck, you're pathetic."

"Shut up!" He grabbed a handful of Leah's hair and twisted. She gritted her teeth but didn't scream.

"Hiding behind a woman."

Tyler jerked Leah to her feet and pressed the knife to her side. "I should gut her like a fish."

"You don't have the balls," Alex said. "You know once she's gone, I'm going to kill you very slowly. You're defenseless without her."

Tyler snarled and then shoved Leah hard, sending her falling to the floor before he lunged at Alex. Tyler was a large man but quick and just as Alex braced for a blow, the man slammed into him. Alex grunted, his bruised and battered body screaming in pain.

Alex drew his arm around to hit Tyler but the man pounded a fist into his ribs. Agony cut through him. Hissing in a breath, he punched Tyler in the jaw and the blow slowed him only for an instant before he hit Alex again.

Leah scrambled to her side and then to her feet just as Tyler slammed his fist again into Alex's bruised ribs. Alex grunted in pain.

Leah ran to a side table, picked up a lamp and hit Tyler hard on the back of the head. The blow didn't knock him out but it got his attention. He turned, his face dark with rage and his fists balled.

Alex, his body riddled with agony, grabbed his knife from his pocket and flipped it open. In that split second, Alex lunged, stabbing Tyler in the throat. Blood sprayed on him and Leah as he stumbled toward her. Tyler, his gaze locked on Leah, dropped to his knees.

Leah stood frozen as she stared down at Tyler's body. Alex reached for his phone and called for backup. He moved toward Tyler and rolled him on his back. The knife had cut through his jugular and he was bleeding out.

Tyler looked up at Leah. He raised a hand toward her, but the loss of blood was too fast and violent. "Whore," he mouthed.

"Go to hell," she said.

His hand dropped and his eyes closed.

Seconds later, Deke came through the front door, gun drawn. His gaze swept the scene as Alex rose and moved toward Leah. He reached out to touch her, but she drew inward, as if she were afraid to trust him or herself.

Her gaze settled on Tyler and the pool of blood swelling around his head. "He's been planning this for months."

He took her chilled hands in his. "I know. I know. It's okay. You're safe."

She tightened her fingers around his and looked at him, tears streaming down her cheeks, mingling with the blood from the nick on her cheek. "Alex, he said Philip did die in that car accident."

Deke took Alex's knife from him and urged the two toward a squad car.

Alex opened the car door for Leah and had her sit down. He limped around to the other side of the car and carefully lowered into the seat beside her. "He was clever. Made us all believe Philip could be alive."

"He hated Deidre so much. The look in his eyes reminded me so much of Philip that last night. Love, hate, rage. I saw them all in his eyes."

He wrapped his arm around her shoulder. "It's okay, Leah. They're both gone. No one can hurt you anymore."

She met his gaze. Pain telegraphed from the watery depths. "I'm so sorry. I didn't want to call you. I knew what he wanted to do to you, and I still called. He said he'd kill Gail."

"I'm not so easy to kill."

Gingerly she touched his bruised ribs. "He said she and Charlie are in the trunk of his car."

Alex knocked on the window and a uniformed officer crossed to him. "Tell Deke to find Radcliff's car. He's locked a woman inside."

The officer nodded. "Right away."

The cop and several others fanned out and moved down the street. Minutes later, he returned. "We found them."

She held her breath. "He's killed them."

"No, ma'am," the officer said. "They are alive. Drugged but alive. We've called for paramedics."

Leah studied the officer's face. "You're sure they're fine?"

"Yes, ma'am."

"They're okay," Alex said.

She faced him. "I'm so sorry to have pulled you into this mess."

He cupped her face. "You didn't pull me into anything. I'm here with you because this is exactly where I want to be."

EPILOGUE

Four months later
Nashville, Tennessee

The half marathon drew record crowds. Runners from around the region and the country had shown up to race on what was one of the prettiest spring days Leah could have imagined. She had been nervous and jittery when the starting horn had blared, and for the first mile, her pace had been too quick. Finally, her nerves had settled and she'd fallen into a steady pace. By the time she'd crossed the finish line, her muscles ached and sweat drenched her body. A glance up at the clock revealed . . . well, not a so-fast run time, but she didn't care. She'd finished the race. She'd made it.

Her shorts and jogging top did a poor job of hiding the scars on her arms and legs, and, overheated as she was, they looked all the more angry. She'd caught several people glancing in her direction, silent questions sparking in their gaze. But she didn't try to hide her scars. She'd survived Philip. And Tyler. She'd come through the fire and, as far as she was concerned, a few scars didn't really matter much.

When Alex and Deke had searched Tyler's home, they'd

found his plans for killing Deidre. He'd pieced together his plan with meticulous detail. Deidre had thought she could outsmart her past and move forward, but Tyler had been quicker. He brought Philip back to life, in a manner of speaking, and begun his plan of terror.

A shiver ran through her as she thought about the pure evil that had blackened Philip's and Tyler's hearts.

The sound of Charlie barking had her turning to see Alex and the forty-pound black dog approaching. Dark sunglasses concealed his eyes and his expression was stoic.

Alex wore jeans and a button-down. He'd rolled up the sleeves, revealing muscled forearms with thick, coarse hair. A thick, black watch wrapped around his wrist. He walked up to her. "Good job, Dr. Carson."

His sunglasses tossed back her reflection, but just knowing he was looking at her made her stomach flutter. "Not the most memorable finish."

"I'll never forget it." He leaned in to kiss her.

"I'm sweaty."

"I don't care." He kissed her on the mouth, cupping her face in his hand. "Salty. And sweet."

Charlie barked and jumped, pulling Leah's attention to the dog. She knelt and rubbed her between her ears. "She wasn't too much trouble?"

"She's fine. And pretty smart."

Alex had once told her he wasn't a dog person, but he'd proven very patient and good with Charlie. "So what do you say we get out of here?"

She rose and kissed him on the lips. "Sounds like a great plan."

Please turn the page for an exciting sneak peek of
Mary Burton's newest romantic-suspense thriller,

VULNERABLE,

Now on sale from Kensington Publishing.

Elisa pressed up against a tree, her round curves scraping against the bark. Her eyes warmed with heat and longing, as if she couldn't believe anyone wanted her with such intensity.

"I can't believe I'm blowing off study group to do this," she breathed. "You make agreeing so easy."

It was easy to trace a calculated hand up Elisa's arm and over breasts that weren't very remarkable. "You're so hot."

As dark sexual sensations sent tension shuddering over Elisa's plain square face, faint thoughts of reason chased after it, tugging her lips into a frown. "I must be insane to follow a stranger into the woods. A few conversations in the coffee shop don't make us friends."

"Are you really looking for a friend or do you want something hot and dangerous?" A slow, practiced, sexy smile always made them forget their worries.

"Hot and dangerous," Elisa breathed.

"You're so beautiful. You have an energy that's so hard to resist."

There were so many Elisas in the world. They were desperate for touch. Desperate for a life with a thrilling excitement that reached beyond work and weighty goals. Desperate to be seen.

Their desperation made them so ripe for the picking. So easy to pluck out of their everyday, safe lives. So easy to convince that a walk on the wild side was their chance to create a new incarnation. To believe this was her chance to prove she was cool. Reckless. Could take chances. Be spontaneous.

A kiss at the hollow of Elisa's neck had her moaning and closing her eyes. She was drunk with desire. Her head tipped back against the tree, and the brush of a hand over her breasts hardened her nipples into jutting peaks.

"Do you want me to squeeze them?" The warm whisper brushed Elisa's ear. "Do you want me to suck them?"

"Yes." The word exploded free, as if she now had no control of her own mind.

"Show me. Show me."

With trembling hands, Elisa reached for the buttons of her shirt and frantically unbuttoned them. In her haste, one button popped and skittered to the ground. She peeled back the cotton folds of her very sensible cotton shirt and re-vealed a pink lacy bra cupping unremarkable C-cup breasts. A large pink bow frantically clung to the stretch of lace banding under Elisa's cleavage, looking as awkward as she did at her little table in the coffee shop.

"Very nice." Forceful hands pinched a nipple hard enough to make Elisa wince.

Elisa's eyes opened, the pain slicing at the edges of the mindless desire clouding reason. A whimper tumbled over her lips, but she didn't complain. Her kind never com-plained or made waves when anyone paid the slightest attention for fear harsh words would chase away what little attention they received.

A gentle kiss on the stinging, reddened nipple nudged away the clouds of worry. "Nice. So hot."

"Really? I'm hot?" A pathetic hope clung to the words as her voice rasped over lips painted a cherry red that made her pale skin look pasty white.

"Yeah. Hot."

Tears moistened muddy-brown eyes. "No one has ever said that to me before."

Ah, there it was, the sign that this girl would do whatever was asked of her in this moment because she was so grateful. Long, strong fingers rested at the hollow of Elisa's neck as her pulse thrummed a crazed beat.

"You're nervous."

"Yes." So blinded with wanting, her voice sounded as if it had been shredded by a knife. Scents of a spicy perfume mingled with the musk of the desire dampening her lace panties.

"You don't have to be nervous."

Elisa lifted her breast, silently begging for more touch. "I can't help it. God, I want this."

Soft, seductive laughter rumbled. "I can smell your fear. Your sex."

She moistened her lips, tasting the cherry flavor of her lip gloss. "You can smell it?"

"Super sexy."

Even white teeth nipped her earlobe and sent a visible shudder through Elisa. "You're wet."

Self-consciousness sent a rush of heat up her face. "I can't help it."

"It's good to want this." Energy pulsed. Hummed. The press of fingers to her moist center had Elisa hissing in a breath. Slow circular motions sent the young woman's eyes rolling back in her head as the desire rushed and threatened to knock her over.

The fingers stopped moving in the practiced caress and rose to Elisa's lips, teasing them open until she sucked. "That's my girl."

"Please don't stop."

"I'm not even close to stopping." Strong hands cupped Elisa's throat and squeezed gently at first.

"Is it going to hurt?" The blurted words stumbled past Elisa's lips before they could be censored.

"Do you doubt me?"

"No. No. I just thought . . ."

A soft chuckle rumbled. "It's okay that this is your first time. You don't need to pretend with me. I like knowing I'm the first."

Elisa searched with moist green eyes and, finding no hint of judgment or censor, eased back against the tree.

"I'm going to make you so hot, I'll slide right into you and you'll want all of it."

"I want to feel hot. Sexy. Like the other girls in college."

"You're so much better than those girls. Most of them come from money and have had it all handed to them. You're smart. Different."

"I want to be transformed." Elisa's words rushed past her lips, as if she sent a request to the heavens.

"You will be." Again, silken words brushed over Elisa like a caress as the sun hung lower on the horizon, pulling with it the remnants of the day's light. Shadows bathed the woods around them, creeping closer with each second. "It'll be like nothing you've ever experienced before."

Strong fingers gripped tighter around Elisa's neck, sending tingles through both the seducer and the seduced. Skin tingled. Thrills shot as the pressure increased. So dangerous. So fun to enjoy such utter control.

Elisa closed her eyes, releasing the reins held most days in a white-knuckled grip. She wanted to be dominated. She wanted to be owned. Mind. Body. And spirit.

When the pressure constricted her airway ever so slightly, the first flickers of doubt sparked. Ah, there it was—the fear, which was far more intoxicating than sex.

"Feels good, doesn't it, baby?" Grinning, the seducer squeezed harder, cutting off all air. The white-hot desire blurring in Elisa's thoughts cooled as quickly as molten metal plunged into ice water. Common sense elbowed past the dark cravings as she shook her head and raised her hands to the still-tightening grip.

"Stop," she croaked.

Pain and fear collided in Elisa, driving more energy and determination into her hold.

"Stop." The word strained to be heard as she dug nails painted a bright purple into ribbons of muscles streaming up powerful forearms.

In these moments, with their bodies joined in such an intimate embrace, their thoughts connected. Elisa, who had so desperately wanted a challenge more physically thrilling than math problems or debate team practice, wanted now nothing more than to break free and scurry back to the safety of her little house. She wanted to breathe. To live.

Malice dimmed all traces of humanity and opened the abyss now hungry for fear, pain, and panic. "Fear is part of the fun, baby. Fear shows us we're alive."

When Elisa's breath caught in her throat and couldn't pass to her lungs, she struggled with a renewed energy and then drew up her knee and drove it, with a desperate force, into bone and sinew.

Anger rocketed, stole breath and strength, and the deepening hold slackened. "Fucking bitch!"

Oxygen rushing into her lungs, Elisa gobbled it up as she raised trembling fingers and shoved back hard. Her fingers pressed to her bruised neck, she pushed away from the tree and stumbled forward, her shoe catching and slipping off her foot, before righting herself and sprinting toward the narrow path that cut through the thicket of woods.

"You can't leave yet, Elisa!"

Screaming, she tripped over a root, bit her lip hard, and nearly tumbled before she caught herself. Lungs filling and refilling with a wheeze, she hurried faster and faster down the path toward Warner Park's main road.

"You won't get away from me, Elisa. I know the woods too well." Jogging now under the light of the full moon, it was easy to follow Elisa's panicked footsteps thundering down the path.

"Wondering where the road is, Elisa?"

Branches cracked and snapped, fusing with her cries and prayers. "I know you're wondering where we are in the park. Let's see, we drove up that main road just a half hour ago and parked in the lot before I kissed you on those lush lips and led you to the entrance of the woods. Thirty minutes ago, excitement and anticipation tingled your skin as you gave me just a peek at those panties and bra you bought just for me."

"Leave me alone! I don't want to do this anymore." She sobbed, sucking in her breath as she raced faster.

"You aren't scared, are you? You know I would never hurt you. This is supposed to be fun for both of us. I want you so bad, baby."

As night squeezed the last of twilight from the trail, tree branches and briars reached out like specters. Their thoughts rejoined this time as hunter and prey. The roar of a truck engine told them both the road was close. A yelp escaped Elisa's lips as she ran faster. She was calculating the distance to the road. Could she catch the attention of a driver? Would she be saved from the nightmare that had ensnared her?

Elisa could flag down a car and then, in a blink, she would escape. And the plans would be ruined. That wouldn't work at all.

"Elisa!" Her name sounded twisted as the dark bent branches. "Elisa! Don't be afraid of me. I don't want to hurt you! I want you, baby."

The woods grew silent, swallowing up the little fawn, who was, no doubt, clenching her mouth shut and swallowing her cries.

Ahead, a fallen log lay across the path, and to the right its large rotted stump was circled by a pile of thick branches. Had she burrowed those purple nails into the dirt, clawing and scraping and hoping the earth would swallow her up?

In the center of the path lay a shoe. It belonged to Elisa. She was close, hiding in the thicket. "Elisa, come out, come out, wherever you are. I won't hurt you, baby. You can run, but you can't hide forever."

A twig broke. Leaves rustled. Another car raced down the road, chased out of the park by the darkness. Time stilled, sharpening all the senses. The hunter noticed the cracked branches beside the path and the freshly trampled path. And then Elisa's soft, soft whimpers echoed in the darkness. The sound led down the path to a pale foot peeking out from under a log.

Five fast footsteps and the hunter grabbed her ankle as Elisa dug her fingers into the dirt, fighting to stay burrowed in her hiding spot. The will to live gave her strength.

"I don't want to do this anymore. I want to go home," she screamed.

Fingers bit into her skin, tearing the flesh, yanking her free of her sanctuary. "Got to finish what you started, baby. Got to finish it."

She drew in a breath, but fisted fingers smashed against her jaw. She crumpled to the dirt, stunned.

Hoisting her wasn't so difficult, nor was it hard to carry her back through the woods to the entrance of a small cave, which had been their ultimate destination since the first day they met.

Elisa fell to the cave's floor with a hard thud. "Please, just let me go. I won't tell."

"I know you won't tell."